MURDER
Freshly Baked

Center Point
Large Print

Also by Vannetta Chapman and available from Center Point Large Print:

The Amish Village Mystery Series
Murder Simply Brewed
Murder Tightly Knit

The Shipshewana Amish Mystery Series
A Perfect Square
Material Witness

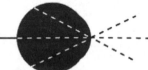

**This Large Print Book carries the
Seal of Approval of N.A.V.H.**

MURDER
Freshly Baked

An Amish Village Mystery
—Book 3—

Vannetta Chapman

CENTER POINT LARGE PRINT
THORNDIKE, MAINE

This Center Point Large Print edition is published in the year 2015 by arrangement with Zondervan.

The text of this Large Print edition is unabridged. In other aspects, this book may vary from the original edition. Printed in the United States of America on permanent paper. Set in 16-point Times New Roman type.

ISBN: 978-1-62899-622-7

Library of Congress Cataloging-in-Publication Data
Chapman, Vannetta.
Murder freshly baked : an Amish village mystery / Vannetta Chapman.
— Center Point Large Print edition.
pages cm
Summary: "When delicious baked goods become lethal, it's time to find a killer in this Amish Village Mystery"—Provided by publisher.
ISBN 978-1-62899-622-7 (library binding : alk. paper)
1. Amish—Fiction. 2. Murder—Investigation—Fiction.
  3. Large type books. I. Title.
PS3603.H3744M86 2015b
813'.6—dc23
                                    2015011749

For Mary Sue Seymour

If I speak in the tongues of men and of angels, but have not love, I am only a resounding gong or a clanging cymbal.

—1 Corinthians 13:1

Author's Note

While this novel is set against the real backdrop of Middlebury, Indiana, the characters are fictional. There is no intended resemblance between the characters in this book and any real members of the Amish and Mennonite communities. As with any work of fiction, I've taken license in some areas of research as a means of creating the necessary circumstances for my characters. My research was thorough; however, it would be impossible to be completely accurate in details and descriptions, since every community differs. Therefore, any inaccuracies in the Amish and Mennonite lifestyles portrayed in this book are completely due to fictional license.

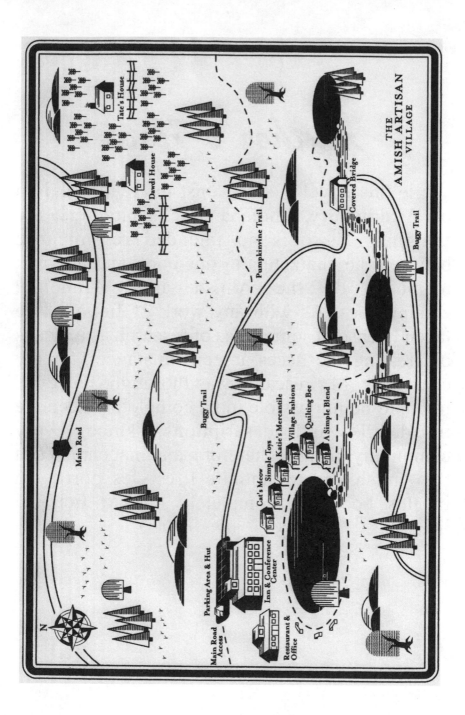

Glossary

ach—oh
boppli—baby
bruder—brother
danki—thank you
dat—father
Dawdy Haus—grandfather's home
dochder, dochdern—daughter, daughters
Englischer—non-Amish person
freinden—friends
Gotte's wille—God's will
grandkinner—grandchildren
grossdaddi—grandfather
gudemariye—good morning
gut—good
in lieb—in love
kaffi—coffee
kapp—prayer covering
kind—child
kinner—children
loblied—praise song
mamm—mom
naerfich—nervous
narrisch—crazy
nein—no
Ordnung—set of rules for Amish living
rumspringa—running around; time before an

Amish young person has officially joined the church, provides a bridge between childhood and adulthood

schweschder—sister

wunderbaar—wonderful

ya—yes

One

The Village
Middlebury, Indiana
May

Amber Bowman was looking directly at Ryan Duvall when he died.

Pam was standing to her right, wearing a skirt made of bright pink and purple fabric, a purple blouse, and a pink scarf. Hannah and Jesse were on her left, both in their customary Amish clothing—Hannah wearing what looked like a new peach-colored apron over a darker peach-colored dress, and a white *kapp*. Jesse wore his dark blue pants, suspenders, and a lighter blue button-down cotton shirt. In that moment, the image of her three closest friends froze in Amber's mind.

Her husband, Tate, had stepped away to take photos of the crowd as they moved through the parking lot, but now he was positioned in front of her closer to the finish line. He was taking pictures to update the website Events page of the Amish Village, the facility where Amber, Pam, Hannah, and Jesse worked. In fact, most of Amber's employees were standing outside on what had begun as a fine May morning—sunny, and a pleasant 59 degrees according to Amber's smartphone. The dogwood trees had finally begun to sport their blooms of yellow flowers surrounded by white petals. The spring flowers her grounds crew had planted nodded merrily in the sunshine. The smell of freshly baked cinnamon rolls caused Amber's stomach to give a nice strong rumble.

It seemed the entire town of Middlebury had turned out en masse to cheer on their friends and family who had chosen to participate in Race for a Cure. Participants and spectators alike wore small ribbons representing the type of cancer they'd battled—yellow, purple, blue, peach, and the ever-present pink. The colors were as varied as the age and particulars of the people. Colored ribbons had been tied to the trees, and balloons swayed in the slight breeze.

Ryan Duvall had crossed the finish line, clearly the winner of his 40-plus division. Ryan had recently turned forty, and most folks felt sure he would win because he'd won the 26 to 39 division the year before. She was just a little surprised he had still decided to compete today.

There was applause, cheering, and good-natured teasing as Ryan raised his arms in victory. Amber saw a mixture of pride and satisfaction in his eyes, quickly followed by a look of surprise. A harsh explosive sound echoed through the morning air, louder than the sound of a firecracker popping, and Ryan slumped to the ground.

"What's going on?" Pam placed a hand on Amber's shoulder and attempted to stand on her tiptoes, but Amber was already moving toward Ryan.

"Where's she going?" Hannah asked, and Pam must have answered, because Hannah began talking to Jesse in a mixture of Pennsylvania Dutch and English. Amber never heard their replies, because at that moment there was a scream, and the good townsfolk of Middlebury, Indiana, became a panicked mob, intent on putting distance between themselves and Ryan's tragic end.

Tate pulled the camera strap from around his neck and handed the camera to Hannah as he rushed forward. Amber and Tate reached Ryan's side at the same moment. Shrugging off his outer shirt, Tate rolled it into a bundle and pressed it against what was left of Ryan's chest.

"Pressure on the wound," Tate murmured, waiting to move until Amber had her hands pressed firmly on top of the cloth.

She glanced down at the wound in Ryan's chest, then looked away as bile rose in her throat. Slowly she forced her gaze back to the man lying on the ground. Ryan's wavy black hair was wet with sweat. His face was unnaturally pale.

"Is he—"

"He's bleeding out. Looks like the bullet went through his heart. I'll check for a pulse." But one look in Tate's eyes told her all she needed to know.

The white T-shirt Ryan had been wearing read "Forty and Loving It." The letters were splattered and torn from the violence of the wound, and the cloth had turned crimson. Tate moved so that he was positioned alongside Ryan's head. Pressing his index and middle fingers to Ryan's neck, he checked for a heartbeat at the carotid artery.

The sounds around them faded to background noise.

To Amber it seemed she heard the cries and shouts as if from a great distance. Some woman continued to scream. A child asked a parent what was wrong. The person who had been running the portable public address system, moments ago announcing the names of each person as they crossed the finish line, now urged caution. The piercing wail of an ambulance added to the chaos. It had been stationed in the parking area in case a runner needed oxygen or fluids.

But fluids wouldn't help Ryan.

Oxygen wouldn't bring him back.

Amber closed her eyes and prayed with all her might—prayed that God would have mercy on Ryan, that God would save him.

She became aware of Pam's hand on her

shoulder, her voice soft and low, her accent Southern, urging her to come away. "Let the paramedics have him, honey."

"I have to . . . I have to hold this." Tate's shirt was now slick in her hands.

Tate stood and shook his head once. Jack Lambright, who had worked at the Village as a boy but had been with the EMS for at least five years now, jumped out of the ambulance and crouched beside Ryan. He spoke into his radio, his voice urgent and clipped. She heard him say "GSW" and "fatality," and then Tate was pulling her to her feet, circling his arms around her.

Amber's teeth began to chatter, and her legs turned rubbery and weak.

"Not here, love. Make it to the curb." He practically carried her there and insisted she put her head between her knees. She pulled in deep breaths, one after another, as her world tilted, then stabilized.

She was vaguely conscious of Tate on one side and Pam on the other. Tate rubbed her back in small circles. Pam asked what the world was coming to that a town couldn't hold a charity run without violence. Hannah and Jesse stood behind her. Amber couldn't make out their words, which were now all in Pennsylvania Dutch, but she knew they were praying.

It wasn't until Sergeant Gordon Avery stepped into the now-cleared area surrounding Ryan's body that she struggled to her feet. Planting her hands on Tate's and Pam's arms to push herself up, she left a bloody residue on both of them.

"I want this immediate area completely cleared," Gordon growled. Nearing fifty, he'd been with the Middlebury Police Department for most of his career, and at nearly six feet tall and 220 pounds of solid muscle, people immediately followed his orders. "Secure the perimeter and the parking lot. I don't want a single person in this crowd leaving until we have a chance to question them."

Cherry Brookstone, a more recent Middlebury PD recruit, stepped forward and said something to Gordon about a complaint filed. She glanced around and then added "restraining order" and "Preston."

"Find him and bring him in. We'll need to question him." Gordon turned to Jasmine, who had been with the Middlebury PD less than a year. "I want statements from everyone. Someone saw who did this."

"I did." The words seemed to come from far away, and they took all the strength Amber possessed to speak them.

Now Gordon turned to stare at her, his expression quickly flickering from surprise to sympathy to disbelief. "You saw the person who did this?"

"No." Amber corrected herself even as she

stepped closer and looked down again at Ryan's body. Tate's shirt had been cast aside and replaced with clean dressings, but even the paramedic had given up any pretense of helping Ryan.

It had all come together in her mind, the moment she saw Jack Lambright kneel beside Ryan. Unrequited love and a tragic ending. Didn't such stories grace the national news nearly every week? And now it had happened, here in their peaceful town of Middlebury.

Amber felt their eyes on her—Tate, Gordon, Pam, Hannah, and Jesse. Even Jack stopped what he was doing to turn and stare.

"No, I didn't see who pulled the trigger, but I know who killed Ryan."

Two

One month earlier

Amber walked through the Village, her crochet bag slung over her shoulder. The temps were still rather cool, and she was glad she'd thought to wear her sweater. Though it was nearly noon, spring was taking its time warming their area of northern Indiana. She'd spent over twenty years in Middlebury, so it sometimes seemed she'd lived there her entire life. And the Amish Village?

The small collection of shops, restaurant, bakery, and inn and conference center seemed as much her home as the ranch house she shared with Tate. Hard to believe it was practically this time last year that she and Tate had been thrown together, solving the first murder to happen in Middlebury in quite some time. God had found a way to bring good out of even those dire circumstances.

At the age of forty-four, she'd fallen in love for the first time—palms-sweating, heart-racing, speech-stealing love. Their relationship broke several stereotypes. They'd been longtime neighbors who barely tolerated one another. Tate was seven years older and not interested in dating—Amber had been looking for love but did not expect to find it next door. Tate farmed—Amber managed a business. The first sparks flew as they puzzled over threatening graffiti, and their love blossomed as they hunted a killer. Tate had asked her to marry him soon after the murder was solved, and they'd celebrated with a small, sweet ceremony on the Village grounds at the end of the previous summer. Not the stuff of romance novels exactly. More like a televised murder mystery series.

Amber still wondered at how things had turned out. She marveled that God had taken the sterile, uniform life she had built and turned it into something amazing. He had given her a chance at true love and a family and joy. He'd refined her faith. He'd offered her a choice—trust him or go on with the life she'd so carefully constructed. When she'd found the courage to accept God's way, life had become more than she'd ever imagined.

Her mind combed back over the verse from Genesis—"You intended to harm me, but God intended it for good."

Ethan Gray's family had found some measure of peace.

And her employees at the Village had grown even closer to one another—resembling a large family more than a workforce.

Then there was the trouble six months ago. Amber didn't want to focus on the murder of Owen Esch. Those memories remained fresh, like a wound not quite healed. Every day was a little better, and she no longer cringed at the sight of the Pumpkinvine Trail. However, some nights she woke with sweat running down her brow and a scream on her lips. Those nights, Tate would gather her in his arms and whisper words of comfort and prayers of healing.

She pushed all of that away as she walked the property of the Village. Spring had arrived. Best to leave the past where it belonged—firmly behind them.

She spoke to several members of the grounds crew as she made her way along the concrete path that circled the pond. They were busy planting pansies in a rainbow of colors—pink, white, and yellow, all with dark purple centers. Jesse Miller stood on the other side of the pond, speaking with Preston Johnstone. Jesse removed his hat, revealing brown hair that had been recently cut in the traditional Amish style, then placed it back on his head. One Amish, one *Englisch*, and yet it seemed they'd become good friends. Such was the way in Middlebury, or so Amber chose to believe.

Both men raised a hand in greeting, and she waved back.

The first shop on the path around the pond was the yarn shop, The Cat's Meow, which happened to be her destination. She stopped in front of the store to admire the window display. Bushel baskets in their natural pale wood color were scattered throughout, and one was filled with different types of yellow yarn, another with shades of purple, and a third with soft pinks. Amber stepped closer to the window and looked at the yarn nearest the Amish-made cradle. A circular basket was filled with every shade of blue Amber could imagine.

Yes, that was what she needed to work on next—a baby blanket for Collin and Brenda's baby.

She still couldn't believe Tate was having another grandchild. Technically, she was too—

though Collin had experienced trouble accepting her as his stepmom at first. Things were still not quite smooth between them, but they were less tense than they'd initially been. Collin had called over the weekend to tell Tate they'd learned the baby was a boy, and he'd insisted that Amber be on the line when he shared the news. That was a sign of improvement in their relationship—in the past she'd always received news secondhand from Tate.

The child wasn't due until mid-August. Even she could finish a baby afghan in that amount of time.

She pushed open the door, and the bell over the doorway announced her entrance. Hannah and Mary were already sitting in the chairs near the back of the room, spreading their lunch out on the table in front of them. A sign at the register read, "We're knitting in the back. Come join us."

"We were afraid you'd skip." Hannah pushed back the strings of her prayer *kapp* and smiled.

She would turn twenty-three in a few weeks, but to Amber she seemed older. Perhaps it was because she knew her so well, or because they'd been through so much together. In spite of the twenty-plus years between their ages, they'd become fast friends. Hannah's chestnut brown hair peeked out from under her white *kapp*, and her brown eyes sparkled behind her glasses.

"After Mary convinced you to take out your

border last week, we thought you might avoid our little get-together."

"I needed to take out the border. I'd done it all wrong!"

"You're a *gut* student, Amber." At first look, Mary was the exact opposite of Hannah. Thirty years old, she tended toward heavy, whereas Hannah was slim. She only recently began dressing in colors other than gray, blue, and black. Hannah preferred pastels. And every strand of Mary's blonde hair was carefully tucked inside her *kapp*.

The ways they were similar—their kindness, professionalism, and faith—were what mattered. That and the fact that both girls were to be married in six weeks caused Amber to think of them as related. They weren't kin, but they were in the same church district. They would also become sisters soon, since they were marrying brothers—Andrew and Jesse.

"I'm a slow learner." Amber rattled the bakery bag in her hand. "But I bring sweets, so you all allow me to keep coming."

"Classes are for everyone who wants to come, but the sweets are *gut* too." Mary reached for the bag and peeked inside. "Snickerdoodles. My favorite."

That earned a laugh as Mary said those same two words no matter what was inside a bakery bag.

The bell over the front door tinkled again, and Martha Gingerich stepped into the store. Also Amish, Martha was tall and thin to the point of resembling an athlete. In fact, Martha did enjoy playing softball and volleyball and even ice skating. Her hair was a golden brown, and her *kapp* always slightly askew as if she'd just come in from enjoying some game. According to Hannah, she wasn't ready to settle down quite yet. What mattered to Amber was that she was an excellent employee who handled the front desk of the inn like a seasoned professional.

Carol Jennings, the manager of The Quilting Bee, rounded out their group. Older, *Englisch*, and quite proper in her dress and speech, Amber had been surprised when Carol joined their group.

"Everyone's here. Time for a hen fest!"

"Time to teach you to read that pattern you were supposed to make progress on last week." Mary moved to the chair next to Amber and insisted she show her what she'd done with the pastel-colored lap blanket in a ripple pattern.

"I was thinking I could start on a baby afghan—"

"*Gut* idea, but after you finish this one."

"Yes, except I'm not as excited about this one anymore." Amber stared down at the yellow, purple, and green mess she'd made. Somehow her ripple looked more like a strange, geometric object.

"The problem is that you forgot you have to count. Pull it out to here"—Mary pointed to a spot four rows down—"and we'll go over the pattern together."

"But what about the baby afghan?"

"Finish this one and I'll be happy to sell you more yarn. Your grandbaby's not due until the end of summer, right?"

"Yes . . ."

"Then start pulling out those rows."

Amber sighed and did as instructed. Soon she was focused on counting the way Mary had shown her. Somehow she'd forgotten to do that while she was watching the History Channel with Tate. She supposed most of these gals could crochet and pay attention to something else at the same time, but perhaps she wasn't quite in that place yet.

Conversations swirled around her as each woman nibbled on her lunch and worked the yarn she'd brought into a special gift. The Stitch Club, as they called it, was one of Amber's favorite times of the week. They brought whatever they were working on—crocheting, knitting, needlework, even the occasional quilt. Not only was Amber learning something new, something useful, but she was nurturing friendships at the same time. Friends had been an area of her life she'd neglected for too long. It was sometimes difficult when you were the boss, but she was determined to accept every opportunity to meet with these special ladies who had become an important part of her life.

She was focusing on her counting—single crochet in eight, skip two, single crochet in eight, three in the next stitch—when she realized the conversation around her had stumbled to a halt and everyone was staring at Martha, who had flushed a rosy color.

"Ryan? Ryan Duvall?" Hannah leaned forward.

"*Ya*. It's not such a big deal. I don't know why you're all staring at me as if my *kapp* has slipped off."

"But Martha, Ryan is *Englisch*." Hannah reached for a snickerdoodle.

"I know he's *Englisch*."

"And you're going out with him?"

"Not going out exactly. He asked if I'd like to see some of the new foals at his place, and I said yes. You know how I adore anything that allows me to spend time outdoors."

Carol *tsk-tsked* as her needle sped in and out of the variegated yarn that was different shades of green. "I don't know that spending time with Ryan is a good idea, but his family has raised quality horses for the folks in our town for two generations. I pass their place every morning, and I always look over to catch a glimpse of the new foals. One is a beautiful flaxen chestnut."

"Ryan Duvall?" Mary shook her head and

tugged on the ball of yarn she was knitting. "He's twenty years older than you are."

"Eighteen, and we're not courting. We're looking at his horses."

"Ryan can be . . ." Mary paused and glanced around the circle. Finally she settled for gently saying, "He can be charming. Be careful."

"I'm not sure charming is what you intended to say." Amber set her crocheting in her lap so she wouldn't add too many stitches while she was talking. "Is he a player?"

All three of the Amish women stared at her, but Carol nodded in understanding. "I'd say he is. That's a good description. Nice enough guy, but he tends to mislead the ladies."

"That's what player means?" Hannah nudged Mary and barely suppressed a giggle. "I thought you were going to say he plays football or, worse than that, hockey. Both games seem so violent."

"They wear pads. I've explained this to you—" Amber couldn't resist the urge to defend her Colts.

"Ryan is as old as your *dat*, Martha." Mary's tone clearly expressed her disapproval.

"I'm not dating him, and he's not as old as my *dat*, who turned fifty last month. Ryan is actually a good deal younger."

They seemed to realize there was no changing Martha's mind, so the subject turned to other things and Amber resumed her counting and

26

crocheting. When they left forty minutes later, she caught a snippet of the parting conversation between Carol and Martha. Carol, who was something of a mother hen to all the girls, had her arm looped through Martha's and was saying, "Promise you'll be careful. Yours wouldn't be the first heart Ryan has broken . . ."

Amber certainly didn't want to see any of her employees experience heartache, but wasn't that a part of growing up? In the last year they'd dealt with two murders, several break-ins, and an explosion in her office, not to mention that wicked creature left in her home to kill her.

As she walked back out into the April sunshine, she thought that heartaches were something they could deal with.

They were a normal ingredient of life, albeit an unpleasant one.

Courting and breakups and rebounding were part of the natural cycle of human relationships.

What was the worst thing that could happen?

Martha would fall for Ryan, he'd move on to someone else, and they'd all go out for ice cream to mend her hurt feelings. Not a problem. That was the phrase that kept bouncing through Amber's head as she made her way back to her office.

She'd never met Ryan Duvall, but he was not a problem.

Three

The ponds situated on the south side of the Amish Village provided a peaceful invitation to the motorists hurrying along Highway 20. Preston Johnstone knelt by the drain that allowed water to flow from the large pond to the smaller one. Sun glinted off the water, causing him to squint when he looked up. He'd been working for over an hour when he felt the familiar sensations he'd come to dread.

The sounds around him faded.

His hand began to tremble slightly.

His throat instantly became dry.

Suddenly the sun was inexplicably brighter. He reached for the bricked wall and felt gravel beneath his fingers, hot and dusty. The familiar weight of his uniform and rifle brought him no comfort.

They were coming.

He needed to get up, move back to the observation post, and warn everyone.

He needed to run.

"Are you okay, Preston?" Joshua Lapp stood in the water, wearing waders several sizes too large, with a foolish grin on his face.

All of nineteen years old, he'd probably never been out of Middlebury, Indiana. Though he wore a wool cap, it didn't completely cover his dark brown hair, which was cut in the typical chili-bowl fashion. He had the calm, pleasant expression Preston had seen on Amish boys all his life while growing up next to them, playing ball together, even sometimes chasing after the same girl. Joshua wore a plain blue cotton shirt and black pants under the waders.

In that moment, Preston envied Joshua his innocence and his simple life.

Sweat poured down his back and an odd mixture of dread and relief flooded through his veins.

He'd slipped back again.

But he was okay.

He was home.

"You kind of went away for a minute there."

"I'm fine. Thanks." He wasn't fine, but saying he was seemed to relax other people. He needed a long drink of water, something to wash the desert from his mouth, from his memory. An image of Zoey popped into his mind. His thoughts wanted to brush over their most recent conversation, but now wasn't the time. For now, he needed to push the memory away. Zoey had been so adamant, and perhaps what had just happened proved she was right, but he couldn't make such a decision squatting next to the Village pond. He needed to focus on the task at hand.

"This is a pretty cushy job I have."

Preston forced the remnants of his memories back into that locked place in his heart. He turned toward Joshua and tried to make sense out of what the boy had just said. "Yeah."

"It's as if I'm getting paid to play in the water."

He couldn't help smiling at the boy's enthusiasm. "You won't think you're playing if a snake pops out of that drain."

"It's too cool for snakes. We both know that." Joshua used a hoe to pull more debris from the drain, which was situated near the top of the earthen wall.

The pond they were working on was the largest on the Village property, and the shops encircled one side of it. A concrete walk continued around the far side. When the water level reached within a foot of the top, it went through the drain and filled the lower pond. Though they'd had rain most of February and the first half of March, the storms had tapered off the last few weeks. April had actually been dry, causing the water level to finally drop enough for them to be able to clean out the drain—a project they did at least twice a year to keep the water flowing from one pond to the other.

Joshua directed the debris toward Preston, who deposited it into a ten-gallon bucket.

"Snakes don't always act predictably," he reminded Joshua.

"Snakes! You grew up here. You know how rarely we see a poisonous snake."

"Just trying to keep you alert."

"You don't have to supervise me," Joshua persisted. "I've cleaned out drains before." He pulled out another glob of leaves, sticks, and a plastic cup.

"Sure. I know that. But I have to do something to earn my wage, and supervising you seemed like my best option today."

"Rumor has it you like to get your hands dirty."

"That so?"

"Folks say Amber offered you a desk job and you turned it down."

Preston scoffed at the idea, but he didn't outright deny what Joshua said because it was true. Amber had tried to put him in charge of ordering, shipping, and receiving. While he didn't mind unloading whatever supplies arrived, he didn't want to spend all day staring at a computer screen. His flashbacks seemed to lessen when he was physically busy, and sheer exhaustion allowed him to sleep at night. He'd told Amber he was worried about staying fit, which wasn't exactly a lie.

Too often what he said was a half-truth. He'd spoken with Tate about that, and they'd discussed ways he could maintain his privacy but still be truthful with people.

Amber had accepted that he didn't want the

31

promotion, and she hadn't seemed all that surprised. He was content in his position as assistant manager of maintenance. More than likely she understood and appreciated his reasoning. She was intuitive like that, reminding Preston in many ways of his own mother. Nancy Johnstone had passed while he was overseas, and though it had been many years, he still missed her.

If Amber had insisted, he would have taken the new job. Instead she offered the new position to someone else, and he'd continued his duties in maintenance. On some level he realized that he would do whatever Amber or Tate needed him to do. Both of them had literally saved his life. He owed them a debt he would never consider repaid.

"Look at this." Joshua held up the hoe. Dangling off the end was something that sparkled. He moved it carefully toward Preston, who plucked it off the end of the garden tool.

The bracelet was covered with mud and green sludge, and a piece of gum was stuck to one end. Preston was glad both he and Joshua were wearing rubber gloves that stretched up to their elbows. The stuff people dropped into ponds—on purpose or inadvertently—wasn't for the faint-hearted.

"A guest lost this before Christmas. She mourned it like a best friend who'd moved across the world without saying good-bye." He picked up his canteen and rinsed off the piece of jewelry.

"Not much to look at now—covered with all that sludge after sitting in this pond for six months."

"The diamonds are still good, and I suspect it's more the sentimental value than its actual worth that had her so upset. Elizabeth kept her address in case it showed up."

"Take it on over. We're practically done here."

Preston moved to the other side of the gravel road and studied the reverse side of the drain. The water was flowing through unobstructed. "Good work, Joshua."

"*Danki*, boss."

Holding out a hand, Preston pulled Joshua up onto the bank.

"I'll bag this up and take it to the Dumpster."

"Good deal. Then get out of those waders before you fall over. If you stay on my crew, we're going to have to order something that fits you better."

Joshua had developed plenty of muscle and strength since coming to work for Preston's department, but at five foot five, he was definitely the shortest member of the team.

Preston was halfway to the office when Hannah popped out of the yarn shop, nearly bowling him over.

"I'm so sorry. I was hurrying and wasn't looking where my feet were pointed."

"Is there an emergency?"

"Hopefully not. I was headed to check on Seth. He hasn't had a disaster in at least two weeks. We're overdue."

"I peeked inside A Simple Blend as I walked by. He was sitting at the table folding to-go menus."

"Sounds safe enough." Hannah hesitated before she brushed her *kapp* strings behind her shoulders and stepped closer. "Could I ask you a question?"

"Of course."

Preston moved toward the building, grateful for the shade. He liked Hannah. She was a good kid, and Jesse, the young man she was marrying, was one of the best workers on the property. There was also a possibility the reason he liked Hannah and Jesse so much had more to do with their shared history, the unlikely web of murder they had been caught up in together not once but twice. Preston was grateful those days were behind them.

"Do you know Ryan Duvall?"

"Sure," Preston answered cautiously. "I've known Ryan most of my life. It's a small town."

"It seems that he's taken a shine to Martha."

Preston crossed his arms and rested his back against the side of the building. "Ryan has a short attention span."

"*Ya.* So I've heard, and I hate to see Martha get hurt."

"Is she serious about him? I'm surprised she'd date outside of your faith."

"You know about *rumspringa*, right?"

"Sure. I see the occasional teen with a car or sporting the newest smartphone." An image of Joshua popped into his mind. The kid had purchased a dilapidated 1976 Ford short-bed truck. Faded paint, torn upholstery, and a broken air conditioner/heater unit did nothing to dampen the boy's enthusiasm for the old Ford. "Are you saying Martha is indulging in her taste of freedom from the *Ordnung*? And that she's doing so with Ryan?"

Preston had lived in Middlebury all his life, except for the time he lived overseas on Uncle Sam's nickel. He knew all about *rumspringa*, *Ordnung*, and the difficulties involved. In that respect little had changed since his days in high school.

Hannah frowned and puckered her bottom lip. "Our rules allow Martha to experience things freely in the *Englisch* world, within reason. I'm not worried about her receiving criticism for dating an *Englisch* man, though she insists they're not dating. Why a man as old as Ryan would be interested in a young girl like her—"

"It wouldn't be the first time such a thing happened."

"I'm more worried about Martha's heart. She has little experience in these things." As an afterthought she added, "She's always been rather shy."

"If I see Ryan I'll certainly suggest he move on if he's not serious—and I doubt he's serious."

"Thank you, Preston."

For a fleeting second Preston thought Hannah was going to stand on her tiptoes and kiss his cheek. Instead she reached out, squeezed his arm, and hurried on toward A Simple Blend, the coffee shop she managed for the Village.

Preston checked his pocket to make sure the recovered bracelet was still there and then set off for Amber's office.

The day was taking more twists and turns than a country road, but that didn't surprise him. If there was one thing he'd learned, it was to be patient and things would change. In this case, he was hoping they'd change back to calm and unremarkable.

Four

Preston walked into the restaurant and immediately relaxed. The familiar smells of hot coffee, fried chicken, and vegetable casseroles filled the room. He could close his eyes and envision each one, and he would have loved to stay and enjoy a big lunch. Instead he worked his way down the hall, resisted the sign proclaiming "Bakery—This

Way," and jogged up the stairs. The area opened into a nice-size waiting area, and beyond that were Amber's office, a conference room, and Pam's office. Elizabeth wasn't at her desk. She tended to take her lunch after everyone else.

Amber's door was open, so Preston passed the secretary's desk and tapped on the door frame.

Amber was typing ninety to nothing on her computer. She held up one finger, finished what she was doing with a flourish of keys, and then glanced up. When she did, Preston was struck once again by what a kind person she was. The grin that spread across her face was genuine, and her hazel eyes practically danced. It seemed to Preston that in Amber, God had provided the sister he'd never had, and he was grateful for that. An image of the park bench he used to sleep on crossed his mind, but he brushed it away. Even in his darkest days, God had a plan, one that often made no sense to him. Fortunately that plan had included the woman in front of him.

"I didn't think my day could get any better, but now it has." She came around the desk and enfolded him in a hug. The gesture of affection was so natural that Preston almost didn't flinch.

Amber grabbed his hand and pulled him toward the two chairs near the window, which overlooked the Village property.

"Tell me everything you've been doing, and how is Zoey? We were out of town, so we didn't see either of you at church last week."

"Zoey's good." Preston stopped there. If he started talking about Zoey, if he poured out his heart to Amber, he'd be an hour behind in his work. So instead he reached into his pocket and pulled out the bracelet.

Her eyes widened as she reached for it. "Is that what I think it is?"

Preston nodded. "Joshua was helping me clean out the drain at the top of the larger pond. Those diamonds winked at us through the muck and grime."

"Mrs. Stinson is going to be so thrilled to have it returned. Her father gave it to her for her eighteenth birthday."

Preston raised an eyebrow, and Amber laughed.

"I know. I received a fifty-dollar savings bond for my eighteenth—"

"My pop took me out for a steak dinner. I thought I was all grown up."

"As the daughter of a Texas oilman, Mrs. Stinson has lived a different life than you and I have. I suspect whether you're rich, poor, or middle class, your memories of those formative years are precious. Think about it, Preston. She must have received this in 1944. What a different place the world was then."

Preston's thoughts immediately went to World War II. His grandfather had served in the US Navy, and he'd grown up hearing stories of the

Pacific battles. No doubt, his decision to join the military could be traced back through his family tree. With a start, he realized Amber was still talking about the bracelet and the elderly woman who had inadvertently dropped it into the pond.

"I have a feeling it's the memories attached to this that bring her joy, not the market value." She held the bracelet in her hand and rubbed at the grime with one thumb.

"I told Joshua pretty much the same thing. It's a shame about the gunk and rust, though."

"Oh, I don't think there will be any rust. No doubt it was fashioned from the highest-quality gold. We'll send it to Carson's Jewelers and have it cleaned up."

"I can do that for you."

"Would you?" Amber patted his hand, then turned it over and dropped the bracelet back into his palm. "Thank you, and I will contact Mrs. Stinson and let her know we'll ship it to her home in Midland via Priority Mail and with insurance."

Preston stood to go, but Amber wasn't finished with him yet, or maybe she had never planned to let him off the hook so easily.

"Zoey is a sweet girl."

"Yes, she is, though she's hardly a girl."

"Have you thought any more about her suggestion?"

"I'm still thinking on it." Preston stopped there.

He wasn't about to go into all the reasons Zoey's idea wouldn't work.

"I want you to know that I spoke with the owners of the Village, and they are fully supportive, as am I." Her curly brown hair bounced when she nodded. Preston had noticed that she was wearing it that way—curly—rather than taming it into straight submission. The style made her look younger and also more relaxed.

She seemed to be waiting for him to agree. Instead he shrugged and remained silent.

"You're a stubborn man, Preston Johnstone." She started to say something else, then stopped herself and apparently reversed directions. "Would you two like to come over for dinner sometime soon? When Zoey is free?"

Preston stared out the window at the blossoming trees. Some days he could actually believe he'd been given another chance, and that this time things might turn out the way they should.

"I'll ask Zoey about her schedule and let you know, but I'm sure she'll say yes."

"Excellent, and tell her she doesn't have to bring a thing. Tate loves to cook."

Preston once again tucked the bracelet into his pants pocket and headed back out, stopping to say hello to Elizabeth as he did. She lowered her half-glasses and gave Preston the concerned-grandmotherly look, asking how he was getting along in the *Dawdy Haus*. "If there's anything you need, anything at all, you tell me and we'll put a purchase order or work requisition in."

"The house is fine, Elizabeth. Thank you."

"You don't have to do plumbing repairs yourself. We have a budget for those sorts of things." Her gray hair was cut in a short bob, and when she shook her head it swayed slightly back and forth.

Preston thanked her again, which they both knew meant he wouldn't call the next time. The way he looked at it, Amber had given him a second chance, a job, and a place to live. He could handle a backed-up drain or leaking faucet.

He made his way to the parking area, stopping to tell Joshua where he was going and asking him to relay the message to the maintenance secretary. As they spoke, they walked over to Preston's car—another step toward normalcy. It was a Volkswagen Beetle, 1964, and he'd been slowly restoring it.

"You put in the new seats."

"Last week."

"And you covered them yourself?"

"Zoey helped. She's better with a needle than I am, but with both of us working on it we were able to re-cover all three seats in a single weekend."

"I like the black leather. Should last a *gut* long time. What's next? New blue paint job? New convertible top?"

"I'm still fine-tuning the engine. The paint job can wait, and the top"—he ran his hand over the ivory-colored ragtop, which was stained in places but didn't leak a drop—"the top is good as is."

Joshua looked at Preston with an admiration that caused him to squirm. The last thing he had any business being was a role model for some kid who was about to be married. Not with his history.

Joshua waved a hand as Preston pulled away.

He drove toward the jeweler's. He didn't forget his promise to Hannah, but it occurred to him that in this case it might be best to give the situation a little time. He'd agreed to talk to Ryan to calm her nerves, but even though he didn't know him all that well, he was certain the situation would take care of itself. Ryan would be on to another girl before Preston had time to chase him down.

Five

Hannah worried the strings to her prayer *kapp* as she walked beside Jesse. They were making their way home from the Village via the Pumpkinvine Trail. They didn't hold hands, but they walked close to one another, pausing first to look at the blossoms on a black cherry tree and then to stare at a woodpecker who was busily pecking away for insects high in a maple tree.

They stood for a full five minutes and watched a doe standing in the center of a field, the afternoon sun slanting down around her.

Hannah knew Jesse would kiss her before saying good-bye at her house. She loved the private moments they shared. They made her think ahead to their marriage and the life they'd be embarking on together. She couldn't imagine feeling closer to him. In the quiet moments standing and watching the doe, it seemed their hearts beat in the same rhythm. In those times when he did pull her into his arms and kiss her lips, she marveled that she fit so naturally within his embrace, her heart tripping and her emotions soaring like the birds flying from the trees.

It was as if they were connected by an invisible cord, whether or not they were actually touching.

It was as if they were slowly becoming one person.

After the doe sprinted away, they continued down the trail.

"You're sure it was Letha who had been riding with Ryan?" Hannah kicked at a pebble as they made their way slowly toward home.

Letha was the manager of Village Fashions. Though she was Amish, Letha had never been married, and now she was old enough to be Hannah's mother. As far as Hannah knew, the woman had never so much as shared a buggy ride with an eligible man.

"*Ya*, it was Letha. There's no mistaking her dark hair—nearly black. Very unusual for an Amish woman, *ya*?"

Hannah shrugged. Letha's hair would have been covered with a *kapp*, but often that only accentuated how raven black her hair was. She was fairly easy to pick out in a crowd.

"She got out of his car in the parking lot earlier today."

"Well, she is certainly more his age, but I'm still confused."

"Confused about what, Hannah Bell?"

"Men, I suppose."

"All men?"

"No, not all." She pushed him playfully so that he brushed up against an Eastern Redbud in full bloom, causing tiny white flowers to shower down onto both of them. "Some men confuse me."

"Like Ryan."

"*Ya*. Why does he date both *Englisch* and Amish? You said you'd seen him in town with a woman from the city. And why date young girls as well as women his age? And why so many? I would think it would get terribly complicated."

"I don't know that Ryan sees it as dating. He's a friendly guy."

"Perhaps among the *Englisch* that's okay, but it most certainly is not acceptable in our community."

44

"There was that time when your *bruder* Ben tried dating one girl in our district and another in Shipshewana."

"It didn't work out so well for him, now did it?" Hannah smiled at the memory.

"*Nein*. I still can't believe those girls found out, spoke to each other, and then—"

"Both showed up at the ice cream shop where he was seeing one girl for lunch and the other for dinner."

"That was a bad idea. Too much ice cream can give you a terrible stomachache." Jesse dodged to the right to avoid Hannah's swipe.

"They straightened him out for sure and certain, and then no one would date him for a good month."

"He had to eat his ice cream all alone."

"Oh, Jesse. You act as if it's all fun and games."

"It is—"

"Until someone gets hurt," they said in unison.

"Ben never intended to hurt either girl, and I don't think Ryan does either." Jesse twined his fingers around her hand. "If the girls think what he's doing is wrong, they don't have to go out with him. It's not as if he sneaks around."

"I know Martha's parents would be happier if she were seeing a nice Amish boy her own age."

"*Ya*, after all, look at how happy your parents are that you've made such a fine catch in me."

"Jesse Miller, you're not a fish and I didn't catch you."

They'd reached the lane leading up to her home, and instead of arguing with her, Jesse dodged into the shadow of the large Red Maple, pulled her into his arms, and kissed her thoroughly. For a moment, Hannah forgot about Martha and Letha and Ryan. For a moment, all she thought of was Jesse and the blessing of their life together.

But later that night the subject of Ryan came up again while she was helping her mother put her sister to bed.

Mattie had grown in the last six months.

She'd also changed in ways that surprised Hannah.

Perhaps it had been too long since her brothers were small, or maybe now, looking at her little sister, she was realizing she could have her own child within the next year. Maybe. If it was *Gotte's wille*. For many girls it was several years before their first baby arrived.

Mattie was now speaking short sentences, and her vocabulary seemed to increase every day. More pointedly, though, she was sharing her opinion—which was often contrary to everyone else's.

"Stay Hannah." She stuck out her lower lip and threw herself into Hannah's arms, crocodile tears spouting from her eyes.

"It's bedtime for you, Mattie, but not for

Hannah. Now, no more arguing." Eunice entered the room Hannah shared with Mattie. She switched on the battery-operated lantern they kept on the table between their beds.

Her mother was a little shorter than Hannah and a good twenty pounds heavier. She'd removed her *kapp*, and her hair hung in a long braid down her back. Once the color of wheat, it was now mixed generously with gray. Good humor softened her tone, though she must have been exhausted. A farmer's wife woke early and went to bed late! Somehow Eunice managed to do all that was needed without complaining, though she did insist that each member of the family help. Even Mattie had chores, such as putting water out for the chickens (most sloshed on the ground) and helping with their feed (she'd often stand in one place and feed a single chicken).

Eunice set a small cup of water on the night-stand close to Mattie's bed.

"Stay Hannah!" She clung fiercely to Hannah's neck as if she were in a runaway buggy and fearing for her life.

"Sweetheart, sit beside me and I'll read to you while Hannah brushes out your hair."

Mattie finally relented, curling up next to her mother, who opened the old family Bible to the book of Genesis, chapter seven. In a soft, gentle voice, she began reading.

"The LORD then said to Noah, 'Go into the ark, you and your whole family, because I have found you righteous in this generation. Take with you seven of every kind of clean animal—' "

"Dogs." Mattie walked her fingers across the page.

"—'a male and its mate, and two of every kind of unclean animal, a male and its mate—' "

"Dogs!" Mattie insisted again.

"—'and also seven of every kind of bird, male and female, to keep their various kinds alive throughout the earth.' "

"Dogs, *Mamm*. Dogs!" Mattie pointed to the page, though it was filled with words, not pictures. Even the words were in German, but that didn't slow Mattie down.

"Yes, God put dogs on Noah's ark."

Hannah had unbraided Mattie's hair and now ran the brush gently from top to bottom. Her sister's hair was a warm blonde, and it already reached to the middle of her back.

"Cats!"

"Yes, I suppose there were cats too." Eunice smiled at Hannah over the top of Mattie's head.

"Camel!"

Both Hannah and Eunice laughed, and soon Mattie was joining in.

"I imagine your *bruder* taught you that word." Eunice closed the Bible and pulled down the quilt on Mattie's bed.

"Camel!"

"Is Dan actually going to purchase a camel?"

"He's ordered one, though it may be some time before it's delivered."

"Horse!"

"We'll have *Englischers* stopping by to take pictures." Hannah frowned as she returned the brush to the drawer of their nightstand.

"Unlikely. Manasses practically has a herd at this point. I'm sure he'll be the better photo op."

Mattie had escaped and begun jumping around the floor like a dog, or maybe she thought she was mimicking a camel. Eunice patted the spot beside her.

Mattie returned to the bed, her expression suddenly serious. She placed the palms of her hands together and closed her eyes, all thoughts of rebelling long gone, though she continued to whisper the names of various animals.

When Hannah and Eunice bowed their heads, Mattie grew quiet, then slipped one small hand into her mother's and the other small hand into Hannah's. In that moment, life was so right and so precious that Hannah felt a physical ache. She wanted to freeze time, to pretend things would never change.

It was after they'd tucked Mattie into bed and moved downstairs to work on their crocheting, that Hannah mentioned what was on her heart to her mother.

The sound of her three brothers and father in the kitchen, rummaging for a late-night snack and talking about the weather, provided a comfortable, familiar background.

"I'm going to miss all of this after the wedding."

"You'll be down the road, only a few minutes away." Eunice didn't pause as her crochet needle pulled the warm blue yarn so that the ball twisted and turned where it sat in the basket beside her chair. Hannah suspected it was a throw blanket she was making, and that it would be a gift for her and Jesse. She knew full well that it was a work of love, as Eunice had been up longer than any of them and no doubt would have liked to have gone straight to bed. But she sat in the rocker, working the yarn, and listening to Hannah's foolish fears.

"*Ya*, I know we won't be far away. Jesse's parents will begin work on two extra rooms now that the crops are all planted—one room for us and the other for Andrew and Mary."

"The four of you will be very close, Hannah. I'm so pleased you are marrying at the same time. You'll be able to share your joys and your burdens."

"But I'll miss"—Hannah's hand came out and waved toward the upstairs and then the kitchen —"all of this."

Eunice smiled at her over the top of her reader glasses.

"Change is difficult, even when it's something we've looked forward to for many years."

Hannah pulled out the dish towels she'd been knitting for Mary and Andrew. She had eight completed, but she was hoping to give them an even dozen. The yarn was a nice cotton blend—an off-white with a light dash of pink, Mary's favorite color.

"Do you ever worry?" Hannah asked. "About us all moving away and being left here alone with *Dat*?"

"*Nein.*" Eunice rocked as she crocheted. "The chatter of *kinner* will be replaced with the sweet sounds of *grandkinner*. Yet another kind of change, but a natural one."

"Which of the boys will stay to help *Dat* with the farm?" Hannah's brothers were twenty, seventeen, and sixteen. The oldest two had girlfriends, but neither seemed to take their relationship seriously the last time she'd asked. Of course, that could change quickly. Look at her and Jesse!

Six months ago, they'd been best of friends, and Hannah had worried they'd never be anything more. Now they'd soon be wed. Relationships had a way of changing suddenly and permanently. She'd eyed each girl the boys sat with during singings and wondered if they would one day be her sister. More change.

"We can't possibly know who will stay and who will have their own place to farm. It will depend on what your *bruders* decide to do and whom they marry—the situation of the family they are marrying into. Then there's Dan's fascination with camels, which might keep him here, or he may go to Pennsylvania—"

"Pennsylvania?"

"*Ya*. There is much he could learn there. Some of your *dat's* family live in the Lancaster district, and several of the men have worked with camels for years. As Manasses told us, the milk is good for those who are sick—people with Crohn's disease and diabetes. Perhaps it can also help those who have chronic intestinal problems. Instead of the supplements, they can drink the camel's milk and be able to digest it, providing them the nutrients they need." Eunice shook her head. "Even the *Englisch* doctors don't fully understand the benefits yet, but it seems as if it will be a *gut* profession for your *bruder*."

"I didn't know he was thinking of leaving." Hannah stared at the half-made dish towel in her hands and wondered what stitch she had been using.

"Visiting is a better word. He doesn't plan to stay."

"*Mamm*, why didn't I know about this?"

"We speak of it at dinner, but sometimes you—"

"Daydream?"

"*Ya*." Eunice again smiled. It wasn't a criticism as much as an observation.

"What else have I missed?"

Her mother seemed about to share more news, hesitated, then shook her head as if she had thought better of it.

"The point is that your *dat* and I understand this is a time of change, and that it's natural. You don't need to worry about us being alone. You'll be down the road, and Mattie still has many years before she is gone."

"It's hard to imagine her married."

"True. Whoever *Gotte* intends for her husband will need to be a patient man."

"And it might help if he likes all the animals *Gotte* put on the ark."

They both resumed their crochet work, and then Hannah's mind drifted to Martha and Ryan.

She spoke to her mother of her concern for Martha, who seemed hopelessly naive, and how she didn't understand Ryan Duvall one bit.

"We can never truly know what's in another person's heart, Hannah. We can pray for them, and you can do your best to be a true friend to Martha —not only in word but also in deed. Talk to her, listen to her, and be there if she needs you."

It was with those words of wisdom ringing through her heart that Hannah slipped back upstairs to her room and fell into a restless, troubled sleep. In her dreams, she and Amber were once again scouring Middlebury, following a shadow that she could never quite make out.

Six

Amber knew better than to work late in the evening. She'd already spent a half hour revisiting her Stitch Club project from earlier that day, and now she had an urge to confirm that everything was running smoothly at the Village. She hesitated for a moment, then reached for her tablet. It wouldn't hurt to check her e-mail one final time before heading to bed. She wasn't sure why she had fallen into the habit of doing so. Who would e-mail her at ten in the evening? Yet habits die hard, and she was able to rest better knowing nothing at work needed her attention.

Plus Tate enjoyed watching the local late news. They both finished up by the half hour. He'd been winking at her for the last twenty minutes, causing laughter to bubble up and goose bumps to scatter across her arms. She'd known that marrying Tate had been the right thing to do—he was steady, practical, and kind. Plus she loved him! What she hadn't realized was that being married to him would be so much fun.

Leo stared at her from his place in the seat of the rocker, his feet tucked neatly underneath him. The golden-colored cat had adjusted easily to their new home with Tate. Though he was pretending to sleep, he'd open his eyes occasionally to study her. She could hear his purring from across the room.

She logged on quickly, thinking there would be nothing of importance, and she could beat Tate to their room. The smile on her face quickly faded when she saw the subject line for the top e-mail, "Poisonous Sweets."

Glancing at Tate, she decided not to interrupt his concentration—his attention was completely focused on watching the local sports report. The Northridge Raider High School softball team was off to a strong start for the season and had apparently fared well in the first weekend tournament.

Amber's finger hovered over the "Delete" button.

Perhaps it was spam.

Opening it might release a data-eating virus.

Then again, her spam filter should have caught any e-mail that looked even remotely sinister. She'd recently installed all the updates. Surely that had beefed up her tablet to protect her against any type of malware.

In the end, it was her curiosity that caused her to click it open.

A small squeak escaped her lips as she quickly read over the short message.

Tate muted the sound on the television.

"What's up? I haven't heard that sound since

Leo brought in a—" Tate stood and moved beside her on the couch. "Tell me what's wrong. You're pale as the patch between Trixie's eyes."

Any mention of their donkeys usually lightened Amber's mood, but not this time. This time she placed the tablet in Tate's hands and pointed toward the screen.

Kindness is a virtue
Meanness is a sin
Better watch your bakery pies
For poison I've slipped in

"Prank e-mail?" Tate scanned to the top of the screen. "I don't recognize the name of whoever sent it."

"Because it's not a name. It looks like random letters and numbers. I'm surprised my spam filter allowed it through."

"It must have been addressed specifically to you. Most spam goes out to a batch of folks. That's the main way it's caught."

"I don't understand, though. Why me? And what does it mean?"

"That someone wants you to throw away all of tomorrow's pies. Do you have any new competition in town?"

"Not that I know of, and wouldn't that be rather obvious? Why not walk up to our house and nail a note on the door?"

Tate set the tablet on the end table and pulled her into his arms.

"Anything new going on at the Village?"

"No. Nothing."

"Have you fired anyone lately?"

"No."

"Turned down someone for employment who might be angry?"

"Not that I can remember, but Pam does most of the hiring now."

"You can call her first thing tomorrow."

"But—"

"No one is going to be in your bakery eating pie at this hour. You can rest easy. The restaurant and bakery are closed by now, correct?"

"They should be."

"Not to mention this is a hoax. It's designed to rattle you."

"Mission accomplished." Amber snuggled into his arms and breathed deeply, enjoying the smell of him and the steadiness, reminding herself how far she'd come in learning to trust God with the details of her life.

Tate kissed the top of her head.

"We've been through too much to let some teen punk rattle us."

"What makes you think it's a teen?"

"Cyberbullying? It's a classic teenage move— anonymous and instantaneous."

Amber supposed he was right. She couldn't

think of one person who would be angry with her or the Village. Things had been going smoothly since—

She pushed the thought of Owen Esch from her mind.

That murder was solved, and they'd all moved on from the events of the previous fall.

Tate was probably right.

She was overreacting.

With a conscious effort, she slowed her breathing and forced her shoulders to relax. She'd show the e-mail to Pam in the morning. Her assistant was like Tate—not easily shaken. If necessary they'd go see Georgia, the bakery manager. The last thing she needed to do was call Gordon Avery after ten o'clock at night. She'd been through two murder investigations with the Middlebury Police sergeant. He deserved a rest from her meddling. Not that this would be meddling. A girl needed to protect her business, not to mention her customers.

It was with the conviction that everything was okay that she went to bed, convinced the note was indeed from a spammer with poor poetry skills.

Preston struggled up the rocky slope, placing his hand against the mountain wall. Instead of dirt, he touched rock, gravel, and grit. The sun blazed down on the four of them—Toby, Bogar, Frank, and him. The harshness of the

58

sun cast everything and everyone in an uncompromising light. It hadn't rained in the last sixty days, not since he'd arrived in northeastern Afghanistan. He moved slowly and methodically, careful to avoid kicking up dust. Something wasn't as it should be. He couldn't put his finger on it, couldn't single out one thing that was out of place, but his instincts told him something was wrong.

His instincts told him to run.

He gripped his rifle more tightly, ignoring the slickness of his palms and the way his heart thumped and thundered in his chest.

Toby was ten meters in front of him, Frank ten meters behind. When Toby held up his right hand, they both stopped instantaneously.

So they felt it too. The thing that was wrong. The danger lurking close, closer each moment.

Preston scanned the slope below them and the valley that spread out to the south. Nothing moved. Even the animals sought what shade could be found at this time of day. The image before him was like something out of a picture, an ageless vista that had withstood countless armies and men.

Toby signaled for them to continue. He'd barely lowered his arm when the first explosion shook the ground, and then Preston's regiment leader vanished.

One moment there, the next—gone.

It was as if he had dropped over the ridge, but Preston knew he hadn't. Through the dust and smoke he could see what was left of Toby's pack. The man hadn't even had time to scream.

Preston turned, the cry of "Go back!" attempting to claw its way out of his throat. Frank's eyes met his for a split second, and then the man turned and was running down the mountain trail, retracing their steps.

Preston tried to sprint after him, but his legs refused to budge. He stood there, frozen, moving nothing except for his eyes—scanning to the right, where Toby had been, then to his left, at Frank who was beating a path to their previous location. In front of him, sunlight glinted off metal. Preston raised his rifle, took the shot, and saw the insurgent fall to the ground.

He turned to run after Frank, but found his way blocked. Seized with an instinctive panic, he closed his eyes and took a deep breath, then forced his legs to move. He would crawl if need be, but he would find a way over or around the rock and gravel debris that had fallen, obscuring the path.

His boots scraped against the trail.

Desert sounds slowly returned—first the cry of a hawk and then the sound of the wind rushing across the sand below.

Sweat poured down his back.

Their fallback position seemed a hundred miles away.

He stopped to rest, scan the horizon, and drink from his canteen. He needed to close his eyes—if only for a brief second. He needed to wipe away the image of the sights he had just seen, but it seemed that they had been carved upon his heart. He closed his eyes and vowed to rest no more than two minutes.

When he opened them he was crouched in the mouth of a cave looking out over the desert. The sun's rays were still beating down, but there was an angle to the light now. Darkness would fall within a few hours. How long had they been there?

Frank lay beside him, a makeshift tourniquet wrapped above his right knee, the leg below the tourniquet a bloody mess. It took only a brief look to understand that no doctor would be fixing what was left of Frank Cannopy's right leg. Had Preston placed the tourniquet? How had he moved the man from the ridge to the cave?

How?

And why?

Why didn't he carry him back to camp?

"Are they still out there?" Frank's voice was barely a whisper, but still Preston flinched.

If they were found they had enough ammunition to stop the first dozen who attempted to breach the cave where they were hidden. Their chances against an entire group of Taliban, and that had to be who had attacked, were slim. Against an RPG or grenade attack they had no chance at all.

He turned toward Frank, and in doing so he knocked over their packs. The sound echoed through the cave, amplified by the rock walls, signaling their exact location to whoever was out there.

Preston blinked once, twice, and then a third time before he realized he was in the *Dawdy Haus*, crouched in the corner of his bedroom, not in the province of Nuristan south of the Hindu Kush Valley. He blinked again, reached up, and wiped away the sweat dripping down his face and into his eyes, mixing with salty tears.

His arms began to shake.

He stayed where he was, waiting for the episode to pass and for his heartbeat to return to normal. It took several moments to realize he was holding his bedside lamp across his chest, clutching it as if it were the rifle that could save his life—their lives.

Slowly his breathing evened out.

He closed his eyes and prayed for the peace God promised. Prayed this was the last time.

Prayed that he would find a way to leave that other life, that other world behind.

Finally he stood, his legs wobbly from crouching for so long. How many minutes had he been there, in a defensive position in the corner of his bedroom? He walked to the light switch on the wall and counted to three before he switched it on.

The scene that met his eyes was one of destruction.

His bed was a shambles, the mattress on its side and the sheets a pile on the floor. The nightstand, the one he'd grabbed the lamp from, was knocked over, and one of the legs had broken in the process. The battery-operated alarm clock had skittered across the floor. The sole picture in the room, a print of an Indiana sunrise over a farmer's field, had been knocked crooked.

With his back to the wall, he slid to the floor and studied the chaos in front of him. He didn't remember any of it. He remembered the battle well enough—the smell of gunfire was still strong, causing bile to rise up in his throat. He could see the image of Toby—what was left of Toby—and he could remember now that what remained on the trail of his commander and friend was more than the piece of pack he'd seen in his dream.

He covered his face and allowed the emotion to pour out of him, until his shoulders shook and his throat ached. He cried for Frank and for Toby, but also for every soldier who had endured that terrible battle. He wept for the ones who made it and the ones who didn't.

And when he thought he had no tears left, he cried for the normal life that he'd never have—the life he longed to share with Zoey but knew he couldn't.

How could he ask her to endure scenes like this night after night? How could he be sure he wouldn't hurt her while he was lost in the past?

He was home, but a part of him was still over there. And he wasn't sure he could ever bury the part that had died. He wasn't sure he would ever be truly free of his past.

Seven

More coffee was what Amber needed. Turning right, she bypassed the building that held her office and headed toward A Simple Blend. She'd received a text from Pam, and they were meeting at eight thirty to talk about the poison poetry e-mail. In the light of an Indiana spring morning, it all seemed rather silly. So Amber decided to start her day in her favorite way.

Tate made excellent coffee, so she didn't need to visit the Village shop to receive her daily dose of caffeine, though she wouldn't turn down an extra cup. No, that wasn't the reason she went. She went because she liked stopping in to see Hannah before their day began. She'd grown close to the young girl in the last year. In her mind, it was like taking a moment to wish her younger sister a good day.

Which was somewhat ironic since she had a younger sister—Madison, to whom she was quite close. Madison was married and living in Biloxi, Mississippi. She had visited over the Christmas holidays, bringing her two daughters, though her husband couldn't take off the extra time from work. Chase was a pastor at one of the larger churches in Biloxi. He received vacation time, but they tried to save it up for family trips during spring break and the summer.

Madison had agreed that Hannah was like the baby sister they'd never had.

They had laughed about that, remembering how they'd dress their mother's Chihuahua in clothes meant for their dolls. The poor dog had suffered mightily at their hands, though they'd always rewarded him with extra treats. That could have been the reason he'd been nearly as round as he was tall.

Amber walked into the shop and was greeted by the smell of recently brewed coffee and the sight of freshly baked pastries. When Hannah had first taken over the shop, the pastries were delivered by an outside firm. Hannah had asked why they didn't use what was in the bakery. Amber had broached the subject with Georgia, who readily agreed as long as she could have one extra employee to help in the early morning hours.

The move had netted them a bigger profit as well as happier customers.

"Tell me you have one of Georgia's apple Danishes left."

"We're barely open. Of course I have one." Hannah laughed as she pulled it from the display case, then poured her a cup of her favorite blend. "And if we'd started running out, I would have saved one for you."

"Am I that predictable?"

"*Nein*. The days you don't stop by for a fresh Danish, I sell the one I set back to Jesse."

Three customers stepped into the shop, and Amber carried her Danish and coffee to a corner table. She enjoyed watching customers come in and out of the shop, and she also liked the way Hannah interacted with them. Some of the tourists were bold and asked Hannah questions about her dress and way of life. Others stole overt glances when Hannah had her back turned, as if by looking closer they would understand what it meant to be plain. Hannah withstood it all in good humor.

Hannah was about Amber's size—five and a half feet, with a slight build and chestnut brown hair. They could have passed for sisters, except

Amber was an inch shorter and her hair was naturally curly. For most of her life she had fought those curls, but days before they were married Tate told her how much he liked her "natural" look. She decided to experiment with wearing it that way. Once she did, she couldn't remember why she'd ever spent so much time trying to rope her hair into a hairstyle that wasn't hers naturally. She loved having a good haircut, but she wouldn't spend another minute on straighteners, blow dryers, or flatirons.

She'd been set free.

When the customers left, Hannah grabbed a mug of hot tea and joined Amber at the table.

"What did you think of yesterday's knitting class?" Hannah clasped her hands around the warm mug.

"I liked it. I like seeing what other people are making. It's encouraging, even though I'm crocheting and most of you are knitting."

"One needle or two, that's the only difference."

"So you say, but remember when I tried knitting? It looked like I was making a tube sock, the way it curled."

Hannah started to laugh. "*Ya*, your crocheting is much better."

"It's faster too."

"For you it is, and probably for me. My *mamm*, though? She knits faster than I can crochet."

"Your *mamm* is an amazing woman."

Hannah blushed as if she were the one who had been complimented, but she also nodded in agreement. Then she cleared her throat and sat up straighter. "I saw Preston yesterday as I was leaving the yarn shop. I asked him if he would maybe speak with Ryan."

"About Martha?"

"*Ya.* I don't think she understands that Ryan isn't serious about having a relationship. I don't want her to get hurt. Also, Jesse told me he saw Letha get out of Ryan's car."

"Our Letha?"

"The very same. Surely Ryan isn't dating them both."

"Letha is closer to my age, and as far as I can remember is not very interested in dating."

"Except now maybe she is. Maybe Ryan is thinking of the Village as a one-stop shop for his dating needs." Hannah frowned as she worried the strings of her prayer *kapp*.

"It would be nice if we could protect those we love from heartache, but it isn't always possible."

"*Ya*, Jesse said something similar. Still, we can try, and if Preston knows him and can set things right before they go too far . . ."

"Why isn't Martha dating someone her own age, someone from your community?"

Hannah sipped from her tea before she answered. "We were in school together, Martha and I. She was always the quiet one, the scholar our teacher never caught talking or dawdling on the playground during break—though she loved the games of softball and volleyball. Still, she would always be the first one back in the schoolhouse door. She always had her homework done and ready."

"A teacher pleaser, huh?"

"I guess you could call her that, but she acted this way everywhere—school, home, even here at work. Martha's always been a people pleaser. She does what she thinks will make others happy."

"But?"

"I'm not sure." Hannah tapped the table as she stared out the window. "Her younger *schweschder* married last month. Maybe it's caused her to reconsider things."

"She's a pretty girl."

"True, but in a plain community it isn't always about who is the prettiest. Sometimes it's about who is the most interested. If one boy asks you to a singing and you say no, well, nothing much is thought about that. If you turn down several boys who ask you, though, then boys start assuming you're not interested."

"Not too different from my high school."

Hannah cocked her head, but didn't agree or disagree.

"So why did Martha always say no?"

"I couldn't tell you, but when we were in

school she was always quiet and never very social. She wasn't rude or anything, but she seemed to prefer being alone."

"We call that being introverted, and many people feel that way."

"Maybe so, but suddenly something has changed with Martha. Perhaps it's the thought of being the one still home with her parents. It could be that she's started to realize what she'll miss—having a home of her own, a husband to love her, children. It seems to me that maybe she decided she wanted to date, but no one asks anymore . . ."

"Until Ryan did."

"Exactly, though looking at horses isn't actually a date."

"Sometimes what starts out as *not dating* turns into that very thing." Amber thought about her and Tate and the incident with the donkeys and the storm and the vandalism that had brought them together. That certainly had not been a date, but it had led to one, which had led to another. Now they were happily married.

She glanced at the time on her phone. She had ten minutes before she was supposed to meet with Pam, which reminded her of the e-mail they needed to discuss. "Say, Hannah. You haven't heard of anyone who is unhappy in their job, or maybe angry about something that happened here at the Village, have you?"

"*Nein*. Why?"

Amber considered how much she should say, but in the end she remembered how helpful Hannah had been in the last two situations they'd encountered. If it weren't for the girl sitting across from her, she could have died both times. Hannah might be young, but she was also mature.

So Amber turned on her tablet and showed her the e-mail.

Hannah's eyes widened as she read it. "Sounds like a bad joke."

"I thought so too. I spoke with Georgia before I came over here. She assured me that no one has access to her baking supplies except for her and the employees directly under her. She told me to stop worrying."

"Did you?"

"A little." Amber smiled as she stood and collected her keys, tablet, and purse. "I came here, didn't I?"

"But it's hard to resist my *kaffi*."

"True."

"What will you do?"

"I'm meeting with Pam to discuss it in a few minutes. If you hear of anyone, though, anyone at all who might be upset with me or someone here at the Village, let me know. For once I'd like to stop a situation before it spins out of control."

Eight

Hannah desperately needed a break. She needed to go talk to Martha.

She usually waited until Seth had arrived and their morning rush was over. Seth Kauffman was eighteen years old, over six feet tall, and had brown hair and mocha-colored eyes. Hannah had noticed some of the girls at church meeting gazing at him, then giggling behind their hands. It seemed to her that everyone was changing, growing older, growing up! She especially noticed the difference in Seth, who now worked for her. He no longer seemed like a young teenager.

Walking into the coffee shop ten minutes before his shift was due to start, Seth greeted her and then made his way calmly to the back room, where his apron was stored on a hook. He'd definitely changed over the last year. There was a time when she was afraid to leave him alone in the coffee shop, even for a fifteen-minute break. But Seth had matured. He did occasionally still find himself in the oddest situations, but those instances were fewer and farther apart. The last one Hannah could remember was when he'd been working on their front window display and broken one of the crates they used to set merchandise on. Instead of telling her, he'd gone out and bought superglue, then proceeded to glue his fingers together.

Fortunately Pam Coleman, Amber's assistant general manager, had happened by. She knew the remedy for super-glued fingers—salt! "My grammy always said a pinch of salt could cure a world of ills."

They'd scrubbed Seth's fingers with a salt paste, and the rough residue had melted away. Pam was good with homemade remedies. She would have made a wonderful Amish person, though she did not dress plain, and to be truthful, there were few black Amish. Hannah had certainly never met one.

One part of Hannah's mind said that Seth was overdue for an accident, as she'd suggested to Preston the day before. The more charitable part of her mind said that perhaps he was growing out of such foolishness.

"Would you like me to clean out the syrup containers while you're gone?"

"Can you do it without spilling?"

"I only did that once."

"Or putting the syrup back in the wrong containers?"

"That was a little funny." He sobered when he saw her disapproving expression. "Not very funny, though. I'll be extra careful."

"You're doing well, Seth. One day you may be the manager here instead of me."

Seth froze, a large container of raspberry syrup in his hands. "Why would I do that? I like working for you, Hannah."

"You know as well as I do that plain women don't work after they marry—not usually anyway."

"You could." His face reddened, but he pushed forward. "Until your first *boppli* arrives you could."

"What?"

"I don't think Jesse would mind if you kept working after you marry, and our bishop tends to leave such decisions to the family."

Hannah simply stared at Seth. She'd been so busy preparing for her wedding and worrying about Ryan Duvall and her friends that she honestly hadn't given any thought to whether she would continue working. She liked the idea of being home with little ones, but . . . but what? That was what Amish women did! She'd miss the coffee shop, though. It had become her private little haven.

"We'll see. It's not something you have to worry about today. I'll be back after a short break."

"Take your time." He waved her away, the look on his face still a bit unsettled. Apparently it had never occurred to him that things would change. Hannah was only a few years older, but already she was learning that things always changed.

There was no point in being anxious about it, as change was the one constant in anyone's world. Come to think of it, her mother had said something similar during their talk the night before.

She didn't pause to look in any of the shop windows though they were filled with colorful spring displays that normally would have enticed her. Instead she walked straight to the inn and pushed open the door. The reception area always brought a smile to Hannah's face. Tall, clear vases held bright, silk spring flowers. Amber insisted on artificial displays because some of the guests were allergic to fresh floral arrangements. A light lemony scent filled the air, indicating the furniture had been recently dusted. Sunshine poured through the blinds, which were partially open. The couches and chairs positioned in the sitting area were upholstered in cheerful floral prints. A few *Englischers* lounged in the chairs, but most of the area was empty.

Martha and Jake stood behind the counter. Martha was filing some paperwork and Jake was straightening pens and paper.

"You two look bored."

"Hardly." Martha closed the file in her hand and tucked it into a drawer. "We just had a rush, folks checking out early to drive through the countryside. They want to catch the Amish farmers for some pictures."

Hannah laughed. "I hope they started early. My *dat* had the plow hitched up by six this morning."

Jake shook his head as he placed his elbows on the counter and stared out the front window. "That is too early for anyone to be working outside."

Jake wore his black hair long and pulled back into a ponytail. Hannah didn't know many men who had long hair—in fact, she couldn't think of any others. When he'd first come to work at the Village, Hannah had thought him rather strange. Now she knew him better. She understood he wasn't strange, only different. Jake was an artist, but instead of paper and paint, he created art on computers. She didn't completely understand how he did this, but he'd showed her a few things and they were quite good. He called it graphic design, and Amber had recently hired him to help redo the Village webpage.

Hannah stepped closer to Martha and lowered her voice. "I was wondering if you could take a break now."

"I guess. Things should stay quiet around here for another half hour or so."

"This won't take long."

Martha turned to confirm it was okay with Jake, but he waved her away. "Get out of here. I can handle a few checkouts on my own."

"Fifteen minutes. We won't be any longer."

Hannah and Martha hurried outside and over to a bench.

"What is it? Is something wrong?"

"*Nein*. I wanted to know if you went to Ryan's after work yesterday."

Martha smiled and folded her hands in her lap.

"You did!" Hannah lowered her voice. "Sorry. I didn't mean to shout, but I can't believe you actually did it. I thought you would change your mind."

"I did not change my mind." Martha's eyes practically sparkled. "I'm tired of being the shy, quiet Martha everyone thinks of as their *schweschder*. If Amish boys don't want to ask me out, then I'll go out with *Englischers*."

"Is that what this is about?"

"Maybe. Or maybe I woke up one morning and realized that life doesn't stand still. I'm not getting any younger, you know. I don't want to end up like some of the old women in our district who never had a chance to experience romance or love or having their own family."

"But, Martha, you're nowhere near as old as the women you're thinking about—and yes, I know who it is you're referring to."

An image of Katie Schmucker popped into Hannah's mind. Katie had been married, but when her husband died it was as if a part of her heart died too. She never remarried, never had children, and she'd lived in a room at her brother's for as long as Hannah could remember. Then there was Letha Keim, who loved working at the Village but was still single. Why she had never married, Hannah couldn't begin to guess. As far as she knew, Letha had never even attended singings, and of course now she was too old for such things.

"You're not that old," Hannah said again.

"Maybe not, but I think it sneaks up on you. I'm not going to let that happen to me. I'm going to do something about it."

"Something like go out with Ryan Duvall?"

Martha hesitated, staring down at her hands. When she did look up, there was a smile tugging at her lips. "He's very sweet, Hannah. And he knows about our ways. He's lived here all his life."

"Still, he's not Amish."

"That's true, but we only went to see his father's horses. They're *wunderbaar*. All sorts of buggy horses and work horses too. The foals are a sight for sure."

"And . . ."

"And what?"

"You're seeing him again, aren't you? I can tell by the way you keep smiling as if you have a special secret."

"He offered to take me to Goshen to dinner at the Hibachi Grill."

"When?"

"Thursday night. It's the next evening he has free. I'm sure his father keeps him very busy with so many horses."

"I'm sure."

If Martha recognized the sarcasm in Hannah's voice, she didn't react to it. "I don't even know what a Hibachi Grill is, but it sounds like fun!"

"You said yes already?"

"Of course I said yes. Do you think I want to stay home and eat with my parents every night? Always one of my *bruders* or *schweschders* has something happening with their beaus or their spouses, and I sit there—like a cat everyone ignores. I'd much rather be at the Hibachi Grill."

Hannah took a moment before she answered. She had the feeling anything she said would push Martha closer to Ryan. And what did she actually know about him? Nothing. Only what she had heard, which wasn't actually a fair basis to decide whether or not you like someone.

She knew from Jesse that Ryan had given Letha a ride to the Village, but perhaps a ride with an *Englischer* did not mean the same thing as a buggy ride with an eligible Amish man. Perhaps this wasn't her business.

Finally, she pulled Martha's hands into her lap, and waited until she raised her eyes.

"Promise me you'll be careful, *ya*?"

"Of course." Martha jumped up. "I should go back inside. Jake's *gut* with the computer, but if we have a rush of folks checking out he'll need help."

As Martha walked back into the inn, Hannah couldn't help noticing there was a new spring in her step and a healthier color in her cheeks. Perhaps this would all blow over in a couple of weeks, but in the meantime, she'd be supportive of her friend.

That's what friends did.

They stood by one another, even through the murky waters. But as she walked back toward the coffee shop, she prayed that those murky waters would clear quickly. She didn't want to be worrying over Martha and Ryan and Letha. It was enough to think about her job and supervising Seth, not to mention preparing for her upcoming wedding.

And then there was Amber's disgruntled poet.

Why would anyone claim to taint the Village pies with poison?

Another mystery, and the last one they'd solved had involved uncovering a murderer. Fortunately, this didn't seem quite so serious.

Delusional? Maybe.

Dangerous? She doubted it.

No one would have access to the bakery supplies unless Georgia personally handed them the key. The woman ran a tight shop, and for once Hannah was very glad for that.

She didn't doubt for a minute that everything would be cleared up in a few days. By the time May rolled around, they would be laughing at the problems of the month before.

And hopefully by then, Ryan Duvall would be out of their lives for good.

Amber's morning had gone well.

She'd met with Pam. Together they'd gone over the mysterious e-mail from the night before, and they had both decided it was the product of a sick, bored person. There was nothing to worry about. This in no way compared to the incident with Owen Esch or Ethan Gray.

Relieved, Amber had gone about her morning with a quieted mind and a reassured heart. She'd tackled her in-box, clearing it out completely, and she'd fielded a couple of phone calls regarding the upcoming Race for a Cure. This was to be their first time to serve as host. To her surprise she stared at her calendar and realized the date was fast approaching with less than four weeks to prepare. Pam was handling the bulk of the details, but there were still a few matters Amber needed to address. She was happy to get those out of the way and focus her attention on the day-to-day running of the Village.

Her stomach grumbled, reminding her it was time for lunch. She stood and collected her keys and tablet, then glanced toward her main computer. Three new e-mails had popped up in her mailbox. Read them now or wait?

She decided to deal with them before leaving. She was meeting Tate for lunch in town. They were to grab a sandwich and then stop by the local nursery. It was Amber's first time to have a real home garden, and she was beside herself with enthusiasm—something Tate tolerated with a smile and a warning that they'd have to weed all the rows she was insistent upon planting. Their vegetables had been set in the ground, and now she wanted to add a few flowers. The lunch would probably stretch to two hours. She'd already cleared her calendar, but the e-mails . . . well, they might be something she needed to deal with.

When she clicked the little mail button, her heart skidded to a stop. She stared at the screen, unable to accept what she was seeing. Two of the e-mails were from Elizabeth—one with the weekly comments from their webpage and the other a forwarded message from their local newspaper requesting an interview.

It was the third e-mail that caused her to feel as if she were sinking back into an all-too-familiar nightmare.

Another anonymous e-mail.

This time the subject line read "First Warning."

Amber didn't know whether to be worried or irritated as her finger hovered over the Open button. She could just delete it, but if she did she'd spend the rest of the day wondering what it said.

Sitting back down in her chair and pulling her mouse closer, she opened the e-mail, fully expecting a skull and crossbones to greet her before her computer crashed.

Never read anonymous e-mails!

She'd seen the advice a dozen times, but . . . she had an inquisitive nature. Surely her malware would have filtered out any malicious programming.

If I had wanted our business blabbed to the entire Village I would have done so myself. It would have been a piece of cake to involve your precious friends. I don't want that. I want this to stay between me and you.

Keep Hannah out of our business. It would be tragic if something happened to the poor girl—right before her wedding and all.

I'm guessing you showed our previous correspondence to your uppity assistant and goody-two-shoes husband as well.

Stop!

Or you'll force me to do something we'll both regret.

Amber tried to breathe, but she felt as if a giant hand were squeezing her heart. She read the e-mail again, and then one more time after that. The words didn't change. The threat was plain as could be. She was once more in the crosshairs of a crazed killer—or wannabe killer—and this time she was supposed to endure it alone.

Nine

Preston hurried toward the Village restaurant, intent on his mission. Several times a week he purchased a sack lunch as well as the local newspaper. He went to visit his dad at least every other day, always stopping to buy him a current paper. His father wasn't much of a reader. He'd recently turned eighty-two and had some trouble focusing on an article for any amount of time. Perhaps that was a side effect of his dementia. He might not read a lot anymore, but he delighted in completing the crossword puzzle out of the paper every day.

Preston's relationship with his father had been a rocky one since his return from Afghanistan. Initially he had lived with his dad, but that hadn't worked out so well. His dad was still mourning the loss of his mother, who had died while Preston was overseas. He also didn't understand why Preston was having problems adjusting to civilian life. He couldn't understand or even comprehend what PTSD was.

Preston still winced at that diagnosis, but he had at least reached the place where he no longer denied it. Post-Traumatic Stress Disorder was a real illness that many people suffered from, not just soldiers. Realizing that had been the first step on his road to recovery, and he'd been able to at least admit he had a serious problem. Soon after that realization he'd moved out of his dad's home and begun living on the streets of Middlebury.

Folks thought living on the streets was difficult, and it was problematic in many respects. But it wasn't as hard as seeing the disappointment and confusion in his dad's eyes. Then there had been the time he'd come out of a flashback, and he was holding an iron skillet and swinging it wildly to protect himself. His father had stood a few feet away, frozen, unsure how to handle what he was seeing. Preston had moved out the next day.

He would have tried to lease an apartment, but he soon discovered that holding a job was going to be a problem. He'd do well for a week or so, then he'd have an episode at work. If he had told any of his employers he had PTSD, they would have kept him on, would have probably offered counseling of some sort. But he was still in denial as to the extent of his problem at that point. For a time he'd tried coping with alcohol and drugs. Those things had numbed the pain, but they hadn't resolved anything.

The dreams and flashbacks continued to plague him, even when he slept in the park. But he woke from them more quickly, and there was seldom anyone close enough to him to be in danger.

It had taken some convincing for him to move off the streets. Tate and Amber had been persistent, though. At first he'd stayed in the barn on the Amish Village property. He'd worked each day, and begun eating regular meals again. When Amber married, she suggested he move into the *Dawdy Haus* because she was moving into Tate's home. He'd been less sure about that, but agreed to it on a trial basis.

The best part of the entire situation was that his dad had since moved to a retirement home across the street from the Village. Preston was able to check on him often. When any type of issue arose, the staff there called the Village, and Preston was able to leave work and be at his dad's side in a matter of minutes.

Preston stepped into the restaurant, bypassing the line of waiting guests and moving down the hall to the bakery. Georgia was bustling behind the counter, fetching cinnamon rolls and freshly baked cookies for the folks waiting in line. Spring had come to Middlebury, a fact reflected in the size of the crowds. When she glanced up and saw Preston, she motioned toward the register with a tilt of her head.

"One turkey on wheat, today's and yesterday's newspaper, and two whoopie pies." Georgia was probably five feet and a couple of inches, but she was a presence in the bakery. There was no doubt that she was the captain of this particular ship. Preston guessed her to be in her fifties. She was neither heavy nor thin, and her hair was a solid gray teased into a bouffant hairdo like those the older women wore.

"I didn't—"

"I did. Your father doesn't receive many sweets at that home, and I happen to know he doesn't have a problem with his blood sugar. It's fine to be healthy, but everyone can use a dash of sugar now and then."

"Thank you, Georgia."

"Don't mention it." The woman's voice was all business, but the look on her face was pure compassion.

At times Preston found people's kindness more difficult to bear than his own problems. Alone, he could turn off his emotions, attempt to look at life's problems in an objective way—unless he was huddled in the corner of his bedroom. He pushed that memory away as he headed across the Village property to where his dad now lived.

Grace Homes had been built two years earlier. It could barely be recognized as a place for old folks, unless you looked closely. Each home had wheelchair access. They were also placed in semicircles with paved paths leading around and behind them for easy access to the recreation center, which was positioned in the middle of the property.

Preston had been living on the streets for a little over three months when his dad sold the house and moved into Grace. At the time, it felt like another small piece of his heart had died. Seeing the home he had grown up in sporting a "For Sale" sign in the front yard had been a real blow. Those months he was homeless, he had regularly walked by the old house. He'd needed to see it, to be sure everything looked okay. Only on rare occasions did he actually stop.

The morning he had first seen the Realtor's sign, he had stood frozen on the sidewalk, staring at his childhood home.

His pop had greeted him with a wary hand-shake and a cup of coffee. That was the way it was between them. They never mentioned the night he had torn apart the kitchen, or the fact that he was living on the streets. Those things sat between them like a solid wall, which they could peer over but never break through.

"What's going on, Pops? Why the 'For Sale' sign?"

"Better to do it while I can. Your mom would want that." He'd gone on to explain that the doctor had confirmed an Alzheimer's diagnosis with a genetic test. He was in the early stages and wanted to take care of such decisions while he was still able.

"Nights are the worst." Gerald had looked away and then glanced back at him. "I guess that's something we have in common."

After that Preston had stopped by each day to help him box up the few things he'd be moving with him. The rest was sold in an "estate sale"— a fancy term for giving away the accumulations of a lifetime.

Once more Preston had locked his emotions down and done what needed to be done. Like Afghanistan. Like that day he struggled to forget.

One "blessing," as Amber would call it, was the windfall his father had made on the sale of the home and three acres. The house had been paid off when Preston was still in high school, and property values had risen in spite of the recession five years ago. The money had been put into a fund to pay for Gerald's home at Grace. Preston supplemented that nest egg with a sizable portion of his check—something Gerald would never know. Preston didn't do it so his dad would know. He did it because it was the right thing to do.

The second blessing had been Zoey.

He rang the doorbell at his pop's house and waited. Unlike the traditional nursing facility, residents at Grace lived in homes they shared with several others. Each resident had their own bedroom and bath. A nurse and orderly also lived in the home, staying four nights and then off three. The weekend crew stayed Friday through Sunday.

Zoey opened the door, and something tight inside of Preston's chest loosened.

She was a vision of beauty and peace to him.

Zoey's eyes danced as she pulled him into the foyer.

Preston was six feet, and Zoey was a good six inches shorter than him.

Her nurse's scrubs accentuated her curvy figure. Today she wore green the color of summer grass. Cats danced across the fabric, reminding him of a blanket he'd had as a child. Zoey's blonde hair bounced and curled around her face. Preston's mom would have called her a strawberry blonde, whatever that meant.

He'd plunged his fingers into that hair a few times, but not often. He had recognized the moment he began falling in love with Zoey. It was when he'd first seen her reach forward to wipe a little broth from his father's chin. Yes, she was his nurse. Yes, it was her job. But the expression of kindness, well, it had been his undoing.

And now?

He didn't know.

As he'd cleaned his bedroom that morning, setting aside the pieces of the broken nightstand to fix that evening, he'd vowed that he would break off their relationship and tell her to find someone else. Zoey deserved a better life than he could offer.

Ten

Standing in the entryway, her blue eyes smiling at him, her hand on his arm, Preston's resolve weakened. Life without Zoey? His mouth went dry and his throat tightened at the thought.

What he wouldn't give to spend the rest of his life with her, to offer her the home and love she deserved. If only there were a way.

"What is it? What's wrong?"

Preston shook his head. He had no idea how to explain to her the hopelessness of his situation. She always waved such concerns aside, as if they were no more serious than a pesky summer fly.

"Your dad's doing well today. We were about to sit down to lunch."

He followed her into the dining area. Seated around the table were six residents, including his dad. While the grounds and the room might belie the fact that this was indeed a nursing home, one look at those gathered around the dining room table spoke the truth. Three had suffered strokes and obviously favored their "good" side. Two had had broken hips. Their walkers were positioned against the wall behind them. And then there was his father . . . Posture still erect, his father stood behind his chair, waiting for everyone else to sit. He had neatly combed his solid-white hair, and he wore black trousers with a light blue golf shirt.

In that moment, Preston saw the soldier his father had been—confident, astute, and unerringly polite. They were qualities that had been bred into every commander. Preston saw in his father the man he would have liked to become. He saw in his father what he would have been if he hadn't failed so miserably.

The ache passed when his dad caught sight of him waiting in the doorway. "Preston, it's good to see you, son." The smile and warm eyes assured him that everything would be fine.

His dad's greeting was followed by a fairly rousing chorus of "Preston's here" and "Look who's come to visit," as if him stopping by for lunch was a surprise. As if he didn't do the same thing every other day.

Preston glanced at Zoey, and they shared a knowing smile. They often laughed about how his visits took the entire group by surprise. It was one of the few silver linings in working with the elderly in general and specifically those with dementia—it took very little to brighten their day.

Lunch passed with news of grandchildren, recent doctor appointments, and baseball predictions.

They'd learned to steer clear of politics. Even the oldest in their group seemed to still harbor strong political opinions.

Preston waited until he had helped his dad to his room to pull out the whoopie pies from Georgia. Some of the residents had specific dietary restrictions, but his dad was still free to enjoy a daily sweet. Preston cut the individual-size pastry in half with a knife Zoey had provided and handed half to his dad. Gerald accepted the freshly baked treat with a smile as he sank into his recliner. They didn't speak as they each enjoyed the pleasures of sugar, molasses, and chocolate.

Preston collected the napkins and refilled his father's water cup. "How ya doin', Pops?"

"Good, real good. Wish I had the crossword puzzle, though."

It was another of their little traditions. Preston pulled the newspaper out of the paper bag he'd brought with him and turned it to the puzzle.

His father's slow smile was all the reward he needed. Gerald immediately picked up his pen and became engrossed in the puzzle. Preston hadn't seen his father work a crossword puzzle with a pencil since he'd come home from overseas. It was another measure of the sort of confidence in the man Preston envied.

They sat that way for a few minutes, Gerald working the puzzle and then slipping into his afternoon nap, Preston enjoying the moments of quiet. Finally he sighed, stood, and placed the lap blanket over his dad, where he rested in his recliner.

Then he picked up their trash, the bag holding the extra whoopie pie, and the other newspaper before stepping out into the hall. Zoey was helping the resident in the room next door into bed, but she popped her head out and asked him to wait for her.

When she joined him on the front porch, he handed her the newspaper.

"Could you give it to him tomorrow, in case I don't make it over?"

"Of course." She snagged his hand and pulled him over to the porch swing. "Are things busy at the Village?"

"They are. Springtime tourists are arriving, and we want everything in tip-top shape."

"That's understandable."

"This is for you." He handed her the bag with the extra whoopie pie.

Zoey shook her head in mock disgust when she pulled out the pastry. "You're trying to fatten me up, Preston Johnstone."

The playfulness left her face as quickly as it had arrived.

Preston waited. He could tell when Zoey had something to say. He'd learned her little nuances. When her eyes crinkled it meant she had something to share that would make him smile. When she worried her fingers through her curls, as she was doing now, it meant she had something to say that he might not like.

He decided to make it easy for her. "Whatever it is, best be out with it."

Zoey nodded.

"I know you still aren't convinced that this is the best course, but I followed up on your application for a service dog." She held up a hand to stop his protest. "Remember, you indicated on the form that it was okay for them to talk with me on your behalf? Today I received a call from Tomas Hernandez at ICAN. They have a service dog ready. One that has been trained specifically to deal with PTSD—"

"I appreciate your concern, honey. I really do." Preston laced his fingers together and stared at the ground. When he finally glanced up, Zoey was watching him closely. He knew how much she cared. There was no doubt in his mind that she was doing what she thought was best, but sometimes her optimism clouded her judgment. "Even if I thought it was a good idea—and I still don't know how you talked me into applying—I don't have the money. Service dogs cost upwards of ten thousand dollars."

"Tomas says he's willing to cut that price dramatically. He has a real heart for wounded warriors."

Preston tried not to flinch.

"I'm no warrior." The words came out like a growl, and he reached for her hand to soften them. "I appreciate what you're trying to do, Zoey."

"You didn't let me finish."

He gazed off into the distance and reminded himself how important she was to him—a fact that rubbed right up against the revelations he'd had after his destructive flashback the night before.

"Tomas says there are funds within the VA to help pay for the dog."

"And the rest?"

"There is no rest. He's cutting the price, and the VA will pay the remaining amount with a grant. You can have the dog, Preston. You can go see it—today if you have time. Tomas is in Fort Wayne this week."

Preston wanted to tell her no. He wanted to explain to her that he couldn't be trusted to care for an animal. He wanted to remind her that the data was still too new on service dogs with people who suffered from PTSD. He wanted to tell her that surely someone needed that dog more than he did.

He wanted to say all those things, but he looked into her eyes and he couldn't.

This might be their only chance, because he could not—he would not—subject her to what he had been through the night before.

So he said yes.

He didn't actually believe it would help, but since he didn't have a better idea, he agreed.

Amber hurried straight over to the Village bakery, Tate close to her side. Now they stood in the kitchen, staring down at the peach pie Georgia had set in the middle of the large baking counter. A skull and crossbones had been etched into the piecrust, apparently before it was baked since some of the peach filling had dried on the inside of the drawing, making it look even more sinister. Sitting beside the pie, tented as if it were announcing peach pies for sale, was a note.

Thoughts were tumbling through Amber's mind, bumping into each other and creating havoc.

Was this the same person who wrote the e-mails?

It had to be. Didn't it?

"Are you even listening?" Georgia crossed her arms, still clutching the rolling pin she normally used to roll out fresh piecrust. "I asked if you called the police."

"Yes, Gordon should be here any minute."

The words were barely out of her mouth when the Middlebury police sergeant walked into the room. He was dressed in his jeans and flannel shirt, indicating he was giving up time on his day off to answer her call. She'd once again called

97

him directly rather than calling through the police switchboard. He didn't seem overly aggravated about that intrusion. Apparently he'd decided to take her direct calls as a compliment, or perhaps their friendship had progressed that far.

But she couldn't have called the police switchboard, could she? That would be widening the number of people who knew what was happening, and she'd been specifically warned against that.

Would the person doing this know?

Would they hurt Hannah or Pam or Tate?

Gordon's hair remained black without a speck of gray, and his six-foot frame was as muscular as that of a much younger man. They had once dated, but that was before Tate, before her life had changed. Fortunately they'd remained friends even after her marriage.

"Anyone touch it?"

"Not since I found it." Georgia sounded slightly offended.

"And when was that?"

"Thirty minutes ago. I've been guarding it since."

She raised the rolling pin in explanation, and Amber had no doubt she would have used it should anyone try to swipe the evidence off her countertop.

"All right. We'll call in Cherry to fingerprint the area."

"We had the entire crew working this morning." Georgia grimaced and glanced around the large industrial kitchen. "I refuse to watch any of those crime shows, but I do read. It doesn't take Agatha Christie to figure out you're going to have too many fingerprints in this room to be of any use."

"True, but we want to do all we can to catch the perp. There's always a chance we'll get lucky and the material this counter is made of will allow us to easily lift the prints."

Amber cleared her throat. "All the counters were cleaned with bleach before Georgia walked out of the room. She checked the supplies in the pantry, and when she walked back in, the pie was sitting in the middle of the counter."

"All right." Gordon had taken out the small notepad he used, or had used for the two previous incidents. "And where were you when this happened?"

"At lunch, with Tate. We were picking out flowers for—" The words caught in her throat and she felt as if she were going to be sick.

Could this really be happening?

Who was doing this, and why?

"Are you okay, Amber?" Tate asked.

"I'm fine."

"You looked a little green there for a minute."

"No, I'm fine. I ate something that didn't agree with me."

"All right." Gordon glanced back down at his

pad. "So you were with Tate when the call came in from—"

"I called her." Georgia gave him an exasperated look. "And if we could hurry this along, I have baking to tend to."

"This is a crime scene now. I'm afraid we're going to have to bring in the forensic team."

"Oh . . ." Amber tried to think of a way to stop him. "It's probably just a harmless prank. Don't you think?"

When Gordon only stared at her, she added, "Maybe Cherry could do her thing and then we could just throw that pie away."

"We're not throwing it away. We're sending it off to the lab."

At least no one had been hurt by this lunatic so far, and Amber prayed they wouldn't be. If lightning rarely struck twice in the same place, what were the odds that they would encounter three murderers in one collection of Amish shops? None! She refused to even think that might happen.

But she was considering it and going over the two e-mails in her mind. Why would anyone go to such lengths to frighten people? To frighten her?

"The poison design in the crust seems obvious enough." Gordon made another note on his pad.

Georgia tapped the rolling pin against her palm.

"Amber, I heard you received an anonymous e-mail last night."

"How—"

"Few things stay a secret in small towns," Georgia muttered. When Amber offered no explanation, she asked permission to leave and return to her work. "At least I can get the supplies reordered."

She left the room in a huff, obviously exasperated by the entire situation.

Amber opened her tablet and showed Gordon the e-mail she'd received the night before. "Do you think it's the same person?"

"The odds of having two angry folks who are both bad poets are slim to none."

They both stared down at the note left beside the pie.

Don't taste it
Don't share it
Just throw it away
If you try my bakery pie
You won't live to see another day

Amber shook her head. "Why would they even leave this note? If you've gone to the trouble of creating a poisonous pie, and you've risked being caught by bringing it to the Village kitchen, why leave a note warning us not to eat it?"

Tate was taking a picture of the pie with his

101

phone's camera. "Whoever the person is doesn't seem to want to hurt anyone."

"You think so?" Hope filled Amber's voice.

Gordon cleared his throat. "At the same time, the threat is escalating. First the e-mail, now the pie and note. Obviously they're trying to get your attention."

"Oh." Despair crept back into Amber's heart. It was spring and her life was going well. She did not want to be dealing with another creepy, crazy person.

"We'll send the pie and the note to the lab. Perhaps it's a hoax. Maybe there's nothing in the pie, and the note we'll keep as evidence even if there are no fingerprints."

"And if there is poison in the pie?"

"Then we'll find out who did this and arrest them." He reached out and squeezed her arm. "Stop worrying. This looks like the work of an amateur to me. If they'd wanted to hurt someone, they would have baked it like a normal pie and slipped it into the bakery case."

Georgia had walked back in with a clipboard and pen, intent on noting her supply of baking goods. Overhearing Gordon's comment, she adamantly protested the idea that anyone could slip something into her kitchen.

Gordon stopped her in the midst of her protest. "This could be a person who works here, Georgia. It's not your fault that you didn't see them, and no one's accusing you of negligence. You can't be everywhere at once."

"I still don't get it." Amber rubbed her forehead where her headache beat with increasing pressure. "They couldn't know who would receive this pie—and no one would serve or buy a pie with a skull and crossbones on it anyway. And certainly not if they read the note. If they're angry enough to poison someone, then it seems like they'd find a way to be sure it went to that person."

"If they work here, they could do that," Tate said. "They'd know which pie it was and could slip it onto the plate of the customer it was designed for."

"That's diabolical."

Gordon nodded in agreement. "It would serve two functions—sickening or killing the target, and dramatically hurting your business."

"The bakery?" Georgia asked.

"The Village?" Amber blinked in disbelief.

"Guests who have been poisoned tend to sue the establishment, if they live long enough to contact a lawyer. If they don't, their family will sue. Either way, the Village could be found guilty of negligence. I read about a poisoning case in California where the restaurant was successfully sued even though the perpetrator was caught and not an employee of the establishment."

"Should we close the restaurant?" Amber's

stomach once again turned, joining her throbbing head in increasing her misery. She hadn't even considered such drastic actions.

"Not yet. Let me have this analyzed first. In the meantime, you both need to keep your eyes open."

"Should I alert the other employees?" Georgia was now twisting her apron in both of her hands.

Gordon glanced around. "Yes, I think that's a good idea. We want to let whoever this is know that we're taking their threat seriously, and that we're on the offensive."

Oh, Amber was taking it seriously—if Gordon only knew. But she couldn't tell him. If she did, the person would get wind of it, somehow.

Both Amber and Georgia nodded.

"And call me if you see or hear anything suspicious."

"Sure . . ." Amber's voice faded as she considered the second e-mail on her tablet. Should she show him? Or should she keep it to herself?

"Are you okay, Amber?" Gordon stepped closer. "You're acting a bit strange, even for you."

Amber wanted to protest, but she didn't have the energy. "I'm not feeling too well," she answered truthfully.

"You need to go home."

She nodded, then added, "We'll call if there's another incident. And Gordon, thank you for coming in on your day off." Amber touched his arm as Georgia moved toward her office.

"Life in a small town can grow boring at times," Tate admitted.

"Boring is good from a public safety standpoint." Gordon shook his head. "I wouldn't want more crime in Middlebury. But your cases have a way of keeping me on my toes."

"My cases—"

"There's hardly ever a dull moment at the Village."

"It's not like—"

"I'm not saying it's your fault."

Gordon's smile assured her he was teasing, and that—more than anything else—helped her to relax. They'd catch the poison poet. When they did, she was going to schedule a vacation. This sort of thing had a way of making her feel older and exceedingly tired.

Take care of the spring rush of tourists.

Find out who is sending the e-mails.

Apprehend the poison poet.

Schedule a three-day weekend away with Tate.

Maybe she'd stretch it to five days and reserve them a berth on a cruise ship.

The thought of the ocean calmed her. She could see herself sitting by the ship's pool with a novel and a waitress bringing her fruit-flavored tea. Yeah. That was the ticket. She nearly added it to her to-do list, but then her phone rang.

She glanced at the display and some deep instinct told her the news wouldn't be good. "I need to take this." She pushed the Talk button and stepped out of the restaurant.

Eleven

For reasons she didn't quite understand, Hannah felt as twitchy as a cat. It was past two in the afternoon when she closed up the coffee shop. She had twisted the key in the lock of the door and checked to make sure it had clicked into place. Turning away from the shop, she practically jumped out of her *kapp* when she realized someone was standing directly behind her.

"I didn't mean to scare you." Pam Coleman smiled as she tucked her hand inside Hannah's arm. "My grammy would say you look like a kitten caught in the milk pail."

Pam was Amber's new assistant. She'd joined the Village the year before, after Hannah had first taken over running A Simple Blend—after she'd found Ethan Gray sprawled among the coffee beans, dead.

"Still making the lunch bags? I need to buy one of those."

Hannah looked down at her lunch bag—quilted in new spring fabrics of pink, yellow, and blue. Then she glanced at Pam. The assistant manager of the Village had black hair, cut shoulder length. She was not a small woman, but she carried her weight and height well. She always wore interesting clothes that accented her dark brown skin, and her personality was as bright and strong as her style of clothing. Today she wore a sky blue dress covered in different types of kites.

Kites! Flat kites, boxed kites, bowed kites—in green, yellow, pink, red, even purple—all flying against the rich blue fabric. Hannah couldn't imagine using the material to quilt or wear, but she had to admit that it looked fun on Pam. It made her think about flying kites with her little sister. It made her forget her worries, if only for a moment.

"Lunch bags?" Pam reached over and tapped the bag.

"*Ya*, I do still make the lunch bags, and I sell them at The Quilting Bee." She nodded toward the shop next door.

"I'll buy one. I could use it to carry a snack, since most days I eat lunch in the restaurant. Have you tried the fried chicken over there? We hire the best cooks."

Hannah nodded. "Their food is nearly as good as my *mamm*'s."

"Huh. What does a girl have to do to get an invitation to your house for dinner? On second thought, if your mom's chicken is better than what we serve, I'd probably come away homesick. You need to go south, Hannah, at least once. Go and sample our famous Southern cooking. You would love it."

Hannah nodded, then switched her bag from one hand to the other. "But you didn't come by to talk to me about chicken."

"I didn't." Pam pulled Hannah toward a bench. "Tell me about Martha. How is she doing? Amber's so consumed with the poison poet—"

Hannah flinched at Pam's name for their newest pest. She kept trying to forget about the threatening e-mail Amber had shown her. She had been so looking forward to spring, and she didn't want it marred by another dark mystery.

"And then she received that unexpected call from Preston—"

"Is he okay?"

"Sure. Something about a dog. Nothing to worry about."

Hannah couldn't imagine Preston with a dog. He seemed to work a lot of hours. When would he spend time with it? And why was Amber involved?

"Let's talk about Martha, though. Amber was worried because of this guy Ryan Duvall."

"*Ya*, Martha is sort of seeing him."

"The guy is older, right?"

"Much."

"And he's something of a player, if I understand correctly."

"I'm not sure about that, but he has a reputation for seeing more than one girl at a time."

"Do you think he's dating Martha?"

Hannah replayed the conversation she'd had with her friend earlier. She didn't want to betray any confidence, but then Martha hadn't told her anything that wasn't public knowledge. No, it wasn't where they'd gone or planned on going that bothered Hannah. It was her friend's mannerisms—the way she blushed, the dreamy look in her eyes, and the determination in her voice.

"Martha thinks he is," she finally answered.

"Probably not any of our business." Pam fingered the purple scarf she wore draped down the front of her dress. "We wouldn't normally involve ourselves in an employee's private life."

"But this time is different?"

"It might be. Earlier today a little bird told me Ryan is also seeing a couple of other women here at the Village."

"I knew he had given Letha a ride, but I hadn't heard that he was dating anyone else." More importantly, Hannah wondered if Martha had heard.

"He gave her more than a ride. He definitely took Letha Keim out last night."

"You're sure? Usually Letha works late on Mondays and stocks the deliveries she received earlier for the clothing shop."

"Apparently they were having dinner at Mancino's."

"I know his parents own a horse farm, but still, how can he afford so many dinners at restaurants?" Hannah placed her lunch bag on her lap and stared down at it. She was certainly grateful that her love life wasn't complicated. Jesse had never shown any interest in anyone else. If he was distracted at times, it was because he was planning something on the farm or worrying about something at the Village.

"Who says he can afford it? Sometimes men run up a large credit card bill and then borrow the money."

"Who would lend it to them?"

"Women in love do things they wouldn't under normal circumstances. I knew a gal in San Antonio . . . she fell for this cowboy on the rodeo circuit. Next thing we knew, she'd cleaned out her bank account to loan him enough for his next gig. He headed west and she never heard from him again."

Hannah didn't know what a rodeo circuit or a gig was, but none of that sounded good to her. Would Ryan attempt to do the same to Martha? Did Martha have any money saved?

"Still, it doesn't seem like our business—not really." Hannah didn't add that she'd spoken to Martha about Ryan earlier that day. Maybe she was overstepping the boundaries of friendship to be worried about her friend's romantic affairs, but certainly it had nothing to do with the Village. Did it?

"Normally I'd agree with you, but we both know Amber and Carol look over you girls like mother hens—which is how this ended up on my to-do list."

"So Ryan is seeing both Martha and Letha. What can we do about it?"

"Maybe nothing. But another little bird told me that at this very moment Ryan is over at the restaurant enjoying a meal with Georgia. I thought we might hop over there for a piece of pie. I'll pay. What do you say?"

"Why me?" Hannah's voice cracked on the question. She wasn't sure how involved she wanted to be with this guy. He sounded more and more like a disreputable person. On the other hand, if they could help Martha in some way, she'd certainly be willing to do that.

Pam had stood and was motioning Hannah to her feet. "I've never had the pleasure of meeting Mr. Duvall. I'm guessing that you have?"

"I've seen him around town. He's lived here all his life."

"Wonderful—a homegrown Casanova."

"A what?"

"The thing is, I'm fairly new in town, so I haven't had the opportunity to make Ryan Duvall's acquaintance yet. I want to make sure

111

this little piece of information about Georgia and Ryan is true. I need you to go with me and identify him. For all I know Georgia entertains a different man at every lunch. I don't want to assume he's Duvall."

"We don't have to speak with him?"

"Nah. I'll leave that to Amber, unless he does something to irk me. Then I might have to set him straight."

Hannah didn't know what Ryan could possibly do to annoy Pam, but she did know she wouldn't want to make the assistant manager angry. Pam was one of the nicest managers Hannah had ever worked for, but she'd seen her disposition quickly change when she perceived one of their own was being mistreated. In her opinion, Pam resembled a momma bear more than a mother hen. Pam Coleman was one person whose good side she'd rather stay on. If it meant eating a free piece of pie, that was something she could do with no problem at all.

Besides, it wasn't like they were going to talk to Ryan.

She decided to enjoy the chance to sit in the Village restaurant and treat herself to some freshly baked dessert. There was more work waiting for her at home, but she'd eaten her lunch hours ago.

Her stomach growled, confirming it was the right thing to do.

A tickle in the memory section of her brain, however, told her to be prepared. If there was one thing she'd learned in the last year, it was that often things did not turn out the way you planned.

Preston tried not to glance at Amber as he steered his Volkswagen onto US 33 South. They were twenty minutes into the trip, and still he had no idea what to say. Fortunately, that was rarely a problem for Amber.

Today she seemed chattier than ever. She'd updated him on the health status of Tate's donkeys—all good, the impending birth of his grandson—in August, and Ryan Duvall's dating status—busy. The last news had claimed Preston's attention for a moment, until he remembered where he was going and what he was doing. Then he slipped back into the circle his thoughts insisted on following.

Zoey. Last night. Dog.

Last night. Zoey. Dog.

Dog. Zoey. Last night.

Any way he looked at it, he arrived at the same conclusion. Though he didn't much believe it would work, agreeing to a service dog seemed to be his one hope for a normal life—if it worked, which he doubted.

"You're awfully quiet over there, even for you, and yes, I realize you aren't known for your long speeches." Amber chewed on her thumbnail, something he'd never seen her do before.

Was she as nervous about this trip as he was?

"Thanks for coming with me, Amber. I didn't expect you to drop everything when I called. I just wanted your permission to take off for the afternoon."

"Of course I wanted to come with you. You're like family, Preston, and this is an important day. I still can't quite believe they have a dog for you. People normally wait for years, right?"

Preston attempted a smile, but his heart wasn't in it.

What was he doing?

Why had he agreed to this?

Amber turned so that her back was against the door of the Beetle and studied him. "Having second thoughts?"

"I'm not sure I had first thoughts—other than this won't work and someone else probably needs the dog more than I do."

To give her credit, she didn't argue. He had no doubt she had countless arguments, the same as Zoey. But when it came down to it, this wasn't a logical decision. It was a decision of the heart. It was a step into the unknown because of his love for Zoey.

"And I still don't know how you got dragged into this." Preston focused his eyes on the road.

"That one's easy. Zoey called me right after you did. She couldn't take off with no notice, and your father's in no condition to go. There was no one else to replace her—except me or Tate, and my dear husband was too dirty from gardening for a quick get-away. So *voilà*! You're stuck with me."

"I should be able to do this myself."

"Their policy requires you to bring a family member. I know I'm not technically related to you, but I'm happy to stand in."

"I appreciate that, Amber. I do." He shook his head, then glanced at her, surprised to find a smile on her face. "This change in my life is happening very fast, and I hate that we both took off the afternoon from the Village."

Amber looked out the front, then side window. Green fields stretched as far as the eye could see on both sides. The sky was Easter-egg blue, punctuated by the occasional fluffy white cloud. The field to the west was being worked by an Amish farmer who had harnessed six Belgian draft horses to his plow.

"You're a bright spot in my life, Preston. You and Tate and Hannah and Pam. What would life be without friends? Sometimes I think I live in a fairy tale." Amber's voice had softened. She reached up and tucked her hair behind her ear before turning again to look at him. "It's easy to forget that when I divide my time between the Village and my home and . . . problems. It's easy to forget all that is around me and how God has blessed our area. You've done me a favor today, Preston. You've helped me remember what I love about living in Indiana."

He had no answer to that, so he nodded as if what she said made sense.

Then he remembered about the dog, and something in his stomach clenched as tight as the spark plugs on the old Volkswagen. When he'd first purchased the Bug, he had thought he'd never get those things off—time and weather had cemented them on good. Now he thought his stomach would never feel normal again.

"Have you ever owned a dog?" Amber pulled a ball of yarn and crochet hook out of her purse, and he almost smiled. Her attempts at crocheting had once been a source of humor around the office, but he heard she was actually improving.

"High school." He hadn't thought of Skipper in quite a long time. "Crazy little dachshund."

Amber smiled as she continued to work the yarn with the crochet hook—to the back, front, and then through. It certainly looked peaceful to watch her do it. "I pictured you with a hunting dog—something big and clumsy."

"Skipper was my mom's dog, but somehow he attached himself to me. He'd wait by the door until I came home, and then—even when I banished him from my room for tearing up something—he'd sleep in the hall outside my bedroom door."

"What happened to him?"

Preston shrugged. "Old age, I guess. I found out in one of the letters Mom sent overseas."

"How often did you receive mail?"

"That depended on several factors. If you were on a base, the mail came fairly often—though it might take two to three weeks to get there by the time it was re-routed. If you were out on a mission, you might not receive any."

Preston was staring out the windshield at the green grass and fields of corn on either side of the road, but suddenly his throat was dry—painfully so. He tried to swallow and couldn't. He ran his fingers over the dashboard, and felt gravel biting into his fingertips. His hand began to tremble slightly, and he clutched the wheel all the harder.

Amber was saying something about cats and dogs, but her voice faded behind the noise from the engine and the road. He tried to focus on her words and on steering the car, to keep his mind locked on where they were going, not where he had been. But he felt himself falling back. He saw the shoulder he was pulling onto, but over that in stronger images and brighter colors he saw blood and carnage and desert. Then he was helpless to stop himself as the world he had left behind crashed in around him once more.

Twelve

They weren't exactly spying. Hannah and Pam sat in a corner booth, watching Georgia and Ryan across the room. The two looked somewhat odd sitting together, Hannah had to admit that. Georgia was in her fifties. Wasn't that too old for romantic relationships?

"I think she's changed her hairdo." Pam squinted across the room.

"*Ya*, looks like a new cut."

"And hasn't she lost weight? She looks thinner to me. I wouldn't be thinner if I worked in a bakery. I'm full-size as it is. Who loses weight while they bake pies and cakes and cookies? I smell a rat—or a diet. Something's off."

Hannah realized that what Pam was saying was true. Georgia's hair looked much more fashionable and she'd definitely lost a good ten pounds. She even looked as if she might be wearing a hint of lipstick. Since when did Georgia Small wear lipstick?

It was disconcerting to study her. She'd always thought of Georgia as . . . Georgia! Not remarkable. Not attractive and not ugly. Georgia was simply as she should be, as she'd always been. But something had changed. Something had caused her to change. Was it the man sitting with her?

Ryan looked like someone who had stepped off the cover of an *Englisch* magazine. He wore jeans, a T-shirt, and a flannel shirt over that— standard fare. But on Ryan Duvall it looked as if he'd had the clothes chosen especially for him. Black hair curled haphazardly over his head, falling into his eyes when he laughed at something Georgia said. His hands, face, and neck were tanned a golden brown, perhaps from working outside with the horses. Though he had turned forty, or so Hannah had heard, he had the look and build of someone younger. There was no gray in his hair, no circles under his eyes, and not a hint of fat anywhere on him—which was saying something since he was busily consuming a rather large piece of Dutch apple pie covered with at least two scoops of ice cream. Other dishes were scattered around their table, so plainly he had enjoyed lunch as well.

If Georgia had noticed Hannah and Pam, she showed no indication. Instead she seemed completely focused on the man across from her.

"You're sure that's him?"

"I'm sure." Hannah pushed away her empty plate. She'd chosen the chocolate peanut butter pie, and she'd devoured every crumb.

"I don't like him." Pam narrowed her eyes, pointing a fork in their direction as she continued

119

to study them. She'd ordered red raspberry cream pie, and a little of it clung to her fork.

"We don't even know him. Not really. We only know his name and that his family raises horses."

"Yes, but the bigger question is what could he possibly want with Georgia?"

Hannah pushed up her glasses but didn't respond.

"Don't look at me that way, Hannah. There's nothing wrong with Georgia, but she's not exactly the catch of the day. Why is Ryan here? Unless he was able to coax a free meal out of her."

"Perhaps he is going to pay for it."

"Not the point." Pam sat back and sipped her coffee.

"What is the point? Why are we here, watching them? I feel like a spy in one of Amber's novels."

Pam laughed at that. "Spies are supposed to blend in. We would not be good at that. I'm a big black woman in a kite dress, and you are one of the most well-known employees we have."

"Me?"

"Sure. Between your sweet personality, the way you've turned the coffee shop around, and your help in solving murders . . ."

"My help? I'm not sure I helped much—and besides, we didn't actually solve them."

"I know what you mean. It's more like we stumbled into the middle of a mess during the last one, and thank goodness I wasn't here for the first. Though come to think of it, if there hadn't been a first I wouldn't be working here now. I owe Ethan Gray, I suppose, God rest his soul."

Hannah didn't want to dwell on Ethan and his death. She certainly didn't want to think about Owen Esch's death. They'd put all of that behind them. The Village had been peaceful for the last six months, and she preferred it that way.

Ryan and Georgia stood. He air-kissed her cheek and they continued to talk for a moment.

"Looks like they're finished, and I can report to Amber that the rumor Ryan was here to lunch with Georgia was true. Let's skedaddle before they have a chance to catch up with us at the register." Reaching into her purse, Pam pulled out a couple of dollars for the tip and left it on the table.

They did skedaddle, but they didn't avoid Ryan.

When they'd reached the register to pay, the checkout girl had run out of tape in her machine. Pam assured her it wasn't a problem as the girl fumbled under the counter and began the clumsy process of putting in the new tape.

Hannah was drumming her fingers against the counter, and Pam was checking her cell phone for messages, when Ryan walked up behind them.

"Afternoon, ladies."

Hannah stared at him and nodded, but didn't speak. What would she say? *Yes, good afternoon.*

It is a fine day, and by the way, we enjoyed snooping on your and Georgia's lunch date.

Was it a date?

Pam looked Ryan up and down, but she also didn't respond. The cashier finally had the machine working. Pam pulled out her Village ID, which was a mere formality. Everyone recognized her as the assistant manager. The girl wrote her ID number on the receipt and wished them a nice afternoon.

Ryan stepped up to the register and Pam moved to the side while she returned her ID card to her purse. They couldn't help but hear Ryan say, "Here's our receipt. Georgia had to attend to some business in the kitchen, but she signed the bottom. She said you'd know what to do."

The girl murmured, "No problem," but Hannah knew instantly that it was going to be a problem. Pam's eyes had flashed as she straightened her posture and turned to Ryan.

"You must be Ryan Duvall. I'm Pam Coleman, the assistant manager here at the Village."

If Ryan was surprised Pam knew his name, he didn't show it. Instead he reached for her hand and shook it, smiling as if she had just made his day.

Ryan pushed a few wavy strands of black hair out of his eyes. "Nice to meet you. I've heard great things about you."

"You have heard things about me?"

"All the girls speak of you highly."

"The girls?"

Ryan hadn't realized he was backing himself into a corner, but Hannah knew. Pam's voice was changing, morphing into something in between one of their preachers on Sunday morning and the stern Mennonite teacher who had taught Hannah in third grade. Pam's change in demeanor wasn't a good thing, but Hannah couldn't think of any way to warn Ryan. All she could do was take a step back and exchange an anxious glance with the cashier.

"By girls you wouldn't happen to mean the three women from the Village you're dating . . . at the same time?"

"I didn't—"

"Because where I come from, that's just rude."

"How did you—"

"And then you show up here and have Georgia buy your lunch? Men should buy the lunch. I might be old-fashioned, but I'm right."

It seemed to Hannah that Ryan finally understood that he was struggling against his reputation. Instead of arguing, he stood silently, head bowed slightly, looking almost repentant and waiting for Pam's lecture to run its course.

Fortunately for him, Pam was done. She made a "humph" sound and turned to Hannah. "Ready, dear?"

Hannah was more than ready. She wanted to be

home helping her mother with the housework. She did not want to be in the middle of an escalating feud.

Unfortunately, Ryan was a slow learner, or maybe it was just his outgoing nature rearing its head. For whatever reason, he called out, "Nice to meet you both, ladies. It was a pleasure, and you both look stunning in your spring frocks."

Hannah had to practically drag Pam out of the restaurant.

Pam was actually sputtering by the time they'd stepped into the afternoon sunshine. "Frocks? Did he actually say *frocks?* I chided that man and he told us we looked *stunning?*"

"I believe it's only his way. He didn't mean anything by it."

"Oh, he meant something. He can give us that sweet *I'm innocent and you are oh-so-special* look, but it doesn't work on this girl. I've learned to recognize a cad when I see one."

"What is a cad?"

"A scoundrel, a rascal, a scalawag."

"A Casanova?" Whether it was Hannah's expression or her attempt to understand *Englisch* slang, she at least managed to calm Pam a bit.

But as they walked toward the parking lot, Ryan mercifully nowhere in sight, Pam scrunched up her face and refocused on the issue at hand.

"Oh, I'm glad you took me to meet him, Hannah."

"I didn't. Going to the restaurant was your idea."

"And it worked perfectly. Now I know what we're up against—good looks, witty remarks, and dangerous eyes."

"Dangerous how?"

"Charm. He's full of charm! But we'll protect our girls. No worries there. I'll speak with Amber as soon as she returns, and we'll find a way to keep the likes of Ryan Duvall from messing with our employees. We're actually doing him a favor. Playboys like Ryan? They could find themselves in a perilous situation."

"Perilous? As in risky?"

They'd reached the Pumpkinvine Trail. Pam was about to turn back toward the offices, and Hannah needed to be on her way. But she couldn't pull back the question, and she did want to know the answer if only to calm the worries that had begun to churn in her stomach.

"Have you never heard the quote, 'Hell hath no fury like a woman scorned'?"

"*Nein.* I haven't."

"Some English dude wrote it. By English I mean British, and he wrote it a few centuries ago. It's in a play, and some crazy college professor of mine thought we needed to read it."

"And what does it mean—this saying?"

"That Ryan Duvall should watch his back, or he could end up regretting his lifestyle. A woman

125

scorned is a force to be reckoned with. Mr. Duvall wouldn't be the first person to pay for their indiscretions."

Hannah said good-bye and hurried away down the Pumpkinvine Trail, and as her tennis shoes slapped against the pavement, they beat a rhythm, a pattern to the words Pam had shared.

Hell hath no fury
Like a woman scorned.

Thirteen

Preston managed to pull the car to the side of the road before the sunshine and Indiana countryside faded completely from his consciousness.

Bogar crouched in front of him, wrapping a field bandage around his chest. Preston stared at the wall of the cave as Bogar worked. He didn't remember being hit by shrapnel. Though the pain was excruciating, he was alive. He was grateful to still be breathing, but he understood there was no guarantee they would survive the next few hours. He found himself petitioning God. Within his heart he cried out for God's mercy and protection. It was what his mother would have called a foxhole prayer. It was a last-minute, desperate place. He realized all those things, but in that moment he also understood that God held their lives in his hand.

Bogar was talking under his breath, but Preston couldn't make any sense of what the man was saying. The words insurgents and Taliban fell around them, like shrapnel dropped onto a concrete floor. Preston tried to focus, to string the words together into a coherent sentence, a thought just out of reach, but he had no success. Looking down, he saw that his uniform was wet with his own blood.

The pounding of his own heartbeat had been throbbing in his ears. Slowly it receded, and he was able to hear and understand what Bogar was saying.

"Got you in the clavicle. Lucky." Bogar continued to wind the bandage up and down and around.

"Lucky?"

Bogar tapped Preston's chest, the exact part where his heart was thudding like a train barreling down tracks. "An inch lower? Would have been good-bye, Preston. Yeah, I'd say you're lucky."

Preston nodded, and Bogar turned his attention to Frank.

"You okay?"

"Preston fixed me up."

"Good."

The reality and terror and memory of what was happening crashed in on Preston with full force. The attack, running after Frank, pausing to aim, and then searing pain.

"Did you get them, Bogar? Did you get any of them?" Preston heard the iron in his own voice. He wondered where that had come from. Just a month ago he'd been a scared kid, assigned to the northern province of Afghanistan. He was a member of the 503rd infantry regiment, and he was well trained, but a part of him was still a scared kid. He could see that now. What he couldn't see is how they were going to get out of this cave alive.

Artillery and even RPGs continued to rain down on their position. Preston had the uncomfortable feeling of being a fish in a barrel. Sure, they'd found a place to bunker down, but how long could they hold the position? Every few minutes dirt and rock spewed outside the mouth of the cave. They could very easily be buried alive. It might be better to chance it on the outside, to make a run for the base.

"I fired a couple hundred rounds." Bogar took a swig from his canteen, then swiped the back of his hand across his mouth. "Chances are I hit a few. I fired until my weapon went hot and jammed."

"How many are there?" Frank had lost too much blood. He was barely able to keep himself in a sitting position, but Preston knew what he was thinking. He knew what the man wanted to do before he even said it.

Frank glanced at each of them and then toward the mouth of the cave. "My weapon still works. You set me up out there, position me just outside with my back against that large rock, and I can still shoot."

Bogar shook his head. "There's a hundred insurgents, at least. Maybe more."

Preston tried to raise his right arm and found he couldn't. It was as if a giant weight were holding it down. He could shoot with his left, but not as well.

Bogar picked up Frank's weapon, checked it, then turned to Preston. "Stay with him."

"I'm coming with you."

"Stay with him. That's an order, soldier." The smile from Bogar belied the tone in his voice. He outranked both of them, and he knew it. He was also in his element when in battle. Some primal, instinctive portion of his brain responded well to danger.

Preston nodded once.

Their eyes met, and then Bogar was gone, out the mouth of the cave.

Preston watched as he hunkered down by the large rock Frank had motioned toward.

Bogar didn't look back, didn't say anything, merely stepped out into the afternoon light. He'd raised his weapon and was firing left to right in a wide arc when a bullet tore through his chest, throwing him back inside the cave.

Amber didn't know what to do. She'd never witnessed someone having a flashback, but she had an idea that was exactly what was happening.

"Preston? Preston, can you hear me?" Amber crouched beside him. She'd jumped out as soon as the vehicle had stopped, running to the driver's side of the car and opening the door. They had slid to a stop on the shoulder of the road. Preston had done his best to brake and steer before he disappeared to wherever it was he'd gone. Fortunately there were no cars around them. They were completely surrounded by row after row of corn.

"What . . ." Preston shook his head, but at least his eyes were seeing again. The blank, slack expression had been replaced by one she recognized—frustration, confusion, and a tinge of embarrassment.

A wave of relief passed over Amber. Her heart rate slowed and the panic that had been clawing at her throat backed away. But her stomach didn't settle and her mind continued to chase multiple questions round and round. This day was not going well. First the day's anonymous e-mail, then the possibly poisonous pie, and now a blackout with Preston. She wanted to go home and pull a quilt over her head.

Preston turned toward her, swung his legs out of the car, and tried to stand.

Amber helped him up. She made sure he was steady before she let go of his arm.

He leaned against the Beetle and stared out across the road, across the fields.

Clearing his throat, he asked, "Are you okay?"

He turned his head, looked at her briefly, and then glanced away.

"I'm fine," she assured him. "And you don't have to be embarrassed. You did a good job guiding the car to the side of the road."

Preston could only shake his head and stare at the ground.

"It was another flashback, wasn't it?" Amber faced the Volkswagen, placed her hands on it, and allowed the warmth to seep into her palms, into her consciousness. It was turning into a fine spring day, but as they'd rattled toward the side of the road a cold dread had seeped through her. One that had to do with what was happening back in Middlebury. It robbed her of her joy. She didn't want to be in the middle of another investigation, and she sure didn't want to be enduring a lunatic's attention all by herself. How could things get any worse?

Were those feelings what Preston dealt with

every day? How often did he suffer these episodes? "Was it a flashback?"

"Yeah."

"Any idea what brought it on?"

"No." He reached a hand up to the area between his neck and his shoulder, right along the breastbone. He touched it once as if he needed to make sure he was okay, then he stuck his hands in his pockets.

"You were telling me about your dog, Skipper. And then we started talking about mail—how you received your mail while you were serving overseas."

"I guess."

"That must be what did it." Amber turned and rested her backside against the hood of the Beetle. "Does this happen every time you talk about the war?"

"No." His mouth felt dry. "Do you have any water?"

"Sure." Amber scooted around the front of the car, reached inside for her bag, and pulled out a bottle of water. "I haven't even opened it yet. No danger of contagion from my germs."

He made a valiant attempt to smile at her joke as he reached across the roof of the VW for the water, but soon a scowl consumed his expression.

"You shouldn't be with me, Amber."

"Fiddlesticks!"

"I'm dangerous. I could have killed us—"

"But you didn't. You fought it, and you drove the car to the side of the road. You kept both of us safe." When he didn't respond, she walked back around the VW and put her arms around him. She stood there holding him in the afternoon sunlight, waiting to move until she felt the tension leave his arms.

Amber had never had a brother, and she didn't think Preston had a sister. He'd confessed to her once that some days it seemed he could hardly remember his mom at all. Some days he had to pull out the photograph of her that he kept in his backpack to help him remember. As they stood there on the side of the road, the Indiana sun warming the tops of their heads and fields of green stretching out on all sides, she realized God had given him the sister he'd never had. And she'd been given the brother she had always longed for.

Amber didn't speak; she only waited.

Finally, he patted her back and stepped away. "I'm good."

"Then let's go get your dog."

"Maybe you should drive—"

"No. We're not going to give in to this." She went back to her side of the car, plopped into the passenger seat, and pulled her seat belt across her chest. He leaned into the VW and stared at her a moment, as if he was seeing something else. As if he wasn't solidly in their reality yet.

Then he rubbed his hand across the top of his brown crew cut and lowered himself into the Beetle, buckling up and starting the ignition.

"But Preston?"

"Yeah?"

"For the rest of the drive, let's talk about the Colts or the Cubs."

"Sports is good," he agreed.

The rhythm of Amber's heart settled into a regular pattern as they scooted down the road, five miles below the speed limit. She had always known that Preston dealt with demons from his past. He'd never told her specific details about the things that haunted him. She'd known about the flashbacks, though. He'd been abundantly clear before moving into the *Dawdy Haus*. In fact, he'd even printed out a list of symptoms for PTSD from a medical website and given it to her and Tate. She'd known, but knowing about something was very different from experiencing it.

She vowed to herself in that moment that she would see Preston whole and healthy again. Maybe the dog would do it. Maybe Zoey would. Or maybe it would be a combination of the people and things around him—the community God had placed him in. One way or another, she was not going to give up on this young man. He meant too much to her.

As did her friends.

She'd find a way to catch the numskull who was threatening her family—and Hannah and Pam were family. God wouldn't give her more than she could handle with his help, even though she felt overwhelmed at the moment. She'd pray for guidance, and wisdom, and strength. Somehow, they would all make it through to the other side of this storm.

It was with that resolve vibrating through her heart that she pointed out their exit as they entered the outskirts of Fort Wayne.

Fourteen

Hannah was barely in the door of her house when her mother handed her a large covered casserole bowl, tucked inside a quilted casserole carrier. Hannah had made the carrier the month before, using leftover pieces of spring-colored fabric and mimicking a fence rail pattern.

"Take this over to Sarah. It's a light chicken broth with some fresh vegetables. I tucked a loaf of fresh bread in the carrier too. Sarah had a treatment again today and can't be feeling very well."

"I go too, Hannah. Mattie go!"

Hannah sent a questioning look at her mother, who nodded her permission.

"Perhaps seeing this sweet girl will cheer her up."

Mattie threw her arms around her mother's legs. Eunice straightened the prayer *kapp* on top of her youngest's head, and then cautioned her, "Mattie, you mind your manners and don't be too loud."

"I'll whisper," Mattie said in a hushed tone.

"And no running around. Sarah is sick."

"Okay." Mattie took exaggerated, hushed steps toward the front door. Hannah claimed Mattie's hand once they were out on the porch. Sarah's home was two houses down from theirs. Each home fronted the county road, though the houses actually were set back a bit. It took less than ten minutes to walk there. Long enough for Mattie to expend the majority of her energy skipping along, pausing occasionally to pull a few flowers, and singing the words of two hymns she'd managed to mash together—"Precious Memories" and "Surely Goodness and Mercy." The result sounded like, "memries and GOOD nights."

"Remember, Mattie. Not too loud."

"Sshhhh." Mattie placed a finger across her lips and smiled up at Hannah mischievously.

"And no bouncing about."

"Okay, Hannah."

They walked up the porch steps, and Hannah knocked lightly on the door. Sarah didn't answer —her husband did.

"Afternoon, Reuben."

The older man nodded as he opened the

door wide for her to pass through. He looked exhausted, but Hannah wondered if that was from the emotional strain more than the physical task of looking after his wife.

Squatting down, he touched Mattie's nose. "How are you today, little Mattie?"

"I'm qui-et." She held out the wildflowers she'd pulled, a little marsh marigold with bright yellow flowers. It grew in the ditch beside the road. The single blue Jacob's Ladder she'd pulled from Eunice's garden.

Mattie had squeezed the stems so hard, the flowers drooped somewhat, but Reuben acted as if he'd just been handed a prize heifer.

"For me?"

"*Nein*! For Sa-rah." Mattie continued to speak in a hushed voice that could probably be heard throughout the entire house.

"Is she sleeping?" Hannah handed him the casserole carrier.

"She was, but woke up a few minutes ago. I know she'd love to see both of you. I'll just set this . . ."

"Soup—chicken and vegetable."

"In the kitchen." He peeked inside. "Some of your *mamm*'s fresh bread too. Tell her *danki* for us."

"I will."

Reuben limped off toward the kitchen. He'd hurt his leg a few years ago while farming the southern portion of his field. Hannah could still remember Sarah's look of desperation as she ran down the road, crying for help. This was before the cancer had changed their lives. At the time, Hannah wondered what that would be like—to love someone so much that their pain was yours. But she realized as she watched Reuben limp into the kitchen that theirs was a mutual devotion. He was suffering with Sarah's illness as much as she was.

Clasping Mattie's hand, Hannah led her back to Sarah's room. Sarah offered them a wan smile as they paused in the doorway. She raised a hand and motioned them in. She was a few years older than Hannah's mother, but she looked as if she'd aged considerably since the chemo had begun. Today she was sitting up in her bed, and though the afternoon was warm, she had the quilt on her bed tucked snugly around her thin frame. Hannah noticed the quilt was the star pattern, one she had first learned when quilting beside her *mamm* and Sarah.

Her *kapp* was on the nightstand beside her, and the sunlight streaming through the window reflected off her bald head.

"Hey, Mattie."

"Sarah!" Mattie started for Sarah's bed, but Hannah pulled her back.

"Sarah's sick today, Mattie. No climbing on the bed."

Mattie stuck out her bottom lip. Then Sarah patted the side of her bed, and Mattie's pucker turned into a smile.

"Mattie is qui-et, Sarah."

"You are quiet."

"We brought flower soup!"

Sarah raised an eyebrow at Hannah, who shook her head.

"Flower soup? That sounds yummy."

"*Nein*! Flowers and soup." Mattie scooted forward and placed her small hand on top of Sarah's head, her expression turning to a scowl.

"Don't worry, my child. My head will be covered with gray hair again before the fall corn is ready to harvest."

Reuben walked into the room carrying a tray. On it was a cup of the soup, a slice of the fresh bread, and Mattie's flowers in a juice cup.

"Now look at this. I'm going to get spoiled if you all keep this up."

Mattie helped her with the napkin, patting it across Sarah's chest and moving the flowers closer to the soup bowl, in case she hadn't seen them.

"Very pretty, Mattie."

"Look what I found, Mattie." Reuben held up a basket of small wooden toys.

Mattie clapped her hands and hopped to the floor beside the bed, settling on the crocheted rag rug. All of her attention turned to pulling the wooden animals—a horse, a cow, a dog, even a

139

sheep—from the basket and setting them up in a line.

Sarah continued to watch her, but the smile she'd put on for Mattie had disappeared. Sarah was one of the most positive people Hannah knew, but on chemo days, it seemed as if she couldn't quite find the energy to summon up her usually sunny self. It was as if she was waging a war on the inside, a war that took a good amount of her energy and nearly all of her attention. The lines in her face were etched more deeply, and the smile only came with an obvious effort.

"Bad treatment?" Hannah pulled a straight-back chair closer to the side of the bed and sat on it.

"All the treatments are *gut*. They kill the bad cells and allow the ones I need to flourish."

Hannah nodded but didn't trust her voice. Her throat felt suddenly tight, and tears caused her vision to blur. Why did life have to be so painful? And why did such terrible things happen to people she loved?

"Don't be crying for me, Hannah. The doctors are doing their best, and *Gotte* has a plan for my life. Now help me with this soup."

So she did, and Sarah made a valiant attempt, eating nearly half of the broth and vegetables. How could she gain her strength back if she didn't eat? How could such a small amount of broth be enough nourishment?

"Tell Eunice the vegetables have a nice flavor." She rested her head against the pillow. Hannah removed the tray and set it on the small table next to the bed.

Reuben had disappeared after bringing in the food. She guessed he didn't often have a chance to leave Sarah's side. Suddenly she was glad they'd come. If she could ease his burden at all, then it was worth the small effort to visit. Sarah had closed her eyes, but she reached over and laid her hand on top of Hannah's.

"Tell me what is new at the Village."

So Hannah told her about the pink, purple, and white flowers that had been planted, the line of spring print calico fabrics Carol had purchased for the quilt shop, and the details of her wedding plans. Finally she mentioned the recent stir over Ryan Duvall.

Sarah opened her eyes and studied Hannah. "Are you worried about him?"

"*Nein*, but I am worried about Martha."

"Martha was always a quiet one. You don't have to concern yourself over her, though. All children go through a *rumspringa*. Martha is only going through hers a little later than others."

"And what of Ryan?"

Sarah waved away her concern. "The *Englisch* are different from us. Martha will realize that in time."

But would she realize it before Ryan broke her

heart? Hannah didn't ask that question. Mattie was now lying on the carpet, bouncing the animals over Hannah's feet. Soon she would tire of the game and be ready to go.

Instead of belaboring the problem with Martha and Ryan, Hannah changed the subject. "Nearly all of the advance preparations for the race are done."

"The race for cancer?"

"*Ya.* The fundraising supports research for a cure and better treatments. Many *Englisch* doctors are working on it. Perhaps soon there will be a treatment that is not so difficult."

Sarah didn't answer that, only opened her eyes to stare out the window.

"Everyone calls it a Race for a Cure, and that's what the posters say as well. Amber ordered quite a lot of ribbon of the different colors that represent different cancers. We're to put it around the trees at the starting line, along the path, and at the finish line. Already we've had more people sign up than last year when it was held downtown."

"That's *gut.*"

"It is, Sarah. We're putting the names of people we're praying for along the race route. I'd like to put your name, if you don't mind."

"That would be nice. Maybe I'll be there to see the runners."

Hannah doubted that, but at least Sarah was

envisioning a time when she would be feeling better. She hadn't given up hope.

Hannah helped Mattie place the animals back into the basket. By the time they picked up the tray and crept to the door, Sarah was already asleep. Something about the way she lay there, the sun still shining in and falling on her where she rested in the bed, reminded Hannah of an infant—of one who had to depend on others. Sarah was depending on them—on Reuben and Eunice and even Hannah and Mattie. They were all her family, in one sense. And they'd do whatever they needed to do to help her recover from this dreadful disease.

Fifteen

The facility for Indiana Canine Assistant Network was not what Preston had expected. He didn't know what he had envisioned—a sad little animal shelter maybe. Or a cold, institutional place for training animals.

ICAN was like something out of a canine's dreams—if dogs dreamed. As they parked and walked toward the building, he noticed a blue canopy covering a concrete slab. Several dogs pushed and pulled on a chew toy, while another lay on its stomach, watching the tug-of-war. Though ICAN was on the outskirts of Fort

Wayne, the property itself looked like something in Middlebury. Trees lined the walk, and the medium-size building had been constructed underneath the shade of a grove of maple trees.

Preston could just make out a creek passing through the back corner of the property. He stopped and studied someone who was working with a dog down by the creek. That dog, as well as the ones under the canopy, all wore blue halters.

"Nice digs," Amber murmured.

"Looks like a boarding facility where the rich and famous leave their pets."

Despite Preston's flashback, they were on time for their appointment, and Tomas Hernandez was waiting for them inside the door of the main ICAN building. He was approximately Preston's age, and he looked as if he spent a fair amount of time working out at a gym. His handshake was firm, and he had no problem maintaining eye contact as he introduced himself. Preston had learned through the years that most people who knew about his PTSD would glance at him and then look away—as if they were afraid they might set him off. Somehow they were uncertain it was safe to be around someone like him. And maybe it wasn't. Today's flashback had proven to him once again that he could never be sure his PTSD wouldn't take control.

"I'm glad you could make it," Tomas said

144

after introductions were made all around.

"Nice place you have." Amber looked left and then right.

Preston was surprised there wasn't a smell to the place. When he was a teenager, he'd taken Skipper into the vet for his mom. He could still remember the way the place had smelled of cats and dogs and antiseptic—and maybe fear.

"Thanks." Tomas walked them back to a small office. "This is only a satellite facility. My main office is at our facility in Indianapolis, but I travel here occasionally to deliver a dog."

"I hope it wasn't a wasted trip for you." Preston sat in the chair Tomas indicated, but he didn't relax.

"We'll get to that in a minute. First I'd like to tell you a little about ICAN. We've been in business for fifteen years. Our dogs are trained by adults incarcerated in Indiana correctional facilities. I like to tell folks that up front since some people have a problem with it."

"What kind of problem?"

Tomas shrugged. "Occasionally potential participants don't like the idea that the training takes place inside a correctional facility, that a prisoner has been working with their dog. Who knows why? I just like to put the details out there at the beginning so that we can ascertain if it will be a problem."

"Everyone deserves a second chance," Preston

said. He was thinking that he understood the truth of that statement better than most.

"What kind of dogs do you use?" Amber asked.

"Retrievers and Labradors." Tomas handed them both a folder full of literature about ICAN. "I don't expect you to read all that now, but scan over it and call me if you get home and have questions. I'll cover the high spots today, but the brochures go into more detail, as does our website."

He spent the next ten minutes explaining how the dogs were trained through a vigorous program with positive reinforcement, performed by both correctional inmates and ICAN volunteers. Their organization had begun training dogs for children with Down syndrome and cerebral palsy. After a few years they branched out to providing service dogs to children and adults who suffered from Type 1 diabetes. And more recently they had begun training dogs for folks with PTSD, especially veterans.

"I see your average wait time is three to four years." Amber had been glancing over the brochures as Tomas spoke.

"Zoey and I sent my application in a few months ago." Preston shook his head. "How is it possible that you called me so soon?"

"It's an unusual situation. We had trained Mocha for another vet who won't be needing her now. After looking over our applicants, you seemed like the best fit for her."

Preston and Amber shared a smile at the name. Mocha. He'd first come to the Village, first met Amber, because of what had occurred at the coffee shop. Coincidence? Or a sign that this was the right thing to do?

"The person you'd trained her for won't need her . . . what does that mean?" Preston fidgeted with the folder but didn't open it. "Why wouldn't he need her?"

"I can't share information about another client."

"I'm not sure I feel comfortable taking a dog that should have gone to someone else—"

"I understand." Tomas met his gaze and seemed to come to a decision. "I can tell you that this particular person decided to pursue other avenues of treatment. Service dogs aren't for everyone, which is why we ask you to come out and spend some time here. It's important that you are a good fit for each other."

Preston nodded as if he understood, but he wasn't sure if any of it made sense.

"You have doubts."

"I just don't see how a dog can possibly help me."

"You've been diagnosed with PTSD, right?"

Preston nodded in one quick, short motion. His condition wasn't something he discussed openly, and never with someone he'd just met.

"Where did you serve?"

"Afghanistan."

"Do you relive your combat experience . . . to the point that it interrupts your daily activities?"

"Yes."

"Do you isolate yourself from others?"

"I guess . . . some."

"And do you startle easily?"

Again, Preston nodded.

"On a scale of 1 to 10, how severe would you say your symptoms are?"

Preston remembered waking in the *Dawdy Haus*, his bed a shambles, the mattress on its side, and the nightstand broken. He remembered the pain in his legs from crouching in the corner of the room.

He glanced at Amber, and he knew she was thinking about their trip there, him fighting to maintain control as he pulled off to the side of the road.

He glanced out the window and thought of Zoey, the hopeful look in her eyes, and his fear that he could never offer her a safe home.

He was ashamed of those things. If he couldn't be honest in front of Amber, who was like family to him, and in front of Tomas, who obviously wanted to help, then he had little or no chance of getting better.

"Eight or nine. Some days a ten." He swallowed, his throat suddenly terribly dry. "Some days are better than others."

"Our first PTSD dog went to a vet from Iraq. Let's call this guy Sam." Tomas smiled, apparently pleased with having found a way around the privacy issues by providing a fictitious name. "Sam had frequent flashbacks. When he did, his brain and body reacted as though the danger was real, as though he was once again in combat. His sister was afraid to leave him alone, and the entire family worried about him driving. He found it hard to hold a job or maintain any sense of normalcy."

"Sounds familiar," Preston muttered. "You're going to tell me a dog cured this guy? I have a hard time believing that's possible."

"It wasn't instantaneous. A dog isn't a magical antidote against PTSD. In this case, we provided him with a Lab named Simon. Simon helped Sam with some physical issues, but more importantly the dog could recognize the first signs of a flashback."

"Recognize how?" Amber sat forward in her chair.

"I'll be honest. We don't understand the how, but we've seen it work time and again. Perhaps they're able to recognize certain repetitive behaviors you have that signal you're about to suffer a flashback."

Preston thought about his recent flashbacks—

each time he'd had a sense of falling, felt as if he were actually touching the grit and gravel of the desert, and become painfully thirsty. Did his heart rate spike when that happened? Did he clutch his hand or swallow repeatedly? He didn't know, because he was always falling, falling back into the past.

Could a dog sense his distress?

"A dog trained to assist someone with PTSD will learn to recognize when his or her master is slipping into a flashback. When that happens, he'll provide tactile stimulation—"

Amber looked as confused as Preston felt.

"A cold nose to the palm of your hand, a short bark, even brushing up against your leg can bring you back before you suffer the full flashback. Service dogs can also turn on lights and safety-check a room, or turn on lights in a bedroom while you're sleeping to pull you out of a flash-back."

"A dog can do all that?" Amber glanced at Preston and smiled. "I might need to trade in my cat, Leo."

Preston decided at that point he needed to admit the two things that were worrying him more than anything else. "Zoey said there's a grant, from the VA, to pay for the cost of the dog, but it seems to me someone might need those funds more than I do."

"You're going to have to trust me when I say

that it looks to me like you're the best fit for Mocha."

"All right. But what if I'm not a good dog owner? What if I have a fit while driving and crash the car, injuring her? What if I forget and leave the door open and she runs off? What if—"

"We could talk what-ifs for a long time, couldn't we? I've read through your application, and it sounds like you have a good environment for a dog."

Preston thought about the *Dawdy Haus* and the Village. Both would probably be ideal for a dog.

"As far as your symptoms and you possibly causing harm to Mocha, if I thought that was possible, let alone probable, I wouldn't have asked your friend Zoey to have you come in."

Preston stared at the pictures on the wall in Tomas's office, pictures of dogs and children, dogs and adults, dogs and veterans. He'd never even considered owning a pet. How could he? Until a year ago, he'd been living on the streets. A pet, a dog, would be one more step toward normal. And what if Mocha could help him? Preston fully believed God was healing the broken places in his heart and in his mind. But he understood it was a process. Was Mocha part of that process? Had God arranged things so that what had been impossible was now possible?

Suddenly he knew he had to take that leap of faith. Not only did he have a strong conviction that it was the right thing to do, but he wanted to do it. He wanted to be well, completely well, and if Mocha could help with that, then who was he to argue?

"I'll do it."

Tomas's smile was instantaneous. He slapped the folder down on the desk and stood. "All right. Let's go meet Mocha."

Sixteen

Amber walked into her home, breathed in the smell of sizzling vegetables, and dropped her purse and tablet on the coffee table. There was a time when she would have checked e-mails as soon as she walked into the house, especially when she'd been away from the Village for an afternoon. But that time was long gone. She understood now that if someone needed her, they would have texted or called. Any e-mails could wait, and she wanted to see her husband.

Then there was the fear of finding another anonymous e-mail. *Ack!* That would ruin her appetite. Come to think of it, her appetite was already ruined, which was a rare event indeed.

Tate stood in front of the stove, dressed in blue jeans and a flannel shirt, stirring whatever was making that heavenly smell.

"Look who's home."

"Look who's cooking."

Amber walked up to her husband, slipped her arms around his waist, and rested her cheek against his broad back. Home. To think a year ago she had barely known Tate Bowman. Now he was such an important part of her life that she didn't feel whole and at rest unless they were together. How did something like that happen so quickly?

And should she tell him about the second e-mail? But what good would it do? And if somehow the person found out, then she might be pushing them over the proverbial edge.

"You haven't even asked what I'm cooking."

"It doesn't matter what it is. I can smell it, and I'm smitten."

He placed the spatula on the plate he'd been using to slice vegetables, lowered the heat under the pan, and turned to gather her in his arms. "Smitten with me? Or with stir-fried vegetables, rice, and smothered chicken breasts?"

"Yes!" She raised her face to his and waited.

When he kissed her, kissed her thoroughly, she wanted to suggest they forget the dinner preparation. Who needed food when you were in love? Then her stomach rumbled, protesting against the idea of skipping the chicken.

"The lady of the house requires sustenance." Tate ran his thumb over her bottom lip, kissed her once more—this time a short, sweet caress—

and then handed her the spatula. "Stir that while I finish making the salad."

As she stirred, she briefly told him about Mocha, then about Preston's flashback episode on the way to Fort Wayne.

Tate frowned as he handed her a glass of iced tea. "Were you in danger?"

"No. He somehow managed to pull to the side of the road as the flashback overcame him. I was more frightened about what was happening to him than the possibility of us having an accident." She described how he'd gripped the wheel with both hands and how his expression had gone slack. "He slumped in a stupor as soon as the vehicle rolled to a stop. It was like watching someone have a seizure. It broke my heart, Tate."

"It's a miracle neither of you were injured. I knew he has flashbacks, but I didn't realize they affected his driving."

"I suppose he can't choose when or where they happen."

"But this dog—Mocha—is supposed to help stop them?"

"That's what Tomas told us."

They sat at the table, and when Tate clasped her hand in his, Amber understood fully how much she had to be thankful for. Not only the fact that she and Preston hadn't been hurt, but that she had a warm and loving husband waiting for her when she returned home. God had provided in so many ways, even as he was now providing for Preston, even as he had provided the meal they were about to eat.

Surely he would also provide an answer to her latest dilemma.

They bowed their heads. As usual, Tate's simple but sincere prayer summed up all Amber was feeling—gratitude, love, and humbleness.

He squeezed her hand when her head remained bowed. "Something worrying you?"

Instead of answering that question, she began to tell him more about Preston and Mocha. "I wish you could have seen them. I was tempted to record it on my phone."

"I doubt Preston would want that shared."

"Maybe not." Amber tried a bite of the smothered chicken. Delicious! Her man could cook.

Cooking.

Baking.

Poison.

Sweat broke out along her forehead and she reached for her glass of water. "At first he was hesitant, like a father with a new child, as if he was afraid he might break the dog or something. But Mocha is a sweetheart. She sat in front of him, patiently waiting for him to make the first move."

"And then?"

"Then they focused on the commands Preston needed to learn. Tomas walked him through what training they had done, how Mocha is supposed to react if Preston has an episode, and gave him a list of to-dos and not-to-dos."

"Such as?"

"Table scraps. That's a big no-no."

Silence settled around them as Tate enjoyed the dinner, and Amber pushed her food around on her plate. She had taken another two bites— one of the smothered chicken and one of the stir-fried veggies—when her cell phone rang. At first she thought to ignore it, but then the house phone began ringing.

"I'll get that," Tate said.

"And I'll find my cell."

They pushed back from the table simultaneously.

Leo stared at them from his perch on the stool near the kitchen window. No doubt he couldn't understand why they were abandoning a perfectly good meal, and he'd been unimpressed by the conversation about Preston's dog.

"Don't even think about taking a bite," Amber cautioned. The cat had never been one for table scraps, but if there were ever a meal to start him down that path it now sat on the table. Steam still rose from the chicken, and the smell was simply tantalizing.

Walking backward, Amber kept her eyes on the

cat, who showed his disinterest by raising a paw and commencing to clean his face. She darted into the living room, retrieved her cell, and was back in her seat in time to hear Tate's end of his conversation.

Georgia, he mouthed. "I'll tell her. No, it's good that you called. We'll be over in a few minutes."

One glance at her phone's screen told Amber that Pam was calling. This worried her even more than what she'd heard of Tate's conversation. Pam was adamant about not interrupting Amber's time off—she claimed that the *newlyweds* needed their time alone. Only a major emergency would have caused her to call.

Tate began covering their plates and placing them in the microwave as Amber took the call. Even as she spoke to her assistant, Amber gathered her purse, her tablet, and a light jacket. "Call the police, not nine-one-one, but the administrative number. They'll patch you through to the closest officer."

By the time she hung up, Tate had snagged the truck keys. This was one emergency she knew he wasn't going to let her handle alone, and based on her history over the past year, that was probably a very wise decision.

Seventeen

Amber reminded herself to pray as they drove the short distance to the Village, parked, and walked to the bakery. Her natural inclination was to worry, but she was trying to change that. She was trying to mature in her faith, and now would be a good time to put that into practice.

When they reached the parking lot, she saw a Shipshewana police cruiser had already pulled up outside. Apparently Gordon Avery's shift had ended. Cherry Brookstone reached the bakery door at the same time they did. Cherry was young, thin, and muscular, and had long red hair to match her name. Her green eyes nearly twinkled into a smile—nearly, but not quite. Amber and Cherry had not always agreed on things, but after the last murder they seemed to have at least found a common ground of respect.

Amber still thought Cherry was too young and too arrogant, but she admired her skills and her dedication to her job. As for what Cherry thought, well, who could tell? The woman hadn't actually called and invited her for a cup of coffee. For some reason they seemed to stay just a few feet shy of an actual friendship.

"A poison poet, huh?"

"Apparently, though the poet part is a stretch. The last note left showed a real lack of creativity. It's almost as if a teenager were writing it, based on the poor rhyming scheme—" Amber stopped short as she realized she was discussing the case with a police officer. She was doing exactly what the e-mail had told her not to do—if in fact both e-mails had come from the same person. And why wouldn't they have? What were the odds of two crazies popping up at the same time?

They stepped into the bakery.

An older woman was seated in a chair that had been brought over from the restaurant and placed near the cash register. Georgia stood behind the counter, a scowl on her face. It flitted across Amber's mind that Pam was right—Georgia had changed. But she couldn't think of that right now. She had to focus on the crisis at hand.

Pam squatted in front of the woman, attempting to calm her. The two other bakery employees were scurrying back and forth behind the counter, trying to fill orders despite the chaos. Most of the customers had stopped to stare at the woman in the chair, who was now wailing and moaning. For a moment, Amber gave in to the fear that the woman had been poisoned, but Pam had specifically said the pie hadn't been cut.

"Mrs. Webster, I need you to calm down." Pam knelt in front of the woman with steel gray hair teased into a tall beehive hairdo. She fanned

159

herself with a bakery brochure, pausing now and again to moan.

Amber, Tate, and Cherry hustled toward the register.

"I'll fetch her a glass of water," Tate said.

"Ma'am, I'm Amber Bowman, and I'm the manager of the Village."

"If you're the manager . . . oh. Oh, my."

"Are you hurt in any way?"

"Hurt? Am I hurt? If you were doing your job this wouldn't have . . . oh." The woman put her head back and fanned her neck. "I could have been killed."

Her voice rose sharply as she pondered her near-death experience. Then the careening noise Amber had heard from the door began again.

"She's in shock." Cherry pulled her radio off her belt. "I'll call in the paramedics."

"No! Oh, no paramedics."

"Ma'am?"

Mrs. Webster gathered all her energy and pulled herself together, sitting up straighter in the chair and leveling her gaze at Cherry. "Have you seen the way those young men drive? Haven't I been through enough today?"

"What exactly—"

"It's the horror of it, is all. I need a moment. Oh."

"I need you to calm down, ma'am. Otherwise procedures state that I need to call medical personnel to obtain a professional opinion."

Mrs. Webster was neither large nor small, and at least seventy years old, but she was astute. Amber noticed the way she cut her eyes to the right and the left, checking to see how big her audience was. Finally she leaned forward and spoke in a theatrical, hushed voice, meaning that everyone in the store could hear her. "You need to take my statement. There's a murderer loose—"

A collective gasp escaped from the crowd, and they seemed to simultaneously move back in one giant step, as if they needed to put some distance between themselves and the danger wrought by the poison poet. Mrs. Webster had made sure everyone around her knew what the note said.

"The police can take your statement." Pam stood and straightened her blouse, which was a warm yellow decorated with peacocks. "But there is no murderer loose. All we have is a pie with a note on it. No one has been hurt, officer."

Tate arrived with the glass of water and handed it to Mrs. Webster. She took a long, slow sip, returned the glass to Tate, and then focused her gaze on Cherry. "My name is Mrs. Irene Webster, and I found that . . . that dangerous pie and that awful note on a shelf over there."

She pointed to her right, nearly knocking the glass out of Tate's hand in the process, then repeated her name and gave her address and phone number to Cherry. She was adamant that the officer have all of her contact information.

"It was over there, and I almost purchased it without reading that note. I almost took it home." She fluttered her eyelids as if the thought was too painful to entertain. "If I had, if I'd cut it and eaten a piece, I could be dead!"

Cherry didn't look up from the pad where she was writing down Mrs. Webster's statement. "Where is the pie now?"

"I have it," Georgia said. It was the first time she'd spoken since Amber had walked through the door. The new hairdo and makeup disoriented Amber. She felt like she was talking to a stranger, not the woman she had known for years. "And before you upbraid me for moving it, I used a dish towel, not my hands. I don't think I contaminated it in any way, unless I smudged some prints. I couldn't just leave it out on the pie table, though."

Cherry and Amber stepped toward the counter.

The note was on the same type of paper as the first, what looked to Amber like a piece of plain copier paper. It had been typed or printed from a computer. And the poetry was as bad as ever.

Cyanide might be sickly sweet
But put it into a treat you eat
Next thing you know your adversary
Will be gone and life will be merry

"Her cadence is all wrong," Amber muttered.

"Cadence?" Cherry had taken a picture of the pie and the note with her phone. "What cadence?"

"You know, the rhythm. She doesn't have enough beats per line."

"It's not a crime to be a bad poet," Pam pointed out.

"It should be." Amber's mind wasn't completely on the bad rhyme. She was wondering if she'd received another e-mail. And why now? What had instigated this rash outbreak of threats?

Cherry turned her back to them and spoke into her radio, which seemed rather rude to Amber, but who was she to say? She was just trying to run a Village that was now being frequented by a bad poet with a taste for drama and poison.

"I'm sorry I called and interrupted your evening," Pam said.

"No, I'm glad you did." Amber turned to Georgia. "Are you all right?"

Georgia waved away her concern and pulled on her apron, which did seem less snug around her middle. How much weight had the woman lost? "I'm tougher than whoever this twerp is. I just wish they would pick someone else's bakery to mess with. Two times in one day is a bit too much excitement for me."

"I wish whoever is doing this would get some help—see a doctor or a shrink or a priest," Pam said. "These sorts of things put people on edge, and we don't need the bad publicity."

Amber bit her lip to keep from answering. How many people were in the room? A dozen? More?

Was the person watching to see how she'd react? To see if she would mention the e-mails? Whoever it was must be on the property, because they knew she'd spoken with Hannah. Or maybe they'd only suspected it. They couldn't have heard the conversation, since the two had been in the coffee shop alone.

"Not to mention these situations tend to attract drama queens." Pam offered this comment in a low aside that only Amber and Tate heard. Pam and Tate shared a smile that should have helped to lessen the tension, but Amber quickly stared at the floor.

"Say, what's wrong with you?" Pam's voice was colored with concern. "You're not acting like yourself. This person isn't creeping you out, I hope. Because we are going to catch them, just like the last time. And when we do—"

"Perhaps we could allow Cherry to do her work."

Pam's eyes nearly bulged out of her head.

Tate said, "I think Pam was trying to be encouraging."

"And I appreciate it. I only meant that maybe we should stay out of her way."

"Since when do we stay out of the way? What happened to the person who tracked down Owen's killer?"

Amber couldn't speak, couldn't push any of the words out, so instead she shook her head no. Pam was no longer watching the officer or the woman in the chair. She was staring at Amber as if she'd suddenly shown up in Amish clothing.

Cherry turned back toward them. "I want this area cleared of both personnel and customers. I have crime scene techs coming in to dust for fingerprints."

Tate began moving customers toward the door, suggesting they have a cup of coffee and snack in the restaurant.

"Complimentary coffee," Pam added. "And thank you all for your patience."

"I couldn't possibly drink coffee now," Mrs. Webster proclaimed. "And who knows when I'll be able to eat again. This has completely upset my system."

"That's a real shame." Amber pulled a card out of her bag and handed it to the woman. "This is good for a complimentary meal in our restaurant. I do hope that you'll stop by when you're feeling better—"

"I suppose I could eat something."

"Excellent. Pam will help you to a table."

Amber stepped away from the woman, wondering how long this night was going to be, when she bumped into Cherry.

"Thank you for coming," she mumbled.

Tate was once again at her side. "It's probably just some nut, craving attention. Don't you think?"

"Possibly, but I scanned the folks in the room, and in my opinion none of them appeared to be likely candidates." A squawk came from Cherry's radio and she reached to turn down the volume.

"We should go." Amber tugged on Tate's jacket sleeve, but he appeared not to notice.

"Maybe they like seeing their . . . *work* in the paper." Tate glanced around the now-empty room, and then put his arm around Amber. "It doesn't mean they were here to witness it personally."

"Could be."

"Do you have the results back from the first incident?"

"That was less than twelve hours ago, so no. Even if there had been a murder, which there wasn't, the crime lab couldn't move that fast."

Tate pulled Amber even closer. "So we have two pies that may or may not be poisonous."

"You also have three incidents in two days."

If you only knew, Amber thought. There had been four—and the one Cherry didn't know about scared Amber as much as the others.

Cherry stared up at the corner of the ceiling, as if trying to remember each incident. "The e-mail Amber received last night, the pie that appeared on the counter with a warning note, and tonight's pie and note."

"That's a little too close together for my liking," Tate said.

Amber leaned closer to him, and murmured that she had a headache and would like to go.

Tate nodded, but continued talking. "This time they mentioned a specific poison—cyanide. Why would they tell us what they'd put into the pie?"

"Maybe just to frighten folks. A specific threat is more disturbing than a general one. It's as if this person is desperate to get their point across."

"Which is?"

"That pie is dangerous? That poisons are easily accessible? That the Village bakery is a terrible place to eat?"

Amber scowled at that last one. She was proud of their bakery. It had always been a bright spot in the Village. Checkered curtains adorned the windows. Shelves were nicely spaced out, and the displays were inviting. Instrumental hymns played over the speakers. Wonderful scents floated in from the kitchen.

"Why me?" she asked. "Haven't we had enough trouble this last year? Why now? Why again?"

Cherry ran her fingers over her right eyebrow, as if she could stir up a good answer. Finally she said, "It seems you attract the worst kind. Let's just hope this time it doesn't end in murder."

Preston had pulled up to the *Dawdy Haus* when he saw Amber and Tate pass by in their vehicle.

"I wonder where those two have been." Zoey

gave him a suggestive smile and a wink. "Probably out on a hot date."

Preston shrugged.

"Don't you think it's sweet? The way they found love in their later years."

"Neither is that old," Preston reminded her. He reached into the backseat of the Volkswagen and pulled out several packages of dog supplies.

Zoey picked up the dog bed and hugged it to her chest. It was made of some plush material that she was convinced Mocha would love. "They're not that young, either. I'm thankful that you and I found each other early in our lives."

Preston grunted as he jostled both bags to his left arm and unlocked the front door. He'd never have guessed a dog would need so much stuff, but Zoey had walked through the discount store with Tomas's list, rapidly filling his cart. He wasn't sure the *Dawdy Haus* was big enough for him and this beast.

While he unbagged the supplies and set them on the table, Zoey made them each a mug of hot decaffeinated coffee. Then she pulled the bag of oatmeal cookies from the refrigerator—a bag he had picked up at the Village bakery because he knew they were her favorite. It was that way between them now—easy and natural. But his life wasn't easy or natural, and he needed to help Zoey to see that.

"Want to sit on the front porch?"

"Sure." He took one of the coffee mugs and the cookies from her, then led the way outside.

"I love it here," Zoey said. "I know people say the Amish life is peaceful and simple, but that's not what I mean, or it's not the only thing. It's that the majority of people around here have chosen to keep their life simple. They've embraced the quiet, rural life, and they value it."

Preston watched her as she pulled her feet up and tucked them underneath her. She was like a cat—finding a place she liked and luxuriating in it.

He cleared his throat. "I feel like there are some things we need to talk about."

She studied him over her coffee mug and waited. He didn't want to spoil the moment, but he'd also been waiting for a chance, waiting until they were alone and there wouldn't be any interruptions. He'd learned in the military that when you had something unpleasant to do, you needed to do it. Procrastinating only made it worse.

"You know how I feel about you, Zoey."

"I do?" A smile played on her lips.

"I'm crazy about you. I've never met anyone who could make me feel . . . kind of like you were saying, at peace. Or maybe it's that with you my life is more on the path it should be. My priorities are better. My spiritual life—well, it isn't great, but it's improving every week."

"Still meeting with Tate?"

"Yes. He's been a big help to me, and so has Pastor Mitch."

Zoey reached for a cookie and nibbled around the edges. "I hear a *but* coming."

He set his coffee mug down on the small table, planted his feet firmly on the ground, and leaned forward so his elbows were resting on his legs. He studied her and tried to discern her expression in the near darkness.

"You know what I'm getting at."

"Maybe."

"I care about you, maybe too much to see you stuck with someone like me, someone who is still broken." He held up his hand to stop her protests. "I know. It's better. My entire life— every aspect of it—is better than a year ago, but what if this is as good as it gets? What if the nightmares never stop and the flashbacks . . . what if someday I hurt someone? What if that person I hurt is you? How could I live with that? And why would you want to risk it?"

Zoey carefully placed her coffee mug on the table, then moved out of her chair and squatted down in front of him. Gently she placed her hands over his. "You told me you love me—"

"I do."

"And I love you. For now that's enough. We don't have to figure out the future or even decide what happens next. God will take care of the details."

He reached out and touched her face, kissed her softly, allowed his hand to slide down her arm. And in that moment, sitting on his front porch with a million stars making an appearance overhead, it was easy to believe that what she said made sense. It was easy, for a little while, to stop being afraid.

Eighteen

Hannah had been waiting at the end of her lane for Mary. When she saw her friend walking toward her, she waved and stepped onto the Pumpkinvine Trail. Hannah had known Mary all her life. Though Mary was eight years older, they'd always been a part of the same church district, and then more recently they'd both worked at the Village.

It would have been difficult for Hannah to describe the changes in her friend over the last six months, since the death of Owen Esch and since Andrew had returned home. In some ways Mary was even more pensive than before. She would get that faraway look in her eyes and forget she was in the middle of a conversation. Those times, Hannah knew she was remembering Owen, was praying for his family, and was struggling against the guilt that perhaps she could have done something more. She couldn't have. She'd admitted as much to Hannah one cold night in the middle of winter. Still, she sometimes battled feelings of remorse. Owen had been a close friend, practically a brother to her, and she mourned his loss as one would grieve over the passing of a family member.

But those moments of introspection were becoming less intrusive with each day that passed, and there were other changes in Mary as well—good changes. Though she had recently turned thirty-one, there was a spring in her step and a lightness in her laughter that hadn't been there before she'd allowed herself to love Andrew Miller.

Mary had always had a sweet tooth, and she was still on the heavy side of plump. However, that no longer seemed to affect her self-image. She now wore dresses made with fabric of lighter colors. She took more care in her appearance in general, not to the point of pride, but simple things that reflected her mood. Today for example, she carried a knitted handbag—one made of a variegated yarn with splashes of peach interwoven with sky blues and off-whites. Mary was the manager of the Village's yarn shop, The Cat's Meow, and Hannah was certain she'd made the new bag herself. Her blonde hair was still carefully pinned beneath her *kapp*. Not a strand escaped into view, but in a dozen small ways she had relaxed. She was in love. She was happy, and Hannah was beyond thrilled that they would soon be sisters-in-law.

"*Gudemariye*," Mary called.

Hannah waited until Mary was closer, then linked her arm with her friend's. "And *gudemariye* to you, Mary."

"You're in a fine mood."

"Why wouldn't I be? It's a beautiful April morning, both Andrew and Jesse are home today—working on our rooms—and we're to be married in a month."

"Some days I feel as if I'm walking through a dream."

"*Ya*. I know. It probably won't feel that way when we're living together in the crowded Miller house."

"Andrew and Jesse, the two of us, their four younger *schweschdern*, and their parents." Mary laughed as she ticked off the number of people who would be in their new home.

"That will be—"

"Ten! Ten people in one house. Even more crowded than our home."

"Or ours." Hannah loved her family, and she would actually miss sharing a room with her little *schweschder*, Mattie. However, she'd only be a little ways down the road, and soon Mattie would be riding bicycles, attending school, and traveling down the Pumpkinvine Trail to visit. They would see each other often.

"The rooms they're adding on sound like the perfect temporary solution."

"I haven't seen them yet. Have you?"

"*Nein*, but Andrew described them to me—a room for each of us and a bathroom to share in between."

Hannah sighed. "I wouldn't mind if we did have to share a bathroom with everyone else. It's no different than what we've always known. I just want it done and finished. I'm ready to be a bride!"

Mary smiled. "You're young and impatient. When you're my age you'll learn to savor the moment, even when it includes waiting."

"Pooh. You sound as if you're ancient. You're only—"

"Thirty-one."

"Thirty-one is still young, and besides, *Gotte* had a plan for you, a plan that included Andrew coming home and falling *in lieb*."

They continued discussing wedding details as they walked. Although they intended to keep their celebration small, they expected to be feeding nearly five hundred people. If each couple invited only twenty-five couples, they would still reach five hundred guests because most families had at least ten members. Fortunately, they'd found when they compared lists that they had many dupli-cated names.

"The tables will be set up the week before," Mary reminded her.

"That's in three weeks!"

"*Ya*, and the food prep will start at the same time."

"I've helped in a lot of weddings, but I'm learning it's a completely different thing when it's your own." Hannah shook her head, hoping to clear it. Some days she was excited, others a bit stressed, but always under that lay a stream of joy that soon she would be with Jesse every morning, every day, every night.

"Have you begun sewing your dress?" Mary's question pulled her from thoughts of waking next to Jesse.

"*Nein*. My next day off is on Monday. *Mamm* and I plan to begin then. She's a fast seamstress."

"It's *gut* that we bought the fabric when we did."

Hannah nodded. "I heard there were so many weddings this year, in Middlebury and Shipshe, that the places where we normally purchase our fabric had to order more of the wedding material."

"*Ya*. I heard the same."

"I stopped by the downtown store last week," Hannah confessed. "Just to walk up and down the aisles a little."

"Tell me you didn't buy anything."

"*Nein*—"

"Because you know we'll receive gifts."

"I just couldn't help looking, though. The thought of having our own home . . ."

"We won't have our own homes," Mary reminded her. "But we'll have our own rooms, which is almost as good."

"And someday our own homes. You'll see."

They had reached the parking lot of the Village. Mary switched the bag she carried from her right arm to her left. "Just stay away from any shopping temptations."

Hannah rolled her eyes but nodded in agreement. She wasn't going to buy anything. She wasn't *narrisch*.

They crossed the parking lot, waving at Henry but not walking close enough to the attendant's hut to speak with him. As they walked between the bakery and the inn, something yellow flapping in the breeze caught Hannah's attention. She stopped, pushed up on her glasses, and then moved in the direction of the bakery.

"Wrong way, Hannah. Are you so *in lieb* you've forgotten where your shop is?"

But Hannah wasn't listening. She was hurrying toward the bakery and toward the thing she had hoped she would never see again.

It reminded her of Ethan Gray, his death, and the turbulent weeks that had followed.

It reminded her of Owen Esch and the tragedy that had ensnared Mary.

It was harmless, of course, but the sight still sent her pulse racing. The tape was a mere three inches wide. As she drew closer she

176

recognized the yellow, black stripes, and bold letters.

CRIME SCENE.

Its very existence across the door of the bakery proclaimed that once again the law had been broken and someone at the Village was involved.

Nineteen

Preston's morning started with a nightmare.

He stumbled out of his bed, stubbing his toe on the bedside table, unable to remember the details of his dream. He was able to taste the grit of the desert, and he knew that he'd returned, once again, to that terrible day. Had he dreamed about the attack? About his friends? Or about the countless hours of waiting for rescue?

He couldn't remember, so he splashed water on his face and stared at himself in the bathroom mirror—bloodshot eyes from too little sleep and wrinkle lines that he hadn't noticed before. Time marched on, or so he'd always heard. So why was a large part of his heart and mind trapped in the past?

Why couldn't he simply let it go?

Cranking the shower all the way to hot, he allowed the steam that filled the room to melt away some of the tension he'd woken with. The details of the nightmare were not important. What did matter was that he'd wakened, his T-shirt wet with sweat and his hand reaching for a weapon that wasn't there because he kept his firearm safely locked away.

Would Mocha have intervened? Or did she only alert when he was in real distress, attempting to drive off a perfectly good road? Would Preston wake to find the rather large dog on his chest, barking and pleading with him to come back from his terrifying dreams?

"Get ahold of yourself, Preston." The habit of talking to himself was not a result of his battle experience. He'd done it since he was a teen, staring in the mirror, waiting for those first signs of manhood—actually longing to shave—and seeing only new acne.

"Today's a new day. Today's the day you become a dog owner." He stripped off the sweat-soaked clothes he'd slept in and stepped into the shower, forgetting to move the temperature away from all hot. He yelped and jumped out of the way of the searing stream of water.

Adjusting it, waiting, slowing his breathing, he thought back over what the preacher had said on Sunday. "Listen to God. Make time to listen." He'd always thought of himself as a good listener, but listen to God? How did a person even do that?

As he showered, shaved, dressed, and ate a light breakfast, he attempted to slow his thoughts, to still his worries, and to listen. He did not hear a voice telling him how to straighten out his life. No direct words from God. He did hear a cardinal outside his window, a slight breeze in the trees, and Amber's cat meowing on the doorstep.

After putting a little feed out for the ginger cat—how could he resist, the feline practically insisted on it—he picked up his keys and cell phone and headed off to work, opting to leave his VW Beetle at home. The walk was one of his favorite parts of each day. And though he hadn't heard God, hadn't received a word, he felt calmer and more centered for his time spent listening. Perhaps that was sometimes how a word from God came—through the natural rhythm of nature.

He was later glad for those few quiet moments, as the day grew more chaotic than usual with each passing moment. His phone chirped when he'd covered less than half the distance to the Village—a text from Amber, asking him to stop by her office first thing. Once he was there, she told him and Elizabeth about the previous night's excitement.

"How long will the bakery be closed?" Elizabeth asked. She was older, competent, and reminded Preston of a cross between his commanding officer and his grandmother.

"I'm hoping to open it back up first thing tomorrow, but I'll have to hear from the police department before that happens."

"Any idea why this person is picking the Village bakery to harass?" Preston sipped the coffee Elizabeth had handed him and considered what he could do to help the situation, but nothing came to mind.

"None. Why even warn someone that you're going to poison them? It all makes no sense."

"Unless they're doing it for the drama." Elizabeth removed her glasses, little reading cheaters that were attached to a jeweled chain, and cleaned them with the hem of her blouse. "Whoever this is wants attention. They're not doing it in secret. Maybe they enjoy the limelight."

"I hope they enjoy a jail cell, because that's where they're going to end up." Amber drummed her fingers against the top of her desk. "I suppose that didn't sound very charitable, but I'm completely frustrated with this entire situation. I've phoned the Village owners, and they have offered any resources we need, even suggesting we could hire private security personnel."

"To guard the pies?" Elizabeth donned her glasses and stared at Amber over the tops of them.

"Exactly. Every aspect of this threat is ludicrous. I told them we'd think about it, but at this time it doesn't feel necessary." Amber sat back, sipped her coffee, and then focused her gaze on Preston. "Pam was here late, so I told her you could handle this morning alone."

"No problem."

"But I still want you out of here by two."

"Not necessary. I can call Tomas and—"

"You'll do no such thing. Mocha's coming today, Preston. We're not going to let a poison freak who indulges in bad poetry ruin this day."

"If you're sure."

"I am." Amber shared a smile with Elizabeth. "This is a new beginning, Preston."

"I never thought of myself as a dog person."

"I never thought I'd be running an Amish Village."

"And I certainly didn't expect to still be working well into my sixties." Elizabeth stood and picked up the empty coffee mugs. "Turns out I actually enjoy my job. A rare thing if you believe what you read in the paper. As far as the dog, never discount what God can do through his creatures. Be glad he didn't send you a donkey."

It was with that image that Preston went about his morning work, muttering, "A dog. God is going to solve my problems by sending me a dog?" Could be worse, he supposed, just as Elizabeth had suggested. What if he had a service donkey that followed him everywhere? Like Balaam's donkey, perhaps it could warn him when he was about to encounter an angel. The thought lightened his mood. Suddenly it didn't seem to be such a huge deal that he'd agreed to take ownership of one yellow Labrador.

He spent the next six hours attending to minor emergencies, directing projects by the maintenance crew, and preparing the bakery to reopen the next day. The police had called Amber and okayed removing the crime scene tape, though they warned her that the forensic results were still not back. That was the only detail she shared, but Preston knew she was relieved to be able to reopen. She was preparing an announcement to put in the local paper, post on the door of the bakery, and put in customer bags.

Preston was so focused on moving quickly from one task to another that he barely noticed the lunch hour, pausing long enough to grab a vitamin drink from the lunchroom vending machine. Then the alarm on his phone was ringing, reminding him that it was nearly two. It was time to go home and accept delivery of his dog.

Though he'd met Mocha the day before, this felt different. This was at his home, on his turf, and it was permanent. Preston and Zoey sat on the front porch and watched the small SUV make its way down the lane. "ICAN" was painted on the side with large blue letters.

Zoey reached over and squeezed his hand.

"Nervous?"

"Maybe a little."

"This is a wonderful day, Preston. I'm proud of you."

He started to ask her why, what had he possibly done to merit her praise, but then Tomas was pulling in front of the house. He opened the car door, walked around to the back, and opened the hatchback. Now that the car was closer, Preston could see there was a wire mesh separating the two front seats from the back. He supposed when you regularly transported animals, you made adjustments to your vehicle.

Tomas called to Mocha. She jumped out, shook herself thoroughly, and followed him to the porch.

Preston made the introductions.

Zoey shook hands with Tomas and then knelt in front of Mocha. "You're a beautiful girl." She reached out and ran her hand from the top of Mocha's blonde head down her back. The dog panted appreciatively, but for the most part she kept her warm brown eyes on Preston.

And he could feel it.

As crazy as it sounded, he could feel the connection between them, like a rope that tethered them together. Was that possible after only one afternoon together? A part of his heart that he'd kept guarded for a very long time opened up when he looked into Mocha's patient gaze.

His life was filled with complicated things. His past in Afghanistan. His time living on the streets. Even his feelings for Zoey. When he looked at Mocha, when he reached down and settled his hand on the dog's head, he was reminded of the simplest things in life—a parent's love, God's goodness, and the trust and loyalty of a dog.

"Let's take a look around," Tomas suggested. "I'll walk you through some of the procedures we use to help a dog adjust to her new home."

Preston had carefully set out the supplies he and Zoey had purchased the night before. Using the list Tomas provided, they had purchased dog food (the healthy, expensive kind), one bowl for food and another for water, and, of course, the large, circular pet bed Zoey had chosen. Preston had argued that they should wait, that Tomas or even Mocha might change their mind. Zoey had smiled, pushed those lovely blonde curls back away from her face, and said that she liked the bed in the red plaid best.

It was that easy for her—not *when* or *if* he would take the dog, but whether the bed should be plain, puppy print, or red plaid. Preston realized in that moment that life was easier for Zoey, probably because she met it head-on with an undying optimism. And he couldn't blame it on the fact that she hadn't seen battle. She fought terminal diseases, dealt with difficult families, and endured a heavy workload every day. He thought about their discussion the night before— even faced with his disabilities she was opti- mistic. Was it because she had an easier life? No, the difference was that Zoey had been blessed with a positive view of life, and he had been blessed with Zoey.

They spent half an hour going over the commands Preston had learned the day before. Each time Mocha responded as she'd been taught. Each time she leveled that thoughtful gaze at him and waited expectantly. He could feel her creeping into the protected places of his heart. He could feel her becoming a part of his life.

After they'd given Mocha time to check out the backyard and sniff around the perimeter of the house, they went inside. Mocha gobbled the food he set out and lapped appreciatively at the water. Then she glanced up at Preston, as if to say, "What's next?"

So they all traipsed down the hall where the red plaid bed now sat in the corner of his bedroom, the same corner he'd crouched in a few days before. The irony of that wasn't lost on him.

"It looks to me like you've done everything I asked." They returned to the small dining room table, and Tomas walked Preston through the paperwork.

"You're sure I don't owe you anything?"

"All remaining costs were covered through the VA grant. We're good." Tomas slapped him on the back and they walked out to the front porch. Tomas stood looking out over Preston's front yard and beyond that to the Village property. "I couldn't have envisioned a better place for Mocha."

"Thank you, Tomas." Zoey stepped closer to Preston and tucked her hand inside his arm. "We know you did a lot to make this possible."

"I only did my job, and I'm glad to be of help. We appreciate your service to our country, Preston. If Mocha can repay even a small portion of the debt this country owes you, then I will feel like we all have a reason to celebrate."

He thrust his hand toward Preston, who hesitated only a moment before shaking it.

"That's it?" he asked. "We're done?"

"We are. You have my number if you have any questions. I'll stop by once a week to see how you two are doing. Of course, I'll text you first to make sure I'm coming at a good time."

"What if I . . ." Preston swallowed and started again. "What if I mess it up? What if I mess her up?"

"That's not going to happen, Preston. I wouldn't leave Mocha unless I was sure you were a good match."

Mocha pressed against his leg, and Preston couldn't help but lower his hand to touch the top of her head. Was she worried about him? Could she tell that his heart was beating in a triple rhythm?

"As far as training, we went over the basic commands yesterday and again today. If you come across something you don't know how to handle, give me a call."

Preston nodded. He wanted to thank him again. A part of him wanted to tell Tomas that he was overwhelmed by his trust. That he appreciated this new beginning. But Tomas was already moving toward his car, then smiling and waving as he backed up before driving away.

If Preston expected Mocha to be distressed or look longingly after Tomas, he was mistaken. The dog turned around three times, then curled into a circle, her head on her paws, her eyes glancing occasionally at Preston.

"It looks like you're the proud parent of a yellow Lab." Zoey stood on her tiptoes and planted a kiss on his lips. "This is good, Preston. Don't look so scared."

"Easy for you to say." He tried to growl, but there was a grin spreading across his face that he couldn't stop.

"Uh-huh. How about you feed me some lunch?"

"Lunch?"

"I bet you didn't eat."

"I didn't."

"Then let's eat."

Preston pulled her into a hug, resting his chin on top of her head. "You want to eat?"

"I do."

"And then what?"

"Then I say we take Mocha for a walk."

"A walk, huh?"

"Yeah, there's someone else who is dying to meet her."

Mocha looked up expectantly, as if she understood every word of what they were saying.

"Pop's going to love her," Preston agreed.

Mocha's tail slapped a beat against the porch floor, but her eyes—they were as patient and calm as the clouds drifting lazily across the sky.

Twenty

Amber did not feel up to continuing her normal routine, but she was afraid any change in what she did each day might set off the person sending her the threatening notes. Yesterday had been a nightmare. Two potentially poisoned pies in the same day. Two notes declaring the poison poet's nefarious intentions. And then the personal e-mail to her.

The stress was beginning to take its toll, and she was having trouble hiding it from those who cared about her. Tate had quizzed her twice the evening before, finally suggesting she try a hot bath and go to bed early. Pam had left a message, telling her to call if she wanted to talk.

She might have to avoid those she loved most until she figured this thing out. She couldn't afford to arouse their suspicions.

That was one of the reasons she decided to go ahead with her weekly luncheon with one of her managers. The lunches were never with a group of them. That would have ruined what she was hoping to achieve. No, the purpose of the luncheons was to spend some one-on-one time with each of the managers, to get to know them a little better, to become more of a family.

Today's luncheon was with Letha Keim, the manager of Village Fashions. If anyone thought it odd to have an Amish woman in charge of a clothing boutique, their doubts fled when they walked into the little store. The clothes displayed were simple, but they were not Amish. Instead Letha had an eye for dresses that were cut well, blouses that weren't too busy but had a special accent, and pants that complimented many different shapes and sizes of women. Of late, she'd begun to add a variety of accessories— everything from jewelry to scarves to socks and shoes. Again, they weren't *plain,* but they bore a marvelous simplicity and charm.

Village Fashions and Letha Keim were a bright spot in the Village shops—but then all of the shops had been quite successful. Amber daily thanked the Lord for her group of managers and their workers. Together they made a prosperous and productive team.

The Village bakery had reopened late morning, and both the bakery and the restaurant were busier than ever. Amber and Letha stood outside the main building, watching the crowd of folks come and go.

"How about we head to town?" Amber asked. "We could eat at that small coffee shop in the back of the furniture store."

"*Ya, gut* idea. They make delicious sandwiches."

So they climbed into Amber's little red car and motored the few blocks to the downtown area. The sky had turned cloudy and rain was predicted, but at the moment it was merely a cool spring day. Coffee and a hot sandwich sounded perfect to Amber.

Letha wasn't as shy as most Amish women. She wasn't small, but neither was she particularly large—she was what Amber's mom would have called sturdy. Little about Letha was what a stranger would expect to see in the Amish. She was outspoken and had a quick sense of humor. Though in her early forties, she had never married. And her dress—well, it surprised even Amber. Though she stayed within the conventions set by the local *Ordnung*, she always managed to wear something slightly unconventional.

"Cute socks." Amber stirred creamer into her coffee and smiled at Letha.

"These?" Letha stuck her foot out from under the booth where they were sitting. She was wearing tennis shoes, fairly common among

Amish women, but her socks were white athletic anklets embroidered around the top with spring flowers. "I'm carrying these in the shop now. Aren't they fantastic?"

Part of the reason Amber had made Letha manager of Village Fashions over five years ago was that the woman had an excellent eye for what would be popular. Amber had no doubt that she'd soon see guests sporting embroidered athletic socks.

As she sipped her coffee and relaxed in the cozy atmosphere of the coffee shop, Amber felt the weight of stress she'd been carrying slip away. "You enjoy your job, don't you, Letha?"

"What's not to enjoy? I get to order things with the Village money, and we all know women love to shop. My job—it's like shopping all day long." She reached into her purse, a Vera Bradley bag covered with bright spring flowers. "Have I shown you the new lipsticks?"

She pulled out a small tube imprinted with a designer logo. Amber took the lipstick and studied it. The label claimed the lipstick contained aloe and sunscreen and was lemon flavored.

"It's available in a variety of light tints."

"It was a smart move to begin carrying a few cosmetics."

"*Ya*, and Amish women can wear this as well as *Englisch*."

"Lipstick?" Amber peered over her steaming coffee. "I'm skeptical."

"Because you don't understand our ways—not completely. Makeup is forbidden, but this is a lightly colored cream good for the protection of lips from exposure to the sun. I researched it before purchasing. Our bishop can't possibly have a problem with it, especially since we've had two instances of skin cancer in the last year —one that was on the lips."

The girl at the counter, a friend of Hannah's if Amber wasn't mistaken, called out their names. They suspended their conversation while Amber picked up their grilled sandwiches and Letha collected napkins and refilled their coffee mugs. After pausing for a moment of silent prayer, Amber bit into her ham and cheese on rye and nearly groaned.

"*Gut, ya?*" Letha smiled over her BLT.

"It is. Nearly as good as what we make at the Village."

"We have a *gut* restaurant."

"And bakery," Amber reminded her. "Georgia and Stanley see to that."

"Those two make a pair. Georgia's domain is the bakery and Stanley's is the restaurant—and never the two shall meet!"

"Two strong personalities, that is for certain."

"Don't admit to Stanley you like the sandwiches here. He's convinced he operates the best restaurant in a hundred miles—says we'll be having bigger crowds than the Blue Gate soon."

"He's enthusiastic about his job, but I believe there are enough tourists for our Village here in Middlebury and the Blue Gate in Shipshe."

"*Ya*, many eat lunch at one and dinner at the other." Letha wagged a finger at her. "A highlight of coming to Amish country is enjoying the food."

They both savored their meal for a few moments before resuming their conversation.

Pushing away her plate, Letha stood and refilled their coffee mugs once more from the containers by the sandwich bar.

"Decaf for me this time," Amber called out. The last thing she needed was caffeine-induced jitters all afternoon.

When Letha returned to the table, she slipped the tube of lipstick back into her purse.

"So you seem to like walking on the line of what is allowed. Am I right, or am I imagining that?"

"*Nein*, you're not imagining it, though I don't walk on the line so much as I was born with an inquisitive nature. If a rule has an obvious reason —for instance, the fact that we don't own automobiles—then I have no problem with it."

"Because you want to keep your families close to home—no speeding back and forth to South Bend for a dinner or to Indianapolis for a day of shopping."

"Exactly. Those rules are for the best to uphold

our community and beneficial for the members in their desire to be plain and close to *Gotte*. But embroidered socks or lip balm? Both are harmless."

"Some would say that those things encourage vanity."

"I'm not vain because my socks make me smile or my lips aren't dry and cracked. Those folks—the ones who say no to anything new—they are stubborn, and their opinions are detrimental to our community."

"What about the Vera Bradley bag?" Amber was teasing Letha now, but it was hard to resist.

Letha smiled as she popped a piece of her snickerdoodle cookie into her mouth. "Our *Ordnung* does not address handbags . . . yet."

Amber had bypassed the cookies and settled for a small cup of fruit for dessert. The cookie looked tastier.

"I don't mean to pry, and you can certainly tell me this is none of my business—"

"But you're my boss. I would never be so rude."

Both women grinned at that. Letha indeed had never been rude, but she was known to completely change the subject when the conversation entered an area that she didn't want to discuss.

"It really is none of my business. I'm speaking as your friend now, not as your boss."

"And we are *freinden*, Amber. That once came as a surprise to me."

"Why? We're both good businesswomen, and we both care about the people of Middlebury."

Letha nodded, then moved her hand in a *go on* gesture.

"I've heard a man named Ryan Duvall has been visiting the Village a lot of late."

When Letha didn't respond to that, Amber pushed forward.

"Someone said they noticed you getting a ride from him."

"Now you're telling me there are rules about who I can ride with?"

"No, I'm not. We both know there are no rules about that. But Ryan Duvall? He's *Englisch*, right? What gives?"

Letha didn't answer immediately. Just when Amber thought there was going to be an abrupt conversation change, Letha leaned forward and tapped the table. "A solid man is sometimes hard to find. *Ya*? Even in the Amish community—most of the men my age are already married or else they prefer to remain single."

"Single Amish men?" Amber asked in a tone of pretend shock.

"It's rare, *ya*, but we have a few here in Middlebury. For whatever reason, they've decided the single life is preferable. Maybe they're shy. Or maybe they've watched their *bruders* and *schweschders* marry and have a dozen children and decided that's not the life for them. Who knows why—" She waved her hand as if the rationality for such behavior was inconsequential. "For whatever reason, my time for courting has certainly come and gone."

"And then Ryan came along."

"He's been a customer for years, stopping in to purchase an item for his *mamm* on her birthday or Christmas."

Amber thought it was more likely that he was purchasing gifts for one of his many girlfriends, but she didn't suggest as much to Letha.

"Yet there are rules in your *Ordnung* about remaining separate. In all the years I've been here, there hasn't been a single conversion from *Englisch* to Amish—not for marriage, not for any reason."

"Such conversions are rare. I read in the *Budget* about a couple in Maine—the girl was *Englisch* and converted. Perhaps it's easier for women than men to give up the conveniences of modern life."

"So—"

"So why am I seeing Ryan? Is that what you want to know?"

Amber felt suddenly foolish. It wasn't her business what Letha did in her private life. She was out of line asking such questions. And she would have let it drop, but that mothering tendency was difficult to deny. The Amish in her employ . . . it felt like her place to look after them. That was also an illusion, though. She knew better than anyone that the Amish were perfectly capable of looking after themselves.

Letha finished her cookie and neatly folded the napkin into quarters. "You and I—we're nearly the same age."

"I'm forty-five."

"And I'm forty-two. So you know what it's like—to be our age and unmarried."

"I liked my life before I met Tate. In fact, I was rather content." She suddenly remembered dating Gordon Avery and being dissatisfied with that relationship. She remembered putting "date" on her to-do list. "Maybe not content, but you know—"

"I do." Letha sat back, a mischievous smile playing on her lips. "Do I expect Ryan to become Amish? *Nein*. Do I expect him to offer me a proposal of marriage? *Nein*! I don't have those kinds of pie-in-the-sky expectations. He gives me rides. We share an ice cream cone occasionally. He brings me flowers."

"Flowers?"

"Only once or twice."

"Oh my—"

"It's a chance for me to experience something I haven't. If I decide I like it? Perhaps I'll turn a more favorable eye on those old grumpy Amish bachelors."

"Grumpy, huh?"

"You can't imagine." Letha stood and nodded

toward the restrooms sign. "I need to make a stop."

"No worries. I'll check my e-mail while I wait." Amber scanned the dozen e-mails that had come in since she'd left for lunch. At first she didn't notice the anonymous note, maybe because this time the subject line was "Good Job."

Glancing around to make sure no one was paying her any mind, Amber clicked on the icon to open the e-mail.

Good job last night.

It would have been a mistake to show sassy Cherry Brookstone our private correspon-dence. Too bad the police already knew about my first e-mail, but you won't make that mistake again.

Will you, Amber?

Because you have so many friends and loved ones, and you want to protect them. Always the mother hen, always wanting to have your cake and eat it too.

Which is why you'll do whatever I demand.

I'll send you instructions soon.

Amber started to read the e-mail again, but then Letha was at her side and she quickly stuck her phone into her purse.

"Bad news?"

"What? No. Why do you say that?"

"I suppose it was your expression. You looked as if someone had died."

"Oh. No." Amber gathered her things together. "Just work stuff."

She darted out of the coffee shop before Letha could ask any other questions.

A few folks said hello as they made their way through the furniture store, but Amber barely heard them. She needed to hurry back to her office. She needed to figure out what she was going to do. This person was sending her instructions? About what?

Amber and Letha had stopped outside the store entrance, staring at the rain that had begun to fall. Standing under the awning, they waited for a letup and watched an elderly couple. The man had parked as close as possible to the front steps. He walked slowly to his wife's side of the car— and yes, it was obvious that the white-haired woman was his wife. Anyone could tell in one glance. From the way their eyes met and how words were unnecessary, from the small smile on her face and the softness in his eyes. Theirs was a marriage forged through time and strong as the tallest of trees that lined Main Street. Amber couldn't have said how she knew that, but she did.

He popped open an umbrella, and then helped her out of the car. She tucked her hand in the bend of his arm. Slowly they made their way into the store, pausing to nod a greeting and collapse the umbrella.

Letha turned toward her, the smile now gone, her voice suddenly serious. "Who doesn't want that, Amber? Devotion is a beautiful thing."

Amber didn't answer, because she was thinking of Tate and the many ways he had changed her life. She was thanking God that he had offered her a second chance the year before, a different chance, even at the age of forty-four.

"The bigger question, the one I think you wanted to ask me, was whether I know that Ryan is also seeing Martha and Georgia."

Amber tried not to react to that, but apparently her expression gave away her shock. Letha knew? But then why . . .

"Martha is a child. Ryan will tire of her quickly enough. And Georgia? Well, she's an efficient baker, but she's not a barrel of laughs to be with. A new hairstyle and trimmer waistline doesn't change a person's personality. And no, I'm not saying that I am the perfect date." Letha leaned forward and reached out a hand, allowing the rain to splash through her fingers. "I believe I've learned to appreciate life, though."

She tossed a smile over her shoulder, then dashed for the car. Amber blipped the "Unlock" button and darted after her.

They drove back to the Village in silence. When

they'd entered the parking lot, Amber reached out a hand to stop Letha from leaving the car. "If there's anything you need from me—"

"I'm *gut*. Besides, you are too busy to bother with my personal life. You have your hands full with running this place and catching the poison poet."

"Oh, I don't plan to—"

"People are actually betting on who will catch the perpetrator this time—you or Hannah."

"They're betting?"

"I'm not. That would be wrong." Letha clasped Amber's hand and squeezed it. "*Danki* for lunch, and for caring about me enough to ask the hard questions."

Then before Amber could grab her umbrella— the one she'd left in the car before—and follow her, Letha was gone, hurrying toward her shop in the rain, which had at least lightened.

So she sat in her car and thought about the most recent e-mail. The sender said Amber would do whatever was demanded because she "had so many friends and loved ones." Was she reading too much between the lines, or did that ring of jealousy? Was this person a loner? Did they envy Amber for her friends or for her recent marriage?

As she stared out at the rain, her thoughts turned to love and marriage and dating and aging. She could see the corner of her and Tate's property from where she sat, and she could see the back side of the Village. Her life was so full, so satisfying, and she wanted others to experience the same—even her employees like Letha. But she had to admit that people were often at a different place in their lives. God was still in control, and he would certainly look out for Letha and Martha and Georgia.

She'd probably be better off turning her attention and efforts to the person who was fascinated with poison pies and bad poetry, to the person sending her the anonymous e-mails. Surely they were all from the same person. She had absolutely no intention of attempting to "catch the perpetrator." She'd be happy to leave this one in Gordon's capable hands. She had sworn that her days as an amateur sleuth were done.

Now it seemed as if she was being pushed back into that role again, and this time she was going to have to solve the mystery on her own.

And she was not going to let this person dictate every aspect of what she would and wouldn't do. She'd follow their instructions to a point. She'd keep the e-mails to herself. What good would it do to share them? Gordon already had the one. Perhaps he would find out who was sending them before anything terrible happened. Until then, it never hurt to ask a few questions, and that was exactly what she planned to do.

Twenty-One

Disaster struck on Friday. Hannah was cleaning up A Simple Blend. Seth had the day off, so she had stayed through the lunch rush and was now preparing to close the coffee shop.

She'd swept the floor and returned the broom to the utility closet. Then she'd remembered that it was her day to put out food for the lanky cat haunting their shrubs. Hannah would have been happy to catch the pitiful thing and carry it home. They could always use another barn cat. But the stray was not interested in being caught.

Seth had named him Buttons because his black nose looked like a button set in the middle of his white face. His tail and paws were a dark gray, and though he was on the small side, he was mighty in his own eyes. Hannah had watched him stalk birds, hiss at dogs, and sidle up to folks and purr as if he were the sweetest thing this side of a whoopie pie.

At first she'd been worried the feline might have rabies, but Jesse caught Buttons the previous week and studied his collar. Attached to it was a tag. He confirmed that Buttons had his current vaccinations before dropping him with a shout when the cat swiped and drew blood.

"Guess he doesn't like to be studied." Hannah

had laughed in spite of the look on Jesse's face.

"You can never know the mind of a cat—sort of like a woman."

"Let me disinfect that." She'd insisted he come inside and wash the scratch. Then she had found the antibiotic ointment in their new first aid kit, applied it, and covered the entire thing with a bandage.

"It's a cat scratch, Hannah Bell. Are you going to worry over every little injury when we marry?"

"Of course I will. It's part of a woman's job." She'd dodged out of his way when he'd tried to kiss her, but her heart had skipped a beat and she'd once again counted the days until their wedding.

The cat was apparently from over in Goshen. When they called the number on the collar, it was a veterinary clinic. The receptionist looked up the tag number and told them the family had moved out of town and left no forwarding address. Buttons officially became the Village cat that afternoon, and each shop manager took turns feeding him.

After setting out food and clean water for Buttons, Hannah stepped inside the shop and locked the back door. She fetched her purse from the storage room and returned to the front of the shop to check things one last time. Seth would be working Saturday morning on his own, and she wanted to make sure everything was perfect for him. Yes, Seth's infamous accidents were becoming fewer and farther between; however, an ounce of prevention went a long way toward ensuring another wouldn't pop up the next morning.

She made certain his checklist was on the back counter where they mixed drinks, made sure it was in plain sight, and then turned back toward the front of the store.

The thumping of her heart skidded to a stop.

She was staring at the pie, sitting in the middle of the fresh baked goods case. The pie that had not been there ten minutes ago. It had not been there when she'd walked out back to feed Buttons. She would have noticed it.

The note was typed on a sheet of paper that had been folded in half, then tented beside the pastry, as if it were announcing a special.

Arsenic and lace
May sound very quaint
But it will leave you thirsty, damp, and cold
This poison pie is deadly to behold

How did the pie and note end up in her pastry case?

Who had put them there?

And why?

Her hand shook slightly as she picked up the phone on the counter. Should she call Amber? Or the police?

She opted for her boss, since this wasn't technically an emergency. No one had been hurt —yet.

Ten minutes later Amber was standing in her shop.

"Why are you acting so *naerfich*?"

"Huh?"

"Nervous."

"I'm not nervous. Well, I am. This whole"— Amber waved her hand to encompass the baked goods case, the coffee machines, and the entire shop—"thing makes me angry and nervous. It's crazy that we're going through a criminal investigation again."

"*Ya*, but you keep looking out the window as if you expect someone to jump inside and force pie down our throats. You're making me *naerfich*."

"Sorry." Amber continued to pace back and forth.

Fortunately they didn't have to wait long for Sergeant Avery.

"Arsenic, huh? Seems our poet has a wide range of taste in poisons."

"Is there poison in it?" Hannah asked.

"We can't know until we have it tested, but arsenic is fairly simple to test for. Unless the perp is messing with us and actually has a different poison hidden inside this apple pie."

Amber hugged her arms around herself. She'd

206

forgotten her tablet, which she always carried with her, and she was still splitting her attention between the shop and the windows. "What about the other pies? Was there anything in them? I left you a message earlier, but—"

"I know, Amber. I was planning on returning your call."

Hannah was aware of the fact that Gordon and Amber once dated, but since Amber's marriage to Tate it seemed the two had become good friends. It was almost like watching a brother and sister toss around a subject, only this subject was a deadly one.

"Why was this in my shop?" Hannah asked. "I don't know if I'm more frightened than angry or more angry than frightened."

Amber reached out and rubbed her back. "I know the feeling. This is getting old very fast."

Gordon walked to the window, pulled out his cell phone, and had a private conversation. He paced back and forth a few moments, saying inane things like, "Uh-huh. You're sure? Got it."

Nothing he said helped Hannah at all, though she and Amber were listening with all their might.

Then he turned back to them. "I've called this in to the crime scene tech. They'll be here in an hour or so."

"An hour?" Amber's voice rose in disbelief.

"They've been a little busy. I'll get to that in a

minute. Now back to your phone call. The reason I didn't return it was that I was waiting to hear from the lab." Gordon walked back across the little shop, and he didn't stop until he was standing directly in front of them. "The lab sent me an e-mail on my way over, which I checked in the parking lot. I called them just now to confirm their results."

"And?" Amber was standing behind the counter with Hannah. Now she leaned across, as if she could shake the answer from the sergeant.

"And there was nothing in the first two pies—nothing harmful that we could detect."

Hannah flopped down on the stool next to the register, instantly relieved. Strangely, Amber only seemed more agitated. She tapped her fingernails against her front teeth, and continued to dart glances out the window. Something else was going on here, but Hannah had no idea what.

Pulling the strings of her prayer *kapp* to the front, she ran the fingers of her right hand from the top to the bottom—once, twice, three times. It was a childish gesture, one she'd indulged in since she was a six-year-old trotting off to school for the first time. Childish or not, the motion soothed her, and it helped her to think more clearly.

"This is *narrisch*. Why would someone claim to put poison in a pie, write notes to warn us, but then not actually do it?"

"Because they are *narrisch*—crazy people tend to abound in my life!" Amber again crossed her arms and let out a sigh of exasperation.

"I wish I had a video of you two," Gordon said.

"Why?" Hannah asked.

"Yeah, why?"

"Because you look like Holmes and Watson—only you're stumped!"

"Who are—"

"I'll explain later." Amber pointed to the note, to the words *arsenic and lace*. "This is plainly a case of someone more into Agatha Christie than Sir Arthur Conan Doyle."

"I've heard of Agatha Christie. You even lent me a few of her books. But who is Conan Doyle?" Hannah felt as if the conversation was spiraling away from the important fact that someone had snuck into her shop and left a threatening note.

"The good sergeant is suggesting that I'm a sleuth and you're my sidekick."

"Oh." Hannah pushed her *kapp* strings to the back. "Maybe you're *my* sidekick."

Gordon nodded at them both. "It's good to see you both still have your sense of humor."

"Sure we do. But Gordon, this could be serious." Amber licked her lips, hesitated, and then plunged onward. "What if whoever this person is has a courage problem? What if they want to do something terrible but haven't been able to yet? What if this is building up to an actual murder?"

"It's possible, but not likely." Gordon pulled a stool over to his side of the counter. "I understand that you two are very concerned, and I'm not discounting the seriousness of this. There's a chance—as you suggest—that they could be building courage for the real thing. I don't think so, though. Statistically, a perp who leaves warnings with no real threat behind them is someone craving attention."

When they continued to stare at him, he added, "We will catch whoever is doing these things. However, I wouldn't be too worried about another murder on your doorstep."

"They weren't exactly on my doorstep," Amber muttered.

"This seems to me to be similar to a teen who repeatedly calls in a bomb threat."

"Doesn't that sort of person finally snap and plant a bomb?"

"Hardly. They don't have the means or knowledge. The threats are usually a way of venting their frustration about a certain situation."

"So you think it's someone here at the Village? Someone who's frustrated with their situation?" Hannah started mentally checking off each employee at the Village. It didn't seem any of them could be capable of such a thing.

"Not necessarily." Gordon cleared his throat.

"The Village isn't the only place these pies have shown up."

"What?" Amber and Hannah responded in harmony.

"What do you mean this isn't the only place?" Amber asked.

"There've been more? More pies?"

"And more bad poetry?"

Gordon held up a hand to stop them. "Still under investigation, which means I can't discuss it. However, you'll probably read the basic facts in tomorrow's paper, so I can share those."

Hannah felt as if she were in a dream. This was all so bizarre. In one sense she felt like she was reliving the nightmare of Ethan Gray's murder as well as that of Owen Esch. But in another sense, it felt surreal, like a bad joke—something that couldn't really be happening.

"Yesterday, a pie similar to the ones you found showed up at two other establishments."

"Where—" Amber stopped herself and impatiently waited for Gordon to tell what meager details he could share.

"The grocery store as well as the other bakery here in town. The notes with them were similar to the ones you've received."

"And now another one here." Hannah stared around the small, closed coffee shop. Someone had been here, maybe even when she was in the back room. What if she'd walked in and surprised the guilty party? What would have happened?

"Yes, now here. So we have a pie first found in the Village kitchen, then one was found displayed on a shelf at your bakery."

"The next two were off property." Amber looked around, spinning in a circle, no doubt looking for her forgotten tablet. Not seeing it, she ticked the pies off on her fingers.

"Those two happened while your bakery was closed," Gordon pointed out.

"So this person must have a connection to the bakery here." Hannah pushed up on her glasses. She suddenly felt like they could figure this out, if they just kept the fear at bay and thought about it logically.

"Possibly," Gordon said. "Or maybe it's simply the closest target."

"They moved to a place in town when our bakery was closed." Amber stared out the window. "But they could have come here yesterday. The coffee shop was still open."

"That's true. We can't always understand the behavior of a perpetrator, but if you look close enough you'll usually see a pattern and possibly a motivation—though sometimes even that eludes us."

"Knowing a motive would be good," Hannah said. "But what we need is a name. It's wrong to scare people, and it's disruptive for Village personnel and guests. Even if the threats aren't harmful in and of themselves, they create an atmosphere of fear."

Amber jumped at the word *fear*. Clearing her throat, she said, "Like the woman in the bakery Tuesday evening. Some of her response was drama, but I think she might have really been frightened when she read the note from the poison poet."

"We'll dust again for prints here in the shop and especially on the tray holding the pie. Whoever is doing this will slip up, and when they do we'll catch them."

But suddenly Hannah had new things to worry about. Sergeant Avery would catch this person— she had no doubt about that. But what was wrong with Amber?

And what was she going to do about it?

Twenty-Two

Hannah's day had been a disaster, but it took a turn for the better on the way home. She didn't end up leaving the shop until nearly four. Since she'd arrived in time to open early that morning, she felt as if she'd worked two days in one— which probably explained why she nearly walked into Preston as she made her way toward the Pumpkinvine Trail. The rain had pushed through and the afternoon was cool but clear.

"Hi there. Where are you going with such a dour look?"

Hannah started to explain, but then she noticed the yellow dog waiting patiently at Preston's side.

"Oh my. Preston, you didn't tell me you got your dog. You didn't come to see me!"

"Yes, well, we've spent the last couple of days adjusting."

"He's beautiful."

"She."

Hannah covered her mouth with her hand, stifling the giggles that threatened to escape. "She. I'm so sorry."

"No worries. Hannah, meet Mocha. Mocha, this is my friend, Hannah. You can pet her if you want."

"But her jacket says 'Service dog, do not pet.' "

"Yes, well, that's for the general public. You're like family."

Hannah knelt on the ground so that she was eye-to-eye with the dog. Mocha was large, nearly two feet tall if Hannah were to guess. She had a long, dense coat that apparently was brushed often—it fairly sparkled in the sun. It was her color that captivated Hannah—a lovely blend of gold and cream.

Mocha.

Perfect.

"I take it you approve."

"I do!" Hannah scratched the spot between

Mocha's ears and gazed once more into the dog's warm brown eyes, then sighed and stood. "She's lovely, and so well trained!"

"Mostly well trained, though she does like to chase Leo."

"Amber's cat?"

"Yes. He insists on coming back to the *Dawdy Haus* each day. I never minded the company, and we've sort of fallen into a habit of me feeding the guy each morning."

"What does Mocha think of that?"

"The two haven't exactly made friends yet."

They had stepped onto the Pumpkinvine Trail. "You don't have to walk me home. I'm sure you're exhausted."

"Actually, I spent most of the day in safety training."

"Safety?"

"OSHA stuff." When Hannah only stared at him, he added, "Occupational Safety and Health Administration. Half the managers went today. The other half will have the pleasure next week, including you."

"Oh, yes. I did receive that notice. Sounds boring."

"It is, though I suppose we should all learn to deal with blood-borne pathogens."

"Yuck."

"Exactly."

"I'm more worried about poisons than

pathogens." She proceeded to tell Preston about the day's events.

"Sounds irritating, but not exactly dangerous. Not yet, anyway. Are you sure you read Amber's response correctly?"

"I'm telling you, she was more nervous than I've ever seen her."

"And she wouldn't talk to you about it?"

"We had no chance. As soon as Sergeant Avery left, she took off. It was almost as if . . ." Hannah stopped, feeling strange even uttering the words, feeling as if she was betraying her friend.

"Spit it out, kid."

"It was almost as if she was afraid to be alone with me. I know how bizarre that sounds."

"Maybe she had something else on her mind, or somewhere else she needed to be."

"*Ya*, that explains her being in a hurry, but it doesn't explain her strange reaction. I'm telling you, she was about to jump out of her skin." Hannah paused and glanced around, surprised to see they'd reached the lane that led to her house. She'd been so caught up in recounting the day's events that she hadn't noticed they'd walked the entire way from the Village to her home.

"Thanks for letting me share my worries with you, Preston. And congratulations on getting Mocha."

Preston reached down and touched the top of Mocha's head.

Hannah had turned away and was starting down the lane when Preston called out to her. He closed the gap between them, maybe so he wouldn't have to shout.

"Would you like me to check on Amber? Do you think it's that serious?"

"I do believe it's serious, and yes—I think it would be *gut* if you stopped in to see her."

"All right. Mocha and I are going to walk a little farther, then turn around. I'll go by her house. I've been meaning to introduce Mocha to Tate."

"*Danki*, Preston. You're a *gut* friend."

Her burden lighter, she turned back toward home. Whatever was wrong, Preston would figure it out. He had a knack for that sort of thing. And Amber wouldn't be able to resist Mocha. She'd see the dog and stop to pet it, and then the barrier that she'd created around herself would fall. She'd share whatever was bothering her. Hannah felt sure of it, sure enough to put her worries away and focus on home and her wedding plans.

Preston was surprised when he reached Amber's house and she wasn't home. He'd purposefully extended Mocha's walk so he would arrive there after five.

But no little red car sat in the driveway.

So he walked up the steps and rapped on the door.

Tate answered, wearing an apron and holding a large spoon in his right hand. "Come on in. I was just stirring the pot."

"What pot?"

"The dinner pot." Tate clapped him on the back, and then said to the dog, "You must be Mocha. It's an honor to meet you."

Preston couldn't help smiling when Mocha lifted a paw to shake.

"Can I get you anything?"

"Perhaps some water for Mocha, if you have an old butter tub or something else to put it in."

"I can do you one better than that."

Leo arched his back and hissed when they walked into the large kitchen/dining room.

"Do these two know each other?"

"Yeah. They met yesterday morning and again today."

"I know Leo is still going to your house every morning. I can sit on my front porch and watch him make his way down to your back porch."

"Probably I shouldn't be feeding him. It just encourages his wanderings."

"Do you remember what happened with Ethan Gray? Given the way that ended, I'd say we should spoil the cat in any way possible."

Leo had resettled in the window seat, which offered a view out over the back of the property, his paws tucked underneath, his eyes still on Mocha.

Tate walked to a far cabinet, opened it, and pulled out a large red water bowl.

"For the granddogs," he explained as he filled it with tap water and set it on the floor.

Mocha looked up at Preston, waiting for permission. Preston nodded, and the dog trotted to the bowl and began to lap up the water.

"I'd heard she was well trained," Tate said, "but that's amazing."

"You haven't seen anything. They actually taught her how to dial nine-one-one, in case . . . you know, in case I have an incident."

"Special phone?" Tate asked.

"Yes. Large numbers. Tomas brought one when he first delivered her to my place. Mocha—she's a special dog."

"And have you, you know, had a need to check out her skills yet?"

Preston smiled as Tate set a glass of water on the counter for him, next to his own glass with iced tea. The man knew him well, knew that water was his drink of preference. "It's hard to be sure about that. I've only had her two days. I might have had the beginnings of a flashback last night. I woke to Mocha standing beside the bed, whining, and pushing her cold nose into my hand."

Tate shook his head. "I'd say this dog is a godsend."

"Indeed."

"Thanks for coming by and bringing her."

As the minutes ticked by and Amber still didn't show, Preston and Tate took their drinks out to the front porch. Sitting in the rockers, watching the sun begin to set, with Mocha lying at his feet, the day seemed almost perfect to Preston.

But it wasn't perfect.

Something was wrong. Preston could sense it like a storm arriving from the west.

He could tell Tate was aware of it too. He drummed the fingers of his left hand against the arm of the chair, and twice he checked the phone in his shirt pocket.

Finally Preston cleared his throat and broached the subject they were both avoiding. "Hannah's pretty worked up about this poison poet."

"Given what she's been through—what we've all been through—the last year, that's not surprising."

"I believe she's more concerned for Amber than she is for herself."

Tate didn't comment on that directly, but he nodded and the lines across his forehead deepened.

When Amber finally drove up, Tate let out an audible sigh. "Don't know why I was worried. She would have called if there had been a problem."

Preston wasn't so sure.

Something was definitely off-kilter, and it didn't take a genius to see the toll it was taking on Amber. Her eyes continually darted left then right. The scarf she'd been wearing had worked its way nearly off her neck, but she didn't seem to notice. And she repeatedly ran her right hand through her hair, as if the gesture comforted her in some way.

"Late day at the office?" Tate aimed for a breezy tone.

"Yeah. I had . . . had some things I needed to take care of."

"Preston stopped by to introduce me to Mocha."

The dog had sat up as soon as Amber pulled into the driveway. Now she cocked her head, keeping her eyes on Amber and waiting. But Amber barely seemed aware that she was petting the dog on top of her head as she walked into the house, murmuring that she needed a minute to clean up before dinner.

"Do you think Hannah was overreacting?"

"No. I don't." Tate leaned forward, elbows braced on his legs. "I knew she hadn't been sleeping well, but I thought it was due to this poison thing going on at the Village."

"Maybe it is."

"Could be, but that answer doesn't feel right. We made it through Ethan Gray's investigation just fine. I don't need to remind you how that ended."

Preston shook his head. That investigation was

the reason he wasn't still living on the streets. No, maybe he wasn't giving credit where credit was due when he looked at it that way. God had used that investigation to bring Tate and Amber into his life, and coming back into the community—back into the fold—had cleared the way for Preston to find his way off the streets.

"Could be the stress is taking its toll," Preston said.

"It's possible, but this doesn't seem nearly as stressful as finding an employee dead in the coffee shop as with Ethan's death, or having someone killed with a bow and arrow."

"Owen's murder was difficult for the entire community."

"And especially Amber. After all, it happened a little over a mile from our home."

They both considered those past two incidents for a few moments.

"Maybe it's more cumulative. We saw that a lot in the military." Mocha moved closer to Preston as he allowed his thoughts to comb back through those memories. Although they weren't as painful as they had once been, he supposed he would always have a physiological reaction to those days. "We had one guy . . . he did great in every encounter. Never cracked under pressure, always performed his duties superbly. Then on the way home, he fell apart—just seemed to emotionally and physically collapse. The medic said it was the cumulative stress that got him. Took three months in a VA hospital to pull him out of it."

"I understand what you're saying." Tate stood and motioned him inside. "But this is my wife we're talking about, and I'm not waiting to let whatever is accumulating cause her to collapse. We're going to deal with whatever is wrong today. It's my job to take care of her, and that's exactly what I plan to do."

Preston thought they were headed inside to dinner—Tate had been stirring a large pot of stew when he arrived. Cornbread was already baked and cooling on the counter. The man was turning into quite the cook, another testament of his love for Amber. He'd told Preston that he actually enjoyed it, that it made him happy to know that Amber was coming home to a warm meal and a snug house.

But the woman standing in the middle of their living room didn't look as if she even realized she was in her house. She'd dropped her tablet and purse on the coffee table and was clutching her phone, pacing back and forth, muttering something under her breath.

"Amber, honey, why don't you sit down and rest?"

Amber looked up in confusion, as if she didn't remember that Preston and Tate were there. As if she was surprised to see her husband in her own living room.

"Sit?"

"Yeah. Let's just sit down together. Dinner probably needs another ten minutes, and Preston and I would like to talk to you."

"Talk to me?"

Instead of answering, Tate led her to the couch, then sat down beside her.

"Preston stopped by to introduce Mocha, but he's also worried about you."

Amber didn't reply to that, opting instead to stare at the dog.

"Hannah told him what happened at the Village today, in her shop. She was worried that you didn't take it so well."

"What does that mean?" Amber asked sharply.

"I don't know." Preston spread his hands out, palms up. "You weren't acting like your normal take-charge self, I suppose. She was concerned and asked if I knew anything, if you were okay."

"Why would you know if I'm okay?"

Tate sighed. "He works closely with you. Probably Hannah thought he might be able to shed some light on why you're so stressed. I'm sure she only wanted to help."

"Maybe I don't need any help." Amber popped up off the couch. "In fact, I'm sure I don't."

"Honey, what's wrong?"

To Preston's dismay he saw tears in Amber's eyes, but she didn't give in to them. Instead she tossed her hair and snatched up her tablet and purse. "The only thing wrong is that I need to clean up before dinner. Now, if you'll excuse me . . ."

She hurried out of the room before either man could respond.

Tate stood and moved toward the kitchen, Preston and Mocha in his wake. "I've seen her this way once before. It was before I asked her to marry me, when I first told her how much I cared about her. I don't know if it was the pressure of a new relationship, or the fact she was frightened about jumping into a new phase of her life." He began to spoon stew from the large pot into bowls, glancing over at Preston as he continued. "It could have even been the last two murder investigations. Amber, she isn't a cop. She's a person with a big heart, and sometimes she cares too much. Anyway, she sort of freaked out then too. I had hoped to settle this tonight, but that doesn't look likely. I think if we give her a few days, she'll share with us what's on her mind."

Preston nodded, though it seemed to him that a few more days might land Amber in a hospital bed. When she returned to the kitchen, she didn't eat—opting instead to stir her stew around in her bowl without ever taking a bite. As far as conversation, she limited herself to mono-syllables and excused herself before they were half done.

They finished their meal in silence, and Tate thanked him for coming over and sharing his concerns. As he walked home, Preston had the distinct feeling Tate was fooling himself. Things were not going to get better in a few days. At the rate things were going, they were destined to get much worse.

Twenty-Three

Amber waited until Tate's breathing evened out, until she was sure he was in a deep slumber. Then she slid out from beneath the blankets, donned her robe and slippers, and quietly made her way to the kitchen.

Flipping on the light over the stove, she placed the teakettle on the burner and set the flame to low. Going through the familiar routine helped to calm her nerves. By the time she had her tea brewed and was sitting at the kitchen table, she knew what needed to be done.

First she needed to pray. She had to stop dodging this way and that. She had to calm down. It wasn't as if someone was standing in her home, threatening her family with a knife. But somehow this seemed worse. It was so insidiously evil. What sort of person claimed to put poison in food and frightened people with personal threats?

But even someone who was that bent on doing

harm wasn't outside of God's reach. So she prayed—for herself, that she would remain calm, calmer than she had been the last twelve hours. For wisdom, that she would know what to do. For her family, that God would keep them safe. And finally for the person who was bent on evil, that God might soften their heart. Maybe they would turn themselves in! Perhaps they would become convicted of their sin and regret the steps they had taken. Regret could be a fabulous motivator.

By the time she'd finished praying, her tea was cold, so she popped it into the microwave. Then she retrieved her tablet and a pad of paper. Surely if she thought of this logically, she could find a solution.

She pulled up the most recent e-mail from her anonymous tormenter.

At this point you're probably wondering why you? There are many reasons, but the best is that your life is too perfect.

That fact, more than any other, irks me.

When you began poking your nose into my business, I knew I had to step forward and do something.

I think it's time for Amber Bowman to eat a little humble pie.

Amber shook her head in disbelief, not needing to read the rest, not needing to read the crucial portion. She had committed the e-mail to memory when she'd first received it. She'd been in her office, preparing to head home, weary and dejected. The e-mail had set her off—simultaneously frightened and angered and frustrated her.

Whose business was she poking into? She cared about a lot of people, but as far as she knew, she wasn't actually interfering with anyone's life. Not even Letha seemed to think so when she'd asked her about Ryan. She'd thanked Amber for caring enough to "ask the hard questions."

And how dare someone call her life perfect?

She'd lived a lonely, hardworking existence the first twenty years she'd been at the Village. Sure, she'd enjoyed her job, but she had worked hard at it, and no one could have called those years perfect.

Then she'd endured two murder investigations, and yes, she had even helped to capture the culprits.

In the midst of those terrible events, God had seen fit to bless her with Tate, to show her real friendship through Hannah and Pam and Preston. She would not apologize for any of those things.

It seemed wrong to do so.

It seemed ungrateful.

And yet she was edgy. This delusional person

was operating on two fronts—the pies left with the threatening notes and the e-mails to her. Why?

She placed the question at the top of the sheet of yellow lined paper. She'd rather have been working on her tablet, but she no longer trusted any of her technology to be secure. This person was adept at crossing normal tech barriers, such as spam filters. Could they also break into the server that automatically backed up both her tablet and her work computer? She couldn't risk it, so she settled for jotting notes on the piece of paper.

And did the degree of computer skills mean the person was *Englisch* rather than Amish? She added that question to her list.

Motive? The person wanted to gain something. What?

Gender? It would be easy to assume a woman, but assuming could land her in deeper trouble.

Background? Whoever was doing this had some experience in baking, obviously. If she listed every person in Middlebury skilled in the kitchen, the names would include at least two-thirds of the area's population.

Sighing, she flipped to a clean page on the tablet.

It was time to face the biggest question. Who was this person? She stared at the blank page for several moments before she slowly began to list names, going with her gut instincts as she considered each person she came into contact with daily. With each name she wrote down, it felt as if her heart were enduring a blunt force. These were people she knew. People she might count as friends, or at least close acquaintances. Who could harbor such resentment toward her and yet keep it hidden all this time?

Finally she turned to a third page and drew a line down the middle. The left column she titled "Steps to Take." Across the right she wrote "Things Not to Do." One thing was for certain—the perpetrator was spying on her at work and possibly at home.

She could not go to her family or friends for help.

She could not continue to arouse their suspicions.

She could not go to the police—not yet.

Last, she could not afford to ignore the e-mailer's demands.

So what could she do? Try to placate the person, keep them calm. She could keep her eyes open, and pay attention to everything going on at the Village—and this did center around the Village, though two pies had shown up elsewhere. Something told her that was a distraction. This was a vendetta against her, and it was something else too. But what?

She could and would keep her family and friends at a distance—she drew a circle around this one. It wasn't in her nature, but she'd do what she must. And sharing these personal threats with them, even sharing them with Tate, could only drag people she loved into the middle of something that might be about to explode. She wouldn't do that again. Tate had been in danger when they caught Owen's killer. Hannah and Jesse had nearly been hurt by Ethan Gray's killer. No, she wouldn't allow that to happen again. She'd do whatever was necessary to keep them out of it.

At the moment, that seemed to include eating a little humble pie. For whatever reason this person wanted to see her publicly humiliated. All right. Amber had never been a prideful person, and she didn't mind being ridiculed if it bought them some time. So she turned to yet one more clean sheet of paper and began to list her five biggest faults.

Preston had gone to sleep worried and distracted. Even brushing Mocha hadn't helped, though that was something he'd learned to enjoy in the last few days. The dog was a good companion. She filled places in his life, in his heart, that he didn't realize were vacant.

She offered unconditional love, even though they'd known each other only a few days. Perhaps that was why folks were crazy about their pets. Preston had never understood it before, but now he did. Looking into Mocha's trusting eyes, he knew she was a blessing straight from God, just as Tate had said.

He'd been thinking of those things as he prepared for bed, and he'd immediately fallen into a restless sleep.

It seemed the dreams began as soon as his head hit the pillow. Twice he startled awake, only to find Mocha sitting patiently by the side of his bed. Each time, she'd licked his hand once, then padded to her bed in the corner of his room and settled down on it.

The second time he gulped down the glass of water he kept beside his bed, and quickly fell into another agitated slumber—straight into his past.

Frank lay against the wall of the cave. He lay so still that Preston worried he might have died.

"Frank. Frank. Talk to me."

The man who had been his friend since he'd arrived in Wanat stirred, glanced left and right, then stared into Preston's eyes. "It's not looking so good."

"No, it's not. But we're going to find a way out of this."

"Bogar?"

Preston shook his head. He'd somehow managed to drag the man's body to the back of the cave and cover him with his own

232

jacket. Though the night had turned cold, it was better than leaving him exposed to the night air. That had seemed disrespectful and the final nail in their respective coffins. He had to cling to the hope that help was coming.

"You're bleeding," Frank said.

"Not a problem. I can still fire my weapon."

"If you'll move me . . ."

"I'm not moving you anywhere."

"Move me to the front." Frank's expression twitched into a smile. "We go down fighting if we're going down."

Preston didn't struggle with the decision for long. If they were attacked while in the cave, they had no chance of surviving. Sure, they could take quite a few of the insurgents out with them, but they wouldn't survive it. The numbers weren't on their side.

Their only hope was to hold their position and wait for reinforcements.

Grudgingly he checked Frank's leg. If anything, it looked worse than before, more swollen, darker, and hot to the touch. The bleeding had slowed, but he had lost too much blood before Preston had managed to put the compress on. How did Frank manage to stay conscious? How did he endure the pain? Perhaps he was in shock; however, Preston knew Frank was a fine soldier. As long as he was breathing, he'd defend his brothers-in-arms.

As gently as possible he moved him to the front of the cave. By positioning him against the wall, Frank was able to rest his rifle on a boulder and scope the right side of the openings. Preston took up position across from him, covering the left side.

They'd been waiting, in the dark, for over an hour when the firing began. The sound of artillery filled the night, and smoke soon made breathing difficult. Once again he found himself crying out to God, praying for mercy and grace.

Preston woke to a blinding light and Mocha's sharp bark.

The dog sat less than two feet in front of him, barking at regular three-second intervals.

Somehow Preston had fallen from the bed and crawled toward the bathroom door, dragging his covers with him.

"It's okay, girl. I'm okay." The words came out in a shaky murmur. Mocha stepped closer, licked his hand, and waited. He reached for her, and she practically climbed into his lap. "I'm okay. Good girl. Good dog."

Sweat slicked his skin, and it took a moment to firmly root himself in reality. The clock on the nightstand proclaimed it to be two a.m. Preston's first reaction to the flashback was "not again," but as he studied his bedroom, he couldn't help

comparing what he saw to the previous ins
—the one where he'd broken the nightstand
woken crouched in the corner.

This time nothing was broken.

In fact, the room looked exactly as it had whe.
he'd turned off the lights—the only difference
being the tangle of covers he'd pulled with him as
he'd crawled across the floor, crawled across the
cave. His dream came back to him in an instant.

They'd needed more ammo, and he'd crawled to
the back of the cave to retrieve what Bogar still
had on his person. The man had been blown back
into the entrance of the cave when he was hit, and
now he lay under Preston's jacket. As Preston had
crawled to the back something had come through
the mouth of the cave. He'd thought it was a
grenade or other type of IED. However, it hadn't
been an improvised explosive device or a grenade.
It had been an IFAK—an individual first aid kit.

He'd understood in that moment that they were
rescued.

He'd understood that it was over.

Mocha whined again, cocking her head and
staring at him with her dark eyes.

"You did good, girl. You did real good."

He hadn't torn up the room. He hadn't
endangered anyone. And Mocha had done what
she had been trained to do.

For the first time in many years, Preston felt
hope surge through his doubts.

Twenty-Four

annah wished just one day would proceed as she had planned. She had not intended to go into the Village on Saturday, but she ran out of the paper they were using for wedding invitations. Usually she would purchase such items at the general store in town, but with her employee discount, the stationery sold in Katie's Mercantile was less expensive.

"Go on. We've finished the cleaning here." Eunice wiped Mattie's mouth. Hannah's little sister had managed to wear more of her banana and peanut butter than she'd swallowed.

"I'll help clean up this little one first." Hannah took the dish towel from her mother and smiled at Mattie. How she would miss her little sister when she moved to Jesse's.

Yes, she'd be only a little way down the road.

Yes, she'd see her several times a week.

And yes, she was being a tad sentimental.

However, the sense that things were changing, quickly and irrevocably, sometimes overwhelmed her.

Mattie lightened the mood by touching her fingers to Hannah's lips and attempting to share what was left of her lunch.

"*Danki*, little girl."

"Danki, wittle girl." Mattie cocked her head and then reminded Hannah, "Mattie's big, not wittle!"

"Of course you are. Big enough to pick up your toys in the sitting room?"

"Ya. Down, Hannah. Let me down."

Hannah managed one last dab with the dish towel at the corner of Mattie's mouth before her sister dashed off to the living room.

"I'll be back in an hour," she called to her mother as she pulled her purse off the peg in the mud room.

"Don't rush. Mattie and I are going to read a story, and then perhaps one of us will take a nap."

"No nap." Mattie had picked her letter blocks up from the floor and dumped them into her toy basket. Now she was plopped down beside them, pulling each one out again.

The last glimpse Hannah had of her family was her mother easing into the rocker, Mattie on the floor, and her brothers and father out in the field. It was a peaceful, comforting image that immediately embedded itself in her memory.

As soon as she arrived at the Village, she saw the large group of people outside Letha's dress shop, but she ignored it, heading to Katie's to purchase her stationery.

Katie pulled her aside as soon as she walked in the door.

"Did you see it? Over by Letha's shop?"

Hannah gently removed Katie's hand from her arm. She was clutching it hard enough to leave a bruise. "See what? I didn't see anything other than a lot of people outside, which is normal for a Saturday."

"The note!" Katie lowered her voice as a customer walked by them. "The note on the bulletin board. Did you see it?"

"*Nein*. I saw folks milling around there, but I didn't notice anything else."

"Go and look. Then come back and tell me what we're to do!"

Hannah forgot about the stationery for the wedding invitations. She ducked back outside and nearly ran into Pam.

"I thought you were off today."

"I am. I'm only here to buy paper."

Pam looked at her right and left hands. "Are you hiding it somewhere? Because I don't see any purchases."

"Katie wouldn't even sell it to me. She insisted I go and look at—"

"The bulletin board."

"*Ya*. How did you know?"

"Because everyone is talking about it. Everyone except Amber, who won't say a word. I'd better go with you."

"I don't understand."

"Honey, I don't either, and I thought I had seen it all." She hesitated and then added, "Grammy

238

once told me, 'If you think you've seen it all, put on your sunglasses, because you're about to be surprised.' "

As they walked back toward Letha's, Pam made no attempt to explain what had happened. But the look on her face told Hannah that whatever had happened was serious. Then they pushed their way to the front of the crowd, and she understood just how grave the situation was.

What would have caused Amber to write such a thing? Hannah's mind swirled with questions as she once again read the note from top to bottom.

Nearly as overwhelming as the paper in the middle were the notes people were pinning to every free space on the board. They were written on the backs of business cards, on sticky notes, on receipts, even on what looked like the margin of a newspaper.

The center note had been penned on a sheet of lined paper from a tablet, and it was in Amber's handwriting, that was for certain. Hannah would recognize the slant and precisely formed letters anywhere. But she stepped closer to better study the sheet, because her eyes, her heart, could not believe what she was seeing.

MY FIVE BIGGEST FAULTS
BY AMBER BOWMAN

1. Vanity. I spend an inordinate amount of time worried about how I look.

2. Worry. Where I should trust my friends and my Lord, I often choose to fret over things instead.

3. Envy. Often when I look at someone else's new outfit, new purse, or even new car, I am filled with envy and desire.

4. Pride. I do take pride in the Village, as if it is my own creation, which of course it isn't.

5. Snooping. I often put my nose where it doesn't belong, perhaps for good reason. Still, I now realize that I should mind my own business and not interfere in others' lives.

There was no explanation to follow the list, no hint to explain her boss's sudden need to bare her soul. No indication as to what had occurred to bring about this strange public disclosure.

"When did she put it up?"

"Before I arrived at work, and she usually doesn't even come in on Saturday."

Hannah glanced left and then right before pulling Pam away from the crowd. "But she's here now?"

"She is. She's been holed up in her office all day. She doesn't want to speak to anyone, and she won't explain to me what's going on."

Hannah stared at the people milling around. Some were still posting notes to the board. They said things like, "We love you, Amber" and "God bless you" and "Thank you for all you do." They were people's reactions to this strange situation.

"Does Tate know?"

"Yes. I called him when she wouldn't talk to me. After he saw the board, he went up to speak with her. Stayed about ten minutes, then left without another word."

"Something's wrong." Hannah once again surveyed the crowd. Now she had the sense of a clock ticking, counting down to a terrible moment. That instinct, more than anything else, convinced her of the need to be very careful. "Let's walk."

"What is it? What are you thinking?" Pam fiddled with the buttons of her denim jacket. It had horses outlined on it, and she wore it over a matching long dress.

The horses gave Hannah an idea. She suspected this recent turn of events had to do with the poison pies—otherwise it was a bizarre coincidence, and she no longer believed in those. To get Amber to spill, she would need to entice her away from the Village, from any possibility of being overheard or seen by the poison poet.

Whoever that was, they apparently loved to bake and so were no doubt comfortable in a kitchen. Most of the people Hannah knew who loved cooking intensely disliked barns. They were smelly and dirty. They were the opposite of a clean, well-organized kitchen.

She was certain Pam could be trusted, so she leaned in and spoke quietly. "It's two now. I'm going to gather the others—"

"Others?"

Hannah wanted to explain, but what if someone was listening. Sweat beaded under the edge of her *kapp*, and she reached up to wipe it away.

"Bring her to—" She stepped even closer to whisper the location, pretending to straighten the collar of Pam's jacket. "In two hours. Do whatever you have to, but bring her."

Then she turned and walked away.

If anyone had been watching, they would have seen nothing out of the ordinary. They wouldn't have heard the meeting place. And they couldn't have guessed that Hannah had decided to take action. After all, everyone knew Amish women kept to themselves and took the least controversial path. There was no chance they could have guessed that Hannah was in full support mode, even if that meant involving herself in the midst of another mystery.

She hurried back to Katie's, purchased her stationery, and promised to speak to her about it all the next day at their church service. As she was leaving the store, she saw a display of birthday cards. The fact that it was almost her birthday had totally escaped her attention. With her marriage, the poison poet, and the incident with Amber, growing older was the last thing on her mind.

A birthday celebration?

She couldn't even think about it.

Instead, she hurried back down the Pumpkin-vine Trail and stopped at the phone shack. Once there, she set her package on the counter and made three phone calls. Each person had questions —questions Hannah couldn't begin to answer. Each person agreed to what she suggested. When she'd finished, she realized she would barely have time to stop by her house, tell her mother she wouldn't be there for dinner, and head to Jesse's barn.

It occurred to her as she hurried down the lane that she hadn't asked Jesse first. She'd been certain he would agree to the meeting on his property. He cared for Amber as she did, and he would want to ensure that nothing terrible happened to her.

Hannah was once again struck by how close she and Jesse had become over the last year, so much so that she could know what was in his heart without asking.

Twenty-Five

Amber had pulled many all-nighters when she was in college, but those days were over twenty years in her past. She'd forgotten how miserable the next day could be. At first she'd been merely groggy, then the headache began to pound at her temples, and soon her body was sore—as if she'd actually run a marathon rather than agonized over her lists.

She'd left the house after telling Tate she needed to attend to some things—even though it was Saturday. He'd kissed her, told her he loved her, and nearly pulled a full confession from her lips. But she held firm, clutched her bag close as if in fear he might spy the incriminating sheets, and hurried off to the Village.

Tacking the note to the board was easy enough.

The problem had been what to do after that, so she'd gone to her office and waited for the fallout. It hadn't taken long. She'd had visits from Pam, then Preston, and finally Tate.

Each had asked her what was going on.

Each had expressed their concern.

But she'd turned them all away. It was what she'd vowed to do as dawn had peered through her kitchen window.

Now Pam was once again standing in the doorway of her office.

"We have a situation."

"Situation?"

"Village business. Better grab your purse."

"No. I can't—"

"This won't wait." Pam actually walked behind Amber's desk and helped her to her feet.

"But—"

"Have you had lunch? I bet you haven't eaten a thing."

"I'm not hungry at all."

"Humph. Seems to me that lunch is the most important meal of the day."

"I didn't have time to go to lunch, Pam."

"Understood, but you can't ignore Village business, especially Village emergencies. Now, let's go."

And so she'd allowed herself to be pulled away from her desk, where she was accomplishing nothing anyway.

Pam didn't attempt to explain any further during the drive, and Amber was too exhausted to question her. Whatever it was, she'd deal with it and then return to her office. She fully expected more "instructions" to arrive from her anonymous pen pal at any moment—not that she had ever replied to any of the e-mails. As they drove, she checked her phone several times.

And while Pam didn't ask questions, she repeatedly sent her a questioning look.

Then they pulled into the lane leading to an

Amish home—one Amber had never been to before. On the west side of the house, an extra room was being constructed. Possibly more than one room. The addition covered the entire length of the house.

"Perhaps you should leave your phone here . . . and your tablet." Pam's expression was inscrutable, but there was a note in her voice that Amber had rarely heard before, though maybe once when they'd been accosted outside the meeting of the Indiana Survivalist Group. It was a soft, firm tone—one that left no room for argument.

Amber did as she suggested, and still she was surprised when they passed the house and walked to the barn. What Village business could be going on here? Was this simply a ploy to get her out of the office? If so, why bring her to an Amish farm? Did she even know these people?

Raising her eyebrows, she stopped and put her hand on Pam's arm. "What's this about?"

But Pam only shook her head and opened the door to the barn.

Stepping out of the bright sunshine and into the barn, Amber at first couldn't see much—only silhouettes.

Slowly her eyes adjusted.

She saw Hannah and Jesse, holding hands and sitting on a large bale of hay near the front of those assembled. Close to them were Mary and

Andrew sitting on a bench, confirming what she had suspected—they were at the Miller home and the construction she had noticed was for the two couples about to be married.

Her fingers went to her lips when she saw Tate and Preston and Gordon, who had all stood when she and Pam walked in.

"Why . . . why are you all here?"

"Because we want to help." Hannah stood as well and stepped forward, clasped her hand, and pulled her toward a crate so she could sit next to Tate.

He reached over, rubbed her back, and whispered, "Hannah called us all together."

"I did, and most of you don't even know exactly why." She brushed her *kapp* strings behind her shoulder. "But you came anyway. You came because you care about Amber and you care about the Village. *Danki.*"

"We're happy to do it, Hannah." Mary glanced at Andrew and then continued. "Why are we here, though? What's this all about?"

"I'm not entirely sure I know. What I do know is that Amber's in trouble and we need to help her."

Amber began to protest, but Pam stopped her. She'd sat down beside Amber, and now she reached over and pulled Amber's hand into her lap. Their fingers interlaced, white and brown, a symbol of their friendship that had strengthened over the past six months. It seemed to Amber that they had been friends all of her life. It seemed as if Pam was more her sister than her employee.

"You don't have to deny it anymore," Pam said. "You can trust every person in this room, and no one outside this room can hear you—which is why I had you leave your phone and tablet in the car. In case you still think somehow someone is able to listen in on your conversations."

Gordon was still standing, his feet slightly apart and his arms crossed. He wasn't in uniform, but that did nothing to mitigate his authority. He was her friend, and he was here because of it, but he still had an official capacity. "You need to tell us what's going on."

She didn't know where to start, and she wasn't entirely convinced she should. She hesitated, and in that moment she thought of Preston and Mocha and their need for one another. That image alone persuaded her to speak. If she thought she could handle this on her own, well then, she was as deluded as Preston had been before accepting his service dog. Everyone needed help. A wise person realized it before disaster struck, and Amber could feel disaster breathing over her shoulder.

And if she couldn't trust these people, whom could she trust?

Mocha whined once and then settled on the

ground next to Preston, but not before looking at Amber as if she understood.

So she told them everything. She described in detail the private e-mails from the anonymous person. She told them all she knew and everything she feared. Then finally she explained why she'd posted her note to the Village bulletin board. She recited the note word for word, ending with what she'd been told to do.

Make a list of your five biggest faults. Tack it to the display board outside the dress shop. Place it high where everyone can see. Be sure to sign your name.

And Amber, convince me that you are doing some soul-searching. Otherwise, I might have to take the next step.

"Someone wants to humiliate you." Pam scowled. "Why, though? What are they getting out of it?"

"Some sort of satisfaction." Tate had scooted closer to Amber as she spoke. Now she turned to him, studying his face closely. "You're not angry with me, for keeping all of this from you?"

"No. I might have done the same thing in your shoes. Our instinct to protect one another is strong and natural."

Relief flooded through Amber at those words and at the show of support around her. Though she was still tired and unsure of what their next step should be, she had a glimmering hope that together they could and would catch whoever was doing all this.

"You all have to be sure no one discovers that you know." Amber tried not to imagine what might happen if word of their meeting reached the crazy person tormenting her. "If this person finds out, they're going to do something desperate."

"The perp will know nothing about this meeting." Gordon fetched a crate and set it front and center before sitting down. The group had formed in a semicircle, and now all eyes were on him. "Four of the people in this room live here. Tate and I came in through the back pasture, which is why you didn't see our cars, and Preston hiked down the trail. For all anyone knows, you're here to help the girls with some aspect of their wedding preparation."

"All right." Amber pulled in a wobbly breath and tried to relax her shoulders. She felt as if the tight knot inside her stomach was finally loosening to a manageable ache.

"Let's start with what we know." Gordon pulled out the small pad he kept notes on, which made Amber smile—she'd done the same thing the night before. In fact, her sheets of paper were still in her purse in Pam's car. She didn't need to fetch them, though. She'd agonized over every line. The names, suspicions, and events were etched in her memory.

"The same person who is threatening Amber is leaving the pies and notes." Jesse removed the piece of hay he'd been chewing on. "It has to be the same person. There can't be two crazy people who are . . . you know, the same kind of crazy."

"Agreed, though there's always the possibility that this person is *not* working alone." It felt good for Amber to confess her deepest fears. "What if it's a team or a couple or two family members?"

"Honey, I don't think there are two crazy people left in Middlebury." Pam traced the outline of a horse on the cuff of her jacket. "I'm pretty sure we've put all but one in jail already."

"Technically prison, but I agree with Pam." Tate reached over and gently rubbed Amber's shoulders.

She wanted to allow herself to completely relax, to melt under his hands. But suddenly she felt as if she'd found her second wind. Energy and thoughts zipped through her body and mind. Amber felt as if she'd just consumed an energy drink. It was amazing what having a support group did for one's morale, and a higher morale always meant more zip as far as she was concerned.

"This person is also probably associated with the Village, at least peripherally," Tate said.

Hannah agreed. "How else could she have known that you spoke with me about the first e-mail? She must have been walking by the coffee shop and seen us huddled over your tablet."

"We don't even know this person is a *she*." Amber stared around the room, wondering if she should share the list of suspects she had compiled the night before. "Men bake too."

"She or he also knew what you'd told Tate, when you were standing in the bakery dealing with the threat on Tuesday evening." Andrew gave them a *what* look. "I've heard all the rumors, and I've been listening to what everyone said today. I still have the habits of a reporter— such as remembering dates and events."

Mary nodded. "He remembers all sorts of things that I forget. It's like a steel trap lies in his brain, waiting to capture bits of information."

Andrew smiled as if his bride-to-be had just complimented him, which maybe she had.

"Amber, if I know how you operate, and I think I do, then I would guess you already have a list of suspects." Gordon waited, not very patiently, bouncing his knee and staring at her pointedly.

"Okay. I made a list, but that doesn't mean it contains the right names. I worked on it last night, all night, and the middle of the night doesn't make for the clearest thinking. Plus I hate to call anyone a suspect until I have more to go on than my gut instinct." She paused, then continued. "Some of these people I like. It hurts to even think terrible things about them. It's actually painful to think they dislike me and the Village enough to do something this desperate."

"Don't go blaming yourself," Gordon said. "I know from past cases—and you should know by now—that someone's reason for lashing out isn't always logical. And often it's completely unrelated to the person they're threatening to harm. Many times it's more of a wrong-place-at-the-wrong-time scenario."

Amber caved. She shared the five names she'd been able to come up with the night before. Each name brought a groan or gasp from one or the other corner of the barn. Then her friends started brainstorming. Within fifteen minutes her list had grown to a baker's dozen.

"All right. Let's summarize before people begin to notice we're missing." Gordon stared down at his pad. "Amber has received three anonymous e-mails—the one I've seen and two others that are from the same person. I already have Jasmine working on the first e-mail communication. It hasn't been a priority because we were focusing on the actual crime scenes, but I'll move this to the front of her tasks."

"What if that spooks the person who's doing this? What if they find out?" Amber asked.

"The only people who are going to know are Jasmine and me. It's good to be cautious, but let's not get paranoid." Gordon checked his pad again.

"Pam, Amber, and Tate—you were all three in the bakery on Tuesday evening. I want you to separately make a list of everyone you can remember in the room—everyone. I'll visit each of you tomorrow and pick it up. And no, Amber, it won't look suspicious. This person knows there's a crime investigation going on. It would look suspicious for me not to check in with you."

"What do the rest of us do?" Hannah asked.

"Keep your eyes open. Whoever this is thinks Amber is dealing with it alone. Our perp is on a power high at this point, and we want to maintain that illusion. In truth, we'll have nine people with eyes open and focused on Village property."

"Not so hard for those of us who work there," Pam said. "In fact, a lot of us will be gathering for a quilting getaway next weekend."

"I was going to cancel," Amber admitted.

"Don't! Some of the names on our list? They'll be there. We might learn something."

"I think that's a good idea, but I want you to proceed with caution." Gordon glanced around the group. "Anyone else?"

"It's not a problem for me to visit the Village," Andrew argued. "I don't mind taking my best girl out for dessert . . . though I think I'll stay away from the pie."

Gordon cleared his throat. "On that topic, I want you all to stay away from pies. In fact, stay away from any dessert unless you made it your-self or a family member made it."

Jesse groaned in mock despair, but Andrew grinned. "No worries. I can stop by for lunch."

After a few final words of instruction about being careful, watching their backs, and not handling evidence, Gordon called the meeting to a close.

Each person in the room stopped to speak to Amber, assuring her that everything would be fine, that this time they were ahead of the actual crime, and that no one would get hurt.

Only Preston didn't predict immediate success with no casualties. Perhaps his combat experi-ence made him more realistic, or maybe he would rather err on the side of caution. "Promise me you won't try any heroics this time."

"I don't know what you mean."

"If you think of a great lead, share it with Gordon or me or Tate."

"Of course."

"Don't take off with Hannah or Pam—not alone—not dealing with this."

Amber pretended to be offended.

"And go home to take a nap. You look exhausted."

"Thank you."

"I only say it because I care." A word to Mocha, and he was gone, exiting through the back door of the barn.

Amber spoke to the soon-to-be-married couples. "Keep your focus on your wedding. I don't want it spoiled by this."

Then she hugged Tate, thanked Gordon, and walked back out into the afternoon sunlight with Pam.

"Sorry I had to trick you to get you here."

"I'm glad you did. Fortunately, I was too tired to put up much of a fuss."

"As soon as I saw that list on the bulletin board, I knew something was wrong. Those are more habits than sins."

"A sin can be a habit." Amber opened the passenger side door.

Another benefit of the meeting was that Gordon had assured her no one was spying on her via her tablet or phone. "That type of technology is not easy to acquire or use." Amber picked up her phone, checked her e-mail, and was relieved to see no new messages.

Pam slipped behind the wheel. "I suppose each of those things you listed can be considered a sin. But I don't think you're vain because you care how you look. Your momma raised you to pay attention to your appearance, the same as mine did."

"Worry is a sin," Amber countered.

"Yeah. When it's unwarranted. After the last investigation, I'd say it's plain smart."

Pam started the car, backed it up, and turned

toward the main road. They both waved at Jesse's mom, who was hanging clothes on the line. In the distance, Amber could see Jesse's father working in the field. Jesse had assured her they wouldn't mention the meeting.

"Amish are quite adept at keeping a secret when necessary."

Jesse had looked so much older when he'd said that. Amber had wanted to weep. These tragedies—these events—had stolen her young friend's innocence. And yet, the scene before her was a peaceful one. It served to reinforce her hope that everything would be fine.

"All right. You've got me on the first two—but what about envy? You can't argue that isn't a sin."

"Sure. I suppose. But if you were perfect God would have already called you home. And don't start with pride and snooping. You're proud of what others do. That isn't a sin; it's a kindness. As far as snooping—"

"Yes, how are you going to legitimize snooping?" Amber was actually enjoying listening to Pam whittle away her list of sins.

But Pam's expression had turned grim. She wasn't one to shy away from the facts, even when they were unpleasant. Instead, she frowned at the road and admitted, "If we don't snoop now, someone may be killed."

Twenty-Six

There were no further incidents the following week, but somehow this did not relieve the tension. They all did as Gordon had asked—paid special attention to what was going on at the Village. But they still had no idea who had been baking the pies, writing the notes, and sending the e-mails. None of Gordon's efforts seemed to have turned up any useful clues.

Amber thought maybe this silence was just one more way for the poison poet to mess with her.

She wasn't sure going to the quilting getaway was important after all. But Pam insisted, and finally she compromised and agreed to attend all day Saturday. She skipped the Friday evening activities, claiming she had a personal conflict. In fact, she and Tate had a standing date on Fridays and she looked forward to it all week long. After the stress of recent events, she felt as if she needed that quiet evening more than ever.

Pam picked her up Saturday morning as the sun peeked over the horizon. She looked fresh and stylish—wearing a blouse covered in daisies.

"Who quilts this early?"

"You'd be surprised. These ladies are a little

fanatical. I called the woman who runs the retreat earlier and she said some didn't even go to bed last night."

Amber sipped from her spillproof coffee mug and stared at Pam as she pulled out onto the two-lane road. "You look awfully chipper."

"I'm not one of those who stayed up all night. I went to bed, though did you know that Carol snores?"

"Carol Jennings?"

"The same. We room-shared with two other ladies. I'm not embarrassed that I'm a full-size woman—I'm one of God's creations. But he didn't create me to sleep on a twin-size bed. It doesn't really work for me. Part of my anatomy was hanging off the side no matter how I turned and fidgeted."

"So you didn't sleep well?"

"I slept like a rock. Grammy says that if you have peace with God, you'll sleep like a baby."

Amber couldn't help smiling at that. Pam's Grammy was one person she'd like to meet.

"Last night was interesting. You know I don't even sew, but I had fun pretending I was interested."

"Isn't that lying?"

"Nah. It's always good to learn something new, and I could decide to quilt one day. Maybe after I finish learning French."

"You're learning French?"

"I told you that. If I travel to Europe, I should know the languages."

"You're traveling to Europe?"

But Pam was still defending her behavior at the retreat. "I might even learn to sew like the Amish—by hand and all. A simple needle and thread I can maybe handle, but some of those machines take a college degree to understand. And I don't mean a degree in business like you and I have. Still, I was able to listen and learn. I walked around and glanced at things while I was listening."

Amber considered that for a minute. "All right. So what did your snooping yield? What did you learn?"

"How to thread a machine, for one."

"You don't own a machine."

"And I don't plan to, but you asked what I learned."

"What did you learn about the people we're . . . you know, spying on."

"Mostly that women are the same everywhere. Their tongues wag even when their hands are busy."

"Pam Coleman! That sounds like a biased thing to say. I thought you were a supporter of women—"

"I'm only stating a fact. You can conclude whatever you want from it. Have you ever walked in on two men watching a ball game? Or a dozen men, for that matter. If there's any discussion it's directed toward the television."

"I guess I might have noticed that."

"These women don't even own a television, or at least there aren't any at Diane's retreat center."

They continued on the road out of town. The retreat was situated thirty miles south. Seemed like a long trip. It occurred to Amber that she could be home, taking care of the donkeys, napping with Leo, and spending the day with her husband.

"Why are we even doing this? What good will it do?"

"Sounds like someone woke up on the negative side of the bed."

Pam gave her a look of pity, but Amber waved it away. "I just don't see how attending an all-day sewing event—"

"Quilting retreat. Learn the proper terminology so you'll fit in. I actually think it's a good idea. We need to scope out the people on your list. The Amish ladies were there yesterday and most are returning today. It's interesting to see how they interact with the *Englisch* women. I think we could learn something."

"So you think our perpetrator is a woman?"

"All those pie notes? It's a woman. I've never seen a man who is very handy around the kitchen. I know Tate is—no offense, but he's the exception to the rule."

"He mostly barbecues, and what he's learned to cook in the kitchen he learned while being a widower." The caffeine was beginning to kick in and Amber's mood was improving. Maybe they could learn something. Maybe they *could* crack this case today before anyone got hurt. It was critical for them to make progress because, the more she thought about it, the more Amber was concerned that the poison poet had been inactive for the last week—like the calm before a storm.

They saw the sign for the retreat center and turned down the gravel road. The sign sported bright red letters on a white background and spelled out the word QUILTERS with an arrow below it.

"It's another ten minutes or so from here," Pam said.

The setting was beautiful, with trees over-shadowing most of the gravel lane. The trees had been trimmed recently and brush lined the road to the right and left. The building itself came into view when they'd followed a gentle curve. It reminded Amber of a log cabin, but much larger. It was actually new and modern but constructed in an old-fashioned style. When she stepped inside she was surprised to see the entry opened onto a large, well-lit room that was completely filled with fabric, women, and machines.

Diane hurried from the kitchen. "I'm so glad you could make it!"

Amber guessed they were about the same age. She'd met the woman a couple of times when she'd stopped by to visit with Carol and then a few times at the post office. Diane was pretty, with shoulder-length, reddish hair. She wore jeans, a comfortable shirt that read, "I quilt so I don't kill people," and orthopedic shoes. By her side was the largest dog Amber had ever seen.

"Her name is Liberty."

"She's huge."

"Yes. She's an English Mastiff and fiercely loyal. Really, she's like one of the family."

Liberty gazed up at Diane with adoring brown eyes. She had a light cream-colored coat and a very dark, very large muzzle. Several cats could have fit easily in her mouth. She looked muscular and heavy, probably eighty pounds if Amber were to guess.

"This is our gathering room." Diane moved them into the big work area, where women were already sewing. As Pam had suggested, it looked as if some had been up all night. One was in her pajamas, and a few others were clutching mugs of coffee. "I suppose you know some of the ladies here."

There were several murmured hellos. Amber hoped the women knew she and Pam were attending for purely social reasons. She knew next to nothing about quilting. Lately she'd been too busy catching psychopaths to pick up a new hobby in addition to crocheting.

"Breakfast will be ready in twenty minutes," Diane reminded the group. "If there's anyone still asleep, you might want to wake them."

The room was interesting. Design boards covered most of the walls. There was an ironing center set up in the middle of the room, holding several irons and bottles of spray starch. In opposite corners there were cutting centers with various cutting boards, rotary cutters, and rulers. The rest of the area comprised L-shaped work tables, which were currently holding a variety of machines and all manner of fabric. Within each L-shape was an ergonomic chair. The room had been well thought out, and Amber found herself wishing she could sink into one of the chairs, pull out a bundle of fabric, and begin sewing.

She spent the next twenty minutes walking around the room and studying the quilts-in-progress. Breakfast was delicious and was followed by chat time so attendees could get to know each other. Amber found herself sitting between two women from Goshen who were avid quilters. She mainly listened, and she learned that the quilting process was more complicated than she had imagined. She didn't learn anything that would help with the investigation.

They spent the rest of the morning working on individual projects. Since Amber didn't have a sewing machine, or a project for that matter, she was put to work at the ironing center—learning how to set a seam and then press it toward the darker fabric. The work soothed her anxiousness. She'd begun to relax, to forget her real purpose for being there, when Georgia banged through the front door carrying a large platter.

"Oh, thanks so much for bringing the dessert." Diane was there to help her before Amber could move from her ironing table.

Georgia cast a sour look around the group, then traipsed after Diane into the kitchen.

"What's she doing here?" Pam asked, appearing at Amber's elbow. "I've never seen her away from the Village."

"Beats me. Looks like she brought dessert. Does she quilt?"

"I don't think so. Seems to me all she does is work."

Amber went back to her ironing, but her mind kept turning over what Pam had said. She couldn't remember ever seeing Georgia in town or at church or at a community event. She actually knew very little about her. She'd had lunch with her a few weeks ago, but they'd mostly talked about the Village.

By the time lunch was served, Carol Jennings had arrived with several of the Amish women from the Village in tow, including Hannah, Martha, and Letha.

"Sure hope there isn't a catfight between Martha and Letha, but we've managed to avoid a confrontation between all three ladies. I was just in the kitchen, and apparently Georgia already left out the back door." Pam had held back while the group was filing into the dining room.

"Amish don't fight. Remember?"

"Maybe not, but they don't usually date the same *Englisch* man either."

Amber sighed. For at least a week, her mind had forgotten about Ryan Duvall. Why did the trouble with him have to come up at the same time as the poison poet? Could they possibly be tied together? She didn't see how.

The rest of the afternoon passed quickly, and she was actually sad to say good-bye. "Next year I'll come for the entire weekend," she promised when she thanked Diane.

"We'll convert you yet," Diane said.

"To the dark side?"

"To the quilting side."

Amber, Pam, and Hannah made their way out to Pam's car. The other Amish women had gone back with Carol thirty minutes earlier, but Hannah had begged off from joining them, saying she needed to finish Amber's project. The quilted book bag was slung over Amber's shoulder. Though she hadn't sewn one seam on it, she'd pressed them all and felt as if she'd accomplished something.

They climbed into Pam's car, driving down the gravel road. They'd made it almost to the two-lane when they rounded a curve in the road, and Amber heard Pam pull in a quick, deep breath.

Then everything went wrong at once.

Twenty-Seven

Hannah heard Pam gasp before she hit the brakes. Hannah had still been working with a stubborn seat belt clasp when the sudden stop caused her to fall forward, bumping her head slightly on the headrest.

Pam had already unfastened her seat belt and jumped out of the car. For a big woman, she could move quite fast when she was motivated. Amber turned around and said, "Maybe you should stay in the car."

Hannah nodded, adjusting her *kapp*, which had been knocked askew. She stared out the front window, though, and she could see that someone had pulled brush and tree limbs across the road, completely obstructing their path.

"Someone's messing around," Pam said.

Amber looked up and down the road. "I guess we should move it."

Hannah got out to help. There was no need to wait in the car.

They'd moved about half of the limbs when there was a loud splat against the side of the car.

Green liquid squirted all over the driver's door.

Pam dropped the limb she was moving and strode over to the car. "What . . . how . . ." She glanced left, then right.

She'd backed up when the next splat—this one a bright red—landed on her window. The splatter ricocheted off and covered her shirt, obscuring the pretty daisies on the fabric.

"Oh no. They did not."

Amber had rushed to her side, and Hannah followed quickly in her wake.

"Get down," Amber said.

"Down? I'm not getting down. I'm going after this creep."

Another splat covered the car, Amber, Hannah, and Pam with yellow paint.

"Other side," Hannah said, waving frantically. "Let's move to the other side."

They did, using the car as a shield against the attack on themselves.

"Teenagers," Pam declared. "It has to be teenagers. Or it could be the poison poet. What if it's blood? Or icing? The poet would use poison icing—"

"It's only paint." Amber had wiped some of the yellow off her shirt and was smelling it. "Paint has a distinctive odor. This is paint. Someone has a paintball gun."

Pam leaned forward to smell it, and the color orange burst on her hood.

"It better not be paint. It better wash off. I'm going to find this nut. You don't mess with me, or my car, or my clothes!" The last two words were said in a rising pitch.

When the next paintball hit the top of her hood, paint again flew—this time purple—and splattered into Pam's hair. Her eyes rolled up into the top of her head, as if she were trying to see the paint in her hair. For a moment she looked as if she might faint, but then she shook her head, scrunched up her face, and said, "They're mine. When we catch them—they are mine."

Hannah and Amber exchanged worried looks.

"Who has their cell phone?" Amber asked.

"I don't own a cell phone."

"Mine's in the car," Pam said.

"So is mine." Amber peeked over the top of the car. "I'm going in."

"Do not get that paint inside my car."

"But we can't just sit here. There's no telling how long they can keep this up."

"I'll get it." Hannah removed her apron, which was where the bulk of the paint had splattered, then slowly opened the door, ducked inside, and retrieved Amber's purse.

"Call nine-one-one. Tell them a maniac has us pinned down. Tell them I'm having a hair emergency."

Amber shushed her and keyed in the number.

"We're outside the quilting retreat," she said to

269

the officer, describing the intersection of the two roads. When she explained they were being held in place by a barrage of paintballs, the officer apparently stopped her.

"I don't want to call the administrative number."

She listened a minute longer, then said, "No, we're not in imminent danger, but listen . . ."

"Send them a picture of my clothes," Pam said. "The person holding the paintball gun is in imminent danger."

Amber was shaking her head, pausing, and then trying to reason with the dispatcher on the other end. "I understand that they can't kill us with a paintball gun, but . . ."

She listened another second, and then stared at her phone.

"What happened?" Hannah was squatted next to Pam, who was squatted next to Amber.

"They said not to bother them with non-emergency situations."

"Non-emergency?" Pam's voice rose again, this time in disbelief. "What if one of those paint things hit me in the eye? Would that be a non-emergency? I'd probably lose my job. Who would want a one-eyed assistant manager? Or I could slip on the paint and hit my head. Concussions can be lethal. This situation is brimming with danger, and I think—"

"The police department reminded me I could

be fined for misusing the emergency number. I don't think they fully grasped our situation." Amber stared at the blank screen, then stuck the phone into her back pocket.

"You could call Tate," Hannah suggested.

"I could, but he'd only worry. Whoever this is obviously isn't going to hurt us, though I don't know what they are trying to do." She turned and peeked through the window, and another smack hit the side of the car.

"Stay down." Pam looked at her as if she were crazy. "Every time they see you, they send another paintball. What color was that one?"

"Black."

Pam closed her eyes. "I'm envisioning my car, clothes, and hair clean. I'm sending out positive thoughts to the creepy, disrespectful, sorry little person hiding in the woods."

Hannah had actually been in a paintball fight a few years earlier. A few of the teens had paid a taxi to take them west of Elkhart to the game center there. At the time she'd thought it was fun and a bit wild. She'd never done anything like that before, though she'd confessed it to her bishop the next week. Holding the gun, even though it was only a paintball gun, had seemed wrong. And though they were only having fun, she'd known that she didn't want to do it again. The next time they all went out, they went to the movies. Her *rumspringa* had been rather short-lived, and she was quite glad to have it behind her.

Amber had again removed the phone from her pocket and was Googling paintballs. "This says paintballs contain a water-soluble dye that washes off with a simple spray."

"Spray of what? Turpentine? Oh no. That will ruin my car. That's not going to happen."

"Water." When both Pam and Amber turned to look at Hannah in surprise, she explained about the trip to Elkhart.

"You used a paintball gun?"

"*Ya*. Just that once. And even though we wore old clothes, I was worried about the paint coming out. It washed out, though I did treat it with a stain remover first."

"I suppose that's good news," Pam admitted.

"Uh-oh." Amber was staring at her screen again.

"What? What did you read now?"

"That's the normal paintballs, but law enforcement has access to semi-permanent paintballs to mark leaders in riot situations."

"No. There's no way. This person can't have that kind of access, because this person is a lunatic." Pam fairly shouted the last word, but there was no answer.

The bombardment of paintballs had slowed while Amber was reading from her phone, and then it stopped completely.

"A better question is, why did they want to pin us down?" Amber raised her head to look through the window, but no accompanying paintball splattered.

"It's an expensive way to have fun at someone else's expense," Pam muttered. "Maybe they wanted to send a message."

"I think they're gone." Amber stood, brushed at her clothes, and then walked to the front of the car. "We still need to move the rest of these branches, at least the biggest ones. We could go back to Diane's and ask for help."

"I'm a big woman. I don't need help moving tree branches—and some woman might have put them there in the first place. You just watch the woods and tell me if you see anyone carrying a paintball gun."

Ten minutes later they were back in the car and traveling toward home. Pam had retrieved large trash bags from her trunk, explaining, "These come in handy more often than you would think."

She shook one out of the box, pulled the bottom seam apart, and draped it over her head. "You'll need to cut me some arm holes."

Amber fetched a pair of nail clippers from her purse, and soon they were each wearing a trash bag. Ten minutes outside of Middlebury, the rain started. Hannah looked behind them and saw that they were leaving a trail of paint as it washed off Pam's car.

"What does it mean?" Hannah asked. "Does it mean that whoever was sending the messages and baking the pies was at the retreat? If so, why were they so angry?"

"I'm supposed to be at home." Amber stared out the window. "I'm supposed to be agonizing over the last humiliation, or the next one."

"That's it." Pam tapped the wheel with the palm of her hand. "They knew you were going to be there and the point was to humiliate you. People don't just happen to have paintball supplies in their cars. I wouldn't be surprised if they took pictures and plaster them all over the Village."

"Thank you," Amber groaned. "Now I have something to look forward to."

Hannah leaned forward. "Also, I think the person must have been *at* the retreat center. We saw only women at the retreat, but maybe a man was hiding somewhere, able to hear what we were saying. Anyway, they knew when we were leaving. Who left right before us?"

"Carol. She left with the other girls a half hour before we did."

"So whoever it was waited in the woods, then after Carol left, pulled out the brush and set up an ambush, knowing, I guess, we would be the next to leave."

Amber turned to glance at Hannah and Pam. "But we all agree that we didn't see or hear anything suspicious at the retreat, right?"

"True, but Hannah's also right. Somehow they knew when we were leaving." Pam crossed her arms. "I'm going to find out who it is. Mess with my wardrobe and you are messing with me."

They drove the rest of the way in silence, each, Hannah knew, wrestling with her own thoughts. Their week without incident had come to an end.

Pam had just pulled up to Hannah's house when Amber's phone dinged, indicating a text message. She read it once, then held it up so Pam and Hannah could see it.

Poison squares,
Paintball bullets,
Wizen up
Or there will be more to it.

"This person is a bad writer," Pam said. "That doesn't make any sense."

But Hannah was thinking they must be getting closer, and whoever was behind the pies understood that. This person understood they were in danger of being caught, and as that danger drew closer to reality the person or persons became increasingly more desperate.

Twenty-Eight

Hannah's life resembled an *Englisch* roller coaster. The ups and downs were becoming hard to follow. The next week after the paintball attack had passed quickly, still with no progress made on the poison poet. On the positive side, no new pies had appeared, no one was attacked with paintballs, and no new instructions arrived for Amber. On the negative side, her boss and friend was working herself into a state of exhaustion.

Amber had come up with a new plan designed to "spy on her employees"—those were the exact words she had used when telling Hannah and Preston about it as they walked through the covered bridge on the east side of the property.

"Spend a day with your boss" was ostensibly to help Amber understand more about the tasks and responsibilities of various positions within the Village. A by-product was that it allowed Amber to be out of her office. She was able to see and hear what was happening among her employees.

She had spent one day washing dishes, another taking orders in the restaurant, and a third working on the grounds crew. So far she'd learned nothing, and she was exhausted from trying to complete her office work at night. But she held on to the belief that eventually they would "crack the case." Sometimes *Englischers* spoke in such a strange way Hannah could only shake her head and try not to laugh. Of course, this was no laughing matter. It was serious, and Hannah only wished she could be more help.

Amber stopped in at the coffee shop less often, and Hannah knew that was because she didn't want whoever was threatening her to see them together any more than necessary.

But Hannah understood without Amber explaining her absence. She also knew the stress was taking its toll on her boss—beyond exhaustion. That much was obvious. The day before she'd left her phone and tablet on one of the benches beside the pond. A customer had turned them in to Hannah.

Pam had confirmed that, though they had contained no instructions, the anonymous texts to Amber were still coming; the one about the paintball incident was just the start of a new round. They were all on edge, though Gordon insisted the person would slip up and be caught. The big question was, what would happen next?

Hannah woke Sunday morning with the strong impression it was going to be a special day. She took a moment to study the light coming in the window, listen to the sounds coming from the rooms below, and watch her sister, Mattie, curled up and clutching her Amish doll as she slept.

The doll was faceless, as all Amish dolls were.

It wore a dark purple dress and a black apron, very similar to Mattie's clothing. The doll reminded Hannah of one she'd had as a child—one with glasses, which was a bit unusual. Hannah hadn't wanted to wear the glasses that had been prescribed for her, but it was obvious that she couldn't see well. She'd needed them from a young age. But even after the doctor, her mother, father, and brothers all spoke with her, she still stubbornly refused to wear them.

So her father had fashioned a miniature pair out of wire, careful to cover the ends so she wouldn't scratch her four-year-old hands. One morning she woke to find her doll sitting on the nightstand, wearing the glasses. She had worn her glasses from that day forward, and she had loved that doll.

Probably her dad had no idea how much that gift had meant to her. Had she ever told him? She could think of so many things she wanted to thank her parents for, but then her days became busy and she inevitably forgot.

Suddenly she remembered.

It was her birthday. The last she would celebrate while living in her parents' home.

She dressed quickly and quietly, careful not to waken Mattie so early in the morning, and made her way to the kitchen. Her mother and father were sitting at the table, enjoying a cup of coffee.

Hannah could tell by the rays of sunlight slanting through the kitchen window that it was at least seven in the morning. No doubt both of her parents had been up for several hours. Timothy had already been to the barn and back, and Eunice, she knew, had already accomplished some of her daily household tasks. Outside the window she could see Ben, Noah, and Dan making their way back to the house.

"She must be getting older, sleeping in so late." Timothy smiled, stood to refill his coffee mug, and stopped to kiss her on top of the head. "Happy birthday, *dochder*."

"*Danki*." Hannah spied the cake on the counter. When had her mother found time to mix, bake, and frost it?

"German chocolate—your favorite." Eunice reached across and squeezed her hands. "Happy birthday."

"You're going to spoil me."

"Haven't you heard?" her dad asked. "The Amish don't spoil their children."

At that moment her three rowdy brothers banged through the back door, stopping in the mud room to remove their jackets. Before they were settled at the table, Mattie bounced in.

Her mother had prepared scrambled eggs, sliced fresh bread, and set out jam preserves. But the best part of the meal, in Hannah's opinion, was the chocolate cake. It was a terrible indulgence to eat it for breakfast, but then again she was twenty-three now. She was old enough to make her own decisions—even when they were bad ones. Her brothers readily joined in, and soon all their plates held a good-size piece of the treat. Mattie dropped her fork and decided to go at it with her hands.

Her gifts were practical but delightful.

Her mother and father gave her a new peach-colored dress and a white *kapp*. The dress her mother had made while Hannah was at work. The *kapp* was bought at the mercantile in town. Both were lovely and needed—she'd filled out in certain areas and her old dresses barely fit any longer.

Noah offered her one of the pups he was raising, and Dan joked about letting her help with his camel—of which he hadn't yet taken delivery. It was Ben, her oldest brother, who finally produced a package wrapped in brown paper and boasting a bright blue bow. "We pitched in together to buy it."

The notebook was spiral bound with lined pages and a beautiful cover boasting their native Indiana wildflowers. "We thought you could put your recipes in it," Ben explained.

"*Ya*, if you write down some of the things *Mamm* cooks, maybe Jesse won't have to subsist on *kaffi* recipes."

Hannah endured the ribbing in good form. Her brothers had taken the time to think of her, and that meant more than any gift they could have given. But she also appreciated the journal. Maybe she would use it for her thoughts and memories and prayers rather than recipes. It would be a good way to put on paper the things she wanted to remember—like this morning, this last birthday with her family.

Then Mattie insisted on getting down and toddled into the sitting room. When she returned, she was holding a drawing their mother said she had worked on all week. Written across the top, in her mother's handwriting, was "Happy Birthday, Hannah." And below that was a picture of her family, all standing in the field. After climbing into Hannah's lap, Mattie pointed out each member of their family. The males had surprisingly long arms, and the females each wore *kapps* that looked more like pigtails—but Hannah loved it. The number twenty-three had been added to the bottom right corner. Hannah had attempted to trace it with an orange crayon.

Twenty-three.

The number echoed in her mind as she prepared for church and helped Mattie dress. Twenty-three. And soon she would be Hannah Miller.

Could life grow any sweeter?

Could God possibly bless her more?

Yet as they piled into the family buggy her mind turned to Amber, the Village, and their recent problems. She didn't want to think about those things today. She wanted to focus on her blessings and on the things she had to be grateful for. She managed to do that, until after the warm greetings from friends and family, until after the singing and the sermons, until she found herself shooed outside.

The service had taken place at Fanny and Martin Bontager's farm. Their children were all grown and married and having children of their own, and the oldest son was helping to run the farm. Recently Fanny and Martin had built their own *Dawdy Haus* and moved into it. It was across the parking circle and to the south of the main home. It was a tidy farm, and Hannah realized that one day, after she and Jesse moved to a place of their own, she would be hosting church service. That thought sent her head to spinning.

All the other girls her age were helping with the meal. The boys were setting up the baseball and volleyball games, and the younger children were attended by fathers and grandfathers. She turned in a circle and noticed Minerva Wyse sitting in a rocker on the porch of the *Dawdy Haus*. Hannah walked over and joined her, sitting on the porch steps.

Minerva was one of the oldest widows in their congregation, possibly the oldest person. It was difficult for Hannah to even guess at the woman's age, but she had great-grandchildren. It seemed she had always been among them. Now her skin was pale and wrinkled. When Hannah reached out to touch the woman's hand and say hello, she discovered it was as soft as that of a newborn child. Minerva's *kapp* was pinned precisely as ever and set to the back a little bit because she didn't have enough hair in the front to pin it. She smiled, revealing that she was wearing only her bottom dentures—but the smile was genuine, stretching the wrinkles around her eyes and lighting up her face.

"Happy birthday, my dear. It seems just yesterday that I was young like you, celebrating my birthday and about to marry Jacob."

Hannah didn't remember Jacob. It was possible he had passed before Hannah was born. To hear Minerva talk, she'd walked in the fields with him just the day before. In the last year, the older woman's perception of time had blurred, but in other areas, Minerva was as bright and observant as ever.

"How are you today, Minerva?"

"*Gut. Gut. Gotte* is *gut* to me, my dear." She rocked for a few moments, and then thumped the cane she held across her lap against the arms of the rocker. "And he is *gut* to you, though I can tell you're worried. Goodness, yes. Something is darkening your joy today."

Hannah realized it was true the moment Minerva pronounced it. Though she was enjoying her birthday—the cake had been exquisite, the presents from her family thoughtful, and Jesse was hinting about a special gift he wanted to give her on the way home—behind all that loomed worries about Amber and the Village.

The names on the list—she couldn't stop thinking about them. Amish and *Englisch*. Men and women. All were folks Hannah knew. There wasn't a stranger among the names, and why would there be? Obviously the person harassing her boss was someone from within the Middlebury community. Who else could be so aware of Amber's moves?

But the thought that it was one of them, that it was a neighbor or friend—well, that hurt Hannah's heart.

"I can't talk about it," she admitted.

"Understandable. Some sorrows are not to be shared publicly." Minerva ran her hand over the cane, her eyes focused on something in the distance. "This poison thing, it must be unsettling."

"You know about that?"

Minerva cackled. "I'm old, yes. But I still read the paper, and I still hear the chatter among our group."

"Oh."

"We have spoken of poisons before."

"*Ya.*" Hannah had thought of that after the meeting in the barn. Minerva had helped with the investigation into the death of Ethan Gray. In the end, Hannah had decided not to consult her because this current matter seemed so different.

284

This person was insinuating they had poisons to place into pies, not growing herbs to hide in someone's food.

Arsenic? As far as Hannah knew, you couldn't grow arsenic. And even if you could, the only reason to grow it would be to poison someone. Such a plant in your garden would look rather suspicious. It would be a definite red flag to the police, though Gordon Avery couldn't search every garden. And he might not know an arsenic plant from thyme.

"Baking is close to a person's heart, be it a woman or a man. With your hands you're creating something of sustenance, yes, but also something for pleasure. As you roll out the crust or mix the batter or fashion the frosting, you are envisioning the loved one you're cooking for. It's a true labor of love."

"I don't understand. Why would anyone use such a thing to hurt someone else?"

"We can't know. It's rare that we do understand the mind or heart of another person. Occasionally we have glimpses, yes. And you will find with Jesse, as I found with Jacob, that sometimes you feel as if your two hearts are beating as one." Minerva planted her feet on the porch and stood, bracing her cane to the porch floor. "Just remember, my dear, that cooking and baking and sewing—those are things close to our hearts. For someone to use them to harm or injure . . . it seems to me that would also be a reflection of the heart."

"How so?"

"Perhaps their heart is breaking. Perhaps they are crying out in desperation. Or maybe"—Minerva toddled to the corner of the porch, then turned and studied Hannah—"they are experiencing emotions they don't understand. Whichever is the case, be careful. You're not dealing with a cold-blooded killer this time. You're dealing with an emotionally distressed person—and that can be much more dangerous."

Those words circled in Hannah's mind as their congregation shared a meal, as she participated in the games, and even as she answered questions about her wedding and the progress of the room addition at Jesse's home.

It wasn't until late that afternoon, as she was riding in Jesse's buggy, that she admitted her concerns to him.

"It's worrisome, I know. But there's nothing we can do about it today, and it's your birthday. Let's enjoy this time together."

So she did. Somehow she pushed her questions and worries to the back of her mind and enjoyed the afternoon buggy ride through the April sunshine. When Jesse pulled the buggy into one of the corner parks along the Pumpkinvine Trail, she started laughing.

"Surely we're not about to have a picnic. I

ate enough at Fanny's to last until tomorrow."

"No picnic, but I thought it would be nice to sit in the swings, like we used to when we were younger."

"Can you believe it, Jesse?" She clasped his hand as they walked toward the swings. "We're about to be married—to be man and wife."

"Hannah Bell, you can't begin to know how you satisfy my heart."

"I do?"

Instead of answering, he sat in one of the swings, gently nudging it into motion with his foot. She finally moved in front of him and waited until he looked up at her.

"I satisfy your heart?"

"*Ya.*" He pulled her down, touched her face, and kissed her softly. When she sat down in the swing next to his, he said, "I've always dreamed of having a wife and a home and children . . . but I thought those dreams were for other people. I thought that perhaps *Gotte*'s plan for me was different."

"*Ya*, I was a little afraid of the same thing. I know we're supposed to trust and have faith, but it's hard when you can't see which path your life will take."

"I'm grateful, every day, that our paths are going to be one." He kissed her once more, then laughed lightly. "Speaking of becoming one, I have your birthday present."

"You shouldn't have."

"Oh, so you want me to take it back?"

"*Nein!*"

"*Gut,* because I made it. Taking it back would be difficult." They stood, and together they walked back to the buggy. Jesse reached into the backseat and pulled out a wrapped box the size of a book. "For you, Hannah Bell."

The paper was plain, and the bow fashioned from red yarn. Still, Hannah's heart began to beat in a triple rhythm.

Jesse standing so close.

Jesse smiling at her as if he'd just given her a pot of gold.

Her and Jesse beginning their life together.

She rested her back against the buggy and fumbled with the yarn.

The wooden box had been carved out of maple. The edges were smooth, the corners perfectly formed. Hours of sanding had highlighted the grain in the wood.

Jesse took it from her hands and opened it. Inside the lid he'd carefully carved her initials.

"I thought you could use it for postcards when we travel, or maybe for your sewing notions, or even for the pens you use for your journals . . ."

He probably had more uses for the box, but Hannah never heard them. She threw her arms around his neck, and for the first time that day she allowed all her worries to slip away.

"I'll make you more boxes if this is my thanks."

"You are a wonderful boyfriend, Jesse Miller."

"*Ya?*"

"And I have no doubt you'll be a wonderful husband."

He kissed her then, softly at first and then more urgently. When they pulled apart the last of the sun's rays shot between the limbs of the trees, forming a halo of light and warmth around them.

Twenty-Nine

Preston marveled that his life could change so quickly. He had spent most of the day before with Zoey. It was his second time to attend worship services with Mocha, who lay quietly at his feet as the pastor made the weekly announcements.

The first week there had been a little bit of a stir. Their pastor, Mitch Dodson, had set everyone straight by adding Preston's name to the praise report. By the time he'd suggested they make Mocha an honorary church member, everyone was laughing, and then it was as if Mocha had always been part of the congregation.

Amber had slipped him a note later in the church service. It read, "Tell her everything." So he'd taken Zoey to lunch after church and, in a quiet corner of the restaurant where no one could hear, shared all the details they had uncovered in their meeting in the barn. As he expected, she took it well.

This week as he'd walked into the church, he'd received the normal greetings and a few folks had said good morning to Mocha as well. It seemed a group of folks could grow accustomed to just about anything, including having a service dog in the midst of their worship service.

He and Zoey had talked about the Village situation several times. She came up with a couple of additional names they could add to the growing list of suspects, but other than that she could only caution him to be careful and make him promise he wouldn't be a hero. No worries there. Preston had never felt like a hero, and he saw no reason to start trying to be one now.

However, he would like to spend a few moments alone with whoever was harassing Amber. He'd like to share some of his thoughts with that person. When he was completely honest with himself, he admitted that what he really wanted to do was punch them in the face—but a twinge of guilt reminded him that wasn't the Christian response. That was the old creature, the old Preston, trying to have its way.

He struggled with that realization. What was the Christian response to someone who meant you harm?

Tate suggested they pray, so he did, and it helped to calm his worries. It helped to convince him that God would protect Amber, as he had before. But Preston wasn't certain that things would immediately improve. In fact, he had the distinct feeling their problems were just beginning.

Fortunately it was the busy season at the Village. No one had time to dwell on what might happen. The spring tourists were arriving by the busload. Their charity event, Race for a Cure, was this coming Saturday. Preparations were ongoing and time-consuming, but things were coming together nicely.

And then there was the issue of Ryan Duvall.

Though Preston had pushed that particular situation to the back of his mind, Hannah brought it up as soon as he stepped into the Village coffee shop. As she poured his lunchtime cup of coffee, she talked nonstop about Ryan and Letha and Martha and Georgia. The names buzzed around in Preston's mind, until he began to wish she would slow down.

"What should we do?" Hannah fiddled with the ties of her prayer *kapp* and glanced repeatedly out the window.

"About what?"

"About Ryan. Haven't you been listening?"

"I don't know that we can or should do anything, Hannah."

"But it's going to be a disaster . . . right down the road from here in"—she stared at the clock on the wall—"minutes!"

"You're sure about this? All three of the ladies and Ryan are going to be there?"

"*Ya*. Martha came by and wanted to know how her new dress looked. She was practically turning cartwheels—which is most unlike Martha. I'm telling you, she's convinced she is *in lieb*."

"And Letha?"

"She's going as well! I only found out about her because Helen stopped in for coffee before heading to the dress shop to cover for her."

"And Helen told you Letha was going to the horse auction?"

"*Ya*! Said she wanted to surprise Ryan because it was such a big day—they are showing the quarter horses. Ryan must not know Letha and Georgia are going to be in the audience. He thinks only Martha is coming."

Preston was beginning to see Hannah's point. This had all the potential to turn into a disaster, but he didn't see what they could do about it.

"How did you learn about Georgia?"

"One of the girls from the bakery came in and told me Georgia was all atwitter."

"Hard to imagine."

"She'd been there since three a.m., baking, so she could leave for a very important date. That's what she called it."

"Could have been—"

"And then she wanted to know if what she had on was appropriate to wear to a horse auction."

Preston sipped his coffee while Mocha stared longingly at Hannah.

"Are you sure these dog treats are all right for her? I bought them at the dry goods store downtown."

"You're her new best friend. Go ahead. There's not much chance she'll gain weight, as much walking as we do."

Mocha caught the treat midair and Hannah smiled, her first smile since Preston had walked into the shop. But her attention quickly turned back to her friends.

"Anything could happen. I think they all know about each other, but apparently each thinks Ryan has stopped seeing the other two."

"I would have thought Ryan would have moved on by now. I meant to talk to him weeks ago, and then we got busy with this whole poison poet situation."

"He hasn't moved on at all. We need to go over there and distract two of the girls or I think there's going to be trouble."

"They're bound to find out about each other eventually," he pointed out. He also wondered how the three women all managed to get the same Monday afternoon off, but that wasn't his business either.

"Yes, but it doesn't have to be in public. We should go and intervene."

"How are we going to do that?"

"We'll think of something." Hannah was already turning the store sign to "Closed." "I can't walk there. You need to take me, Preston. I've already asked Seth to finish out the afternoon here."

She looked more desperate and harried than Preston had ever seen her. She was a good kid and only wanted to help her friends. He couldn't really blame her for that. So he sent a quick text to Amber, telling her he'd be off property for a while. He couldn't just drop Hannah off. Who knew what was going to happen?

He called to Mocha, and together the three of them were soon motoring down the road.

The Duvall Complex.

That's what it was called, which had always seemed a little presumptuous to Preston. Mark Duvall had started out with a standard-size barn and a few quarter horses. Over the years the facility had grown until he now employed a half-dozen men to help with the horses, including his son, Ryan. As they pulled into the parking lot, Preston had to admit the place had certainly branched out. Today the auction was being held in an outdoor arena that boasted covered bleachers for the buyers as well as a tack shop, a gift shop, and a snack shop. No doubt Mark Duvall was hoping to appeal to the tourist trade as well as prospective horse owners.

Preston wasn't too surprised to see the bleachers were nearly full. Several of the folks were armed with cameras—no doubt there for the pictures rather than to actually bid on a horse. Other folks were studying a printed sheet of paper, which probably listed the horses and their lineage and size, as well as the order they would be shown.

He barely had time to assess the situation before Hannah was gripping his arm and pointing to the front row.

Martha was seated there. Ryan was standing inside the actual arena, which looked to be a good sixty feet wide and one hundred and twenty feet in length. Rails separated the onlookers from the horses and their riders. Ryan was there to help with the auction, so he was dressed in jeans, chaps, boots, and a western shirt. However, his attention was not on the show that was about to start. Instead he was completely focused on the pretty Amish girl in the front row.

Preston recognized Martha immediately, but she didn't see him or Hannah. She only had eyes for Ryan. She barely seemed to realize that she was in a horse arena.

Ryan had flung his arms over the rail and was peering up at her. Martha had scooted to the edge of her seat, apparently moving closer so they could speak.

What was he supposed to do about this?

Why had he agreed to drive there and become involved?

Then Hannah clutched his arm and pointed to the far end of the arena. They had come in down the middle aisle, and still stood a good ways back. To the right, hurrying toward Ryan with a look of eager anticipation on her face, was Letha Keim. She was wearing the traditional Amish dress, with tennis shoes and little white socks. Though Preston knew for a fact that Letha was forty-two—they'd talked about their respective ages during the winter—the woman looked completely different today. She had a spark in her eyes and a spring in her step.

And she was headed straight for disaster.

"We better hurry." Hannah rushed down the aisle.

Preston closed his eyes, then checked Mocha. The dog seemed alert but calm even among the large crowd. They both followed in Hannah's wake.

"What are you doing here?" Letha had reached Ryan and Martha. She stood there, hands on her hips, demanding an explanation as she stared at her rival.

"It's a free country, Letha." Martha stood to confront the older woman, though she kept her voice low. "I suppose I can come to a horse auction if I want to."

"That's not what I mean, and you know it."

"Letha, maybe—"

Letha Keim turned on Ryan with the fury of a twister switching course. "You stay out of this! You promised—you sat at the table last night and promised me that you were not seeing her anymore."

"You ate with Letha last night?" Martha turned back toward Ryan, a look of puzzlement and hurt on her young face. "But I thought you were—"

"You both thought the same thing I did." Georgia marched up from the left, her purse slung over her right shoulder and a bitter expression on her face. "It would seem Ryan has duped us all."

"No. That's not . . . what I mean is . . ." Ryan glanced left and right, finally catching sight of Preston. He seemed to look to Preston for some kind of help, but Preston only shook his head. This was exactly the type of scene he'd been worried about, and Ryan Duvall had no one to blame but himself.

Hannah rushed to Martha's side as she began to cry.

A small crowd of folks had moved closer to better hear what was going on.

Preston pushed through with Mocha close to his side.

"We should go, Hannah. Take Martha to the car, and I'll give you both a ride back to the Village."

And it might have gone that way. It could have all ended there if not for another foolish move by Ryan. He reached out to stop Martha, putting his hand on her arm. She jerked away, and when she did, she lost her footing and bumped into Georgia, who went down in the aisle.

Ryan vaulted over the railing to help Georgia up. When he did, she took her purse and clocked him with it. Georgia was not Amish, yet the move surprised Preston. Whatever was in the bag must have packed some weight, because Ryan stumbled backward and into Letha, who made an attempt to steady him.

But Ryan still had his eyes on Martha, who had regained her balance and was moving away.

"Don't go, Martha. Let me explain."

"You can't explain this!" The words exploded from Martha with the force of a heart breaking. "Just leave me alone! I never want to see you again."

Ryan moved toward her one more time, and that was when Preston stepped into the middle. "Don't try it."

"Stay out of my way, Preston."

"I'll stay out of your way when the girls are gone."

"Who designated you their chaperone?" Ryan reached out with both hands and shoved Preston.

Calling on all of his restraint, Preston stood firm but didn't raise a hand. Unfortunately, Mocha wasn't so controlled. The yellow Labrador had been well trained, and her primary concern was Preston's well-being. Though he hadn't heard her so much as growl in the past two weeks, he'd also never been threatened in any way. The dog had been standing close, fairly quivering since the commotion had started. When Ryan reached out and pushed Preston, all the dog's training and energy combined into an explosive burst. She literally threw herself at Ryan, barking and baring her teeth, her incisors a few inches from his face.

"Get her off me. Get her off!"

Preston called the dog to heel, and she did so immediately.

But the damage had been done. Ryan saw his chance to change the focus of everyone there from his behavior to Mocha's.

"That dog is a menace!"

"You're the menace, and you're the one who chose to lead on three different women at the same time."

Ryan interrupted with a string of oaths that probably made every woman in the stands blush.

"Maybe you should learn to watch your mouth."

"Don't tell me what to do on my property."

"You mean your dad's property."

"Why are you even here?" Ryan's face had turned the crimson shade of a setting sun. He glanced around at the crowd, looked for Martha, saw that she was gone, then glanced at Georgia and Letha.

"You two saw what happened. That dog attacked me. Service dog? Yeah, right. For what? You're not blind or deaf. You're nothing but a loser who accepted a handout from the VA."

Instead of answering, Letha turned and left.

Only Georgia remained, and Preston wasn't sure she needed his intervention.

"Are you okay?"

"Why I'm fine, Preston." The words were spoken softly, but the smile she gave could have frozen raindrops as they fell.

"I told you to take your mutt and leave—get out of here."

Preston glanced up and saw Mark Duvall hurrying down the aisle. As far as he was concerned, Ryan's father could take it from that point. So he headed back outside, the scene with Ryan forgotten as he turned his attention to the girls waiting beside his car.

Thirty

Wednesday morning, Amber and Pam set out for Martha's home. The day had dawned gray but with the warmth of spring. Rain intermittently fell, reminding Amber of a shower turned on, then off, then on again. Certainly the crops in the fields could use the water, but personally she could stand a little more sunshine.

Martha hadn't come to work the day before, and she hadn't called or shown up for her shift that morning.

"So Preston filled you in on everything that happened at that horse show?" Pam cornered herself in the little red car, watching her boss and sipping her morning coffee.

"He did. And you?"

"Oh, honey. I heard it from so many different sources I could write the article that will surely appear in our local paper."

Amber cringed at the thought. She didn't mind free publicity for the Village, but this was not what she had in mind.

"I hate this sort of thing," Pam admitted. "But I suppose it's better than dealing with some nutcase who might or might not want to poison us. I've been afraid to eat anything besides frozen dinners, and those just don't taste that good. I think I'm losing my womanly figure."

Amber smiled at her assistant. She was not overweight, but she was a big woman. Somehow Amber didn't think she'd look right in a size ten. "We need to solve this quickly then."

"Exactly. But apparently whoever is doing it has backed off. Perhaps when they saw you washing dishes, their need to see you humbled was satisfied."

Amber focused all her attention on the road, avoiding Pam's gaze.

"What aren't you telling me?"

"What?"

"What yourself. You're keeping something from me. I can tell. You get that doe-eyed look as if you're innocent."

"Oh, all right. Check the glove box."

Pam fiddled with the latch, finally opening it, and pulled out the envelope that sat on top of everything else stuffed in there. Inside were three sheets of paper.

"More notes?"

"And more pies. Those are copies—Gordon has the originals."

"Why didn't I hear about this?"

"Because none of the pies have contained poison. We're keeping it on the low-down while Gordon works the case."

"The low-down? Honey, you need a vacation . . ." Pam's voice drifted off as she read the first note.

Oleander can stop the heart
Or give you seizures from the start
Flower petals or broken twigs
Either way you won't need new digs

"Isn't oleander that bush with pink flowers?"

"Yes, sometimes light pink, sometimes dark. Even white."

"We have those all over the south. It's a good

plant for Texas because it doesn't require much care and deer won't eat it."

"They don't eat it because it's poisonous."

"So whoever is doing this could get hold of a few branches or leaves pretty easily."

"According to Gordon, yes."

Amber veered right when they reached the edge of town, following the directions on her GPS to Martha's house. Pam reached out and touched her arm. "I could use another cup of coffee."

"You just had a cup."

"I need another. I have two more notes to read."

Amber pulled into the drive-through of a fast-food joint on the corner. "Will this do?"

"Sure."

But Pam wasn't paying attention; she was reading the next note.

Antifreeze is for your car
But mix it in pie and they won't go far
Seizures result from a little bit
Up the dose and their organs will take a hit

"I know you can purchase antifreeze any-where. This person is sick!"

"Gordon thinks he or she might be indulging in fantasies."

"Of killing people?"

Amber accepted the coffee from the person at the window and handed it over to Pam. She'd ordered herself another as well. She tried to limit her caffeine intake, but she had a feeling she might need the extra boost today. She set her coffee into the cup holder and pulled forward into a parking space that faced the main road.

"Those two came in last week. This last one, the third one, came in yesterday, and it's the one that concerns Gordon the most."

Ricin comes from castor beans
You won't be needing those new blue jeans
It'll burn your mouth, hurt your throat
A few beans baked can make you croak

"I've heard of this one. There was a special on TV about it. That broadcaster guy who died, back in the seventies?"

Amber nodded.

"He was in London and had a pellet fired at him. It contained ricin—"

"Georgi Markov. He died three days after he was hit with the pellet, even though he was in a hospital."

"And how did you remember those details?"

"I didn't. I've been Googling, though I've only been doing it at the library. I still worry that whoever is sending me notes might have a way to access my internet history."

"I don't see how." Pam removed the lid from her coffee and blew on the steaming brew. "I assume these three notes came with pies. Where did they show up?"

"The first was left under the windshield wiper on my car. The second found its way to our back porch, pinned down with a rock, and the last one was at the sandwich shop in town."

"I'm surprised I didn't hear about the last one. This town isn't known for guarding secrets."

"True, but I think Gordon convinced the owner that the best way to catch this person is to keep their name and their activities out of the paper."

Amber restarted the engine and pulled back out onto the road. They were silent for a few moments, and then Pam asked, "So is Gordon any closer?"

"They hit a wall with the computer search. Apparently a distorting proxy was used to hide the internet address."

"A what?"

"All internet activity, including e-mails, can be traced to the point of origin. When a user accesses the internet through a proxy server, it masks or distorts that home address."

"I guess you found that Googling?"

"Yup."

"Girl, shut down the internet and take a step away from the computer. Seriously, when this is over you must take a vacation with that good-looking man of yours. I know I would take a vacation if I had a good-looking man. In fact,

I might not even wait until this incident is resolved. Go now. Go next week!"

"Uh-huh." Amber sipped her coffee and shot Pam *the look*.

"What?"

"You think I should go on vacation?"

"Sure."

"Just take off."

"Absolutely." Pam squirmed uncomfortably in her seat.

"Because I need a break."

"Uh-huh."

"Then explain why you canceled your two-day property management conference in Indianapolis."

"That? Well, I couldn't leave you here alone to have all the fun. I have a feeling we're closing in on this creep. And I want to be here for the take-down."

"Before any takedowns, we need to figure out what we're going to do about our girls." Amber parked in front of Martha's house. It was the typical Amish home—large and sprawling, with a thriving garden to the east side, fields to the south and west, and a giant barn to the north. "It would have been nice if we could have called first."

"Not possible. Who even knows which phone shack to call? These things confuse me, and I've been here nearly a year."

"They confuse me, and I've been here twenty years."

Walking resolutely up the steps of the front porch, Amber was about to knock when several small children appeared on the other side of the screen door. They never said a word, but somehow Martha's mother knew they had visitors. She appeared behind them and shooed them into the sitting room.

Martha's mother was like many of the older Amish women Amber saw—a good thirty to forty pounds overweight, no doubt from the heavy emphasis on starch in their diets. She carried the weight well, and Amber wondered what it would be like to not count calories every day.

"*Kinner* and *grandkinner*, they make for a full and happy house." Martha's mom smiled and pushed back the strings of her *kapp*. "You're Amber, Martha's boss. I've seen you at the Village."

"Yes, and this is my assistant, Pam Coleman."

"My name is Rachel. *Danki* for coming." She bent to answer one of the children. "I suppose you're here to talk to Martha. She prefers not to speak to anyone about this for now."

"Would you be willing to talk with us?"

Rachel only hesitated a moment, then pushed open the door. "Would you like to come inside?"

"Perhaps we could sit on the porch," Amber suggested. Though the rain was still gently falling, the day was warm and the rockers inviting.

"*Ya, gut* idea."

A cry split the morning like lightning crackling across the sky. "That one is not patient. Let me fetch him."

Rachel returned with a baby Amber estimated to be about six months old. He was sucking his thumb and tears ran down his chubby cheeks. "This little man's *mamm* should return any moment. Until then, we will rock."

They'd barely settled into their chairs when Martha's mom began to speak about the events that had occurred at the Duvall Complex.

"Martha, she would barely speak of it, but of course I heard from my neighbors. Apparently it was quite the scene."

"We heard the same," Amber said.

"Martha has always been my quiet one, doing whatever was asked and causing us no problem. She's never even had a real *rumspringa* as far as I could tell—other than seeing this *Englischer*." Rachel rocked her grandbaby and watched the rain. "I tend to worry more about the quiet ones—when they've gone through no period of trying your *Englisch* ways, then sometimes they later wish they had. They have regrets, and regrets are difficult to live with."

"So you knew about her dating Ryan Duvall?" Pam asked.

"A mother suspects when something like this is afoot. I didn't know Mr. Duvall's name, but I was aware that Martha was seeing someone." She paused and then added, "And that he wasn't from within our community."

"How is Martha today?" Amber smiled at a small girl who had opened the screen door, darted out onto the porch, and now stood behind her grandmother's chair.

"Oh, her heart is broken. She will not eat or speak of what has happened. Her *dat*, he says that we shouldn't indulge her, that she must go to work. But I remember . . . remember that age and how strongly one feels such things. I think it's best to give Martha a few days to recover."

"Of course. It's no problem for us to find someone to fill in for her at the desk. I wanted to assure you that I will hold her job."

Pam nodded in agreement and added, "We also wanted to ask if there's anything we can do."

"*Nein.* There's nothing to be done. Time will heal most wounds, and the ones not healed? Those we learn to live with."

Pam and Amber returned to the car and drove next to Letha's. This time the problem wasn't that she'd not showed up for work. Letha had come into work the day before, and today was her regularly scheduled day off. The reason they were going to Letha's was the handwritten note she had left for Amber. She'd actually given it to Elizabeth and told her it was important.

Indeed it was.

Letha did not invite them in. She had walked out to the car when they first drove into the lane. Instead of asking them inside, she stood beneath the willow tree to talk. She wore her traditional dark Amish dress and *kapp*, and on her ankles Amber was happy to see the white socks with an embroidered border. However, the good news stopped there. Letha crossed her arms, a stubborn look on her face, and waited for the inquisition to begin.

"You can't leave, Letha. Over a man? Over Ryan?" Amber had thought of a dozen ways to reason with her, but the woman's silence provoked her into her last resort—guilt. "No one can run the fashions shop the way you do. You know this. We talked about it at lunch. You have a special flair."

"Even I've purchased items from your shop— and I usually go to specialty stores." Pam frowned and then gazed up at the sky. The rain had stopped, but it was temporary. The air was thick and no doubt they were in for the real storm soon.

"Don't throw away what you've worked for," Amber said.

Those words finally loosened Letha's tongue.

"Worked for? I've worked for you. Did you think I was building an empire in fashion? *Nein*. It's not our *plain* way." She said the word *plain* with unmitigated skepticism. "And if you think

310

I'm leaving over Ryan Duvall, you are sadly mistaken. I'm leaving for myself."

"To Pinecraft?"

"*Ya.* I've always wanted to go there. I've had enough with our Indiana winters and our Indiana ways. A change will do me good."

"It might do you good in April," Pam agreed. "Come June or July you might feel differently. Have you ever been in Florida during the summer?"

"*Nein.*"

"You're going to be wishing for Indiana—trust me. I'm from the South. I know how hot and humid the weather can be."

Letha raised her chin in defiance, but didn't offer a response.

"Please reconsider, Letha. We care about you— Pam and I both will miss you so if you leave."

"You've been a *gut* boss and a *gut* friend. You both have." Letha hesitated, then plunged on. "Is my heart broken? *Nein.* But it's sore. I thought I was special to him."

Amber didn't know what to say to that, so she said nothing.

"I'm not a *kind.* I know these feelings will pass. That's why I want to leave before they do. That's why I'm leaving on the bus this Friday. I know two weeks' notice is customary, but I also know you have backups. I need to leave as soon as possible."

"I don't understand," Pam said.

"Don't you? You're a single woman, like me." Letha glanced from Pam to Amber. "It hasn't been that long since you were unmarried."

Amber thought back to the conversation they'd had at the coffee shop when Letha had reminded her of the days before she'd fallen in love with Tate.

"These last few weeks, I have envisioned an entirely different life—one where I'm not alone. I've realized that I want to marry, if it's *Gotte*'s *wille* for me. But I don't see how that's possible here. Not only have I made a fool of myself, but I know all the men in our district as if they were my *bruders*."

Letha pulled Amber into a hug, and then clasped Pam's hand. "*Danki*, both of you. But I will take my chances in a new community. The change, it will do me *gut*."

Amber and Pam finally left, depressed and discouraged.

"How can one man cause this much trouble?" Amber asked.

"I knew that boy was going to be a problem when I first laid eyes on him."

"We might as well go see Georgia."

"Why not? Maybe we can get something to eat. All this coffee is making me hungry."

But they didn't eat.

Georgia was working in the bakery, and she

said she didn't have time to come out and talk with them. So they abandoned their booth and went back into the kitchen.

"If you're here to talk to me about Ryan Duvall, I'm much too busy for such silliness."

Amber and Pam shared a glance.

"Don't think I haven't heard about your visiting Letha and Martha."

"We just got back," Pam said. "How . . . ?"

Georgia waved away her protest with a flour-covered hand. "No matter. Word travels fast."

She dusted the piecrust she was rolling out and set it into a baking pan. Amber noticed she was wearing a pretty pink lipstick, but her new hairdo looked a bit disheveled, as if she'd become frustrated with it and given up. "I don't need your pep talk, and I don't need your sympathy. What I need is to get my work done."

So they'd left her to her baking. There didn't seem to be much more they could do.

As if the day hadn't been depressing enough, they bumped into Preston as they walked toward the office. He was holding a piece of paper in his hand, looking completely dumbfounded.

At first Amber thought it must be another poison note, but then she saw the LaGrange County Court insignia across the top.

"I've been served . . . with this."

Mocha whined, as if she understood her part in the situation.

"A restraining order?" Amber read the sheet twice and then handed it to Pam.

"He's gone too far now." Pam studied the paper before thrusting it back into Preston's hands. "Who does Ryan Duvall think he is? He's the one causing all this trouble and then he issues a restraining order against you?"

"And my dog."

"It's okay, Mocha. You're a good dog." Amber reached into her pocket and pulled out a dog treat.

Preston shook his head in mock disgust.

"What? You let Hannah feed him."

Instead of answering, he refolded the restraining order and stuck it into his back pocket.

"It's no matter to me. I'd be happy not to lay eyes on Ryan for a very long time. How are the girls?"

So they shared their fruitless attempts to bring a sense of resolution to the Ryan Duvall problem. As they discussed the situation, Amber realized the day had been a total failure.

They would have talked about it longer, but Preston received a text that a truck was ready to unload some of the supplies for the Race for a Cure. Pam remembered a meeting she had with housekeeping, and Amber realized she hadn't checked her e-mail in hours. But there was nothing there—nothing out of the ordinary. The last few hours of the workday passed without any escalating events. By the time she went home, she wanted to put up her feet, grab a good book, and forget about any trouble at the Village.

Fortunately, she was able to do just that—at least for one night, before trouble once again found her friends.

Thirty-One

Amber had just climbed into bed the next night when she realized they'd left Leo outside.

"I'll get him," Tate murmured with a groan.

"Stay where you are. I'm pretty sure I forgot to put my phone on the charger. I'll take care of both and be back in a flash."

She found her phone on the table beside the recliner. Plugging it into the charger she kept in the kitchen, she resisted the urge to check her e-mail. No one would have sent her a message so late in the evening. She was halfway back to the bedroom when she remembered the cat.

Usually Leo went outside for a half hour or so, then pawed on the door to ask to be let back in. What had happened to him? Hopefully he wasn't becoming a tomcat.

Amber turned on the front porch light and unlocked the door. Stepping outside she saw Leo, lying on his side. At first she thought he had fallen asleep, but then her mind registered the pie pan, the pool of vomit next to him, and the fact that he wasn't breathing.

Was he breathing?

She fell to her knees beside him and put her hand gently on his tummy. There was a rise and fall, but just barely. She didn't realize she was screaming until Tate came barreling out the door.

"What is it? What's wrong?"

By that point, she had scooped Leo up into her arms. Tears were streaming down her face. She shouldered past him, back into the house, and Tate said, "I'll get the truck keys."

Amber grabbed a small afghan off the couch and wrapped it around her ginger cat. He still hadn't opened his eyes, hadn't acknowledged her in any way.

She found herself praying that Leo would hold on, that they would be able to reach the vet, that some maniac had not succeeded in killing her cat.

Tate drove while Amber held the cat in her arms. She called their vet—Dr. England—on her cell phone and reached him on the first try.

Closing the phone's case, she said, "He's going to meet us at the clinic."

They didn't speak the rest of the way, but Tate reached over and petted Leo, then clasped her hand. Amber prayed. Yes, she knew he was only a cat, but he was her cat and she adored him.

Dr. England—a very large man with a handlebar mustache—met them at the door. Amber had used him for the animals on the Village property and as her personal veterinarian for years. That was the only reason she had his direct number rather than having to go through his answering service. She explained quickly about finding Leo on the porch, the pie pan, and the vomit.

"Is there any reason someone would have wanted to poison your cat?"

Amber and Tate exchanged a quick glance. Tate said, "There is actually a pretty good chance that's what happened. Any idea what they would have used?"

"Quickest and easiest substance to poison an animal?" Dr. England's mustache drooped as his frown grew more pronounced. "Freon. You can buy it anywhere, and the sweet taste attracts them. Let me take this guy to the back. Hopefully you found him in time."

They waited in the front room, the bright lights reflecting off the windows and blocking out any view of the night. To Amber it seemed that they were there for hours, as if the sun would rise before they knew anything, but in fact Dr. England was back within an hour.

"I did a urinalysis, which detected a high concentration of calcium oxalate crystals in his urine—Freon. That's the bad news. The good news is that there was no blood, protein, or glucose in the urine—which means that you found him within a few minutes of his digesting the tainted substance."

"So he's going to be okay?" Amber clutched Tate's hand.

"I can't promise anything, but my opinion? Yes, he's going to be fine. He's a tough little guy, and you did the right thing bringing him here immediately."

"Can we . . . can we take him home?"

"Maybe tomorrow. I've administered ethanol to counterbalance the effect of the Freon, but he needs treatment to correct the imbalance in his fluids and electrolytes." Dr. England stood, shook Tate's hand, and squeezed Amber's arm. "Let me keep him on an IV for twelve more hours and then watch him another twelve after that. Feel free to call tomorrow morning and check on his condition."

"You'll call us if there's any change?" Amber's knees felt weak with relief, and she was suddenly so tired she wasn't sure she could walk back outside to the truck.

"Of course. Now go home and get some sleep." He added with a smile, "You'll want to be rested when you see my bill."

Together Amber and Tate walked back out into the night. As he opened the truck door, she turned and stared up into his face. "You know what this means? Whoever is behind this, they've moved from bragging and planning to actually doing . . . and the next time, they might poison more than an animal. The next time it could be one of our friends."

Preston's eyes opened the first time Mocha whined. She was a good sleeper, a quiet sleeper, and the only time she'd ever wakened him was when she needed to—when she was alerting on his PTSD. This was different. She didn't push her nose into his hand or stand near him with her paws on the side of the bed.

He reached down and found the top of her head in the darkness. "What is it, girl? What's wrong?"

Mocha's answer was another low whine. She didn't leave his side. She was trained to stay with him, especially at night, but there was something raising her hackles.

Preston tossed the covers back. He'd been in a deep sleep. As he stood the details flooded back over him—yet another dream where he'd been running and worried. It hadn't been a flashback, though. This time his dream had been about Zoey and the Village and a dark shadow. There had been an urgency as he'd hurried across the back side of the property, but he'd known somewhere deep inside that he could catch whoever or whatever it was—if he could just move a little faster. He'd felt certain about that, and perhaps his certainty had been why Mocha hadn't alerted to his nightmare. Perhaps his confidence had been obvious even in his sleep.

Maybe she only alerted to fear.

So what had wakened her?

"Let's check it out, girl."

He pulled on the blue jeans he'd folded over the chair next to his bed.

Mocha padded beside him as he walked from the bedroom to the living room. The *Dawdy Haus* was small, which was one of the things he liked about it. He had a glimpse out the front window even before he entered the living room. The full moon was high and bright after the showers and clouds of the last few days. He could easily see the person sitting in the rocker and the long shadow stretching across the wooden porch floor. A glance at the clock told him it was nearly two thirty, much too late—or too early—for someone to be stopping by. Especially without knocking.

Preston motioned for Mocha to sit. He reached up and flicked on the porch light at the same moment he turned the dead bolt lock. Then he pulled open the door and stepped outside to confront his late-night visitor.

One look at Ryan Duvall's face—at the fatigue in his eyes and the wounds across his cheek— told him that the situation had once again changed. He wouldn't be going back to sleep anytime soon.

The porch was cold on his bare feet. The discomfort assured him this wasn't another bad dream.

Instead of inviting Ryan inside, he called to Mocha. She joined him on the porch in less time than it took for Ryan to stand and stuff his hands into his pockets. Preston gave Mocha the all-is-well signal, and she ambled off the porch, sticking close but taking advantage of the unexpected middle-of-the-night bathroom break.

"Preston."

Preston nodded but didn't speak. What was he going to say? That Ryan looked terrible? That he had no business being on his porch? That he should be ashamed of himself for filing the restraining order against him? Come to think of it, he was probably breaching that order being so close to Ryan, though it was the man's own fault, coming to his house this way.

"I didn't know where else to go." Ryan answered in response to the question Preston hadn't asked.

"For . . ."

"Safety? I don't know." Ryan scrubbed his hand across his face, the portion of his face that was unscathed.

It was apparent he hadn't shaved in several days. The stubble was dark and heavy on his chin and cheeks. His clothes were rumpled and his hair unkempt. Then there was the dried blood caked into the long scratches down the left side of his face and across his forehead. He had the look of someone who was on the run, someone who had no place to sleep, nowhere to spend the hours until dawn's light dispelled his fears.

It was that last thought that caused Preston to invite him inside.

"I'll make some coffee. Looks like neither of us is going to get any sleep."

Ryan remained silent until they were sitting at the kitchen table, Mocha lying on the floor between them.

"She seems like a good dog."

"She is."

"I shouldn't have said what I did."

"I know."

Ryan raised the coffee mug to his lips, then set it back down, his hand shaking slightly. "I'm sorry."

Preston nodded. He could easily forget the slights and even the bad decision Ryan had made in filing the restraining order. He couldn't so easily forgive the chaos he was causing in Letha's, Georgia's, and Martha's lives.

"Someone's following me. I don't know who or why."

Preston didn't even think about doubting him. Ryan might be a playboy, and he might make immature decisions as far as his personal life, but a guy knew when someone was watching. Call it primal instinct. His mind flashed back on Wanat and the desert and the certain feeling when you had been sighted in by someone else's weapon. He pushed the memory away, but not before Mocha raised her head and licked his hand once, then resettled.

"How? With a surveillance device?"

"I thought it might be a bug—some sort of listening device. Apparently you can purchase them at Radio Shack now or any of a dozen different internet sites." Ryan stared into his coffee. "So yeah, I went to the PD."

"And?"

"They swept my car and my person. Couldn't find anything. Suggested I get some sleep and lay off the caffeine."

Preston glanced down at their coffee mugs and shrugged. It was none of his business what Ryan did or didn't drink.

"Why are you here?"

"I don't have any place else to go. My parents are ready to disown me after the situation at the horse show—after the scene with the ladies and you. They've suggested I look for somewhere else to live. I left their house on Monday and have been trying to decide what to do."

"Might be a good idea for you to get your own place."

"Except I'm not signing a lease until I know who is following me. Someone is, and I'd rather they not know my new address. Maybe it would be better if I leave town. I don't know."

"So you came here?"

Ryan hesitated, then blurted out, "Everyone knows your combat history. You're practically a celebrity after the piece in the paper about—"

"Mocha." When the local reporter called, Zoey had encouraged him to share his story so others with severe PTSD could know how a dog like Mocha could help them.

"Right." Ryan shook his head. "I was wrong about you and about her. I knew that when I was going off on you, and yes, even as I filed the restraining order. Some things seem to take on their own momentum, and I was angry. Honestly, I was embarrassed."

When Preston didn't contradict him, Ryan continued. "I was even wrong about the way I treated the ladies, though I swear I didn't realize it at the time. I was wrong about a lot of things."

"Have you told them that?"

"I tried! None of them will talk to me."

For the first time since he'd wakened, Preston wanted to smile. If Letha and Martha and even Georgia were learning to be wary, to question people's motives . . . maybe the experience with Ryan had served a useful purpose. Maybe God had used it for good.

"Could it be a brother or a dad following you? Someone who wants a little revenge for how you treated these women? Maybe they want to balance the scales a little, or possibly they hope to catch you doing something you shouldn't be doing."

"Maybe, but Letha and Martha are Amish. What you're suggesting is pretty aggressive. Have you ever seen an Amish guy act that way?"

Preston's mind flashed back on Owen Esch's murder six months earlier. He decided not to mention it. The two situations couldn't be related, and besides, Owen's killer was in prison.

"No, I don't see it." Ryan shook his head, then gulped from the coffee mug.

"What about Georgia's family?"

"One brother. He's a piece of work himself. Drinks a lot, lives out toward Goshen. I don't think he'd notice if I robbed her blind."

When Preston didn't respond to that, Ryan took another long drink of the coffee, and then stared out the back window, out into the night.

"I wouldn't hurt them on purpose, you know. I might not have understood that what I was doing would . . . well, make them feel used. I honestly didn't think they'd even know about each other, and if they did find out, I thought they'd understand that it was a game, entertainment of sorts. Life in a small town can be slow. And I thought . . . well, I thought if everybody had a good time there would be no problem. No harm, no foul."

"But there was harm." Preston thought of telling him about Martha sobbing in Hannah's arms, about Letha's decision to leave Middlebury, even about Georgia's refusal to discuss the situation with anyone. In the end, he remained silent. It wasn't his place to share those things. If the women wanted Ryan Duvall to know their feelings or their future plans, they'd tell him.

"Yeah, I know that now."

"But—"

"I do have a moral compass. I'm not a terrible person, despite what you might think, what you have every right to think. I know my life is a mess right now, but I do know right from wrong."

"So someone is following you, but they're not related to the women, and you don't know what they want."

"Exactly."

"And you'd like me to help you."

"Yes, I would."

Preston didn't blink.

He didn't move at all.

He thought about Zoey and how satisfied he was to have the certainty of her love. He remembered the night he had torn apart the bedroom down the hall, and how hopeless their future had seemed. He thought about driving off the road when Amber was with him, and how frightened he had been that he might have hurt her. He had needed help, but he hadn't known how to ask for it. He couldn't even imagine what form that help would take.

Glancing down at Mocha reminded him of how quickly life could turn around, of how God knew his needs—and began providing for them —before he knew what to ask for.

"If you want my help, you're going to need to tell me what else you're into."

Ryan's face reddened slightly, then he cleared his throat and told Preston the rest of his story.

Thirty-Two

"So you're betting on racehorses?"

"Yeah. Don't look at me like it's the worst sin you can imagine."

"And you were up."

"I was."

"But now you're down."

"Way down."

Neither spoke as the clock ticked past three a.m. Finally Preston stood and refilled their coffee mugs, found the leftover cinnamon rolls Zoey had baked, and brought it all to the table. It wasn't so much that he needed the sugar to think, but he'd learned long ago to eat when he had the chance. This might be one of those situations where he wouldn't have another chance for some time—depending on what Ryan chose, depending on whether he was actually willing to turn his life around.

"So you were down. How much down?" When Ryan only stared at him, Preston named a number. Ryan held out his thumb, pointing down.

Letting out a whistle, Preston asked, "More? How much more?"

When Ryan confessed to the amount, Preston knew there was only one answer to his problem.

"And they came looking for you?"

"Yeah. At first it was only phone calls. They called my bets, and I didn't have the money. I told them I'd get it, but we both knew I couldn't, so they showed up. Here in Middlebury, tonight when I was out taking a walk. I'd left my car near the motel where I've been staying since Monday night. I have my wallet, but that's about it."

That's why Preston hadn't seen a car in his driveway.

"And you ran?"

Ryan's hand went to the left side of his face. "They had a gun, but I didn't think they would use it. Not in the middle of town."

"But they were chasing you in a car, right? If you'd gotten into it—"

"Yeah. That would have been bad. Probably someone would have found my body in the lake."

More likely in a cornfield where wild animals —coyotes and buzzards—would take care of any evidence, but Preston didn't suggest that. No need to rattle Ryan more than he already was.

"I ran through the park, dodged off the path. They didn't expect that, and they sure didn't know their way around Middlebury. By the time I hit the Pumpkinvine Trail, no one was behind me."

"And that's how you scratched up your face?"

"I suppose. I didn't even feel it when it happened."

Preston stood, carried both of their mugs to the sink, and rinsed them out. Then he returned to the table and met Ryan's stare dead-on.

"You're sure you lost these guys in the park?"

"Yes."

"But you think you were still somehow followed here, to the Village?"

"I don't think I was followed. I know I was followed." He pulled his cell phone out of his shirt pocket, swiped through some screens, and then handed it to Preston.

Preston hadn't owned a cell phone until he'd taken the position of assistant manager of maintenance. Amber had insisted he carry one at that point. It was less expensive for the Village to pay for a cell phone than it would have been to install telephone service at the *Dawdy Haus*. Plus she needed to be able to reach him anywhere.

So he'd accepted the phone and become familiar with how much the technology had changed. Things that had been difficult to do with a desktop computer when he'd left for Afghanistan were now routinely done by anyone with a cell phone. He'd caught up to speed as far as the advances in telecommunications, but he was still surprised each time he picked one up and realized that basically he was holding a very small computer.

Ryan had swiped to a screen that was filled with text messages. All the ones he was looking at were from the same number, with no name attached to the tag—only the word *anonymous*. The last one had been at two twenty in the morning, apparently at the time Ryan had arrived at his house. It read—

"Hiding at the Village is a bad idea."

Scanning up, he read the previous messages in reverse order.

"On the trail at this hour?"

"Sleeping in a barn? Isn't that below you?"

Preston glanced up at Ryan, his finger on the word *barn*.

Ryan nodded. "I was in the Amish Village barn tonight—for a few hours—until I realized I couldn't stay there forever. That was when I decided to come here."

The messages continued up for several pages, though they were apparently coming in with increasing frequency. They weren't specific, but there was a prevailing tone of warning, of ill feelings. Finally he set the phone down on the table and pushed it back toward Ryan.

"I don't know who is following you, or why.

My suggestion would be to get a new phone and a different, unlisted number."

Ryan nodded.

"But whoever is sending those texts isn't your most immediate problem."

"Why do you say that?"

"Because there is no inherent threat in them. Last I heard the collectors for the on-line betting network . . . let's just say they aren't known for their tact. They would have promised to break your legs or shoot out your kneecaps or maybe just beat you up badly enough that you'd need to spend a few weeks in the hospital."

"How did you know it was on-line betting?"

"There isn't a casino within a hundred miles of here. You had to work through a bookie or on-line betting, and a bookie wouldn't have let you get down that much. Plus these days the majority of the money from betting is coming through on-line."

"How do you know that?"

"I had a buddy, a few years back. He got in deep. It took four of us emptying our savings to pull him out."

"You did that for him?"

Preston shrugged. "He was in our unit. He would have done it for us. Last I heard, he's stayed out of trouble and is living somewhere in Montana."

Ryan brushed his hand—back and forth, back

and forth—across the table. "So I dodged a bullet this time. But I'm not in a unit. I don't have any friends who would bail me out. I have never had any friends like that. And those three women— the only women I've been seeing these last weeks? They wouldn't have even called nine-one-one if they'd seen those thugs trying to pull me into their Cadillac."

"There's a reason they didn't bother to continue chasing you."

When Ryan only stared at him, Preston continued. "They don't have to chase you. Sooner or later you'll come back. Sooner or later you'll use a credit card to get some money, or your Social Security number to get a job. It's difficult to stay completely off the grid, and you aren't exactly the survivalist type. So they'll wait, and they'll show up again. But next time they'll have more guys. Next time they'll be sure you can't run."

"You're telling me I'm out of options." Ryan's voice had taken on a grim resignation that Preston recognized all too well.

He'd talked to himself in the same tone for years, every time he thought his was a hopeless case. Every time he was ready to give up and needed only one more excuse to do so.

"You're not out of options, Ryan. The question is whether you're willing to do what you have to do."

"What—"

"You go home to your father. I'll drive you."

"No." Ryan stood and began pacing. "No. I can't—"

"You go home. You apologize. You let him bail you out of this mess, and then you work at earning back his respect."

Tears clouded Ryan's eyes as he sank back into the chair. He moved to rub his hand across his face. Then he remembered about the scratches and allowed his hand to fall. "I can't."

"Too proud? Better to live as a servant in your father's house than to eat with the pigs in a foreign land."

"Huh?"

"New Testament—parable of the prodigal son."

Preston thought about his years on the streets, his father living in the house alone, probably wondering if he was still alive, staring out the front window every night and wondering if that would be the night he would come home. Gerald had never reprimanded him. Even after his father had told him about the Alzheimer's diagnosis, he'd never once lashed out at him for being selfish or for abandoning his only family. The day Preston walked back into his life, he'd accepted him as if he'd never been gone. Preston had never imagined that degree of love or of grace. As much as Zoey or Mocha, his father had changed his life.

He thought of his dad, sleeping on the other

side of the Village. He thought of the expression on his father's face every time Preston walked through the door of Grace Homes—happy, smiling, but not surprised. As if he had known his son would come, that his son would be there for him. His father had never stopped watching for him, never stopped believing in him.

"The story of the prodigal son isn't only about the son, Ryan. It's also about the father." And with that he stood, walked to his bedroom, and put on his shoes. By the time he was back in the living room, picking up his keys to the old Volkswagen, Ryan was standing looking out the front door.

"And the phone? The texts?"

"Drop the phone in the pond on your dad's place. You don't need it anymore."

Side by side, they walked forward into the darkness.

As the two of them stepped out onto the porch, Mocha close at their heels, Preston felt somewhat bad that his attention wasn't totally on Ryan and his problems. The evening had rattled something loose in Preston's heart. Hearing Ryan's problems and the details of his various relationships had been a rude awakening for Preston.

He was incredibly blessed to have a simple and peaceful life, to have help with his disability, and to have a beautiful woman he was certain would be willing to share his future with him.

What had he been afraid of? Why had he wasted so much time? And now that he could see clearly how precious each day was, what was he going to do about it?

Thirty-Three

Everyone stared at Amber in disbelief as she shared the details of Leo's poisoning and their trip to the vet's the night before. She was sitting with Hannah, Pam, and Preston in a booth at the back of the Village restaurant. She finished up with the doctor's morning prognosis, and then took a sip from her coffee, though the bitter taste turned her stomach a bit queasy.

"You're sure Leo is going to be fine?" Hannah nervously ran her fingers up and down her *kapp* strings.

"Yes, but it may be a while before we let him wander outside again. At least not as long as this maniac is leaving notes and pies."

"There was another note?"

"No. Not with the pie that poisoned Leo, but Gordon still thinks this must be the same person. He says no note could be a sign that he or she is getting sloppy, not more dangerous."

They were all silent for a moment. Amber was sure they were thinking the same thing she'd said to Tate last night—that one of their friends could be next, no matter what Gordon thought.

Maybe she should tell them about this morning's e-mail, but she wasn't sure. Possibly it would only frighten them more than they needed to be.

Preston frowned down at his food, and then he proceeded to tell them about his meeting with Ryan Duvall. Mocha rested on the floor under the table, brushing up against their feet. They made for a tight fit, but somehow Amber felt the coziness was helping to calm her nerves—that and the information Preston had just shared. Perhaps that problem had finally been resolved.

"So his dad took him back? Just like that?" Amber asked.

Preston nodded as he forked a piece of chicken pot pie into his mouth.

The look on his face was close to bliss, and it was a sight that eased Amber's heart. It would seem that Preston was well on his way to a normal life. She expected an engagement announcement any day, and wouldn't that be appropriate? They might have three spring weddings—Hannah and Jesse, Mary and Andrew, Preston and Zoey. She vowed to double her crocheting efforts—there were afghans to be made, a much more personal wedding gift than something she might have ordered on-line. She was learning, probably from Hannah's example, that home-made gifts often were the most treasured.

"Do you think he's changed? Is Ryan cured

from being a . . . playboy?" Hannah took a sip from her glass of water.

She'd opted for a bowl of fruit rather than pie. Amber suspected she was watching her weight in light of the upcoming wedding. Folks thought Amish women didn't worry about such things. In Amber's experience, every woman did— though perhaps Amish women didn't allow it to become something they dwelled on.

"Who can say?" Preston took a sip of his coffee. "He certainly seemed repentant. Even one night with nowhere to go can change a man's perspective, and I honestly believe he didn't realize the effect his behavior was having on the women involved. Now that he doesn't have to worry about the gambling folks hunting him down—"

"Do you think it was the mob?" Pam glanced around, as if a member of the Chicago mob might be in the Amish Village restaurant, lurking behind a piece of pie and a cup of coffee. "I watched a movie about the mob the other night. Those people are ruthless. They'll kidnap your granny if it will get them the money . . ."

Preston shrugged. "No way to know. I'm just glad the men who were looking for Ryan won't be hanging around Middlebury any longer."

"Have you two alerted Gordon to this?" Amber asked.

"No." Preston glanced away and then back at

her. "Ryan called me from Indianapolis just before I came here. I suggested he call Gordon, but he said his father had just paid the balance of what he owed down there, and he's taken a vow to never gamble again. He said he doesn't want to embarrass his family more by bringing it to the attention of the police."

"Huh. Sounds like he's thinking of someone besides himself. That's a good start." Pam pressed a hand across her scarf, which was covered with different types and colors of butterflies. "Too bad this didn't happen before he hurt Georgia, Letha, and Martha."

No one had an answer to that. Letha had informed them that she was leaving for Pinecraft today. It still seemed like a drastic move to Amber, but she'd learned nothing ever stayed the same. Perhaps the change would be healthy for Letha. Perhaps she could regain her self-respect and rediscover the things that made her happy, with or without a man.

Georgia apparently had returned to her bakery after the horse show incident no worse for the wear. She just wouldn't talk about it.

"I spoke with Martha yesterday. It's good to see her back at work, but she still seems"— Hannah searched for the word—"somber."

"A pretty girl like that, she won't have any trouble attracting attention from a young Amish man. The woods are thick with them around here." Pam looked surprised when they all laughed at her. "What did I say?"

"What about the text messages Ryan was receiving?" Amber motioned for one of the waitresses to come and pick up their dishes. "Did they stop?"

"I suppose they did. I saw Ryan throw the phone into the pond as we were driving up to his father's house, and he called me on his dad's phone this morning. If he's selective about who he gives a new number to, he shouldn't be bothered by them again."

Together they walked outside, after Amber stopped and signed the receipt that would put the cost of their meals on the company ledger. They paused outside the door of the restaurant, watching as the grounds crew added colorful touches to every conceivable surface. The race would support research for every type of cancer, and the decorations reflected that. Balloons would be delivered early the next morning.

Amber and Pam had chosen lavender for the balloons because it represented all cancers. The ribbons and flowers were more specific: pink for breast cancer, violet for Hodgkin's lymphoma, teal for ovarian cancer. She had never realized before how many different types of cancers there were. A quick Google search had revealed over sixty different kinds, and although she couldn't find that many different flowers, she did her best. The American Cancer Society had provided ribbons for participants. The box that had arrived the day before held a rainbow of colors.

It seemed to Amber that the event was bringing together people with different types of trials and difficulties, and that together they would be able to immerse themselves in two common hopes—cures and treatments for loved ones.

"The dating debacle is over just in time." Pam tied her scarf, which was attempting to blow away. The wind was gusting, as it had the tendency to do in the spring.

"Now we can focus on Race for a Cure." Hannah reached up to tug down her *kapp*. "Forecast is perfect for tomorrow. We should have a good crowd." Preston clipped Mocha's leash to her ICAN vest. She stood close to him, pressed against his leg. Her blonde coat sparkled in the afternoon sun, and her fluffy tail swished back and forth in a lackadaisical rhythm. Occasionally she would glance up at him, as if she were assuring herself he was fine.

Amber knew the dog didn't need the leash. She followed Preston as if she were his shadow, but Preston faithfully clipped the leash whenever they were in public. It was a good practice, as the ICAN rep—Tomas—had told them. The day they had first gone to Fort Wayne and met with Tomas and met Mocha seemed about a hundred years ago. The last few weeks had been packed with drama and heartache and uncertainty. They had been more than busy; they had been exhausting. Thank goodness it had all ended well. All except for the poison poet.

"What are you thinking about?" Pam squinted at her. "You have that look, the one that means we're about to find ourselves in the middle of something."

"It's nothing."

When Preston, Hannah, and Pam all looked at her expectantly, she couldn't help laughing. When she did, part of the tightness in her chest eased. "It's the poison poet. I received another message this morning. I still can't imagine what this person hopes to gain by leaving bad poetry in my mailbox or at my office or in the bakery!"

"And why claim to put poison into pies that you then label as poisonous?" Hannah shook her head. "It doesn't make any sense."

"Especially since the lab work showed none of those pies actually contained poison." Pam rolled her eyes.

"But what did the e-mail say?" Preston asked.

"It didn't say anything about Leo, which surprised—and kind of angered—me. But it did say I didn't have to 'worry about poison on race day.' That was it. It wasn't even in the form of bad poetry. Again, Gordon seems to think this is a good sign. Maybe our poet realizes they have crossed a line poisoning a cat. Maybe this is nearly over."

"We still need to know who the person is, though." Hannah crossed her arms. "We need to catch them. How do we go about our lives, when we know they're still on the loose, waiting to wreak havoc?"

"Gordon's doing everything he can. He sent all the notes to the state lab, and the technicians were able to determine that they were created on a typewriter rather than a computer. Whoever owns it has to purchase ribbons for the thing, so they're pursuing the case through that avenue."

"They might not purchase them at a local store," Pam pointed out. "We order our supplies on-line. In fact, we even have a few of those typewriters around the Village. I know because I just updated the equipment inventory."

Amber hitched her purse strap up higher on her shoulder. "Could you get me that list?"

"Sure, but I was headed out to oversee marking the finish line for the race. Would Monday be all right?"

"Monday's perfect."

Preston's phone rang at that moment. He answered it, then nodded and waved at everyone as he walked away, pausing only to mutter, "Someone got the directional signs for the race messed up. I'm heading over to straighten it out."

And so Pam, Hannah, and Amber stood in the afternoon sun on the day before the big race.

Amber, for one, was hoping the poison poet's latest e-mail really did mean all would be well for at least one day—especially with the Ryan Duvall debacle behind them.

Thirty-Four

Hannah was determined to put the fear and anxiety behind her for at least one day. Jesse picked her up early the next morning. Usually they both walked to work, but since it was the day of the race they were riding in Jesse's buggy.

Both wanted to arrive at the Village early. Hannah stepped out onto the porch a few moments before seven. The sun was peeking over the eastern field. She took in the colors painted across the sky for a few moments, appreciating the quiet and the beauty around her. For a few brief moments, she was lost in thoughts of the future—her marriage to Jesse, her move, the children God would surely bless them with.

The sound of clip-clops brought her attention back to the present, and she saw Jesse turning Sadie, the female half of his Morgan Shire team, into her lane.

Sadie looked content to be pulling the buggy so early in the morning, if a horse could be content. Hannah thought they could. The mare was a cross between a Morgan and a Shire. Hannah thought she was the prettiest horse around. Her roan color was only broken by the white on her mane, and she had a habit of nodding gently as she pulled at an even trot.

Hannah called out a good-bye to her mother, who was cooking breakfast for her dad and brothers in the kitchen, and practically skipped to the buggy.

"You have a nice bounce in your step this morning, Hannah Bell."

She climbed into the buggy, leaned over, and kissed Jesse on the cheek, then wrapped the buggy blanket across her lap. At this time of morning in early May, it was still a bit cool.

"I slept well, so I suppose I do have a little extra energy."

"And is that the only reason for your *gut* mood?"

"I'm riding to work with you and Sadie."

"It's going to be a *gut* day, *ya*?"

"I think so, Jesse. I spoke with Martha yesterday as I was leaving the Village. She seemed so much better. It did my heart *gut* to see her smile for the first time since this terrible mess began a few weeks ago."

"So she is over her episode with Ryan?"

"Maybe. She did say he deserves whatever happens to him, but I'm not sure what that meant."

"Sounds a bit ominous."

"I don't think she intended it that way. She mentioned her plans to go to the singing this Sunday—"

"A good sign."

"And then she said Ryan's decisions weren't her problem. That maybe he had changed, maybe he hadn't, but either way whatever happens in the future is a direct result of his actions."

"She seems to have wiped her hands of him," Hannah added meekly.

"Sounds as if she is letting go." Jesse reached over and squeezed her hand, then changed the subject. "This is the last big event of the spring, Hannah. Now we can sit back, rest, and maybe enjoy a little summer fishing."

She slapped his arm. "Jesse Miller, our wedding is in ten days. Have you forgotten that next week we need to deliver our wedding invitations? Not to mention finishing the rooms you and Andrew are building on to your parents' home. Last I checked the walls still lacked any paint."

Jesse's laughter rang out through the morning air. "I have not forgotten. In fact, Andrew and I were working on the rooms last night." He spent the rest of the short ride describing the bathroom they were putting in between their bedroom and Andrew and Mary's.

It was hard to believe that in less than two weeks they would all be living under the same roof. Jesse would no longer be picking her up in the morning. She'd be waking up beside him! A blush warmed her cheeks as they pulled into the parking lot of the Village. Henry Yoder waved them to a stop at the parking booth.

"Busy morning." Jesse glanced out over the top of Sadie. The horse didn't seem concerned about the parking lot full of cars or the crowds of people.

"*Ya.* I came in an hour early, and there were already folks parking their vehicles and walking about. The parking area is filling up fast, but I left Sadie's favorite spot open."

"*Danki*, Henry."

"Amber said I could close the booth and watch the finish of the race. What time do you think I should walk over?"

"Race starts at eight o'clock sharp. It's only a 5k, but there are several categories, so folks will be starting at different times."

"How can they race each other if they start at different times?"

"Each category starts a few minutes apart, to avoid congestion. Also, that way you don't have teens running over the old folks. I'd say close up at eight thirty and you'll be fine."

"That's what I was thinking."

Hannah leaned across Jesse so Henry could hear her. "We'll save you a spot at the finish line, right next to The Quilting Bee."

"I'll be there."

Henry waved them on, and Jesse directed Sadie to a shaded area at the far corner of the parking lot.

"It's *gut* to see so many people, Jesse. Think how much money we're going to be able to raise. Think what it could mean to the people with cancer."

Jesse set the brake on the buggy, climbed down, and walked around to Hannah's side. "You were smiling big enough to rival the sun a few minutes ago."

He helped her down out of the buggy. "Now you have that somber look, which must mean that you're thinking about Sarah."

She didn't want to meet his eyes, didn't want to start crying when she saw the sympathy there. Instead she stared at his light blue cotton shirt. He wore his dark suspenders over them, and in that moment he seemed so solid, so steady, that she wanted to throw herself in his arms and simply stay there. Instead she admitted, "Everyone says her treatments are going well, but it hurts me to see her suffer so."

"Suffering is a difficult part of life, but an important part all the same—as Bishop Joseph reminded us during his last sermon."

"*Ya*, though it's not a part I care to dwell on. We deal with it when we have to, but . . ." Her voice softened as she moved toward Sadie and stroked the mare between her ears. "I remember

Sarah when she was so healthy and able to do anything you or I can."

"Sarah is still under *Gotte*'s care, Hannah. No need for you to worry yourself so. But I understand how it bothers you to see her in pain."

"Reuben is hurting too. I wish you could see him smile each time we visit. Each time Mattie hands him some shiny rock she's picked up or flowers she's pulled along the walk to their house. Her gifts cost nothing, but they ease the pain in Reuben's life. They brighten his world for a moment."

"And those are the things you need to think on. Store up your *gut* memories—Mattie's flowers and Reuben's smiles and days like today." No one was near them in their corner of the parking lot. Jesse stepped closer and pulled her into the circle of his arms.

As she stood there, feeling Jesse's heart beat against hers, it was easy for Hannah to believe that everything was going to be fine. Martha's heart would heal, and Letha would find what she was seeking in Pinecraft. Sarah's treatments would be successful. Their wedding would proceed without a hitch.

It was easy to believe this day would be filled with nothing but joy.

Though Amber had been at the Village until nearly dark the day before, she arrived before sunup the day of the race to help oversee last-minute preparations. She was thrilled to see how everything had come together.

The participants would begin their walk/run at the old covered bridge, then move through Middlebury before returning to the Village via the Pumpkinvine Trail. Bouquets of lavender balloons lined the path as it exited the bridge, where each person would begin their race. Across the finish line was an arch made of more balloons and plenty of streamers in the various colors that represented the different types of cancer. The bouquets of balloons seemed to stretch forever. Each had been sponsored by a different business in Middlebury. Each represented their town and how they were determined to stand together in the fight against cancer.

Amber pivoted in a circle and stopped when she could view the spot where the race ended next to Village Fashions, Letha's shop. A banner proclaiming VICTORY had been hung over the finish line so that each participant would cross underneath it. And above the VICTORY banner was the rainbow of streamers and more lavender balloons.

She turned back to the registration table, which was set up on the left side of the bridge. It was already packed with workers and participants. A large poster near the table assured everyone that all proceeds for entering went to the cancer foundation, which would in turn use them for research.

"The Survivor Table is a nice touch." Pam offered her one of the disposable coffee cups, hot steam rising in the early morning air. The cup was also decorated in multicolored ribbons. The fresh donut her assistant pushed into her hand was wrapped in a napkin that proclaimed current cancer statistics. Amber stared down at the napkin ringed by small ribbons.

New cases per year—1.6 million.
Deaths each year—over half a million.
Top cancer for men—prostate, lung, colon, bladder, skin.
Top cancer for women—breast, lung, colon, uterus, lymphoma.
Five-year survival rate—65.8%.

"You're going to eat it, right? Because you probably won't have another chance to grab a bite until this is over."

Amber didn't even hesitate. She could go back to watching her waistline tomorrow. This morning she was famished, but then again she had been up since five. Who knew there would be so much to coordinate for a race? It was their first year to serve as the host site, and she wanted everything to turn out right.

"The Survivor Table was sponsored by one of

the high school clubs." Amber took a bite of the donut—warm, sweet, and freshly baked. Then she washed it down with a gulp of coffee. "They even created the T-shirts."

"I like tie-dye. I look good in bright colors, but I'm not sure they'd have one in my size." Bright colors didn't quite describe the outfits Pam wore. Today she had on a skirt made of bright pink and purple. The blouse she wore had mid-length sleeves and was all purple. A pink scarf around her neck pulled the outfit together.

"You're not a cancer survivor."

"True, but I survived helping you prepare for this event, and that was no easy task."

"It would have been easier if we hadn't been dealing with the poison poet and the Ryan Duvall fiasco."

Pam nodded toward the registration table where Ryan was signing up to run in the 5k. "I wasn't sure we'd see him today, after what Preston told us."

"What do you mean?"

"You know, the whole"—Pam lowered her voice and stepped closer—"owing the mob thing."

Amber only smiled. It really was nice to have all the dating drama of the last few weeks behind them. In her mind, if Ryan was turning over a new leaf, then perhaps participating in a community event was a good place to start.

Hannah and Jesse joined them. Helen, one of Amber's more flamboyant *Englisch* employees, stood handing out ribbons to participants, friends, and family members. Each ribbon had been fastened with a straight pin. Helen handed the basket of ribbons to Hannah so she could more easily help an elderly gentleman attach his orange ribbon, for skin cancer, to the bib of his overalls.

It was such an incongruous sight—an elderly man with no hair, a large belly, and farmer clothes, next to Helen, who was dressed with her customary flair. Her denim dress stopped just above her knees. She wore long multicolored socks, which reached up past the hem of her dress, and sparkly denim tennis shoes. On Amber the entire ensemble would have looked ridiculous. On Helen it looked chic—especially with her long black hair pulled into a high ponytail and sporting ribbons of every color.

The girl reminded Amber that the next generation was stepping up. Though they were often portrayed as self-centered and disconnected, the truth was that, when there was an opportunity to serve others, they came through.

The old guy grunted when Helen stepped back. "I thought you were going to stick me."

"I wouldn't think of it. Blood might ruin my outfit."

The old man chuckled as he turned away. It

was obvious that the little bit of special attention had made his morning.

Helen reached for the basket of colored ribbons, but Hannah shook her head. "Jesse and I can take care of this. Is there anywhere else you need to be?"

Helen glanced at Amber, who said, "I think they could use your help signing folks in as they register."

Helen shrugged and turned toward the table, but she didn't get five steps before a young boy with a bald head stopped her and asked if she was going to make balloon animals like she had at the Easter picnic. Helen pulled a balloon out of her pocket and squatted down next to him as she blew into it, then pulled and stretched the balloon into the shape of a wienie dog.

"The girl has multiple talents," Pam said.

"Indeed she does." Amber finished her coffee. "Everything looks good here. I think we're ready for just about anything."

At that moment, Julie, a reporter for the *Goshen News* who covered Middlebury events and had interviewed Preston about Mocha, stepped out of the dress shop. Amber was pretty sure she looked their way, but then she hitched her large quilted bag up over her shoulder and turned in the opposite direction.

"Looks like our little event is making the newspaper."

"Which is good," Pam said. "Maybe even more people will contribute to the cause."

Hannah had been listening in on their conversation as she handed out ribbons. "Should I go cover Letha's shop?"

"No. We covered for anyone who wanted the morning off so they could stand with loved ones during the festivities, and technically it's not Letha's shop anymore. She left for Pinecraft yesterday." Pam craned her neck to get a better look across the property. "I wonder what the reporter was doing in there—"

"Maybe she was shopping," Jesse offered with his customary smile.

Amber thought Jesse and Hannah were two of the best employees she had. She certainly was glad they'd decided to attend the event, even though they weren't required to work that morning. She'd gladly approved four extra hours' pay for anyone who had volunteered.

Her thoughts turned to Letha. She'd be missed, that was for certain. Amber had assigned Helen to the store temporarily. It seemed like a natural fit.

"I was still hoping Letha would change her mind," Amber confessed. "It all seems such an overreaction to me."

"It's probably *gut* she isn't here today," Hannah said as she handed both a blue and pink ribbon to a teenage girl. "It's best she doesn't bump into Ryan."

"It is a small town, though. Unless she's moving to Pinecraft permanently, she's bound to see him now and then." Amber hopped to the right just in time to avoid being creamed by a tray of bakery treats.

Georgia brushed past them, carrying a large tray of freshly baked cinnamon rolls. She wore a long-sleeved black top and a blue jean skirt. Over that she had on her Amish Village apron. Jesse hurried over to help her set the tray on the refreshments table. Georgia scowled at the table, moved the tray to the middle, and then turned and strode off back toward the bakery.

"I wonder where Tate is. He's taking pictures for me today." Amber pivoted in a circle, and that was when she spied Martha stepping out the front door of the inn.

The young girl stopped on the edge of the crowd, looked left then right, and finally plunged in. The last thing Amber saw of her was the top of her *kapp*, disappearing into a sea of Middlebury folk—Amish and *Englisch*.

Then she didn't have time to worry about the girls or Ryan Duvall. Their mayor, a cancer survivor herself, had stepped up to the platform and was tapping the microphone.

It was time for the race to begin.

Thirty-Five

Preston had hoped to be near the registration table when the race officially started. But he wasn't exactly surprised that things didn't work out that way.

He'd received a call early that morning about an overflowing sink, which had turned into a minor flooding event in the west wing of the inn. Fortunately, it was on the first floor and limited to two rooms.

Karen was working at the front desk, and she'd found alternate rooms for the guests. Jake helped move the two families, both with young children.

"I'll bet you ten bucks one of those kids stuck something down the drain that shouldn't be there."

"Thank you, but I'll keep my ten." Preston wasn't much of a gambler, plus Jake was probably correct. It wouldn't have been the first time a guest's child had stopped up the plumbing. He'd found hair ribbons, Play-Doh, even tiny Barbie shoes. Drains seemed to exert a powerful pull over children from ages two to ten.

However, Jake's off-the-cuff "I'll bet you ten bucks" did start Preston to thinking about Ryan. He'd had two calls from him since the middle-of-the-night visit on his front porch. The first time was early yesterday morning, to thank him. Although Preston hadn't stayed around to witness the entire reunion, he had lingered long enough to meet the elder Mr. Duvall and to see the look of relief in the father's eyes. Mrs. Duvall immediately came downstairs and started cooking, as if her son might have starved over the course of the last three days. While all three invited Preston to stay, he'd decided it was best that some family reunions remained private.

He'd loaded Mocha back into his car and headed home, too wired to sleep but pleased with how things had turned out.

The second call from Ryan had been later that morning, regarding the gambling debt and his collectors.

"Dad and I are in Indianapolis. He just paid the balance in full."

"No repercussions?"

"Only to his bank account, but I'm going to pay that back. I've seen the light, Preston. I'm a different man now."

Perhaps.

Preston certainly hoped so. Time would tell whether Ryan could change his ways, but he had certainly been highly motivated. He had also mentioned that he was still planning on running in the 5k.

Preston bailed the water out of the sink, dumping it into the toilet. He'd brought his plumbing tools with him, including a new elbow pipe in case the one he was looking at was defective in some way. On inspection, the pipe looked fine. He loosened the upper and lower nuts and pulled the pipe free. He dumped the water pooled there into a pail, unsure exactly what else might come out. Holding it up to the light, he could only see a large mass. So he pulled a long screwdriver from his bag and used it to coax the material out.

The mass fell into the bucket with a plop, but not before he had a good look at it—a metallic-colored goo that reminded him of the gel found inside a stretch-man doll. He could have been imagining that, but the sight triggered a long-forgotten memory. He'd once taken that same action figure apart, wondering what was in there to allow him to stretch and turn and bend. The glop had run down the sink before he could stop it, and yes—it had stopped up the pipe. His father had done exactly what he was doing at the moment. Remove the pipe. Clean it out with a brush. Fit the entire thing back together. The memory brought a smile even as he dropped the goo into the trash can.

Mocha lay on the floor, head on her paws, watching him as if he were conducting a terribly complicated process. She was faithful, that much was certain. He could do no wrong in the eyes of his dog.

He heard a roar from the crowd outside.

The race was starting.

He'd attended the planning meeting with Amber and the other managers. Runners would go first, then teens, followed by children and families. Seniors would bring up the rear of the group. It seemed safest. No one wanted an old guy knocked over accidentally by someone trying to make their best speed.

He had a good twenty minutes before he needed to be at the finish line if he wanted to see the first winner. He spoke to Mocha as he worked, cleaning the pipe and then fastening it back together. "No worries, girl. We'll be done here in plenty of time."

Zoey had been scheduled to work that day, and he'd promised to text her a photo of the finish line. What she didn't know was that he had more to give her than a photograph. He'd driven over to a jewelry store in Goshen and ordered the perfect ring. Perhaps it was too soon, but Preston had decided to go with his heart on this one. Life was short, and he wasn't going to waste another minute of it. The ring might be in today. He'd pick it up, and then he'd ask Zoey to marry him.

Hannah and Jesse stayed at the registration area until things slowed down a bit, then they decided to walk toward the finish line. Quite a group was growing around the arch, although the race hadn't even started yet. There had been an enthusiastic response to the mayor's speech—shouts of approval and applause. Energy thrummed through the crowd, lifting everyone's spirits.

Hannah should have felt happy, but she felt a shadow creeping across the morning. She stepped closer to Jesse, wanting to feel his presence, assuring herself that he was close. Besides, what was there to worry about?

Everything was going smoothly.

Behind them groups of people were waiting to begin the walk or run—whichever they chose. In front of them, at the finish line, tables had been set up with items for the walkers, VICTORY T-shirts, bottles of water, and cups of Gatorade.

"Things are going well, *ya?*" Jesse nudged her shoulder. "Big crowd. Lots of folks will visit the restaurant and the shops once the race is over."

When Hannah didn't answer, he added, "And think of all those entry fees—how much was raised for the cancer research. It's a *gut* day."

"It is." Hannah stopped and studied the scene, slowly turning in a complete circle.

"What's wrong, Hannah Bell? When you become distracted like you are right now, it usually spells trouble. I've seen it before, and it definitely means you're thinking hard about something."

"I don't know if anything is wrong, but something feels . . . out of place."

"Like what?"

Hannah scanned the crowd and noticed two men standing to the far side. They were wearing suits and dark glasses, and they stood out like red roses in a sea of daisies. She lowered her voice and nodded toward them. "Those men in suits. Why are they here?"

"Where?"

"Over there. See them?" She pointed, though she knew it was rude. With more people crowding into the area every minute, she didn't think anyone would notice.

"I see them now. Fancy *Englisch* clothes." Jesse laughed, as if he had made a joke.

"Jesse, there's something wrong about those two."

"Wrong?" He squinted and stared at them with more intensity. "I don't see anything wrong."

"They just seem . . . as if they don't belong." She was thinking they reminded her of a piece of cloth placed in the wrong quilt—not just upside down or turned incorrectly, but completely wrong.

Jesse scratched the back of his neck. "Maybe they're from a newspaper, wanting to cover the event."

"*Nein*. Julie covers the community events. I've met her a couple of times when we had events before. See? She's standing over under the shade of that tree, and she has her camera with her."

"Owners of the Village?"

"Nope. There are pictures of the Campbell family in the conference room. They're much older."

Jesse didn't look convinced, but he shrugged and said, "I'll go and speak to them if you like."

"Something about them makes me *naerfich*." Hannah smoothed down her light peach apron over her new, darker peach dress. She'd so looked forward to this day, but now something seemed . . . off.

"No worries. I'll trot over and see what their story is."

Before she could tell him that was a bad idea, Jesse darted left to skirt around the crowd and toward the men. As she watched him move closer, then come up behind them and introduce himself, the feeling that something was out of place grew even stronger. Anxiety suddenly flooded her heart, causing her pulse to soar.

The men bothered her. As she watched, after Jesse stepped away from them, one pulled out his phone and spoke in it briefly, then returned it to his pocket. He never smiled. He never averted his gaze from the finish line.

Beside him, the other man asked a question, to which he nodded curtly.

They didn't look like someone who worked in offices. Their shoulders were broad, like many of the football players she'd seen on television when walking through one of the restaurants in town. Seems folks were always watching some sort of sports, and that was what these men reminded Hannah of. Too big. Too muscular. Definitely not office workers.

And why would they be wearing suits on a beautiful spring morning? Before she could think of a plausible answer, she looked up and saw Beverly, an employee who normally worked in the inn. She was waving, anxiously trying to attract Hannah's attention. Hannah hurried over to the VICTORY display to see what could be wrong.

"I was supposed to bring the ribbons for those who cross the VICTORY line first, second, and third." Beverly pushed her long black hair back over her shoulder. "I forgot them, but I can't leave right now."

"No worries. I'll fetch them for you."

"They're in a basket next to the inn's computer station, at the front desk."

"I'll hurry." Hannah dodged through the crowd as she made her way around the shops and into the inn. Fortunately the race had barely begun. She didn't think any of the runners would be finishing five kilometers in such a short time.

Pushing through the front door of the inn, she was surprised to see Jake working alone. "Where's Martha?"

"She left a few minutes ago."

"Left where?"

"I'm not sure. She said something had to be dealt with, and she wasn't sure how long it would take. She told me if she couldn't get back, she'd call Pam or Amber."

"That doesn't sound like Martha." Hannah's mind combed over the possibilities for Martha's sudden absence—none of them were good. "You didn't ask her to be more specific?"

Jake drummed his fingers on the countertop and shook his head. "It wasn't my place to interrogate her about it."

"Can you handle any guests who want to check out or in by yourself? I could try to find someone—"

Jake waved away her concerns. "Most everyone is outside milling around. There will be a rush around eleven, but Beverly is scheduled to be back at work by then."

"All right. I'm supposed to pick up the winner ribbons. She left them here by accident."

"Yeah, I saw them earlier." He reached over past the computer and picked up the basket, pushing it into her hands. "I think everything you need is there."

Before she could reply, before she could ask him anything else about Martha, Jake had turned to help a customer who was requesting a late checkout.

Hannah scooted outside.

The weather had turned postcard-perfect

beautiful. She pulled in a lungful of the late spring air and tried to quiet her worries about her friend. Perhaps she wasn't feeling well. Or maybe she had to go home for some reason. She said a brief prayer that Martha hadn't decided to watch the runners. Something told her she didn't need to see Ryan so soon. She hadn't quite healed from his betrayal, if that's what it was.

Hannah plunged back into the crowd, toward the finish line. She was halfway to her destination when a white *kapp* caught her attention. There were plenty of Amish among the crowd, but Hannah would recognize Letha Keim anywhere, even from the back. The woman had a distinctive walk, and she always wore her *kapp* strings pushed behind her shoulders. It was Letha all right, and Letha was supposed to be gone—on the bus to Pinecraft the day before. So why was she milling around the Village?

But Letha was walking toward the right side of the crowd, and Beverly was waiting to the left. Hannah filed her questions away. She'd seek Letha out after the race was finished. Perhaps she had changed her mind. Maybe she'd decided to stay in Middlebury after all.

She made it to the table, where Beverly asked her help with separating the ribbons into categories—apparently the runners were divided further, into age groups.

"The first ones to run should arrive soon."

"Here they are. Take them to the finish line, and I'll organize the rest."

"Thank you, Hannah." Beverly paused to squeeze her arm, then darted off toward the balloon arch. Hannah had never envisioned that a simple race could be so hectic, but then she'd never participated in one. She didn't run much, not anymore. When she was younger, when she had played softball out behind the schoolhouse, she'd enjoyed running the bases.

Times were simpler then.

She hadn't worried about men in suits, or friends who left their work shift, or women who decided things one moment and changed their minds the next.

She'd share all of her concerns with Amber. Her boss would know what to do. Amber handled chaos well, at least she had in the past. Hannah was good at recognizing when something was amiss, but Amber was better at coming up with a plan of action. Perhaps that was why together they made such a good team.

But then she looked at the crowd, ready to let up a cheer as soon as the first group arrived. She forgot all about those little things that more than likely weren't problems after all. Instead, she finished organizing the ribbons, then stepped out from behind the table to look for Jesse. He caught her eye and pointed to an area on a small rise. Hannah glanced that way and saw Amber and

Pam. They'd picked a good spot for watching the action—a place close to the finish line but where they could still easily see over the crowd.

After checking the table one last time to be sure everything was as it should be, she hurried toward her friends. For a moment, she allowed herself to enjoy the morning and believe that all her worries were unfounded. She needed a rest; that was all that was wrong. As soon as the race was over, she would go home and enjoy the peacefulness of the day.

Preston walked toward the front desk of the inn, his toolbox in his left hand, the now-empty pail in his right, and Mocha at his heels.

There was a utility closet behind the desk, and he stepped in there to leave his tools and the bucket. As he did, he heard Jake, who was manning the desk, speak to a customer.

"How was your stay, Mr. Anderson?"

"Good. We always enjoy our stay here at the Village. In fact, we already have a reservation to return in the fall."

"That's excellent. We're glad to hear it."

Jake printed out the man's receipt and set it on the countertop with a pen, instructing him where to sign.

There was something about the scene that caused Preston to pause. Something in the back of his memory about computers and . . . It was right there, but he couldn't seem to reach it.

Then an Amish couple walked by the front of the inn—both dressed in traditional Amish clothing. The woman's *kapp* triggered what he was remembering, what Hannah had told him the day before.

There were two computers in the lobby for guests to use. Hannah had walked in to speak with Martha yesterday afternoon. As she waited for Martha to be able to take her break, she'd noticed Georgia on one of the computers.

"That's interesting. What kind of program is it?" Hannah had peered over Georgia's shoulder.

"Nothing. It's nothing at all." Georgia had quickly closed the program and stood, nearly bumping into her.

"Looked like a map of Middlebury," Hannah had said, aiming for pleasant. "But all those dots . . . what were they for?"

"Lost a pet. I had my cat chipped. She ran off the other day, and I tried to track her on the computer, but I can never seem to catch her."

According to Hannah, Georgia had rushed away without another word. She'd thought it odd enough to mention it to Preston later, only because Georgia had closed the program so quickly. Preston hadn't thought much about it then.

What he was remembering now, however, what he'd remembered when he looked at Jake's computer, was that Georgia hated cats. She wouldn't even feed the stray that hung around the Village. He was surprised Hannah didn't remember that.

So what had Georgia really been up to?

And why had she lied?

Preston shook his head and motioned for Mocha to follow him outside, waving to Jake as he went, continuing to mull over what he had remembered.

So she had lied. Lots of people wanted to keep certain things to themselves. It wasn't that uncommon.

Or so he told himself as he made his way out of the inn.

Thirty-Six

"Where is Preston?" Amber asked.

"Dealing with a maintenance emergency at the inn. I passed him on my way over." Pam looked over her shoulder and then back at Amber. "He'll be here. Don't worry."

Amber nodded, but saying she wasn't going to worry and stopping were two very different things. She and Pam continued studying the crowd as Hannah walked up. It made Amber feel better, the fact that they were all together. These were her friends, in good times and bad. It seemed they had been together through so many tight spots—her and Pam and Hannah. Jesse was somewhere close and Tate was within eyesight. It was nice to be able to share a moment of celebration. The only person missing was Preston, and he'd texted that he would meet them soon.

"Tate's in a perfect spot to see everything," Amber said. "He's even closer than we are."

Pam craned her neck for a better look. "Last I saw he was in the parking lot, photographing the crowd as they arrived."

"Well, now he has a perfect spot near the finish line."

"Nice of him to hop over and give you that kiss, though—you two are like newlyweds."

"We are newlyweds."

Pam tossed her empty coffee cup into a nearby trash can. "He's considerate and he takes his assignments seriously."

"It wasn't exactly an assignment. I asked him to take pictures and he—"

"I like that in a man. Someone who is sweet and doesn't mind showing it, but he's also serious about his work."

"His work is actually on the farm."

"You picked a winner, Amber."

Amber stared across at Tate and nodded in agreement. "Don't I know it, though I'm not sure I picked him as much as he rescued me."

"I'd rather you don't go into that story again. The details always give me the creeps."

"It wasn't all scary." Memories of Ethan's murder and all that had followed flashed through Amber's mind.

Pam was right.

It had been creepy.

She'd had trouble sleeping for weeks afterward. Finally she had gone to meet with her pastor. He'd opened the Old Testament to the book of Genesis, chapter fifty. Amber had since committed much of that story to memory. Joseph, sold into slavery by his brothers. Joseph, suffering at the hands of his family! And ultimately, Joseph offering God's mercy and grace. "You intended to harm me, but God intended it for good."

She'd spent many a night dwelling on that verse, and thanking God that he had been in charge of her life even when she was at her most frightened.

"I don't like stories with critters in them," Pam added.

"That part was creepy—"

"Creepy? Try terrifying. You should know."

"But Tate's proposal was romantic."

"I like stories that include flowers."

"Should I send you some?" Amber smiled over at her assistant.

Pam waved away that idea. "And diamonds . . . stories with diamonds are very good."

Before they could continue batting the topic around, Jesse arrived, slightly out of breath from hurrying toward them.

"Did you ask who they were?" Hannah worried her *kapp* strings as she glanced out over the crowd.

"Who? Is there someone here who doesn't belong?" Pam scowled, as if they might have an intruder in their midst.

"Those men in suits. I thought they—well, I thought they looked out of place."

"No worries, Hannah." Jesse stepped to Hannah's left. "I asked if I could help them, and both men said they were fine. Then I asked if they were here to watch the race, and they said *ya*. I got the feeling they might be with the National Cancer Foundation."

"Did they tell you that?" Pam asked.

Jesse raised his hat, and resettled it on his head. "Maybe not word for word, but that was the impression I got."

"That's odd." Amber brushed her hair behind her ears. "No one called me about sending a representative."

"Maybe they decided to come at the last minute," Jesse said.

"They still bother me." Hannah stood on tiptoe and craned her neck in the direction she'd last seen the men, but they were gone. "They don't look like charity people to me."

"What do charity people look like, Hannah Bell?"

Amber smiled at the pet name. Jesse rarely let it slip in public, though Hannah had told her that he used it often when they were alone. When he did call her that in front of other people, Hannah's cheeks always pinked up like a rose blooming in the spring.

Young love was a wonderful thing to watch.

"Humph. I spoke to someone in that office twice this week," Pam said. "They didn't mention to me that they were coming to visit. I would have made sure they got the VIP suite."

"We don't have a VIP suite." Amber glanced at her quizzically.

"We could make one. Add a basket of fruit and some chocolates—"

Their conversation stopped abruptly as people in the crowd began to clap.

Hannah stepped closer to Jesse and put her hand on his arm. Pam and Amber turned to face the finish line.

The first group, most of whom participated on the high school track team, was soon followed by the second group—18 to 25. Group three was 26 to 39. And then behind them the 40-plus group—the one Amber knew Ryan Duvall would be in. They wore different color numbers that had been printed on copier paper and pinned to their chests. As Amber watched them run down the final stretch of the Pumpkinvine Trail and toward the finish line, it was easy enough to tell which competitors were running together. The third group pulled in behind the second and that was when she saw Ryan—at the front of his pack.

"There's Ryan," Pam said. "Looks like he's leading in his group."

"I'm glad he's here," Amber murmured.

He glanced up, and it seemed like his gaze found hers. He smiled slightly, almost waved, and then he set his sights on the finish line.

Thirty-Seven

Preston stepped out into the bright spring sunshine, grateful to be done with the plumbing problem. He didn't mind the dirty aspects of his job, but anything he could do outside he liked better. Watching the race was no hardship at all. Amber had texted him where they were waiting, and she made him promise he would join their little group.

The text had brought a smile.

It had been many years since he'd felt like a part of a group, probably since his days in the military. That younger man he'd been could never have guessed what he would go through the next few years, and certainly couldn't have foreseen him working for an Amish Village. Which all went to show there was no use trying to anticipate the twists and turns life would take—but in the end, they had been for his good.

He glanced down at Mocha and realized he needed to attach her leash before they made their way through the crowd. When they were indoors, he didn't usually bother with it. Outside, though, he tried to be more conscientious. It wasn't that he was afraid she'd run off—she stuck to his side like she'd been Velcroed there—but other folks seemed more at ease when she was on a leash. She was a gentle-looking dog, with her giant dopey grin. She was also quite large, weighing in at over seventy pounds. He understood that was intimidating to some people, so he kept the leash handy.

Mocha waited patiently at his side, tail wagging, ears alert.

She knew the routine.

He reached into the pocket of his jacket to pull out the leash, and stopped when he heard the pop of a pistol.

Several thoughts went through his mind instantaneously.

Definitely not a firecracker.

Not a car backfiring.

A higher pitch than a shotgun or a rifle.

It was a pistol, no doubt about it.

He had been convinced by the sound, by that place in his memories he didn't like to go. What happened next left no doubt at all.

The pop was followed by a silence, and then the crowd reacted. Even as he began rushing toward where he thought the shot had been fired, people were screaming and running away from the scene. His heart sank as he realized it was the finish line. He couldn't imagine what had happened, but from the reaction of the crowd, he understood it was something terrible.

He ran, never checking on Mocha, but somehow aware that she stayed at his side as they pushed through the crowd, straining against the mass of panicked people. For a moment he moved backward with the momentum of the crowd, but then he put his head down and trundled through —feeling like he had in Wanat, the reality of that bitter memory coming back and merging with the sunny Indiana day.

Mocha whined once and pressed her nose to his hand. He petted her, assured her he was fine, and darted left, then right. One minute turned into two, and two into five. When had the Village grounds become so crowded? All for a charity race? The sound of a siren split the morning, and still he couldn't get any closer.

He caught a few words, "gunshot" and "runner" and "bleeding." It was when he heard someone mention Amber that his pulse rocketed, and he knew he had to find a way past the crowd. He circled right, behind the dress shop, and then suddenly he broke through. The onlookers had formed a ring of sorts, as if an invisible barrier held them back. In the middle of the ring, on the ground, was Ryan Duvall—Preston recognized the curly black hair and the dark eyes that were now frozen open. He wasn't moving, and blood had spread beneath him from a wound in his chest, staining the concrete.

Amber was sitting near Ryan's body, pressing a bloody rag to the wound. Pam placed a hand on Amber's shoulder, bent and said something to her. The ambulance had arrived and Jack Lambright jumped out. Not far behind him was Gordon Avery, shouldering his way through and barking orders.

Preston watched it all from his place at the rim of the crowd. He was about three rows back and could have easily pushed his way through, but he didn't. It wasn't so much that he was frozen by the violence of the event. He was assessing, deciding where he would be the most help or if he could be any help at all.

Tate had been attempting to administer CPR, but he stood, shook his head, and walked toward Amber.

He pulled her up into his arms, and when she nearly stumbled—nearly collapsed there next to Ryan's body—Tate practically carried her to the curb. Now they were opposite from where Preston stood. Once again he hesitated, trying to determine how best to get to his friends.

He could cross the crime scene—it was obvious that's what it was. Two officers from the Middlebury PD were already forming a perimeter, and soon they would string the yellow tape. He could cross or go around. Crossing would draw attention to himself, and he didn't want to hinder Gordon's assessment of the scene. Walking around—that seemed impossible at the moment, as the crowd had formed a tight circle.

So he waited.

Amber sank to the curb, with Tate on one side and Pam on the other. Hannah and Jesse stood behind her, heads bowed. Hannah had a camera strap around her neck. Tate must have handed her his camera when he rushed to help. The sight was incongruous—an Amish woman sporting a camera. But then the entire scene in front of him defied belief.

The paramedic was attending to Ryan.

Gordon finally made it to the side of the body, and that was when Amber struggled to her feet. The look on her face—agony, disbelief, and grief, mingled with a good dose of shock—tore at Preston's heart. He cared for this woman as if she were his own family. She was his family, in every important sense of the word. He couldn't abide the thought of her enduring another murder investigation.

Gordon was barking orders. "I want this immediate area completely clear. Secure the perimeter, but advise everyone to stay put where we can interview them. I don't want a single person in this crowd leaving—"

Preston shifted his attention to the large crowd. A good portion had already fled, though many remained at a distance, watching and talking on their cell phones—some even attempting to take photos.

Then he heard his name, heard it coming from Officer Brookstone, and he knew he couldn't stay in the crowd—hiding like a criminal.

Brookstone was reminding Gordon of the restraining order.

Another officer began moving back the closest circle of witnesses who had stayed, those who were nearest the body.

As one, they seemed to step back.

But Preston didn't, which left him on the front row.

He stood staring, going through the possibilities in his mind and assessing his options.

Preston tore his eyes from Ryan. The man hadn't been his friend, but neither had he been his enemy. He was someone trying to find the right path in life, and now his journey had ended. There was no doubt that he'd died quickly, probably instantly. From the sound of the shot and the size of the wound, Preston would guess the murderer had used a .38 caliber handgun at close range, and obviously no silencer since the sound had carried to where Preston had stood outside the inn.

Amber's voice pulled his attention away from the body. "I didn't see who pulled the trigger, but I know who killed Ryan."

At those words, or maybe it was more the crack in her voice, Preston stepped forward, one foot after another, until he was standing close to Amber and looking down at Ryan Duvall.

Gordon moved back and put his hand on the butt of his firearm.

Amber had insisted it wasn't Preston, that she knew who had fired the gun. Preston heard her as if from a distance. One look at Gordon's face told him the officer wasn't convinced.

Mocha whined, and Preston realized for the first time that he still hadn't leashed the dog. He reached into the pocket of his jacket to pull out the leash, and that was when Gordon raised his gun.

"Hands where I can see them, Johnstone."

Preston froze.

"This is ridiculous." Amber pushed in between Gordon and Preston, though Tate made a desperate attempt to snatch her back. "You're not listening. I know who did this."

Gordon's eyes were still locked on Preston. He held his gun steady, and used his chin to nod. "Hands, up and away from the jacket."

Preston did so, slowly, in as non-threatening a

manner as he could muster. "I was going for the leash—the leash for my dog."

Gordon barked orders to one of the officers, a young woman who looked as if she was fresh out of the police academy.

She stepped forward, met Preston's gaze, and checked him. She ran her fingers up and down his arms, patted down his jacket and the back of his waistband, then checked for an ankle holster. "He's clear."

"May I leash my dog now?"

Gordon nodded, even as he reached for his cuffs. Amber was still arguing with him, insisting he had the wrong guy, when two athletic men in suits stepped up and flashed their ID. "Federal investigators."

"I'm Watkins," the larger of the two said. "That's Snyder. We'd like to offer our assistance."

"Gordon Avery. You're offering assistance on a homicide?" Gordon spoke into his radio, telling someone he wanted the forensic team on scene and he wanted them there five minutes ago. His eyes still locked on Preston, he waved away the two men. "Local matter. No, thank you."

"Agreed. It is local, but if it has anything to do with the poison—"

"Poison? Someone's been poisoned? The last thing we need to deal with this morning is that crazy poison poet." Pam's hand was shaking as she stepped forward and reached out to Amber.

"Come away from there, honey. You can't help Ryan now."

"Who was poisoned?" Amber asked.

"We can't discuss that, ma'am."

Gordon studied the crowd, then turned to the woman who had frisked Preston. Three other officers remained vigilant, spread in a circle around the body, facing the crowd so that they formed a type of barrier between Ryan and the folks who had stayed to watch the tragedy unfold. "Make sure that tape is strung up to create a twenty-foot perimeter. Call in more help if you need it. We want witness reports from anyone who saw anything."

"Sure thing, boss."

Gordon's hand moved away from his cuffs. "I'll be in Amber's office. Call me when the forensics team is done."

"My office?" Amber's hands came up to push back her hair, and Preston could see that she was still trembling. She stared at her hands a moment, as if she couldn't quite fathom how they'd become covered in blood, then dropped them to her side.

Tate was standing next to her on one side, Pam on the other, both trying to steady her. Hannah and Jesse remained perched on the edge of the crowd, apparently unsure where they should be.

"Why my office?"

"Because we need somewhere private, and it's

close." Gordon studied the crowd and shook his head. "Johnstone, you stay in front of me—no fast moves, nothing suspicious, or I'll cuff you and take you in. Tate, Amber . . . let's go."

"You're not taking Amber without me," Pam said. "I'm her backup. I need to be there."

Amber shook her head. "Stay here." Her voice was calm now, certain.

In that moment, Preston realized she had accepted the situation and begun dealing with it.

"Help calm everyone down. Set up a first-aid station in case anyone was hurt trying to run away from the scene." Amber's gaze flicked up and over to Hannah and Jesse. "Do whatever you can to help her."

"I think . . . I think I should go with you." Hannah's voice shook and her face was nearly as pale as her *kapp*. "There's something I need to tell you."

"All right." Gordon nodded toward the men in suits. "On the off chance the poison incidents and this homicide are related, you should join us."

Before Preston could turn toward Amber's office, Gordon added, "And the dog stays here."

It was Pam who came to the rescue. "That is a service dog."

"I didn't ask your opinion."

"Would you deny a blind person his service dog?" Color flowed back into Amber's face. "Do you want a lawsuit if Preston has a flashback

383

and blacks out? Do you want to be responsible for that?"

"What I want is to process this crime scene and find the murderer." Gordon's voice was tired, as if the day had already required more energy than he could possibly muster. He glanced down at Mocha. "Bring her, but keep her out of my way."

Preston clipped the leash onto Mocha's collar. He followed Tate and Amber, and noticed that Gordon stayed three steps behind him as they walked toward Amber's office. Far enough that Preston couldn't grab his gun. Close enough that he could tackle him if he tried to escape.

But he had no reason to do either.

Because he'd had nothing to do with the murder of Ryan Duvall.

Thirty-Eight

When Amber walked into her office she was nearly overwhelmed with the sense of history repeating itself. This was the same room where she'd confronted Ethan Gray's killer. From her window she could look out and see where the Pumpkinvine Trail intersected their property—where Owen Esch had been killed and ultimately she'd been confronted by his killer. She could also see the spot where Ryan Duvall lay, but his body was concealed by the emergency workers and officers who had flanked the area.

Three murders in one year.

All unrelated.

All on her watch.

She wanted to sink into her chair and cry out to the Lord. She wanted to ask why and how and what next.

But she didn't.

She accepted the warm washcloth Tate had brought from the bathroom and used it to wipe the blood from her fingers. There was no removing the dark stain from her shirt, though. It would have to be thrown out. No amount of soaking could remove the spot where Ryan's blood had seeped onto her.

She breathed a prayer for Ryan's soul and for his parents. Did they even know yet?

"Are you okay?" Tate asked.

"No. Yes. I'm not sure." She pulled in a deep breath, and took strength in Tate's hand at the small of her back, Hannah's weak smile, and Preston's steady gaze. She even felt encouraged looking at Gordon Avery's scowl. He was a good cop. He'd figure this out.

The room was already crowded before the two federal agents squeezed in. Elizabeth wasn't working in the outer office. She rarely worked on Saturdays but today had offered to fill in at one of the shops during the race. Tate ducked into the reception area and brought in an extra chair. He headed back for more, but the agents waved him away. One took up a position near the window, the other near the door.

"I'm going to be crystal clear." Gordon glanced out the window, then focused his gaze on their small group. "My instinct tells me to take Preston in for questioning. Preston, I want you to know that I don't say that lightly, and it's not personal. We both grew up in this town, and I admire how you've turned your life around. But when there's a homicide and the victim previously issued a restraining order, it would be standard operating procedure to pull in the involved party."

"Understood." Preston's voice held steady.

Amber noticed he stood at attention, hands clasped behind his back, feet slightly apart. Mocha sat beside him, ears perked as she glanced around the room and then back at her master.

"So tell me why I shouldn't."

"Because I wasn't there. I couldn't have been there to shoot Ryan. I was working in the inn. Call Jake. He saw me leave. In fact, he was checking out a guest when I walked out the door." His gaze went up to the corner of the room, then back to Gordon. "The guest's last name was Andrews, no . . . Anderson. He saw me leave, too, even said good morning. Verify the time Jake printed the receipt for that guest, and you'll know I couldn't have been at the finish line in time to shoot a pistol."

"How do you know it was a pistol?"

"Because it wasn't a rifle. We both know I was in the military long enough to know the difference."

Gordon unclipped his radio, requested the status on the scene, and then directed one of his officers to check out Preston's story.

"Anything else?"

"Only that Ryan and I were on better terms than when he requested that restraining order."

"Better terms? In what way?"

"He showed up at my house Thursday night, the same night Amber's cat was poisoned."

"Your restraining order specifically states—"

"I know what it states. What was I supposed to do? Call you and have you drag him off my front porch at two in the morning?"

Gordon pulled out his notepad and began to write. Amber knew his day was just beginning, that he'd be working straight through as long as he could—or until he caught the killer. She touched his arm and nodded toward the chair behind her desk.

He hesitated and then took a seat.

"So why did he show up at your place in the middle of the night?"

Preston told him everything about the visit, all

the details he'd shared with her and Pam and Hannah.

"Ryan's parents can verify this?"

"Yes. I didn't go inside for long when I took him home. I walked up to the door with him, waited in the entryway after his father answered the door and his mother came downstairs. I waited long enough to make sure he was all right, and then I left."

"Tell me more about this gambling debt you mentioned."

"I don't know anything more. Ryan said they paid the balance in Indianapolis."

"And the people who were looking for him originally, when he still had the debt? Did you see them?"

"I didn't. That happened before he showed up at my house. But he called me later and told me the debt was settled. His father had paid the balance."

Gordon grunted but didn't comment on that.

Silence filled the room, and Amber was suddenly aware of the ticking of a clock, the breeze outside her window, and her own breathing. Finally, she couldn't stand the silence any longer.

"I don't think it was any mob person who did this. Who kills for money? Then there's no chance of receiving what you're owed, and besides the debt was paid."

"In cash no doubt, which is a difficult thing to track." Gordon tapped his pen against the notepad.

"I think it was someone different, someone else completely."

"And why is that?"

"Because Ryan had other problems. It's the reason Preston confronted him to begin with."

"The girls—" Hannah said.

"The girls."

"What girls?" Gordon scowled at his notepad.

It seemed inconceivable to Amber that they hadn't mentioned this to Gordon when they'd met about the poison poet. But then it had seemed that the two situations were unrelated, though they did both start at the same time. Now she wondered why she hadn't seen it earlier, why she hadn't put those particular pieces of the puzzle together.

"Ryan was involved with three of the women here at the Village and possibly others."

Preston shook his head. "He told me that he'd limited himself to Village girls in the last few weeks."

"Names?" Gordon asked.

"Georgia Small, Letha Keim, Martha Gingerich."

"The last two are Amish."

"Correct."

One of the federal agents, the one who was slightly taller and a good ten pounds heavier, cleared his throat. He'd introduced himself to

Gordon, but Amber had trouble remembering his name.

"The name Small—it's someone we're investigating as well."

"Why would you be investigating Georgia?" Amber started to rise from her chair, but Tate put a calming hand on her shoulder.

"We aren't allowed to share that information, ma'am." This from the shorter one with the buzz cut.

"We'll come back to why you're here and who you're investigating." Gordon turned his attention once more to Amber.

"You said you know who killed Ryan. Did you see someone pull the trigger?"

"Well, no—"

"Did someone confess to you?"

"Of course not. It just happened."

"Then you don't know who did it." Gordon held up his hand to stop her protests and answered a squawk on his radio. Everyone in the room could hear the officer confirming that Preston's story was true. Gordon uttered a gruff "Got it" and re-clipped his radio on the front of his shirt.

"Your alibi checked out." He jerked his head to the left, motioning for the federal agent at the door to step aside. "You're free to go."

"I don't want to go."

"Did I ask you?"

"I can help. I spent time with Ryan recently. It

could be that what he was involved in is related to his murder."

"And I expect you to give your statement to one of the officers downstairs."

"How are you going to get statements from everyone who was at the race?" Amber asked. "Some of them left already, before you even arrived on the scene."

Gordon was making a list on his notepad. He paused, pen hovering above the page. "Few of those statements will be useful anyway. They've all had a chance to talk and compare notes. What they saw is tainted by what they've heard other people claim to have seen."

"What will you do?" Tate asked.

"The best we can. In a situation like this, where there's a large number of witnesses and it's impossible to retain them all, we hope someone with credible knowledge contacts us—"

"It was one of the women. I know it was." Amber leaned forward, her hands on her desk, looking directly into Gordon's eyes. "It's been crazy around here the last few weeks. I thought we had it under control. I thought with you handling the poison poet, that I could handle this. But I didn't. I failed Ryan—"

"You can't possibly blame yourself . . ." Tate's voice was both steady and certain. He didn't blame her, that much she knew.

"No. No, I don't blame myself. I blame

whoever pulled the trigger. But it seems to me that one of those women decided to take matters into her own hands."

"Because . . ." Gordon tapped his pen against the notepad.

"Because they felt slighted. They were hurt. People do terrible things when they misjudge a situation, Gordon. When their heart's desire is involved. We know that from experience."

"So you're saying Georgia or Letha or Martha could have—"

"Not Letha," Amber said. "She left town yesterday."

"No, she didn't."

Amber turned to stare at Hannah. She had been standing silently toward the back of the room, her arms wrapped around her waist as if she could protect herself against the dangers of the world, Tate's camera strap still around her neck.

Though her cheeks were stained with tears, she stepped forward and repeated, "No, she didn't. Letha's still here."

Thirty-Nine

Hannah's heart was overwhelmed with the tragedy of what had just occurred. She felt as if sorrow was literally weighing her down, and her desire to sit, or rather lie huddled, was nearly her undoing. Instead she'd insisted on coming with the group, with Amber and Preston and Tate. She'd insisted on being involved because several of the things she'd seen that morning had bothered her. She'd spent the last few minutes watching the group, listening, and praying. The warning bells she had ignored all morning were tearing at her heart. Maybe if she'd spoken up earlier, this wouldn't have happened.

Now her friends were staring at her, as was Sergeant Avery and the federal agents—Watkins and Snyder.

"What do you mean she's here? She left for Pinecraft yesterday." Amber had turned in her chair and was studying her with a concerned look.

"*Ya*. She told us that, and I thought she had. But moments before . . . before Ryan was shot, I had to run back to the inn to pick up the finalist ribbons. As I was leaving, I saw her. She was walking toward the finish line."

"You're sure about this?" Gordon had stood. He looked as if he might dash out of the room at any moment.

Hannah fingered the camera strap around her neck. "*Ya*. I'm sure it was her. I'd know Letha anywhere."

"Any idea where Martha Gingerich was at the time of the shooting?" Gordon sat back down.

"Working in the inn," Amber murmured.

"*Nein.* She wasn't." Hannah felt the heat crawl up her neck to warm her cheeks when everyone once again turned to stare at her. "When I went into the inn, Jake was working the front desk alone. I asked him why, thinking maybe I should stay and help. But he assured me he could handle it. When I asked why he was alone, he said Martha had something come up and . . . and she had to leave. Martha told him she wasn't sure if she'd be back."

A shocked silence filled the room, finally broken by Gordon. "All right. So two of the ladies you think might have a motive to do this were here, probably on the scene at the moment Ryan died."

"They didn't do it." Preston hadn't spoken since Gordon told him to leave. Now he said, "I saw both Letha and Martha after the shooting. They were standing near me, weeping and holding on to one another."

"They could still be guilty," Gordon said. "They wouldn't be the first killers to experience remorse."

"If you'd seen them, you'd know they are innocent. That kind of grief can't be faked. In addition, I heard Letha say she'd stayed so she could tell Ryan that she loved him." Preston shook his head. "She also said she'd refunded her bus ticket. She couldn't bear to leave. Besides— why would they stick around if they'd done it?"

"I've seen stranger things." Gordon once again unclipped his radio. "Can you describe Letha and Martha to me?"

Amber gave him a fairly thorough description, which he relayed to someone still at the scene. As he re-clipped the radio, he muttered, "Sounds like any of a thousand young Amish women."

"What about Pam?" Tate was still standing behind Amber's chair. "She's out there, and she knows what the girls look like."

Gordon didn't even hesitate. "Amber, can you contact Pam? Ask her to find both ladies and take them directly to Cherry Brookstone."

While Amber was texting Pam on her phone, Gordon radioed Cherry and told her to check the women's hands for gunpowder residue.

Hannah listened to all of this activity in a fog of disbelief. But there was one thing she was sure of—her friends were incapable of murder.

Gordon turned his attention back to those assembled in Amber's office. "That only leaves Georgia. Anyone know her whereabouts?"

"We had gone to the bakery to question her . . ." Watkins, the larger federal agent cleared his throat. "About a different matter."

"Poison," Amber said.

Instead of confirming that, Watkins added, "She wasn't there. She'd gone out to watch the race, which is why we were standing at the sidelines."

But Gordon wasn't listening to the agent. He

was staring at the camera around Hannah's neck.

"What is that?"

Hannah looked down, surprised, as if she were seeing the device for the first time.

"That's mine," Tate explained. "I was taking pictures of the winners, but handed it to Hannah when we all reached Ryan's body."

Pulling the camera strap from around her neck, suddenly eager to be rid of it, Hannah caught it in the strings of her *kapp*. Tate freed it for her and handed it to Gordon.

"Where were you standing?" Gordon asked.

"South, so I could catch shots of the runners as they came in."

Hannah had never owned a camera, but some of her friends had owned one during their *rumspringa*. She understood what Gordon was doing as he held the device and stared at it, thumbing through the buttons on the camera. He was looking back through the pictures, hoping to gain an understanding of what had occurred less than an hour before. When he let out a low whistle, goose bumps peppered her arms. He'd found something, maybe something that would help them catch Ryan's killer.

"Talk me through this," Gordon said.

Tate moved around behind the desk. "That's the first group of runners that came through the arch. There's the second. And there's Ryan's group."

"This person." Gordon tapped the screen. "She was in your way?"

"I guess. It was pretty crowded, so I had to continually move around to get good shots."

"But you're facing Ryan's group here. Is there any way to enlarge this?"

Tate touched something on the top of the camera.

"Here he is." Gordon tapped the screen.

"Just before he died."

Amber had also crowded around behind the desk. She was trying to get a look at the screen, but she could barely fit her head in between Tate and Gordon, and she certainly couldn't see over them. Finally she squirmed in between them.

"That's her," she squealed. "That's Georgia."

"All I see is a sleeve."

"But it's *her* sleeve. She was wearing black today, which I thought was odd since it isn't exactly a spring color."

"Many Amish women wear black," Gordon reminded her.

"Look, you can also just barely make out the edge of her Village apron, the one she wears when she's working in the bakery."

Hannah noticed the federal agents exchanging pointed looks.

Gordon turned off the camera, and turned to Watkins and Snyder.

"You need to tell me why you're here."

Preston had listened to the agents with a growing sense of dread. He had assumed they were at the Village on some unrelated matter. Maybe, he had thought, the poison poet and the person who had shot Ryan could be the same person. Furthermore, it was distinctly possible that Ryan's murderer was someone they knew, someone they knew fairly well.

Now he couldn't believe what he was hearing.

"We're not authorized to go into detail, but suffice it to say, there has been suspicious internet activity by this woman. Suspicious enough that we were dispatched from the regional office."

"How can you be looking at her—at anyone's —internet history?" Amber turned her attention from the camera to the agents. "How does someone's internet activity make them guilty of a crime? I could look up all sorts of things— firearm details, composition of a bomb, even poison. That doesn't mean I would ever use those things. I could be plotting a book."

"You don't write books," Gordon muttered.

"That's not the point!"

"Ma'am, we don't read e-mails, if that's what you're thinking. There are sophisticated programs, algorithms, in place. If a combination of terms pops up in anyone's history, then we are alerted. If someone attempts to purchase an illegal substance—a poison, for example, and if the person they're attempting to purchase from happens to be an undercover federal agent, then we're dispatched to deal with the situation."

"You're here to arrest Georgia?" Amber's tone was incredulous.

However, it was starting to make sense to Preston. Who else better to create poisonous baked goods than the woman in charge of the bakery? Only to his knowledge there had never been any poison found in them. Had she lost her nerve—except for poisoning Leo? How then could she be bold enough to shoot someone in broad daylight?

"Wait a minute." Gordon leaned forward, arms on the desk. "I understand that you're speaking hypothetically, but let's move this out of the theoretical. Let's talk about what has been happening here in Middlebury. I sent each of the baked items left by the perpetrator off for analysis. They all came back clean."

Watkins shrugged. "She changed her mind— *this time*. It doesn't mean she won't go through with it in the future."

Preston said out loud, but more to himself than anyone in the room, "For whatever reason she chose to use a gun instead."

"Poisons are always iffy," Snyder said. "You have to get the dosage right or it doesn't work at all. Plus some poisons—like cyanide—aren't easy to purchase. The party in question, she balked before buying from our agent."

"Georgia wasn't that upset." Amber shook her head as if to clear it. "Of the three women, she was the least upset when they found out about Ryan's duplicitous behavior."

"She didn't seem that upset, but perhaps she was hiding her true feelings." Hannah nervously popped her knuckles, something Preston hadn't seen her do in six months, since they'd caught Owen Esch's killer.

At that moment one of the Shipshe officers walked into the office, carrying a gun in a plastic evidence bag. "Someone went to drop a cup into a trash receptacle and saw it."

"So we know she's unarmed. The bakery is downstairs, directly beneath us." Preston glanced at the six other people assembled in the room—two federal agents, a police officer, Tate, Amber, and Hannah. Then there was him and Mocha. Between them, surely they could stop one middle-aged woman.

Gordon checked his watch. "All right. Watkins, I want you to cover the front door of the restaurant. Snyder, cover the back. I'll give you four minutes to get into position, and then I'll—"

"We." Amber was already stepping around the desk, gathering her purse and keys.

"Absolutely not."

"She's my employee, and I'm wearing Ryan Duvall's blood on my shirt." Amber's voice had taken on an uncompromising tone. "Short of arresting me, you're not keeping me out of that bakery."

"I'll go with her." Tate stepped closer, and Preston knew that the need to protect his wife was the foremost thing on his mind. Wouldn't he do the same for Zoey? He'd also step in to protect Amber. They were a family, albeit one made from patchwork.

"There's another exit through the kitchen," Preston said. "Mocha and I can cover it, then you won't have to pull any officers off the primary scene."

"Hannah, you stand in the hall, at the door between the bakery and the restaurant," Amber said. "I'll try to direct any customers out—if there are any customers, which I doubt. The last thing we need is a confrontation involving guests."

Hannah nodded, apparently relieved that she wouldn't need to be in the same room with Georgia.

And then they were all moving into position.

Preston prayed as he hurried toward the kitchen exit, that there would be no more violence, that God would protect all of those involved, and that they would catch Ryan's killer before he or she had a chance to strike again.

Gordon had only allowed them to go because the weapon had been found. Somehow he no longer considered her to be a physical threat.

Preston prayed he was right.

Forty

Amber hurried down the stairs, forcing her emotions to catch up with her mind. She could imagine Georgia committing murder; after the last two homicides it wasn't that difficult to believe anyone was capable—nearly anyone. Not Tate or Pam or Hannah or Jesse. Not Gordon. Not even Preston, though he was once a soldier.

But most people? Driven to extreme measures, yes. Most people probably were capable of lethal force.

Her mind understood this, but her heart was still insisting, *No. It can't be.* She'd known Georgia for over ten years. She'd been a good employee, if a bit difficult to deal with at times —always strict, somewhat unbendable. A real rule-follower. Not always the most pleasant woman, but always a good worker.

And what was the poison scare about? Was Georgia the poison poet? It was almost easier to believe she could be a killer, someone who acted out of a broken heart, than to believe she would intentionally terrify people. Could she be that cold? That calculating?

The dining room was surprisingly busy, but it wasn't their normal morning rush. No, people stood around in clumps, discussing the day's events and wondering when they'd be able to leave.

At one end of the room, an officer was handing out forms—witness reports, Amber guessed. At least everyone's attention was split between the windows and the officer. No one paid them any mind at all.

Gordon held up a hand to stop them from entering the bakery. The customer portion of the store was on the right, then a large counter ran nearly the length of the room, and behind that the workers pulled freshly baked goods from a large window. The window and the door behind the counter connected the bakery to the larger kitchen.

Gordon was counting the time off, giving everyone time to get into position. Amber closed her eyes and pictured it—a federal agent at the front and back doors. Preston in the kitchen. Hannah with them, directing the people she and Tate would hustle out. Gordon confronting Georgia.

If she was there—

At Gordon's signal, they walked through the door.

The room wasn't terribly busy. A few people stood by the windows, staring out at the scene of Ryan's murder. Amber's brain registered the view outside the window—a glimpse of police tape, an officer's uniform, and the still-waiting ambulance. Its lights had been cut. In deference to the dead or because there was no emergency?

For that matter, why was the ambulance still there?

Removing the body would be handled by the coroner.

But she didn't have time to dwell on those things. Tate was ushering folks out, toward Hannah. Amber walked to an elderly couple near the cookie display and asked them to step into the restaurant.

They didn't argue. In fact, they looked a little stunned at all that had happened. Putting down a bag of cookies, they walked toward the door that led back into the main restaurant.

Two girls were working behind the counter, and Amber shooed them out as well.

Then Georgia walked in from the kitchen carrying a tray of pies. Despite the tension, the delicious aroma of baked apples registered in Amber's brain.

Georgia took one look at Gordon, Amber, and Tate and set the pies down on the counter, then put her hands into the large pockets of her apron. "You ran out all of my customers."

"Georgia, Sergeant Avery would like to ask you a few questions."

"About the poison pies? It's about time you came up with some results of your investigation, before someone gets hurt."

"Georgia, I'd like to ask you about Ryan Duvall."

Georgia had begun transferring pies from the tray into the glass cabinet, but she stopped when she heard Ryan's name.

Amber was watching her closely, and she saw —nothing. Georgia's face was entirely devoid of emotion.

"And please keep your hands where I can see them."

She turned and faced Gordon directly, her hands pressed flat against the counter.

"You think I would kill Ryan? Do you think he meant that much to me?"

"I don't know what he meant to you. What I do know is that you were standing in front of him when he died, and you have a motive for killing him. If you did it, whoever was standing next to you must have been so spooked they didn't even realize what had happened. We'll find them, though. We have plenty of photographs taken by those watching the race. Someone saw more than they—and you—realize."

Doubt flickered in Georgia's eyes. It was brief, like the sun darting into the clouds and back out again. But Amber hadn't imagined it, and in that moment her heart broke for this woman.

How had such a thing happened?

Wanting to humiliate Amber as the poison poet was one thing, poisoning Leo was another, but murdering Ryan? Had she nurtured her pain over Ryan until it had become a giant black hole that consumed her?

Did she regret what she'd done?

Tate stepped closer to Amber, his hand going to the small of her back. She was grateful for his presence and for his steadiness.

Gordon shifted to the left slightly, to speak into his radio, probably to call a backup officer. When he did, Georgia turned and darted toward the door that led into the kitchen.

Preston had peeked into the kitchen, where he'd seen Georgia loading pies onto a tray, her back to him. He waited outside in the employee hall that ran from her kitchen to the larger one that serviced the restaurant. Once she'd walked into the bakery, he'd pushed through into the kitchen area and shooed out a lingering employee. Then he had stood watching through the small window in the door as Georgia walked into the retail section of the bakery. He could make out Gordon, Tate, and Amber.

He knew the moment Gordon confronted her by the way her shoulders bunched up, frozen and defensive. Mocha whined once, but he put a hand down to silence the dog. He wasn't nervous, though. It looked as if everything was under control.

Amber and Tate had shooed out the customers.

Gordon was talking to Georgia, though Preston couldn't make out exactly what he was saying.

Suddenly Georgia stopped and placed her hands on top of the counter.

It was when Gordon turned, though, ever so slightly, not exactly taking his eyes off Georgia, but splitting his attention to speak into his radio . . . it was at that moment when Georgia turned and ran toward Preston.

He doubted she even saw him.

She hit the door at full speed, but it didn't budge. It couldn't budge.

Preston was standing on the opposite side when Georgia ran into it, bracing it firmly so it would remain shut. Mocha began to bark, jumping onto the door with her paws.

Georgia fell back against the counter, and Gordon was there, restraining her and leading her away from the glass display.

Preston pushed through the door, Mocha at his side and calmer now.

"You have no proof." Georgia smiled smugly.

Gordon was once again speaking into his radio, ignoring her protests.

"You have no evidence, and I never threatened

him like *this* man and his dog have." She nodded toward Preston.

Clicking off the radio, Gordon gave Georgia his full attention. "Every crime scene contains evidence, Georgia. I have no doubt that we'll find plenty to link you to the murder."

"You won't—"

"We have Tate's picture putting you directly in front of Ryan when he was killed."

Georgia shot Tate a hateful look, paused as she considered Amber, and then dismissed her with a shake of her head. "You are all amateurs."

Preston shrugged when Amber glanced his way. He couldn't explain Georgia to her. The woman was not rational. Perhaps rejection could drive you to such a place, if you didn't have the love and support of others. And if she was also the poison poet, somehow, in some twisted way, she had felt rejected by Amber, too, despite their having worked together for so long. There had to be some reason for her bitterness and desperation.

He remembered what Hannah had told him, about Georgia's use of the inn's computer the day before. Maybe what Georgia had said hadn't been a complete lie. Maybe instead of tracking a pet, she had been tracking a person.

"You watched him. Didn't you?" Preston didn't move a single step closer, but he was suddenly certain of what had happened. "Somehow you managed to put a tracker on Ryan's phone, which is why he showed up at my house, sure that someone was still after him. Only Ryan thought it was the people he owed money to. He said the police had checked his car and his person, but he didn't say they'd checked his phone."

"Ryan was a fool."

"But it was you—sitting at home, tracking him on your computer—right after you poisoned Amber's cat."

"You probably think I don't even know how to use a computer. They're not so expensive now. Anyone can buy one, but you have to be careful. The government could be monitoring . . ." She looked almost smug, as if she didn't understand that she'd practically confessed.

"So you did monitor him. You watched him show up at Martha's and Letha's work, watched him take them to dinner or the movies."

"Stop it!" Georgia practically spat the words. "I don't want to talk about Ryan Duvall."

"And then you couldn't understand why the phone never moved, why it stopped at the edge of the pond. You didn't know he had thrown it into the water."

"Which doesn't mean I killed him." Georgia's face had turned beet red, and she threw repeated glances at the window, as if she could throw herself out of it and be free.

"It will go easier for you if you confess to Ryan's murder," Gordon reminded her.

"I will not. You have nothing. So I was standing there, along with dozens of others cheering them on—as if running a stupid 5k was worth applauding, as if all this activity will do one bit of good for people dying from cancer."

"There will be gunpowder residue on your hands," Amber piped up.

"Hardly. I wash my hands—thoroughly— before I bake." Georgia's full measure of confidence returned when she uttered the word *bake,* pulled slightly away from Gordon, and stuck her hands once more in the pockets of her apron.

In that moment, Preston was sure she had done both—shot Ryan and assumed the persona of the poison poet.

Gordon shook his head, as if Georgia couldn't possibly understand the scope of what she'd done. "I'm happy to hear you have good hygiene habits; however, I'm guessing you haven't had time to wash your apron, and I noticed you like to put your hands in your pockets. No doubt some of the gunpowder residue will have transferred."

Georgia's expression froze, as if she was trying to process what Gordon had just said.

"We'll also match your prints to the weapon— which has already been turned in."

Georgia's eyes narrowed. "I want a lawyer, and I won't say another word until I have one."

"Yes, ma'am. We'll be happy to comply."

Gordon handcuffed her and walked her out of the room, toward the police cruiser that had pulled up in front of the restaurant.

Preston could hear him reciting Georgia her Miranda rights.

"You have the right to remain silent. Anything you say can and will be used against you in a court of law. You have the right to an attorney. If you cannot afford an attorney, one will be provided for you . . ."

Amber rushed around the counter and enfolded Preston in a hug. She must have suddenly realized how much danger they all could have been in. "Are you okay? When I saw Georgia dart your way I was so frightened. What if she'd had another gun? What if she'd shot you?"

"Unlikely she could have shot me through a metal door—"

"What if you'd had one of your flashbacks? What if she'd pushed through the door . . ."

"Amber, I'm okay. Remember? I had Mocha with me." Preston grinned at Tate, who had joined them on the back side of the counter.

"I suppose the bakery and its kitchen are a crime scene now." Tate glanced at the display of freshly baked goods. "Too bad. All of that will probably be thrown away."

Amber squirreled up her nose. "It's as if she put all of her anger toward me into baking—baking pies that were supposedly poisonous. Then the

411

relationship with Ryan pushed her over the edge. It's going to be quite some time before I'll be eating sweets . . . and definitely nothing mixed and baked by Georgia."

Forty-One

Ten days later

The early morning hours passed in a blur.

For once Hannah's brothers had left her alone as she took her time in the bathroom. Mattie had darted in twice, twirling in her new lavender dress and asking, "Isn't it purty, Hannah? Isn't it?"

Hannah's own dress, a lovely bright blue, was also "purty." When Mary arrived, they helped one another with re-braiding their hair especially so, and pinning the white *kapps* for one another. New *kapps*, purchased especially for their wedding day.

Eunice peeked into Hannah's room twice. The second time, Hannah caught her mother brushing tears from her eyes. She'd hugged Hannah fiercely before she darted back downstairs to see to things.

Things.

Like the large amount of food arriving— chickens stuffed with bread filling, creamed celery, vegetables of every type and color, and more freshly baked bread than their entire community could eat.

Like the stalks of celery set in canning jars on the center of each table and rose petals from their garden sprinkled along the tablecloths.

Like the wedding cupcakes, frosted in yellow for Andrew and Mary and white for Hannah and Jesse. They were arranged on a side table, fashioned in such a way that they resembled a bouquet of flowers, waiting for their family and friends to enjoy.

Like the rows of benches set out beneath the giant maple tree, not so far from the swings Hannah's father had built for her and Jesse many years ago.

When Bishop Joseph arrived, her mother appeared again. "He's ready for both of you girls."

"And Jesse?" Hannah clutched Mary's hand.

"Andrew and Jesse are both downstairs already." Eunice stepped forward then, and embraced both girls in her arms, whispering words of blessing and prayers over them.

When she stepped back, Hannah saw Mary's mother standing in the doorway, an expression of satisfaction on her face. "When girls marry they are blessed with an additional family."

Fern stepped forward and claimed both girls' hands. "You two are especially blessed. You'll gain your husband's family, *ya*. But since you are marrying on the same day, and since you will share a home, you'll also gain each other's family."

"It's true, Mary." Eunice wiped at her eyes again. "I feel as if I'm gaining another *dochder*."

"Hannah, I've known you since you were as small as Mattie, but I never thought to dream that *Gotte* would join our families together like he is today." Fern cleared her throat, and then commenced to shoo them out of the room. "The bishop will think you've changed your mind. He's waiting downstairs, in the sitting room."

They walked down the stairs, pausing to peek out the window set midway down the staircase. The view revealed the assembly of guests, and Hannah had the feeling of walking inside a dream, as if none of this was real, but rather a scene her imagination had pulled together.

Both Hannah's and Mary's fathers were waiting at the bottom of the stairs. They embraced their daughters, and then led them into the sitting room, leaving them with the bishop and Andrew and Jesse.

The moment she saw Jesse, Hannah knew her dreams had become a reality. Her mind flashed back to the day Ethan died, the day Jesse had sought her out, sat by her, and merely listened. They'd been friends before that day, but afterward? Afterward they were connected in a way only God and events could conspire to make possible.

He brushed his fingertips against hers as they sat and turned their attention to the bishop.

It was at that moment that Hannah began to tremble, a tremor starting in her arms and spreading to her hands. She understood that the shaking was not a result of nerves or doubts. She trembled because that thing for which she had dreamed so long, that thing for which she had prayed, was finally coming to pass.

She was to spend the rest of her life with the man she loved, and together they would become a family.

"I'd like to read to you from Paul's book, the first letter to the Corinthians and the thirteenth chapter." Joseph's eyes twinkled as he opened the Bible and set his finger on the German text. "You have heard it before, *ya*? But I believe that today the words may sound different. Today these words will have a special meaning for each of you."

Hannah's heart literally felt as if it were going to burst out of her chest.

"If I speak in the tongues of men and of angels, but have not love, I am only a resounding gong or a clanging cymbal."

Happiness surged through her, like the breeze through the trees outside the window.

"If I have the gift of prophecy and can fathom all mysteries and all knowledge . . ."

She glanced at Jesse and found she couldn't look away from his eyes, from this person she already knew so well.

"And if I have a faith that can move mountains, but have not love, I am nothing."

She understood, for perhaps the first time, that their love was about to change. It was about to become something completely different, like the seed in the fields grew and changed to become food for their table.

"If I give all I possess to the poor and surrender my body to hardship, but have not love, I gain nothing."

The words settled over them, like a blessing, which she supposed it was.

Finally Joseph suggested they bow for silent prayer.

Hannah's heart swelled with gratitude. She thanked God for those gathered in the room and those outside, who had already begun to sing, waiting for the ceremony to begin.

Joseph had once again picked up his Bible and continued reading from First Corinthians, describing to them what love *is* and what it is *not*.

Hannah listened, but she also examined her heart as she sat there, the familiar words falling over her. There was so much happiness, and beneath that a little nostalgia, and deep under that still a touch of grief.

The grief was for Georgia, who had seemed like a nice-enough woman. She would now never know the joy of a family, the love of a devoted man, or the peace of looking at each morning's sunrise from her home. According to Amber, she would probably spend the rest of her life in prison.

Her mind briefly flickered over Ryan and his family. Each day she prayed for his parents. Their loss had been the worst Hannah could imagine. With only the one son, they had no one else to fulfill their dreams, no one else to bring them happiness in their old age—though the community, both Amish and *Englisch*, was certainly attempting to step into the gap left by Ryan's death.

Ryan . . . she didn't want to spoil this beautiful morning by thinking of Ryan Duvall, but he was often in her thoughts since that terrible day at the Village. If he had made different decisions, would he still be alive? Or had he lived his allotted number of years? She simply didn't understand, and occasionally that lack of understanding melted into fear.

"Love never fails." The bishop cleared his throat and urged them to again bow their heads in prayer.

Before closing her eyes, Hannah saw Andrew

wink at Mary, forcing Hannah to stifle a laugh. As they began to pray, the sound of their guests singing floated through the window—a stronger, fuller sound now as those assembled warmed to the celebration of this day. The melody was a hymn she knew well. Sung today on this bright May morning, sung just moments before they were to be wed, it sounded different. Hannah heard beneath the melody the chorus of blessings sent out to cover both couples at that moment and for the rest of their lives together.

Joseph stood and gave them one last piece of Scripture. "Remember, my friends, 'These three remain: faith, hope and love. But the greatest of these is love.' "

Then they were walking past the rows upon rows of guests, to the front of the crowd, to the seats that had been reserved especially for them.

Somehow Hannah endured both sermons and yet more singing. She didn't cry until she watched Andrew and Mary step forward, recite their vows, and be blessed by the bishop. It occurred to her then that God had been so good. He had blessed them repeatedly with his favor, and she could count on that blessing to continue for the rest of their lives.

Yes, they would still encounter trouble, but as she stood up and faced Jesse, and caught again a glimpse of so many friends and family gathered for this celebration, she understood that they weren't alone and never would be.

"Do you, Jesse Miller, and you, Hannah Troyer, vow to remain together until death?"

"We do."

Jesse's eyes were locked on hers.

"And will you both be loyal and care for each other during adversity?"

"We will."

It seemed as if their voice was one. She couldn't distinguish hers from his.

"During affliction?"

"*Ya*."

The tremor began again in her arms, but Jesse held her hands gently in his. He held her heart in his hands.

"During sickness?"

"We will."

She thought of Sarah and Reuben, whom she had glimpsed as she and Jesse had walked to the front of the assembly. The tears nearly began to flow again, but she willed them back. This was a time of joy. A time to celebrate, and wasn't the fact that Sarah was able to attend their wedding one more cause for that celebration?

Bishop Joseph turned them toward the friends and family who were waiting and listening intently. He motioned for Andrew and Mary to step forward and join them, and then he said, "All of those assembled here, as your *freinden* and family in Christ, and I, as your bishop, wish you the blessing and mercy of God."

The tears once again spilled from her eyes as Andrew let out a shout of celebration and Jesse slipped his arm around her waist. The clapping seemed to continue forever, and then they were being congratulated. Jesse was repeatedly slapped on the back. Again and again Hannah's hands were pressed between those of people she loved—those she had known all her life and those of friends she had made recently.

All the time her heart was singing that she was no longer Hannah Troyer. She was now Hannah Miller. Her new life had officially begun.

Forty-Two

Amber, Tate, and Pam stood near the gift table, which was piled high with kitchen gadgets, bed linens, and even fabric. Amber thought it was a beautiful sight—all the gifts and blessings for her two favorite Amish couples.

"Why do they need kitchen stuff?" Pam asked. "They're living in the house with the boys' family, right?"

"Right, but in the fall they will begin work on a separate house adjacent to the main one. When that happens, they'll need all these supplies."

"Will both couples live together?" Tate asked.

Amber shook her head. "It will be for Andrew and Mary. Jesse thought he'd be staying at his parents' house, helping them as they grew older. Then Andrew came back. Now Jesse's looking at some land across from Hannah's parents' place. He's been saving his money for years."

"So Andrew is the son who will live closest to the parents," Pam said.

"Exactly. He and Mary will live on the main property, and Jesse and Hannah will move down the road."

"Say, that volleyball game looks fun." Pam craned her neck to get a better look at the young people assembling on both sides of a net that had been erected soon after the wedding ceremony was over.

Personally Amber was trying to avoid the games. She didn't mind a good game of volleyball, but she hadn't actually dressed for it. Wearing their best clothes didn't seem to bother the Amish girls and boys who gathered on both sides of the net, however. The girls had already kicked off their shoes, and the boys were rolling up their sleeves. They looked serious about the game.

"I've never been to a three-hour wedding ceremony before," Pam said.

"All Amish weddings are this way." Amber tucked her hand inside the crook of Tate's arm. "And actually, the wedding doesn't end until later this evening. I think their celebrations are lovely."

"You didn't want a three-hour wedding," Tate reminded her.

"I did not."

"Someone might think you were eager for the honeymoon to start."

"I was," Amber admitted, blushing slightly but enjoying the teasing. In truth, Hannah's wedding had played with her emotions, and she was relieved to lighten the mood a bit. "Seeing Hannah marry . . . it was like watching my own daughter."

"And Mary. A double wedding! I can't wait to call home and tell my momma about that." In a more somber tone, Pam added, "Those girls feel like they belong to us. I sure hope they decide to come back to work at the Village."

"I talked to Hannah and Mary about that earlier this week. Both girls will come back in a week, on a trial basis. If it goes well, they'll stay until—"

"Until the babies start coming," Pam guessed.

"Correct." Tate pulled Amber closer to his side.

Pam added, "Which should be soon by the looks of this crowd. Seems every family has an entire passel of children."

Pam spoke in all seriousness, but Amber nearly laughed because she was right. There were children of all sizes and ages everywhere they looked. Some were playing a different version of the volleyball game on a smaller "court" with a lower net. Others had started a baseball game, and some were toddling around with older siblings. Children were more plentiful than the flowers growing in Eunice's garden, which was a sight to behold.

Amber was thinking about that—children and grandchildren and the natural growth of families —when Hannah and Jesse walked up.

After a round of hugs and congratulations, Pam asked, "Don't you two need to be planning to throw the bouquet or something?"

"We don't have bouquets to throw," Hannah reminded her.

"We're free for a few moments while the others enjoy the games," Jesse said. "Soon we'll begin planning the seating for the evening meal."

"Evening meal? We just finished lunch." Everyone laughed at the surprised look on Pam's face.

"*Ya*, and I have a few ideas of who I'd like to sit next to each other." Hannah grinned as if she'd been planning this for some time. "I think I might have a knack for matchmaking. The evening meal is a chance to sit girls by boys we think might be compatible."

"Unfortunately I won't be able to stay that long." Amber once again enfolded Hannah in a hug. "It was a beautiful wedding, and I wish you all of God's blessings."

Hannah looked as if she might burst into tears, but Jesse jumped to the rescue. "We've been so busy delivering invitations and preparing the house that we haven't heard from anyone at the Village in days. Is there any news on Georgia?"

"You don't want to talk about that today." Pam swiped at an imagined crumb on her mauve-colored dress. It was the only solid-colored thing Amber had ever seen her wear. Apparently she'd asked around about what to wear to an Amish wedding. She had added a scarf stitched with different types of birds. As usual, the ensemble was stunning. "It'll ruin your mood and your appetite."

"*Nein*. It's okay. If there are any new developments, we'd like to know."

"Better to know than to worry," Hannah added.

Amber glanced at Tate, who nodded.

They would read it in the paper or hear it through the Amish grapevine. The news might as well come from her. "Georgia is pleading not guilty to Ryan's murder."

"How is that possible?" Jesse asked, his hand on the small of Hannah's back, his face blanketed with concern.

"Anyone may plead not guilty." Tate glanced out over the crowd. "It's the prosecution's responsibility to prove guilt."

"And will they be able to?" Hannah raised her thumbnail to her mouth, then dropped her hand to her side, suddenly self-conscious about the habit.

Amber shrugged. "Gordon didn't share everything with me, but he did give me a few of the details. The prints on the gun are a match— "

"Good thing someone retrieved it from the trash," Tate said.

"Not the smartest hiding place," Jesse muttered.

"Apparently she thought it would lie in the city dump forever, undetected and no threat to her freedom." Amber crossed her arms.

Pam squinted at them. "The woman is crafty and fairly smart. I think she was going to try to nudge the investigation toward someone who had dated Ryan in the past—someone she was jealous of."

"You don't know that," Amber said.

"No. It's only a guess, but it makes sense to me. She was consumed by jealousy, which is probably what started the whole poison poet thing."

"What was that about?" Preston asked. He walked up holding Zoey's hand, Mocha at his side and a goofy grin on his face . . . until he realized what they were discussing.

Amber hadn't had a chance to speak with him since the wedding began. He and Zoey had arrived as the singing started. She'd spied them as they took a seat in the last row.

"The entire poison thing . . . what was the point?" Preston repeated. "Walter Hopkins, the old guy who works at the police station, stopped in to visit someone at my dad's house. He told a girl that Zoey works with—"

"Rhonda," Zoey said.

"She told Rhonda, who told Zoey—"

"Told me yesterday."

"That the poison thing was a big distraction. According to Walter, Georgia did a lot of research, but she never actually put any poisonous substance in any of the pies—except for the one she left for Leo."

"Why, though?" Amber was glad for the warmth of the sun on her face. Even talking about Georgia, thinking of the people she could have hurt and the people she did hurt, left her feeling cold and unsettled. "Why even bother with the entire ruse?"

"The rumor I heard is that she'd always wanted your job, Amber. She thought you would move on after a few years, but you never did. So she came up with the poison idea. Georgia received extra attention from Ryan because of it." Zoey stepped closer to Preston. "In the beginning, Ryan told her how courageous she was, continuing to work in the face of such danger."

"Hogwash!" Pam placed her hands on her hips. "Where I come from, if you want to poison someone you do it, you don't just talk about it."

Amber couldn't help but smile at Pam's offended tone. "You're not saying that you wish—"

"No. I liked Ryan, even if he was a little immature for his age. Sort of like a high school boy in grown-up clothes."

The conversation stalled as Amber thought of Ryan, someone she barely knew, but now gone. Which was another reminder that they should not take a single day for granted. She wanted to draw her friends closer and protect them from any harm. She couldn't do that, though.

Only God had that sort of ability.

Tate nodded at Preston. "Ryan's parents told me they were relieved you were able to help him. I had a chance to speak with them after the funeral. They said the only way they could bear such a terrible loss was knowing that their last words to each other had been kind, knowing that their relationship had been repaired. They credit you with that."

Preston looked at each of them but didn't speak. So often it seemed to Amber that Preston kept his thoughts to himself, perhaps a residual effect of spending time living on the streets, being disconnected from others. Looking at him now, it was difficult to believe he was the same man. Preston had healed, that much was certain—with the help of Zoey, his friends, their prayers, and one very special dog.

Zoey snuggled closer in the shelter of his arm. "We also visited with Ryan's parents. I know they are hurting. In fact, they seemed to be in shock."

"Who wouldn't be?" Pam ran her fingers down her scarf, adjusting the knot she'd tied to keep it from blowing back and forth in the breeze. "There have been too many murders around here, if you ask me. Even Shipshewana only had the three—I know because I read up on it. Three is enough. We need to focus on weddings and children and improving business at the Village. Normal things that normal people do!"

Amber noticed that Preston colored slightly at the mention of weddings, but he didn't say anything.

Then Andrew and Mary joined them, and the discussion moved to their plans for the future, how the new rooms had turned out, and what they would be planting once the spring crops were harvested. Amber tuned out when they started talking crops, though she noticed that Tate was quite interested in the discussion. He'd been leasing his fields for a few years, but he still remained active in the farming community as a whole. It was one of the many things she loved about him. He didn't retire and sit home doing crossword puzzles—speaking of which, she had one by her chair that she hadn't managed to finish. As far as she was concerned, three across in the local paper was the only type of mystery she was interested in solving. Word games. Maybe a detective novel. That was it. She was hanging up her sleuth apron.

As Pam had said, it was time to focus on family. Preston and Zoey said their good-byes.

The four newlyweds made their way back to the center of the festivities.

And Pam went in search of a recipe for the creamed celery they had served. She'd apparently decided to give cooking a try, or maybe she was going to e-mail the recipe back home.

Amber and Tate stopped to speak with the parents of the happy couples. Both thanked Amber for keeping their children safe. As if she was their protector, their mom away from home, which was often how she felt. But Amber knew God had kept them safe.

He'd sent the federal investigators, Gordon, even Preston and Tate at the moment they had needed help.

He'd allowed her and Pam to figure out enough of the mystery to be on alert the day they needed to be.

He'd protected them the entire time.

And although Ryan was gone, Amber trusted that God would have his eye on Ryan's parents, providing comfort to them in their time of need.

Tate snagged her hand as they walked toward her car. "I noticed you didn't mention Georgia's tracking program, the one you and Pam discovered on the Village computers."

"Gives me the creeps every time I think of it."

"Because . . ."

"Because it's an invasion of privacy, and it shouldn't be allowed. We're not animals or cars or things to be tracked. We're people, and we deserve a certain amount of respect from each other."

"There are always a few—like Georgia—who don't understand that."

"The worst part is that we didn't put the clues together right. Hannah had mentioned that computer incident with Georgia to Pam and me, too, not just Preston. We believed what Georgia told Hannah, that she had been tracking her lost cat. None of us remembered that she hated Buttons. And we didn't connect her hatred of cats to Leo's poisoning, either."

"She was a good liar. And who knew your Village baker could do so much with computers, tracking devices, guns—even paintball guns?"

"But Preston had told us earlier in the day that Ryan thought he was being followed. He told us about the texts. We should have figured it out then. If we had, maybe we could have—"

"Saved Ryan?"

They'd reached Amber's red car. Tate stopped and turned her to face him. "Is that what you're chewing on? Regret? Because you can't solve every mystery, Amber. No one can. You can't protect every person you come in contact with."

She shook her head, but didn't trust her voice. It hurt to realize that her abilities were limited.

It hurt to let go of the illusion that she could intervene in every instance and keep her friends and family out of harm's way.

Once in the car and buckled up, Amber put her hand on Tate's arm. She wasn't ready to leave yet. She liked looking out the front of the car at the buggies, which stretched as far as she could see, intermixed with a few cars. Both were a clear indication of how their community pulled together, not just during times of sorrow but also during times of celebration.

"Today was a good day."

"It was."

"Reminds me of our wedding."

"Hasn't been that long."

"Completely different events."

"Do you think so?" He cornered himself in the car and studied her.

"Yes. We didn't have cupcakes and there was no congregational singing."

"True, but the important thing—the vows and the blessings—they were nearly identical. The rest is window dressing."

It was a funny phrase, as if you could dress a window. She understood what Tate was saying, though. As they pulled out of the parking area, she realized that in many ways they were alike— the *Englisch* and the Amish. Their appearance was different, their window dressing, as Tate would say.

But their faith? It was based on the same Good Book.

Their families? Both committed to one another.

And their friendships—well, there was the proof that where it mattered they were quite similar. And friendship was the one thing Amber knew would see them through—both tragedy and celebration.

Friendship was a gift God had given them, and she planned to nurture every one she had.

Epilogue

The rain fell in a curtain, turning the June afternoon to near darkness. Thunder crashed and lightning slashed the afternoon sky. The temperatures had dropped as the storm rolled in. Preston had been so focused on Zoey, on trying to find the right words, that he hadn't paid attention. He hadn't noticed the telltale signs. Now they were both wet and cold.

They bundled up the picnic, stuffing the tablecloth into their basket, and ran for the car.

Even as he was running, Preston couldn't take his eyes off Zoey. He didn't want to. She was laughing and shivering and soaked clear through to the bone. She was the most beautiful sight he'd ever seen.

He helped her into the Beetle, then ran around

the front of the car and opened the driver's door. Mocha hopped into the backseat before Preston could even move his front seat forward. She sat there, panting, a big sloppy grin on her face.

Preston set the picnic basket in the back, on the seat next to the dog, and then he climbed into the car, pulling the door shut behind him, blocking out the storm.

"Great picnic," Zoey said. She leaned over, planted a kiss on his cheek, and then moved to buckle her seat belt. There was enough daylight remaining for him to make out her smile.

"How about if we just sit here awhile?" he asked.

"Here?"

"Yeah."

"Here in the storm?"

"Yeah."

So they did just that. He started the car and cranked up the heater, thankful that he'd managed to fix it. The air began to warm even as the storm continued to rage around them. They could barely see the park grounds out the front window. The rain was falling in buckets now. A real Indiana downpour. Against the roof of the Volkswagen, it sounded like a hundred drums, beating in harmony with one another.

It sounded to Preston like the beat of his heart, amplified and multiplied until it created a music all its own.

The smell of wet dog permeated the air, and then Mocha did what Preston should have expected. She stood and shook the water from her coat, spraying droplets over the front seat—over both him and Zoey.

"Not exactly a flawless afternoon," Preston said.

"I have loved every minute of it." Zoey squeezed his hand as she accepted the cotton tablecloth he pulled from the picnic basket. "And this works just fine as a towel."

Preston studied her as she blotted her hair. The blonde strands were darker now that they were wet. She proceeded to swipe at her arms and legs. She was wearing blue jeans and a yellow cotton blouse. He thought he could watch her all day, every day, for as long as he lived.

So he turned and fumbled in the picnic basket until he found the small velvet box.

"If you're rummaging around for food, I think we might as well eat at your house. This storm looks as if it's going to last—"

"I'm not rummaging for food. I'd like to ask you something, Zoey." He reached for her hand, turned it over, and placed the box in her palm. Then he reached out to touch her face and nearly laughed at the way her blue eyes widened in astonishment.

How could she be surprised?

How could she not know?

"I spoke with your father last week, on Tuesday."

"You did?"

"I wanted to do this that evening—"

"The night I called you and canceled."

"Because you had to work late." Preston took the tablecloth from her and wiped at drops of rain that still shimmered on her neck. "Then I planned a special afternoon out on the boat."

"On Goose Pond. You couldn't have known I get seasick if I step one foot off dry ground." She ran a finger over the top of the black velvet box, but she didn't open it.

She did reach up and cup her hand around his jaw.

Zoey's fingers on his skin.

Zoey's eyes, wide with surprise and understanding.

Zoey's love filling his heart.

Preston didn't have any doubts, not a single one, that his entire life had led him to this moment.

"I wanted it to be a flawless date that you'd tell our grandchildren about." His voice cracked with emotion, at the tears he refused to shed. "But I'm not going to wait any longer for that. What's important is you and me—together. Not a perfect proposal."

Zoey bit her bottom lip, but still she didn't open the box.

He opened it for her at the same moment he whispered, "Zoey Quinn, will you marry me?"

She didn't answer right away.

Instead she threw herself into his arms, which was no easy feat in the Beetle.

She was laughing and kissing him, and then pulling back when Mocha pushed her way in between them.

"Yes, Preston Johnstone." Tears slipped down her cheeks as she pulled the ring from the box. "I will."

He put it on her finger, and it fit perfectly—of course it did. Her dad had known her ring size. He'd given Preston his blessing and then told him that she had a special preference for white and yellow gold together. The engagement ring held three small diamonds, in a white gold setting, placed atop a yellow gold band. It was modest, but the most he could afford. From the look on her face, he'd chosen well.

"I wanted everything to be just so. I thought a picnic—nothing could go wrong at a picnic." He glanced out the window. The rain was creating large puddles here and there. Mocha lay on the backseat, uttering a contented sigh.

"But those things don't matter. What matters is that you—" He touched the first diamond.

"Me—" He touched the second.

"And Mocha"—he touched the third—"are together."

He closed the box and placed it back into the basket, then clasped her hands in his. "You've changed my life, Zoey. I . . . I still can't believe God brought us together, but he has. And I want to honor that. I want to love you and care for you."

She swiped at her cheeks, glanced at the dog and then at him. "You're good now. Aren't you, Preston?"

"I am, but that doesn't mean things will be—"

"Perfect," she whispered.

"Exactly. Things are better, much better, with Mocha. For so long I was afraid to ask you to share my life, afraid that I would be putting you in danger if I had one of my flashbacks."

"But you're better."

"I am better, thanks to you and Mocha. More than that, I trust that God will continue healing those places in me that are broken."

"You've never told me—"

So he did. He told her about signing up when he was only nineteen, about excelling at everything he was asked to do, and about deploying to Afghanistan. As the heavy rain turned to a light shower, he told her about Wanat, the beauty and harshness of the land. He described the people— men, women, and children he could still see if he closed his eyes. And then he told her about the day of the attack and about how his friends had suffered.

About Frank Cannopy, who lost his leg, and about his commander, Toby Bogar, who didn't make it back at all. He described the blood and carnage. He confessed to the guilt he felt because he had come back whole, but not whole. A part of his heart, maybe a part of his mind broken by what they'd endured.

When he'd finished, when he had no more memories to share, she reached over and wiped the tears from his cheeks.

"I'm grateful God brought you here, brought you to me, Preston."

He turned toward her then, turned away from those nightmares that had haunted him for so long. He leaned toward her, in the little Beetle with a sleeping dog in the back and a storm easing outside their windows. He kissed her, and then she kissed him, and then they pressed their foreheads to one another.

"I love you, Zoey Quinn, with all my heart."

"I love you, Preston." Her voice cracked a little.

He reached up and wiped away the tears slipping down her cheeks, then he kissed her forehead, her cheeks, and finally her mouth. He allowed himself, for the very first time, to melt into the love of this amazing woman God had placed in his life. He allowed himself to believe in what had seemed impossible.

Mocha had rolled over on her back so that her four legs were sticking straight up in the air by the time he started the car and drove them back toward the Village.

They hadn't discussed any of the details—the when or where. But he knew that whatever they decided, Zoey's parents would be there, his father would be there, and their friends would be there— Amber and Tate and Pam. Even Hannah and Jesse. They had become a family, with bonds forged from terrible times and heartbreaking events.

"Let's celebrate with a dinner at the restaurant. Our picnic food is soaked."

"You're spoiling me already."

"Better get used to that."

A hot meal, some coffee, and a piece of freshly baked pie sounded wonderful to Preston. He hadn't been able to eat much for days, since he'd picked up the ring at the jeweler in Goshen. His stomach had been on an aerobics gig until the moment she had said yes. Now he couldn't remember what he had been so nervous about.

As they pulled into the Village parking lot, the last of the day's light broke through the western clouds, scattering the darkness and blazing a rainbow across the sky.

They walked toward the bakery hand in hand —Preston and Zoey with Mocha following at their side, the sound of horses clip-clopping down the road. Somehow Preston knew that even if things weren't perfect, they were as they should be. And that was really all he'd ever wanted.

Author's Note

Cancer statistics included in this story are accurate as of the date this book was written and were taken from the National Cancer Institute. More information can be found at http://seer .cancer.gov.

Nine US soldiers were killed and another twenty-seven wounded during the Battle of Wanat (Nuristan Province, Afghanistan), which took place on July 13, 2008. Preston's participation in this battle is entirely fictional. Soldiers involved in the battle were part of 2nd Battalion, 503rd Airborne Infantry Regiment, 173rd Airborne Brigade Combat Team, Vicenza, Italy.

Service dogs are currently used to treat PTSD. More information can be found at http://www .vetshelpingheroes.org. Donations can be made to ICAN through http://www.icandog.org.

Discussion Questions

1. In chapter 2 Amber remembers the previous trouble they have endured at the Village. She reminds herself of the familiar words spoken by Joseph in Genesis 50:20: "You intended to harm me, but God intended it for good." Discuss a time in your life—or your community's life—when God brought good things out of an evil situation.

2. Preston is struggling with Post-Traumatic Stress Disorder. He wants to believe God's promise of peace, but he's having a hard time reconciling that with the struggle he faces day to day. If you had a friend going through a similar situation, how would you assure them of God's love?

3. Hannah reflects in chapter 12 that she prefers the peaceful days of the last few months. She doesn't want any more danger or drama. It seems that God does bless us with times of peace before trials. Share a verse about God's peace.

4. In chapter 13 Preston offers a "foxhole prayer." Sincere, from the heart, and desperately

honest, he falls on the mercy of God. The Bible tells us to cry out to God in our time of need. Read Psalm 18:6. David was also crying out to God. Discuss a time when you prayed in desperation.

5. We see a lovely image in chapter 20 of an older man and woman walking through the rain into the furniture store. Their love for each other is obvious. What can we learn from older couples in our community about love and faith?

6. In chapter 25 Amber realizes, "Everyone needed help. A wise person realized it before disaster struck . . ." Discuss a time when you had to depend on someone else. How did they come through with the type of help you needed?

7. Martha has her heart broken by Ryan Duvall. In chapter 30, her mother says, "Time will heal most wounds, and the ones not healed? Those we learn to live with." Do you agree or disagree with this statement, and why? What does the Bible say about the broken-hearted? Start with Psalm 34:18.

8. When Ryan Duvall shows up at Preston's house, he is a rumpled, broken man (chapter

31). Strangely, Preston can relate to that, and perhaps that is why he shows mercy to this man who has caused so much trouble. Is this a wise or foolish thing for Preston to do? What does the Bible say about showing mercy to those who would harm us?

9. Jesse reminds Hannah that "Sarah is still under Gotte's care." Sometimes we have to hold tight to the promises found in Scripture. Read the following verses and discuss how these words of encouragement affect your life: Matthew 10:29–31, 1 Peter 5:7, Psalm 118:6. What other verses can you add to this list?

10. Part of this story focuses on cancer, as well as its treatments. Has cancer affected your life in any way? If so, how? What can we do to help those afflicted by this disease?

11. After Hannah is married to Jesse, Amber has the thought that she'd like to "draw her friends closer and protect them from any harm. She couldn't do that, though. Only God had that sort of ability." Have you had any experience with this? Are there folks you would like to protect but have to trust to God's care?

Acknowledgments

This book is lovingly dedicated to Mary Sue Seymour. Mary Sue first offered to represent me based on a romantic suspense novel I had written, which still hasn't seen the light of day. But she didn't give up. In the way of good agents, she suggested a different genre. She suggested I write about the Amish. That was six years and twelve books ago. During that time she has been an exemplary agent and a good friend. I am forever grateful that she took a chance on me.

I'd also like to thank my friends in Middle-bury—both Amish and *Englisch*. You were a joy to visit, very welcoming, and an author's dream as you offered information about your lovely town. A special thank-you to Jeffrey Miller, operations manager of Das Dutchman Essenhaus.

Thank you to Donna, Kristy, and Dorsey, my pre-readers. I also appreciate the work of my editor, Becky Philpott. Thanks to Diane Anderson for her contribution to the ACFW auction and the use of her name. My husband deserves my undying gratitude—he keeps me fed and pointed in the right direction. He also reminds me to step away from the computer, which is advice I need.

445

Northern Indiana has become a place near and dear to my heart. Every time I return (whether physically or through the plot of a story), I am reminded how kind and welcoming the residents have been to me. I count it as one of life's many blessings that our paths have crossed. If you're ever in the area, I encourage you to stop by Middlebury, Goshen, Nappanee, Elkhart, and Shipshewana. Visit the local shops—both Amish and *Englisch*. You're bound to find things you'll enjoy, and don't be afraid to sample the pie.

Finally ". . . always giving thanks to God the Father for everything, in the name of our Lord Jesus Christ" (Ephesians 5:20).

Blessings,
Vannetta

About the Author

Vannetta Chapman is author of the bestselling novel *A Simple Amish Christmas*. She has published over one hundred articles in Christian family magazines, receiving over two dozen awards from Romance Writers of America chapter groups. In 2012 she was awarded a Carol Award for *Falling to Pieces*. She discovered her love for the Amish while researching her grandfather's birthplace of Albion, Pennsylvania.

Visit Vannetta's website:
www.vannettachapman.com
Twitter: @VannettaChapman
Facebook: VannettaChapmanBooks

Center Point Large Print
600 Brooks Road / PO Box 1
Thorndike, ME 04986-0001 USA

(207) 568-3717

US & Canada:
1 800 929-9108
www.centerpointlargeprint.com